T0162388

LAKE
ON THE
MOUNTAIN

DAN SHARP MYSTERIES
Listed in suggested reading order

Lake on the Mountain
Pumpkin Eater
The Jade Butterfly
Shadow Puppet
After the Horses
Lion's Head Revisited
The God Game

JEFFREY ROUND

LAKE ON THE MOUNTAIN

A DAN SHARP MYSTERY

DUNDURN
TORONTO

Publisher: Scott Fraser
Cover designer: Laura Boyle
Cover image: istock.com/CasarsaGuru
Printer: Webcom, a division of Marquis Book Printing Inc.

Library and Archives Canada Cataloguing in Publication

Title: Lake on the mountain : a Dan Sharp mystery / Jeffrey Round.
Names: Round, Jeffrey, author.
Description: Reprint. Originally published: Toronto: Dundurn, 2012.
Identifiers: Canadiana 20190175575 | ISBN 9781459747036 (softcover)
Classification: LCC PS8585.O84929 L35 2019 | DDC C813/.54—dc23

 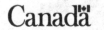

We acknowledge the support of the **Canada Council for the Arts,** which last year invested $153 million to bring the arts to Canadians throughout the country, and the **Ontario Arts Council** for our publishing program. We also acknowledge the financial support of the **Government of Ontario**, through the **Ontario Book Publishing Tax Credit** and the **Ontario Media Development Corporation**, and the **Government of Canada**.

Care has been taken to trace the ownership of copyright material used in this book. The author and the publisher welcome any information enabling them to rectify any references or credits in subsequent editions.

The publisher is not responsible for websites or their content unless they are owned by the publisher.

Printed and bound in Canada.

VISIT US AT

dundurn.com | @dundurnpress | dundurnpress | dundurnpress

Dundurn
3 Church Street, Suite 500
Toronto, Ontario, Canada
M5E 1M2

For my brothers, Mark and Brian

I'll play it first and tell you what it is later.

— Miles Davis

PROLOGUE

1987: The Icy Bier

A COLD SNAP HAD FROZEN EVERYTHING. Record low temperatures setting in the previous week presaged an early winter. The man wheeled his bicycle from the ferry dock over the rocks and down to the shoreline, where the ice had cracked and erupted in little chips, reflecting a bleak sky. The cold's relentless grip on this chill November day was enough to send most men reeling back to their homes as quickly as possible, but this man hardly felt a thing.

He stared at the surrounding shore and the ice encroaching the edges of the battered point. A spumy spray broke at the dock where the ferryboat had just left its mooring in a whorl of ice and black water. A light snow swirled about, landing on the man's coat and brushing his reddened cheeks.

He turned his head to the big boat pulling away from the dock. There were seven cars on board for the return voyage, so few it hardly seemed worth the haul. Most of the passengers were huddled in their vehicles, but a handful emerged to stand on deck braving the elements. If they turned and saw him standing there, would they sense his desperation? Would they glean any hint of who he was or what he was about to do, wondering perhaps if he could go through with it?

A dull sun was setting through the grey skies arching overhead. Soon there would be nothing between him and the chill. He looked up at the mountain looming over the Adolphustown Reach. Somewhere up there, in three hours' time, he had a different assignation. One he knew he was not meant to keep. Just one more broken promise in the grand scheme.

He turned to look over his shoulder. Through the trees he could make out the house he had once called home. It could never feel like home to him again. Not after what had happened. Yesterday lay like a crack in time dividing his old life from whatever remained of it. Everything that mattered had been left behind in that house.

He thought of his wife and felt a cold, clear burning inside. She had beaten him. She had stared across the court-room with coldness and malevolence and spoken the words that brought his doom, describing to them how he had struck her. So she had won, and the victor's spoils were too great for him to bear. But what about his sons? They still needed a father. He'd hardly been that to them.

He took a step onto the ice, feeling its slippery solidity beneath his shoe. For a moment, it took him back to the skating parties when he was a kid. The endless fun, the shrieks of laughter and cups of hot chocolate afterwards. And the daring, going out farther than he should have. He'd been lighter then, a mere pup. Now he weighed more than two hundred pounds. He looked up and imagined himself skating out to where the black swath of water stretched fifty yards offshore, chunks of disembodied whiteness bobbing as the ferry cut a path on its journey to the far side.

He took another step and paused at the uneasy creaking. In a sense, his mind had been made up long ago. He simply had to follow through with his intentions. He would head out for as long as the ice would bear his weight. Then there would be the first cracking and then another and it would be done. He thought about the cold engulfing him, the iciness gripping his skin. Even if he struggled, it would be too late.

If someone were to come looking for him years from now, what would they find? A pile of bones, at best. It would tell nothing of why he had done it. Images spewed from his mind: all the anger, all the labour, all the loss. How would they see him afterwards? As a coward who ran away from his problems? Maybe he was. Then wasn't it better to get it over with, once and for all?

He could still make her pay, he thought. He'd kept meticulous records. Maybe one day it would help them understand his dark motives, the rage that burned, the anger she'd spoken of in court. The diary would help them piece it all together.

A seagull shrieked and bobbed on a stray wave. It seemed to be laughing at him. The ferry had progressed to about the halfway point, slowly sawing through the ice and water. He stood there, a man poised over an abyss. Which would it be, this way or the other, with all of its grim consequences? He could go no farther. He had to choose.

A gust of wind caught his collar, startling him. He turned and looked back to shore. The bicycle caught his eye. He ought to move it, not leave it there as a signpost, if he was going to go through with it.

ONE

2007: Look for the Unexpected

HE WAS LATE AGAIN. It was the third time that week. His son was waiting on the corner outside the dry cleaners, chomping on the yellow crescent of a meat patty and still wearing his team uniform. Dan pulled over and sat by the curb, watching. A smattering of graffiti ran across the brick, swirls and squiggles approaching letters, black on white on red. Nothing actually intelligible except for the cryptic rendering *Babb 2*. But no *Babb 1*. Did graffiti artists disdain the sequential? He watched Ked push against the wall with one foot — the Jordan *Spiz'ikes* that cost more than any shoe Dan had worn at that age — then lean into the brick again. Push away and in, push away and in. It took on a rhythm.

Ked was with the same black kid from the other day — the one Dan had come to think of as the "ruffian." His mind took in outward impressions: skinny face, weird hair, baggy clothes. A low waistband revealed the ruffled edge of blue-grey checkered boxers. At least the boy's jeans were high enough, if he needed to run. What was it with teen-agers and those freaking hoodies? They looked like ghouls roaming the streets, especially after dark.

The ruffian's face was set on neutral. No expression of defiance or curiosity. Certainly no joy. Did that spell devi-ous or repressed? Usually Dan got a feel for kids, but this one gave few clues. He seemed almost catatonic — no junky twitches, no arrogant swagger. It was unnatural.

Dan's training taught him people were composites — aggregates of personalities, upbringings, social milieux. First you looked at the whole and then took in the details one at a time. Being a father confirmed it. You never knew who carried the knife and who might turn out to be a Rhodes Scholar. In this neighbourhood, sometimes the same kid filled both roles. Blue collar workers and artsy boho types eager to be near the film studios lived side by side with the new immigrants who thought they'd found Easy Street. A brave new world of 24-hour convenience stores, tenth-hand junk shops, and self-pumping gas sta-tions, with guaranteed lifetime positions as parking lot attendants, fast food servers, and dollar store cashiers. Roll up, roll up — be the next ethnicity on the block to inhabit this ragtag, burnt-end-of-the-candle cul de sac. A new underclass of hirelings for the least-wanted jobs.

The old Canadians knew they lived in a ghetto at the bottom of Leslieville that held gold for a few, but fool's gold for most. Trapped between the uptight New Agers of Riverdale and the monochromatic, mostly-white enclave known as the Beach (*And don't call it the Beaches!* resi-dents chided), theirs was the forgotten neighbourhood. Above and to the north, Greek and Muslim communities stretched along Danforth Avenue in uneasy communion. To the south there was industry, water filtration plants, and the decay-ridden stench of Lake Ontario.

Ked said something to the other boy, who responded with a gentle upturning at the edges of his mouth. Ah! He was shy, then. Or possibly enamoured of his son. Dan thought about the drink he'd be having at home and the files tucked into his case waiting to be unpacked. He honked.

Ked looked over and said something to the other kid. Hands gestured in teen-speak. Additional clues, these ones more arcane. Ked ran across the street and climbed in back.

"Hey Dad! Find any missing people today?"

"Just you."

"Cool!"

Dan turned to look at him. "Better view from back there?"

Ked grinned. "Nah. I told Eph you were my chauffeur. Don't blow my cover."

"And Eph would be…?"

"Ephraim. New kid. He's cool." His son was mastering the art of the two-second meaningless sound bite.

"Does he need a ride somewhere?"

"Nah. He lives close."

"Is he going to be a friend?" Dan probed.

"Um … maybe." A one-shoulder shrug. "We'll see how it goes."

"He could stand a change of wardrobe," Dan said, catching the boy's retreating form in his side mirror.

Ked snorted. His freckles underwent a quick metamorphosis. "Eph's from an underprivileged family. I hope you're not going to hand me some crap about poor kids being bad influences."

"Hardly."

Dan reversed and swung the car around. Not bad influences, no. But what about the other kind? The kind that determined whether you became a success or failure in life. It added up. Who you hung out with, went to school with, fucked, or married — that sort of thing. It mattered in the end, even if for all the wrong reasons.

He eyed his son in the rear-view mirror. Ked's head was down, focused on his Game Boy. "Good game?" he ventured.

"Pretty good."

"Score any goals?"

"Nah."

Dan nodded. "You'll get there. Just don't neglect your schoolwork."

"I won't," Ked said without lifting his eyes.

"How's your mother?"

"Same."

Dan saw Ked wrinkle his nose the same way Kendra would at such a generic question. "Be specific or be gone," she liked to say. Dan could play that game.

"Same as what?"

"Same as always," came the reply from the backseat.

"That's what you say every time I ask."

Ked looked up. "It's true. What do you want me to say?" His voice rose in pitch, as though puberty wasn't done with him.

"I want you to tell me how she is. Happy? Healthy? Going anywhere interesting?"

"She's fine. She's happy. Not going anywhere. She doesn't ask as many questions as you." Ked bared his teeth at the mirror then turned back to the Game Boy.

"You're really exasperating, you know."

"I know, Dad. I learned it from you."

Cars buzzed past the intersection. Rush hour was in full swing. The streets were packed with the usual muck of traffic heading away from the downtown core. A black Neon swerved into their lane without signalling. Dan felt a prickling of anger on his scalp and back.

"Who taught these losers to drive?"

Ked looked up again. "Other losers?"

Dan braked for a scattering of teenagers running from the 7-Eleven and dodging cars. More hoodies. The smallest of them banged a pop can against an SUV, exchanging glares with the driver and flashing a less obscure hand signal Dan recalled from his own teen years. The light turned red. Vehicles continued to flood the intersection, blocking the way.

"Inconsiderate moron!" Dan yelled through the window.

An Asian woman looked nervously away.

"Too much testosterone, Dad," Ked informed him.

Dan thought again how the city had devolved over the past fifteen years into a rat's nest of frustration and seething tempers. Corporate crime had taken the backseat to a more visible MTV-style menace: street gangs shooting and killing in broad daylight, the corrupt, surly cops who chased them, and the mindless assholes who blocked intersections and drove like the selfish pricks they were. That and the slow-moving immigrants who learned to drive at schools with names like Lucky Driver and navigated as if they were herding caravans in the desert. What did luck have to do with it?

There was a moment's respite as Dan turned down his street. The overhang of leafy boughs made it seem like a vast cathedral. The elation vanished. Once again he had to squeeze past his neighbour's car to get into his parking pad. If she'd pull up another foot it wouldn't be a problem, but Glenda couldn't be bothered to clear his drive. He looked over. She was out raking leaves in the kind of outfit women wore to cocktail parties. She ignored him. He'd been an occasional dinner guest before Steve moved out. Dan liked Steve, but had wondered about his wife. She always seemed a little vacuous and self-absorbed. Maybe Steve liked his women that way.

He got out and slammed the car door. "Fucking princess," he muttered, hoping she might hear but Ked wouldn't.

"You got that one right, Dad," Ked said, shouldering his knapsack.

Juggling his laptop, briefcase, and raincoat, Dan fumbled the key into the lock. As the front door swung open, he smelled something disgusting — like farts, only worse. His first thought was about the garbage. This was more immediate. He looked down and just missed stepping on a large brown turd.

"Not again! That goddamn dog!"

"I'll clean it up." Ked threw his knapsack on the counter and darted for the cupboard to retrieve a mop and a plastic bag.

"I just walked him at lunch time!" Dan fumed, knowing that had been seven hours ago.

Ked bagged the offending litter and knotted the handles together. "Maybe he's mad because you neglect him too."

Dan looked at his son. "Are you saying I neglect you?"

Ked looked up, his face serious. "No, Dad. I'm saying you could be a better dog owner. Even dogs need love."

"He's your dog — *you* love him." He watched his son swipe at the spot with the mop. "He does it on purpose."

Ked looked pained. "He's old, Dad. He can't help himself."

"That's not true. When it's an accident, he hides it in the basement. When he does it at the front door like that — one big piece of crap right where I'll step in it — then it's a big 'Screw you, buddy.'"

Ked giggled.

Dan looked around. "You see — he's nowhere in sight. He knows he's done something bad, otherwise he'd be here to greet us."

"He probably knows you're pissed and he's hiding from you."

Ked finished cleaning and put the mop away. They looked up at the sound of claws scampering over hardwood. The transgressor, a ginger-coloured retriever, stood at the living-room door, tail wagging.

"Here, boy!"

The tail wagged harder, but the dog held his ground.

"Son of a bitch!" Dan snarled.

The dog's ears went down; the tail came to a standstill.

"He's afraid of you," Ked said.

"He'd better be."

Ked knelt and stroked the dog's silky ears. He pointed at the spot he'd just cleaned and looked at the dog. "Did you do that?" The dog's ears went back down; he looked away. "That's a bad boy," Ked said gently.

The dog whimpered.

"He says he's sorry," Ked said.

"Right. Next time he can clean it up, if he's so sorry."

Ked looked at the dog. "Did you hear that, dude? You better behave or Dad'll put us both out on the streets."

The dog's tail thumped enthusiastically.

"You have to learn to speak his language, Dad. Watch his eyes." Ked turned to the dog and opened his arms. "What do you want, Ralph? Show me!"

The dog turned its gaze to the French windows at the rear of the house.

"You want out?" Ked said.

Ralph bounded to the back exit and stood waiting. Ked unlatched the door and the dog tore outside.

"You have to ask him what he wants," Ked said. "He tells you with his eyes. If he looks at the treat cupboard, he wants a reward. If he looks at the fridge, he probably wants whatever you just had to eat. If he looks at his leash, he needs a walk."

"Don't tell me he speaks English."

Ked looked at his father sympathetically, as though he might be just a bit slow. "No, but he can understand what you're saying. You have to learn his language, too."

Dan nodded. "I'll keep it in mind."

"Hey, Dad! I got a new book today."

Ked retrieved a paperback from his knapsack and tossed it on the counter. Dan glanced at a woman's pensive face framed by dark bangs, her cigarette upraised and smoke curling artistically overhead. Harrison Ford's sweaty likeness menaced a library barcode with a hefty handgun. Across the top in red letters: *Blade Runner*.

"It's really cool. It's about this guy who lives in LA after it's been totally destroyed and hunts androids for a living," Ked said. "The only problem is, they look and act exactly like humans, so it's hard to tell who's an android and who's a real person."

Dan grunted.

"You know it?"

"I know it," Dan said. "Only in my day it was called *Do Androids Dream of Electric Sheep.*"

"Yeah — I think that was before the movie, though."

"In the old days."

"Right. Anyway, I think I'm going to like this one."

The answering machine blinked red on the side table. Dan regarded it, appraising what it might hold. He pressed play. A cool voice emerged, the tones submerged beneath a wall of self-assurance.

"Hello, Daniel," said the voice. "It's Bill...."

"Speaking of androids," Ked said quietly.

"He's cancelling," Dan declared, shaking his head. "I knew he would."

"... I wanted to give you a heads-up. Something's come up at the hospital and I can't make it tonight. You and Ked have a good time without me...."

"We will, you dick-head." Dan reached out and cut the message off.

"Why do you date him?" Ked asked. "He treats you like shit."

Dan raised a warning finger. "I can say that — you can't."

Ked rolled his eyes. "I'm just saying ..."

Dan pressed play again. A second voice began. "Hey, Sis — how are things?"

"Does 'Sis' mean sister or sissy?" Ked said.

"Both."

"Hey, Ked," the voice continued. "Happy birthday, dude."

"Cool! He remembered."

"Danny, I forgot to ask if we're having burgers or chicken for supper. I don't know whether to bring white cream soda or red …."

Dan smiled.

"… so maybe I'll bring both. See you tonight!" The message clicked off.

Ked looked up at his father. "Is 'sissy' a bad word?"

"Depends who's saying it."

Ked pondered this. "Did you and Uncle Donny ever date? I know he talks about what you look like nude…."

Dan raised a hand. "Don't believe everything he says!"

"… but I wasn't sure if you ever dated him."

"We dated. It was a very long time ago."

"But was it more than sex?" Ked persisted.

The topic of his father's sexuality had never been off-limits, but of late Ked had become more curious about Dan's private life.

Dan thought this over. "I guess it was, though we may not have realized it at the time. Maybe that's why we're still friends."

"Then why don't you still date him? Is it because he's black?"

Dan shot Ked a look. "You know it's not. Your Uncle Donny just likes to date a lot of men at once…."

"He's a slut!" Ked crowed.

Dan eyed his son. "Ked — don't talk like that."

"Why? That's what Uncle Donny says about himself."

"Nevertheless."

"And you like to date just one guy at a time, right?"

"Something like that."

Ked thought this over. "Do you think you and Bill will ever get married? I mean, for real married, like in a church and everything."

Dan reached over and tugged his son's dark curls. "Why? Do you want to be my best man?"

Ked shrugged. "I would if you wanted me to."

"I'll let you know when we set the date. In the meantime, I've got a bit of work to do ...."

Ked groaned.

"... and you've got at least one guest coming for supper, so let's go get ready."

Upstairs in his office, Dan set his laptop on the chair and cleared his desk. On the walls, Martha Stewart's Corn Husk competed for calm with the green-and-white striped shade pulled down. A single upright oak shelf held investigative reports, half-read anthropological texts, and a handful of slim detective novels, book-ended by Joyce, Pound, Proust.

Dan had three cases to write up before the weekend. Donny would be here by eight o'clock, and that left only tomorrow and Friday morning. After that, the wedding would take up all his free time. If he didn't work now, they might not get done.

He pulled up the latest: a seventy-six-year-old female who hadn't returned from a day trip to Toronto. He scanned the screen. No physical or mental impairment. The woman's daughter had tried to file a report with the Kitchener police; no one would take a formal statement. She'd been advised to contact the Toronto force, who confirmed they'd had notice of her mother's whereabouts on two previous occasions. The bottom of the report carried a familiar name.

Dan flipped through his Rolodex and fingered a card. He had a good guess what had happened. If he were right, Sergeant Carmen Stryker could probably confirm it. He glanced at the clock — nearly seven. If Stryker was still at work, that is.

The phone rang once and someone grabbed it. "Stryker."

"Hey, Carm. Dan Sharp here."

"Sharp! How the hell are ya?"

"Plugging away at it." Dan pictured the beefy sergeant sweating at his desk. "How about you? Still on the desk, I see."

"Fuckers!" the cop growled. "I never get outta here before eight."

Dan heard what sounded like a fist banged onto a desktop.

"You're too good at what you do, my man. If you stopped solving problems indoors, they'd have you back on the streets in a flash."

A hearty laugh. "You got that right! Anyway, what can I do you for? Your mother disappear again?"

"Close. You must be reading crystal balls. I got a misper who came through your office twice before. Wondered if you were keeping her holed up there again."

"Name?"

"Edith Walmsley, age seventy-six. Kitchener address."

"Sounds familiar — she has a history, you say?"

"Oh, yeah."

Dan heard the tapping of keys. Stryker grunted. Then, "Oh, shit — her! Crazy bitch. Yeah, she's here. This time we're keeping her till we make sure her family knows what she does with her spare time. I don't want her coming back with that poor little old lady story."

"Shoplifting again?"

"You got it. More jewellery. This latest price tag might just put her in the big league."

They had a chuckle over the foibles of little old ladies then Stryker had to take another call. "Say hi to the wife for me," he said, hanging up.

"If I had one I would," Dan said to the empty air.

One down, two to go. A drink would serve him well now. He slid the drawer forward and reached for the Scotch. He twisted the top and hesitated. When was the last time he'd worried that he couldn't be bothered to use a glass? Too long ago. Anyway, it was just one. The initial gulp tasted medicinal, iodine on an open wound. The second went down easier.

The next file was more difficult. Two years earlier, a male vic had been found in the Don Valley with gunshot wounds to the face and head. The description was laughably commonplace: white, 175 centimetres tall, 22 to 25 years old, brown hair, heavy tattoo work on the chest and arms. Numerous calls had come in for someone with that description; it never turned out to be him. The case languished in the John Doe files before showing up on a junior officer's desk. It was another month before it was transferred to Dan's.

Dan and the junior officer had perused the photographs together. A tattooed word caught Dan's attention: bog. Dan thought he saw what the problem was.

"What kind of moron tattoos *bog* on his chest?" the underling sneered.

"Maybe a Serbian moron," Dan said. "It means 'God' in Serb. You ask off continent?"

The man's face fell. "How the hell was I supposed to know that?"

"Never assume anything about a man who can't tell you how he ended up on a morgue table," Dan said.

The underling stared at Dan as though he were God in any language. Dan wasn't about to tell him he knew only two words in Serb, thanks to a former lover who'd come and gone with the greeting "Pomoz' bog." *God help you.* Though in this case, it appears God hadn't.

The call came from Bosnia a week later. A woman had reported her son missing two years before. He'd left home looking for employment in March. He hadn't said where he was going but maintained cell phone contact with her until August 16, the day the unidentified body turned up in the Toronto ravine. The Serbian police forwarded the report and a dozen snapshots. The only thing that didn't fit was the age. According to his mother, her son was thirty-two when he disappeared.

Whether he was twenty-five or an underdeveloped thirty-two wouldn't make much difference. Dan looked over the photograph of a mop-haired young man in a navy T. Spiky tattoos peeked from under the sleeves. Dan pulled up the morgue photos. The dead man's face was too damaged to confirm anything, but the tattoos showed a similarity.

The photographs supplied by desperate relatives fascinated Dan. Of course, with hindsight you could read whatever you wanted into them. Those sad eyes might be holding back a lifetime of misery and despair, or maybe they were just bloodshot from drink. That grim stare could belong to someone who'd finally found the determination to leave a hopeless situation, or it might have been masking a simple dislike for the photographer.

The "why" could be more difficult to determine. Some disappeared to punish whoever kept them from whatever was "out there." Occasionally they returned on their own, without finding what they were seeking. Dan wondered if the ones who never showed up again had been more successful. Still others claimed not to know why they'd left or even to have considered who might have been hurt by their actions. Sometimes it was sheer desperation, a last chance to escape whatever held them back. It didn't matter — they just went. Then there were the ones who didn't have a chance to think about it, because vanishing was the last thing on their minds. They had futures, careers, families — and every reason to stay. They turned up in ditches and farmers' fields years later, a pile of bones, a tag of cloth, a collection of dental records. What had made them the target of murderers, the victim of rapists who felt they had no choice but to finish a job gone wrong? These were the most intriguing ones.

The second-last photograph showed a group of young men playing ball near a line of bleachers. Marker arrows pointed to a shirtless figure, his right arm thrown back and a ball in hand. The torso was wiry, the ribs too prominent. A blazon of hair ran up his belly and across his chest. Dan's eyes lingered. If the boy had been alive, he might have found the photo erotic. Being aroused by pictures of the dead made Dan queasy, however. He brought out a magnifying glass and leaned in. On the left pectoral over the heart, he could just make out the word *bog*. Case closed.

He signed off on the file and wondered about his Bosnian counterpart — the one who would contact the family with the news. No matter how a case ended, Dan seldom took pleasure from it. It was work. Whether he successfully tracked someone down or had to pass on bad news had little bearing on how he presented it. He offered his findings quietly, but unambiguously. "Your son died of natural causes." "The dental work confirms it's your daughter's body." "Your wife is alive and well, but no longer a woman." His words fell with simple gravity, as though he were pronouncing a sentence the hearer must bear accordingly.

Some took the news quietly. Others cried or broke down, knowing their lives were changed forever, if not outright ruined. For some it came as a combination of pain and relief at finally knowing. Knowledge could stop the hoping, but it didn't make things better. They were the ones who made Dan's life hell, though he didn't resent them. It was the ones who didn't or wouldn't grieve he resented, as though they'd made his work a failure, like a fireman saving a burning building only to learn it had been condemned. He hated futility — the feeling that his work amounted to nothing. "No return" was unacceptable.

In the course of his investigations, Dan was meticulous. A missing person's past was like a shadow thrown against a curtain, all outline and little detail. Sometimes the smallest point was the telling one. He thought of the junior who'd missed out on the word *bog*. The mistake was understandable, but it was sloppy work all the same. Know thoroughly the nature of what you're being asked to investigate and then look for the unexpected — that was Dan's modus operandi. It was the only way to find the missing, especially if they didn't want to be found.

He stopped and took another pull from the bottle, then settled in again. He brought up the last file and glanced at the overview. He didn't have to read far. Why anyone was surprised when abused teenagers ran away, Dan couldn't imagine. The fourteen-year-old, Richard Philips, had left his home in Oshawa following an argument with his mother and stepfather. The photograph showed a dark-haired teenager with wary eyes and a pouting mouth. Dan wondered who'd taken the shot.

The details were predictable. Richard's problems had started when he was twelve, not long after his mother remarried to a man who never got along with her son. According to his mother, her son had been picked on at school. More importantly, he had sexuality issues. Richard's stepfather threatened him after police nabbed him hanging around a gay cruising area. The boy disappeared two weeks later when the same officer picked him up again.

Dan sat back. He could easily imagine some sadistic homophobe getting his jollies by fucking with the kid's nascent sex drive. At that age, it was hard enough to accept yourself for what you were. To have bullying cops, taunting classmates, and a narrow-minded stepfather harassing you might prove too much for some kids. Running away was one solution. Suicide was the other.

The report carried the usual protestations by the mother and stepfather: they'd given their son everything and didn't understand how he'd become someone they barely knew — angry, resentful, and gay. The first two were

21

usually easy to explain when the history was examined. The third wasn't something you could rationalize to distraught parents, especially the ones who wanted to justify their actions: threats and beatings, doors locked at midnight to teach a lesson to the habitual latecomer and rule-breaker. Self-justification was one thing, but how did you forgive yourself if you locked your door and your kid ended up dead? It happened. Ask Lesley Mahaffey's parents.

Dan looked at his watch — nearly time. He closed the file on the teenage runaway and went downstairs to see what Ked had done to prepare for his party.

TWO

Modern Jazz

KED WAS ASLEEP IN A CHAIR next to the barbecue. Donny and Dan sat across from one another. The remains of a food platter, a dozen empty beer bottles, and a half-eaten birthday cake sat on the table between them. Coloured lanterns threw shadows around the deck. Sleepy nighttime jazz seeped from the speakers and wafted through the backyard.

Donny blew a smoke ring. "This Marsalis?"

"You got it," Dan said. "Is he hot or cool?"

"I'm not sure he's either," Donny answered. "Wynton plays like a white boy. I put him in the same category as Chet Baker."

Dan's face was a question mark. "Are you saying that because he plays classical?"

"Not at all. I think Marsalis is a dynamite classical player. Except for that number two Brandenburg where he sounds like a synthesizer. It's his jazz I have a problem with. It's too stiff and intellectual."

"You don't like Chet either? He's got great tone."

Donny took a drag worthy of Bette Davis then stubbed out the cigarette. "He's Ivy League. I don't like anyone who thinks 'Over the Rainbow' is a respectable jazz number."

Dan laughed and uncapped a beer. "You snob!"

Donny's eyebrows shot up. "Sugar, I work in the cosmetics industry. It comes with the territory. And you can't touch me for that."

It was Donny's revenge for growing up poor, black, and — the ultimate disgrace for a Caribbean son — gay. Somehow he'd discovered he had a discerning nose for expensive scents, the perfumes and nectars of the gods. He now made a living turning up his nose for the same people who'd once snubbed him, advising them on the lotions, potions, and magic formulas they hoped would transform their looks. Maybe even their lives.

"Oh, yeah?" Dan countered. "How cool is it for some of these old black guys to be playing 'Summertime'? That's just tourist shite!"

"Hee-hee! You got me there."

Dan thought for a moment. "Are you saying you can tell whether a player is black or white by how he blows a horn?"

"Sure I can!"

"No way! You're going to have to prove that one." Dan went inside and returned with a handful of CDs, tossing another bottle of beer to Donny. "Test time," he said, slipping a disc into the player.

Chirpy bird-awkward notes wafted upward, drifting among the branches, cool and seductive.

"It's Miles," Donny said after a moment. "Probably from the mid-fifties, which means it's the Quintet." He listened again. "Yeah, that's Coltrane. No mistaking that sound."

Dan whistled. "Very good. It doesn't even sound like the Miles Davis I know."

Donny shook his head. "I can always tell Miles. Ellington called him the 'Picasso of jazz.'"

"Does that make him hot or cool?"

Donny shot him a quick glance. "You have to ask? Miles Davis is the *epitome* of cool jazz. There's no one better. Listen to that sound!"

A rap beat emerged from the player next. Pure street cred. Donny smiled. "Miles again. This is from *doo-bop*, am I right?"

Dan nodded.

"I don't even need to hear the horn. You can't shit me. This was his last album. I'm a true blue Miles fan."

"Damn." Dan shook his head and removed another CD from its case. "Okay, smart ass. Who's this?"

A feathery drum brush dominated the speakers as a stuttering horn searched a pathway between the notes. Donny listened quietly for a moment.

"I'm going to guess Dizzy, and you're a dead man if I'm wrong, 'cause I hate to be wrong when it comes to my horns."

Dan grinned. "Right again."

"I don't know this piece. What is it?"

"It's a live performance of 'Lullaby In Rhythm' from a Paris nightclub. Very early Dizzy. It's a reissue I picked up recently."

"Cool! Catch those brush strokes! That drummer's making love to someone. So's Dizzy. Hear those triplets? Whenever I hear Dizzy, I feel a whiskery set of lips moving to-and-fro across my belly till I'm ready to explode."

25

"So is he hot or cool?"

"He is definitely hot. Listen to that sound — the man's on fire!"

"Define Gillespie's tone in three words or less."

"Hmm...." Donny put a match to a cigarette, cocked his head, and listened. "Sexual ... seductive ... he's all wet and slurpy. He gets right inside your skin with that splatter of notes."

"Too many words. How about 'slutty'?"

Donny exploded in laughter. "You got it. That's exactly what old Dizzy is! Slutty! Whoo, boy! I can feel those bristles on my belly! Just don't tell him he's making love to a man, though. He might get upset."

"You never know. He might like you."

The laughter subsided. Dan switched CDs. A glittery baroque theme gilded the air.

Donny snorted. "Ah, man! That's Marsalis again."

"You sure?"

"You can't fool me just because he's playing classical."

Dan shook his head. "Nope."

"What? Sure it is. That's Wynton Marsalis. I know this piece."

"What is it?"

"Something about the Bright Seraphim. It's by Handel."

"No, man. You are dead wrong on both counts. It's not Handel and it's not Marsalis."

Donny stared, cigarette smoke leaking from his nostrils. "It can't be. Let me see that thing." Donny looked over the CD case, shaking his head. "Well, I'll be damned," he said softly.

"That's Gerard Schwartz playing Scarlatti. He's as white as they come."

"You see? I told you Marsalis plays like a white boy."

Dan smirked. "Gotcha!"

Donny raised a warning finger. "You say a word about this and I'll tell everyone you gave Abe Pittman head in my bathroom because you felt sorry for him when Victor dumped him."

"Ooh!" Dan said. "That's mean. Okay, I promise."

The track came to an end. The night was silent again. Donny turned to look at Ked curled up on his chair.

"You think the kid enjoyed his party?"

"Party of three, with his father and surrogate uncle?"

"Doesn't he have any friends his age?"

Dan shot him a look. "Do you think he'd want me to introduce them to gay Uncle Donny and his dad's boyfriend Bill?"

"I see. We're good enough to fuck, but not good enough to be family, is that it? And what happened to His Royal Highness, anyway? He stand us up again?"

Dan shrugged off the question. "You know — work. Something came up."

"Uh-huh. Something's always 'coming up' at work. When are you going to get wise to that one?"

Dan cocked a warning eyebrow. "Whatever that means, Bill is fine. For now."

"Yeah? Then why's he always running around half-naked, doing E at clubs and acting like he's still in his twenties? He's a doctor, isn't he?"

"He's still a big kid at heart."

"I'll say."

Dan took a pull from his beer and set the bottle on the table. "Anyway, it's not as if I have options."

"And it's not as though you advertise, either. When was the last time you went out to a bar?"

Dan shrugged. "I don't get lucky in bars — I just get drunk. In case you haven't noticed, I'm no beauty."

"No, Sugar, you are not, but you have a very tight, trim body the older boys love because it makes them feel like powerful daddies, and the younger boys enjoy because it makes them feel desired by a hot, sexy man. So everyone's happy." Donny looked askance at Dan. "What about you?"

"Don't be a spoilsport."

Donny glanced over at Ked again. "The boy was asking how come you and I don't date any more."

Dan took another pull on his beer. "What'd you tell him?"

"I said I only fuck white boys to hear them scream, and I don't date you because I couldn't respect you if I did."

Dan threw a hamburger bun at him. It glanced off Donny's shoulder and rolled across the table.

"Asshole! You did not say that. And as I recall, you're the one who screamed on our dates. Good thing I told Ked not to believe a word you say about me."

"Well, I think I once told him his daddy was pretty sizeable for a white boy. He told me his mother said the same thing."

Dan laughed quietly. "Bastard."

"What? It's true! It's a monster."

"You don't need to tell my kid that."

"Don't you want him to grow up to be proud of you?"

"Not for that."

"Suit yourself." Donny crossed his arms and turned away. He waited a moment before looking back. "So you and Miss Doctor are getting along these days?"

Dan shrugged. "He's unreliable and takes forever to return calls, but he's great in the sack...."

"And you say *I* reduce everything to sex!"

"... which you do ... plus I'm going to meet some of his friends this weekend. Did I mention that the wedding we're invited to is on a yacht?"

"Ooh! A yacht even!" Donny made a face. "The girl's classy for a low-down bitch. Where'd she buy these friends?"

Dan stabbed the air with a finger. "You are a total asshole." But he was laughing.

"It's my greatest charm...."

"You have no charm," Dan said, emptying his beer. "One of the guys getting married is Bill's oldest friend. They went to school together. Upper Canada College and a few years of university somewhere...."

"You and your rich boys."

"I was still born in the gutter."

"And you'll die there, if you don't stop dating men like Bill. Like most poor folk, you confuse money with class." Donny peered intently at Dan. "You used to be a regular prolie when I met you — rough around the edges and wet behind the ears — but somewhere along the line you picked up some pretty bourgeois tastes."

Dan snorted. "Really? And what about you?"

"Moi?" Donny splayed a hand against his chest — Marie Antoinette before the tribunal, disavowing all knowledge of privilege. "I'm as middle-class as they come. Which is why you stopped dating me. It's okay, though. I respect you now. But do tell about the wedding. It sounds very recherché."

"Let's have some Scotch first," Dan said, rising.

Donny's hand went up. "I've had enough for tonight. Haven't you?"

"Maybe." Dan sat back and cupped his hands behind his head. "Anyway, I don't know much about the wedding yet, but it promises to be fun. I've never spent an entire weekend on a boat before. Just me and Bill and a bunch of rich folk."

"Rich white folk, no doubt. And where does the prideful event take place?"

"Somewhere in Prince Edward County, half an hour east of Kingston. Ever hear of a place called Glenora?"

Donny took so long to answer that Dan thought he hadn't heard his question. "Yeaaah ..." he said finally. "Something about a freak lake?"

"I don't know anything about a lake, freak or otherwise, but they make a very nice pale ale." He held up the bottle of Glenora Red Coat he'd just finished.

"Oh, is that why...."

"Just sampling the local wares."

"And here I thought you were getting cheap on me." Donny shook his head. "No, man — this place is famous. There's some strange geological phenomenon like nowhere else in the world. It's up on a mountain somewhere. Apparently it has no incoming source of water, but never runs dry...."

"Underground streams?"

"Maybe. I don't remember."

"You sure you don't want another drink?" Dan asked.

Donny put down his bottle and stood. "Thank you, no. I must depart."

"It's about time. I thought you'd never leave."

"And that's the only reason I stayed this long." Donny looked over at Ked. "Say goodbye to the kid for me."

"Take some cake?"

"Please!" Donny made a face. "Keep it for your doctor."

Ralph sniffed curiously at Donny as he passed through the kitchen then turned back to his bed.

"Thanks for coming," Dan said. "Ked was thrilled you made it."

"Me too." Donny filled the doorway. "It was fun to celebrate somebody else's birthday for once."

They hugged as Donny's fingers felt around Dan's midriff. "Still not an inch of fat on you. I don't know how you do it, with all the drinking you do."

"Willpower," Dan said. "That and light beer."

Donny smiled. "You have a good weekend, Sis. And take notes — sounds like it's going to be *trés* elegant. I expect you to come back with lots o' dirt. I want to hear all about how the rich and filthy-minded live. I need to compare notes!"

"I'll tell you all about it when I get back."

An hour later, Ked was packed off to bed. Dan had cleaned up the porch and headed inside. After pouring himself a final drink, he put away the bottles of alcohol. Upstairs in his study, he turned back to the folder containing the file on the runaway, Richard Philips. He read the report again, and again laboured over the photograph. Something about the boy's eyes — some vulnerability — wouldn't let him go. Finally, he closed the file and turned off the machine.

THREE

Coffee and Donuts

DAN'S HEART POUNDED BENEATH THE SHEET. The phone was halfway through the second ring. The caller ID strip glowed green: bell payphone — 3:34 am. It might be Bill calling to say he'd finished his shift, though he usually crawled off to his own place and didn't bother to call — if he even thought of Dan when he left work. Then too, Bill had a cell phone.

Dan cleared his throat and picked up, but the answering machine got there first. A dial tone hung in the air. He stared through the blackness at the receiver. "If you're going to wake me up, you could at least identify yourself so I'll know who to be pissed off at tomorrow."

He smacked the phone down. Anyone in trouble would have left a message. Kendra certainly, and Ked was asleep in the next room, so it couldn't have been anything to do with either of them. But you'd have to be desperate to phone at that hour. His heart was still doing a jazz number.

His thoughts returned to Bill. He might've been arrested with drugs in his pocket at some after-hours club. Once he'd been stopped while driving on the verge of being impaired, but it turned out he'd operated on the cop's mother and got off with a warning. Bill was lucky that way. What if he'd been in an accident? Dan tried not to think about it. In another minute he'd have himself convinced Bill was somewhere out there, hurt or in trouble, and that Dan had failed to be there for him.

He rolled onto his back and stared at the darkness. Anonymous calls pissed him off. He might lie awake for hours wondering who it was. Part of him liked to think Bill would call to say he wanted to come over, screw the late hour. Even with Ked at home, Dan would've agreed. But that never happened. Bill didn't sleep at other peoples' houses.

He tried to drop back to sleep, but with no luck. Sometimes he dreamed of Bill and woke up arguing aloud. They were usually on a train in a foreign city — London, New York, once Miami — headed somewhere that mattered to Dan, but never to Bill. Dan would try to impress on Bill the importance of the trip, but without success. The dreams always ended in confusion, with missed connections, lost tickets, and dashed hopes for arriving wherever they were heading.

Dan's therapist encouraged him to explore how he felt. It didn't take a shrink to tell him all the signs of a heavily flawed relationship were apparent in waking life, never mind in la-la-land when he was asleep. Even intelligent people let themselves be deluded by their emotions.

Bill seemed incapable of affection, elusive and ambivalent about his feelings. Commitment-phobe didn't cover it. He'd make dates and cancel at the last minute. He had excuses — work commitments, family obligations, social networking. Despite the fact they'd been dating a year, they never seemed to get closer. When pressed, Dan found it hard to point to anything meaningful between them. In all that time, he'd met only a handful of Bill's closest friends and not one family member.

"We're not close," Bill had said of his four brothers and two sisters.

In this case, "not close" meant sporadic telephone conversations with his siblings, and infrequent family gatherings of unstated intent. Dan was never invited. At least not by Bill. Even Christmas seemed a duty, though not one Bill felt required a spouse. When Dan pressed him, Bill would shrug and say it wasn't important, shutting down the conversation.

To Dan, the ideal relationship was an easy-going fusion of personalities that allowed both partners to remain healthily independent while knowing each could depend on the other. A state in which late night phone calls were a cause for joy, not alarm, and trust was a matter of course rather than fantasy. Bill was a constant challenge to that goal.

And then there was the small matter of Kedrick. Dan's dates were impressed to learn he was a father, but he sensed their wariness, as though it meant he was already taken. They seemed to doubt he could divide his loyalty between his son and a partner. Maybe they were right — part of him would always be devoted to Kedrick, no matter who came into his life. But Bill didn't demand Dan's loyalty so much as his physical availability. In that, at least, he was easy to please.

It was Donny who'd dubbed Bill the "heartless heart doctor." "It's ironic," he said, "but that man has no feelings for anyone but himself."

They'd been sitting in Timothy's Coffee on Church Street, adrift in a minor sea of T-shirts and denim. Donny had just come from work. He was dressed impeccably in a white button-down shirt, Gucci tie, and black Oxfords — Will Smith behind the perfume counter at Holt Renfrew.

He thrummed a finger in Dan's face. "That man is a self-centred egotist. He expects you to come running when he's free and complains if you won't. On the other hand, he doesn't return your calls for days and whines if you mention it. Where's the equality?"

"He's a busy man." Dan turned to watch the traffic outside the window. "He's dedicated to his work. It's not unusual for him to spend fifteen or sixteen hours at the hospital, even when he's only scheduled for twelve."

Donny hung on noisily and tiresomely like a dog with a chewy toy. "He could still call to let you know. It's not as if you're chopped liver. You're a heavy hitter in your department, too."

"He saves lives. He can't just tell people to come back later."

"Excuse me?" Donny said in that haughty, offended-minority tone he used to give himself the edge in an argument. "And what exactly is it you do?"

Dan's eyes flickered over to the line-up at the counter, where curious faces had turned to take in their conversation. His voice lowered. "I find people who don't want to be found and I return them to places they don't want to be returned to, for reasons that are usually none of my business."

"Fuck you!" Donny said. "Fuck you, you self-loathing faggot!"

He jostled the table and sent coffee spilling from the cups and sluicing over the tabletop. Next to them, an older man with sunken cheeks leaned in sympathetically and offered a stack of napkins.

"Thanks," Donny said, dabbing ineffectually at the mess. He turned back to Dan. "All I'm saying is, you save lives too. Why is your job less important than his?"

"Stop it," Dan said. He didn't bother to pretend to be offended. "I never said my job is less important — it's just more flexible."

Dan hated arguing. Donny always managed to sound right, even when he wasn't, and he had the energy to back it up. But in this case he had a point. Dan may have been a pro at what he did, but somehow he felt like a fraud.

The telephone's anxious ring jarred him, putting Donny and his stained napkins on pause. The ID strip showed a private number now, but there was still no name. It seemed to be his night for anonymous calls. Dan grabbed it before the caller could change his mind again.

"Dan Sharp."

A whispery silence greeted him.

"This is Dan Sharp. Who is this?"

"It's Steve — Steve Jenkins." The voice carried a flatness that made it all but unrecognisable.

Dan's mind bounced around trying to find something familiar in the tone and in light of the unusual circumstances. His former next-door neighbour shouldn't be calling at four in the morning.

Dan's voice softened. "Steve. Did you call half an hour ago from a payphone?"

"Yes. I'm — I'm sorry about the time."

36

"Are you okay?"

"I'm not sure. Could I … could I talk to you?"

Dan threw off the sheets and sat up, his training kicking in like a decathlete approaching the stadium. "Of course. Where are you?"

"I'm in an apartment near Donlands and Danforth."

Dan squinted at the caller ID and read off the number. "Is this the number you're calling from, Steve?"

"I think so. I'd really like to get out of here, though." His words sounded in a slurred monotone.

"Are you on any medications, Steve?"

"Um, no — yeah. I took a tranquillizer, but it doesn't seem to be helping."

"How many?"

"Pardon?"

"How many did you take?"

A pause. "Just one. I'm pretty sure."

"Okay, we can get you out of there. Can you walk? Are you all right — physically, I mean?"

"Yes. I'm okay."

"Do you know the Coffee Time Donuts on the southwest corner of Jones and Danforth?"

"Yes. I'm a block away from there."

"Can you manage to get there? I can be there in five minutes."

"Okay — yeah. Thanks. I really appreciate it, Dan."

Dan arrived with Ked in tow. The shop was garish at that hour. Table surfaces reflected the glare of nighttime windows. Fluorescent fixtures lit up over-sized posters for coffee and bagels, making the racked donuts glow with a blue tinge. Coloured sprinkles and powdered sugar vied with sticky glazes for counter appeal, finding none. A sleepy-looking employee roused himself and approached the register, his hair weirdly illuminated by the light.

"Good morning," Dan said as cheerily as he could manage.

The boy mumbled a few words that vaguely resembled English. Whatever the intended meaning, the sentiment was clearly not welcoming. He wiped his hands on an apron that looked like it had done time in an abattoir. Dan ordered three donuts and a cardboard container of milk for Ked, who looked at him strangely.

Dan frowned. "What? It's good for you."

Ked rolled his eyes. He picked up the tray and went off to a table in a far corner, slouching into the seat.

Dan looked around. One table over, an old Asian man picked at the crumbs on his plate. Or someone's plate. At the far end of the shop, a serious young woman in a beret conferred in quiet tones with a man in a thirties-style suit. Bonnie and Clyde in an idle moment. Dan and Ked were the only other customers. In the daytime, the place bustled with immigrants who didn't share the North American disdain for cheap coffee and lacquered tables. At this hour it looked more like an Edward Hopper study for the lost, the lonely, and the rebellious.

Steve came through the door and stood blinking in the light. Whatever he'd undergone in the four months since leaving Glenda, it didn't look good on him. A cup of tea might have served him in good stead. Dan could have gone for something with a bit more bite.

Ked waved at Steve and turned back to his Game Boy. Steve mumbled an elaboration of his apology for calling so late. Dan let him ramble on about the break-up with Glenda. Steve's hands fidgeted as he related the events that had brought him to his current state. He seemed to be rehashing things to find their meaning or else to locate himself in time, as though he'd gotten lost a few months back.

A moment of silence passed. His tale seemed to have run its course. Steve's hands relaxed as his eyes took on a vacant stare.

"I'm sorry for what you're going through," Dan said. "Is there something I can do to help?"

Steve blinked. "I just thought … I better talk to someone. You were the only one who came to mind. I mean, apart from those pathetic help lines you hear about." He smiled weakly.

At least he hasn't lost it completely, Dan thought. They'd always been friendly, sharing day-to-day concerns across the adjoining fence, but Dan never assumed he and Steve were anything more than neighbours. Over the past year, Steve had brought news of his ongoing arguments with Glenda in what would eventually become a lasting break-up. At the time it felt like simple domestic griping, one man to another. To Steve it had obviously meant more.

"Sometimes when I couldn't sleep, I used to look over and see the light in your study. That's why I remembered you stayed up late." He shook his head. "I'm sorry. I shouldn't have called. I just wanted to talk to someone."

Dan tried for a reassuring tone. "It's all right. I'm glad you called. But I think there's more to it than that, isn't there? Talk can always wait till the morning. Something happened tonight, didn't it?"

Steve's face twisted in an odd half-smile. "What do you mean?"

Dan leaned closer. "I think you were afraid of yourself. Afraid you might do something. You reached some sort of breaking point tonight, didn't you?"

Steve's lip trembled. A tear splashed onto the table. "Does she want me to kill myself? Why won't she even talk to me?"

Dan put a hand on Steve's forearm. "It's okay."

"I did everything for her. Why wasn't she happy?"

In the corner of his vision, Dan saw the old man wander over to another table and start on the crumbs there. He signalled to Ked to give the guy a donut.

Steve shuddered. "I know why," he said at last. "Because she doesn't need me any more. She used to need me. When we were in college together we were terrified of the future. We lived in this one-room dump. We used to cling to each other every night, saying how awful life was. We really needed each other then."

"Then what happened?" Dan said.

"I don't know. Life was getting better. Things were getting easier. Or I thought they were. I worked hard to give her everything she wanted. Then one day she asked me to leave. She said it wasn't working for her. All this time I thought we were happy...." His voice broke on the final syllable. He reached for a napkin and swiped at his eyes. "I gave her the house. Did she tell you?"

"She asked you to leave and you told her she could have the house?"

Steve nodded.

"And she took it?" Dan asked, incredulous.

Steve nodded again. *Of course she damn well took it,* Dan thought.

"I just …" Steve shuddered. "I just want her to be happy."

She is *happy,* Dan thought. *Now that you're out of her life.* He envisioned Glenda raking leaves in her cocktail outfit, just one of a million reasons why he hated the city. Toronto had changed in the years he'd lived there. When had the horrible, selfish hordes moved in and taken over? He thought of the sour contempt with which his fellow citizens viewed the rest of the country, the smug satisfaction they exhibited over their meagre little domain. His neighbour on the other side was no better: a patronizing boor who treated his wife like a piece of real estate, interrupting her whenever she spoke, which was seldom, and raising his voice through the roof the moment he set foot in the door. In the warm weather you could hear him talking non-stop, morning to night. He spoke to Dan with half-disguised contempt, as though he were only being nice to the queer-next-door for form's sake. On the other hand, guys like Steve were a little too nice. "Is there any chance you could —?"

"No. She doesn't want me back." Steve's words slurred again. He seemed to be concentrating to counter the effects of the tranquillizer. "What did I do wrong?" he asked, like a chastised child.

"You didn't do anything wrong. People grow apart for a lot of different reasons."

"I know." Steve blew his nose on the napkin and looked up. "I just never thought it would happen to us."

"I think you need to accept it for now, and go on with your life. Maybe things will change, but you need to get on with things. Are you working?"

Steve shook his head. "No — I'm too much of a mess. I haven't been able to concentrate since this happened."

Dan looked over at Ked, who'd fallen asleep in the chair after giving the old man a donut and the carton of milk. Bonnie and Clyde were holding hands across the table, still speaking in whispers, planning their next heist. The store clerk had disappeared behind his counter.

"I'm sorry," Steve said. "It was selfish of me to call. I didn't realize you had Ked with you."

"I'm glad you felt you could call me." Dan squeezed Steve's forearm. He was thinking that next time he might not get a call till it was too late. He'd hear from Glenda over the fence how poor Steve had killed himself out of grief, trying to sound as if she cared.

"I couldn't stop thinking about those sleeping pills," Steve said, confirming Dan's fears. "I didn't want to disturb you, but something made me do it."

"Calling someone is always the right thing to do. Promise me you'll call any time you feel things are getting out of hand. I'd like to think you'd do the same for me."

Steve smiled ruefully. "Yeah, right — like you've got problems, Mr. Everything's-Under-Control."

Dan wondered if that was really how he appeared to people who didn't know him.

"I think I'm all talked out." Steve yawned. He seemed calmer, a different person from the man who'd walked in the door an hour earlier. "I think we'd better get some rest."

"Are you sure?" Dan said. "I'm not in a hurry."

"Thanks. I'm sure."

They left the donut shop and walked up the street. Ked faltered behind them, as though he couldn't coordinate his footsteps.

"I want you to promise me you'll talk to your doctor about this," Dan said. "You do have a doctor, don't you?"

"Yes."

"Good. Talk to him. Make an appointment today. Maybe a month or two on anti-depressants would help."

"I will," Steve said gratefully. "I promise I will do that." He was nearly Dan's age, but over the last hour he'd assumed the role of dutiful son.

They reached Dan's car. Ked slid into the backseat and lay down without a word.

"I can give you a lift if you want," Dan said.

"I'm only a block away." Steve waved in the direction of Donlands.

The storefronts along Danforth were taking shape, losing shadow in the coming light. A car slid past, somnolent in the pre-dawn hush.

"You should see this place," Steve said. "It comes fully furnished with artificial flowers. Did I tell you? It's like a hotel lobby. It's sort of wonderful and horrible at the same time. You'll have to come over some night. We'll put down a bottle of wine."

For an instant Dan glimpsed the old Steve — friendly, chatty, kind. He was a good person. Someone who should never have to feel alone, with no one to help him sort out his problems.

"I'm always up for a drink and a chat."

Steve shook Dan's hand. "Thanks," he said. "I can't tell you how much I appreciate this, Dan. I feel much better. Truly."

"Good. Keep in touch so I know things are all right. I'm home tonight after work and I'll be in the office Friday morning, but I'm gone for the weekend." Dan pressed a card in Steve's hand. "Here's my cell number. If you need to talk, just call me. Any time. I'm there for you."

He watched Steve walk away, then got in the car and started the engine, hoping he could still catch an hour's sleep. He turned to see Ked slumped in the back.

"How ya doing, kiddo?" he asked. "Gonna make it?"

With eyes closed, Ked nodded his head against the seat. "I love you, Dad," he said softly.

FOUR

Dreams and Schemes

SOMETIMES GOING BACK TO BED for that extra hour was the right thing to do and sometimes it was the wrong thing. Today it had been the wrong thing. Dan fumbled with a dull razor and dressed without realizing he'd put on mismatched socks. At nine o'clock, he spilled half a cup of coffee on his shirt. By ten, the entire day looked like it would be out-of-kilter. His reading glasses felt like a giant pair of daddy-long-legs straddling his head as he finalized the reports on the missing Kitchener woman with her fondness for jewellery and the young Serb who'd placed his faith in God and had the misfortune to come to Canada looking for work.

Shadows passed over the frosted glass with the mumbled goings-on of morning voices outside Dan's office. For a firm that performed feats as miraculous as raising the dead, it might have had a colour scheme to match — beatific tropical shades, joyful rainbow hues. Instead, the offices were battleship grey — dull and cheerless as a December morning. Still, Dan consoled himself it was nothing so invidiously depressing as bubble gum pink or mustard yellow. It was simple, utilitarian, functional. Perhaps that precise shade of grey had been chosen to remind them of the dreary perseverance with which so many of the firm's clients spent their days.

After fourteen years, Dan was one of the senior investigators. Some came and went in the space of a few years after finding more prestigious placement, while others burned out from the perennial themes of human misery that befell so many whose lives they tracked and whose stories were all that was left to record.

Dan had an impressive record of finds behind him and no reason to leave. There were always bigger firms and more prestigious appointments, but he'd made a decent life for himself and Ked. And he hadn't lost interest in his work, which had always been his biggest concern. He didn't need to feign enthusiasm or be admired. He was, despite the predictions of others, unaccountably successful. After all this time watching the others come and go, he had to ask himself: what else was there for him to do?

Dan was on his third cup of coffee, but the caffeine stubbornly refused to kick in. What he really wanted was a drink, but it was only ten thirty — far too early. A bottle of Scotch lay wrapped in a Sobey's bag in the bottom of his desk. He'd hidden it like a schoolboy tucking cigarettes and condoms in the back of his socks drawer. In his mind's eye he watched little feet duck outside and scrabble around the corner to the bar. Let them stay there then.

He tried Bill's number and got the answering service. Bill never slept in, even after a late night, which meant he'd already left for the hospital. If he'd made it home the night before.

"Hiya," Dan said into the phone. "We missed you last night." His voice was gravely with fatigue. He tried to make himself sound jovial. "Give me a call about the weekend. I still don't know who's driving." The plan had been to drive to Glenora on Friday and stay overnight with Bill's friend Thom, the groom. As usual, Bill had been so hard to pin down that basic questions like whose car they were taking were still up in the air. "I'll wait to hear from you. Ciao."

He took another hopeless sip of coffee and opened the file on Richard Philips, the missing fourteen-year-old. The boy's birthdate caught Dan's eye — he was exactly one year less a day older than Ked, which meant that he was now a fifteen-year-old runaway. *Happy birthday, Richard.*

He read on. The boy had been missing for two months. There'd been no body recovered and thus no closure. At the end of August, an anonymous caller phoned Toronto police to say the boy was fine, giving details only someone close to him would know, and adding that Richard had no intention of returning home. He'd been labelled a runaway, plain and simple. Until the police had anything further to go on, the case was shelved.

Dan flipped through the pages to the transcript. The call had been traced to a diner on Church Street in the heart of the gay ghetto. That narrowed the possibilities drastically. Unless a kid had friends to turn to in the city — preferably with money — then hustling was a likely avenue. It was a choice Dan wouldn't wish on anyone, but it was a direct source of income if a kid decided to disappear. It happened often enough, though the parents just couldn't understand why their kids would choose sex with a stranger over the "love" they found at home. Dan could.

He'd had plenty of time to think about it before leaving Sudbury at seventeen. The issue had been simple — why stay where you weren't wanted? He'd said goodbye to his aunt and cousin the night before, then told his father at breakfast he was leaving. Gaunt and grey-faced, the man grunted a response — whether in acknowledgment or disbelief, Dan couldn't tell, just as he could never tell what any of his father's cryptic communications meant.

After an exhilarating day hitchhiking, Dan found himself in Toronto with an empty belly and no bed. He bought three chocolate bars from an all-night grocery and slept on a park bench the first two nights, amazed by the shadowy forms flitting past till the early hours. Now and again, one of them crept close to investigate while Dan held his breath until they left again. It seemed the city never slept — and he had barely. The Yonge Street Mission took him in the third night. He tried pan-handling when his funds ran out, but the people he asked seemed more intimidated by him than sympathetic.

A kid at the mission told him about hustling. There was money to be made, he said, as long as you could stomach the sex. That wasn't a problem. Dan had already experienced sex with older men. He recalled the snuffling, grubbing hands that pawed under his T-shirt and down his sweatpants in the shadows beneath the railway trestle back home. Apparently he had what they liked. He got a reputation for an ability to time his orgasms with passing coaches, earning him the nickname Train Trestle Danny.

When he arrived in Toronto, he was already an adult in body. One Saturday in July he stood on a deserted corner in the downtown strip known as Boys Town. For once he was lucky — in a relative way. The man who stopped his Mercedes to chat up the ungainly teenager with the adult's body had been kind and not unattractive. He reminded Dan of his grade nine shop teacher, Mr. Dalton, a gruff man with hairy arms and shirtsleeves permanently rolled back. Dalton had been an erotic fixation for Dan, who conjured the man's image to trigger his masturbatory fantasies.

Dalton's look-alike invited Dan to his home in Leaside. Dan thought he was talking about a place outside Toronto, but the man assured him it was only a fifteen-minute ride to where they were headed. Money was never discussed. Dan was too nervous to bring it up, and the man had an assuredness that said he knew what he was doing.

As they drove along the tree-lined streets, Dan was struck by how little the neighbourhood offered the casual viewer. He wondered who lived behind the tidy, curtained windows where light spilled over the sills like the first star at twilight. He considered how much you'd have to earn to live there. Certainly more than he'd ever make.

Dan hadn't minded the sex. The man — Bob Greene — was courteous and hadn't asked Dan to do anything he wasn't comfortable with. Afterwards, Dan pocketed the fifty dollars, blushing at Bob's compliments. It was the first time anyone had made him feel attractive.

Bob was experienced at picking up boys. He knew life on the streets was anything but glamorous, and could be hazardous. He also knew hustlers came in two types: the ones you could trust and the ones you couldn't. Most fell into the latter category sooner or later. Bob knew Dan was new at the game. But he was polite and eager to please. The next morning, when Dan didn't seem in a hurry to get back on the streets, Bob invited him to stay for the day.

They spent the morning by the pool. In the afternoon, they walked around the neighbourhood. To Dan, Toronto was Yonge Street — the Eaton Centre and downtown strip with its sex shops, sporting goods chains, and fast food outlets. Beyond that, it seemed to sprawl without boundaries. You could walk all day without reaching the end of it. Here was another gleaming new part of it. With its staid brick homes and sturdy elms, Leaside represented the kind of family environment Dan had never known. It was a world away from the bleak mining town where he'd grown up.

Two months later, Bob picked him up on the same corner. Only this time, Dan didn't leave again for quite a while. The invitation to live in a place with a pool rather than the over-crowded mission was more than enough of an enticement. He stayed with Bob for three years, finishing high school while they lived together. Bob put Dan in charge of his domestic finances, along with housekeeping duties. They'd been more like a couple than an older man and younger hustler. Even then, Dan hadn't admitted to being gay. Sharing Bob's bed for three years hadn't changed that. It was only when Bob died unexpectedly — an epileptic seizure in the shower one week shy of his fortieth birthday — that Dan realized he'd loved him.

In a way, their last year together had been more like father and son than anything Dan had ever known. It would be another five years before he got up the courage to go home and confront his real father face-to-face. By then he had his own son.

Dan looked over the missing boy's photograph, scrutinizing the features. He wasn't attractive, but he wore an air of toughness — probably as a result of the schoolyard bullying — that would go a long way to make up for not being a pretty boy. To survive on the city streets, you needed one or the other.

Dan wondered what the parents were hoping for, information on their son's whereabouts, a reassurance as to his mental and physical well-being, or the whole Corpus Christi? Usually they wanted their children back, even when it wasn't in anybody's best interest. In this case, it was too early to tell.

Teenagers could be surprisingly elusive once they connected with other runaways to help them stay invisible. There was no paper trail of credit card purchases or personal cheques cluttering things up. No Welfare files or ROEs pinning them to specific addresses. Hand-to-mouth was a tough game to play, but it kept them off the radar. Sometimes Dan got lucky when a kid was picked up for shoplifting or vagrancy, though they often lied their way out before he got to them. A twelve-year-old he'd been searching for had stood in a police station two feet from a picture tagging her as a runaway. No one had noticed. Dan found this out later when she turned up half-dead of a drug overdose, alive thanks to emergency resuscitation procedures at the hospital after someone threw her into a cab along with a twenty-dollar bill and closed the door.

He scanned Richard's photograph into his computer and printed a dozen copies, jamming them into his briefcase. He'd put out a few calls — nothing official, just a guy making inquiries around the gay community. Maybe Family Services or Child Find Canada had come across him, though the police would have contacted the brigades of bespectacled middle-aged women wearing their all-weather skirts, hand-knitted sweaters, and freshwater pearls who tirelessly followed up unlikely leads and telephoned to tell you if they'd heard anything, anything at all. If the kid were still in town, someone would come across him sooner or later. Sooner was always preferable.

He'd take the picture around the bars before going home tonight. The bouncers were scrupulous in keeping out underage kids in the evenings, but it was possible for a kid like Richard — half-man, half-boy — to sneak in undetected in the afternoon, especially if he was looking for a daddy. If he had, the bartenders would have noticed.

The phone rang. It was 55 Division calling to say the coroner's office had a possible match for one of his cases and could he come down for a look. They all knew him by name, though most of them called him Sharp, never Dan, except for a couple of female constables he suspected of hitting on him.

He was put on hold. One of his co-workers entered and slapped a photo on his desk. He pointed at the subject's face, an old sharkie they'd been tracing for a dog's age. The man made a cutting motion across his neck. Dan put a hand over the receiver.

"Confirmed?"

A stiff nod. "Just came in. Nasty stuff — looks like gangland. I've got the deets when you want them…."

Fifty-five Division came back on the line. Dan held up a finger while he wrote down the specs. When he turned around, his colleague was gone.

The wall clock crept around to eleven. The numbers swam in his field of vision. It was going to be a long, slow morning. Dan rubbed his eyes. He hadn't hit forty yet, and genetics said it was only going to get worse. Maybe he should stop while he was ahead. Take up a kinder, gentler career. Whatever that might be.

Bob had left Dan enough money to finish university, but Dan balked when it came time to choose. He'd wanted a career that sounded impressive and might be helpful to others. But what was that? Bob had listened thoughtfully while Dan ran through the possibilities: doctor, lawyer, maybe even a minister. But, as Bob pointed out, Dan got faint at the sight of blood, hated debates, and didn't believe in the existence of anything that could vaguely be construed as God-like. That seemed to cancel out his hopes in those areas.

"Go for the money," Bob advised, "but make sure it's something you enjoy. Forty years is a long time to do something you don't like."

Bob tried to steer him toward a vocation where he had aptitude as well as interest, but this proved elusive. Dan had mechanical skills, but the usual choices — plumbing and engineering — held little appeal. And while he had a love of cultural things, music in particular, he had no real artistic inclinations. What Dan knew and seemed to grasp instinctively was other human beings — how they interacted, what motivated and intrigued them. Human resources could always use good people, Bob argued, but discouraged Dan from a career that would cement him in the business world. He was too bright and restless to get bogged down in the corporate mentality.

At the time, it made sense for Dan to attend the University of Toronto and stay with Bob. But then Bob died and his nieces and nephews sold the house. His future uncertain, Dan enrolled in a smattering of courses, hoping to ferret out his interests and potential skill sets shotgun style. He excelled in psychology and sociology but found the disciplines too wide-ranging to hold his attention for long. If he'd been asked what interested him most, he would have narrowed it down to the well-being of other people, but that hardly sounded like a career.

In his second year, he chose a path with the impressive sounding label of Social-Cultural Anthropology, and then got sidetracked briefly by paleontology, thinking he might find himself tracking skeletons in the deserts of Africa. But the dream was more glamorous than the reality — the bone business was already overrun with various social misfits and wannabes who ended up running safari operations for tourists. In the meantime, university failed to stimulate him. He found the academic world labyrinthine, astounded to learn his fellow students might spend years pursuing such abstruse matters as the history of various disciplines without ever tackling the actual subjects.

Ultimately, he didn't take well to studying — possibly because Bob was no longer around to impress or because he'd just lost his home a second time. The centre of his universe hadn't held once again, and it showed. His course advisor summed it up when she told him he had a piercing but restless mind, striking a similar chord to what Bob had said. His papers showed brilliance, but he folded on the exams. She hoped he'd do better.

He might have, but something sidetracked him first. Whatever else those two years had given Dan, they'd brought the realization that university wasn't for him. They'd also given him Kedrick.

FIVE

Kedrick

WHITNEY HALL, DAN'S RESIDENCE in second year, housed an interesting collection of humanity. He made friends with the staff, who quickly sensed his orphan status. One in particular, a talkative night porter, painted from midnight to dawn then packed up his artist's gear and went home. But from ten p.m. to midnight, the artist held court. He'd established a cult appeal among the student body, having known celebrities and worked briefly as a bodyguard for an English movie star.

Among his coterie was a young Syrian named Arman, who had a habit of wearing as little as possible around the residence. In deep winter, Arman stalked the halls like a restless lion, dressed in sleeveless T-shirts and loose-fitting sweatpants. The porter's room was small, and Dan often found himself crowded in next to this silky-skinned Arab. One evening, bored or tired, Arman leaned his head on Dan's shoulder. Dan flinched.

Arman turned a cool gaze on him. "Afraid of being touched?" he asked, with his superior-sounding English accent and comically raised eyebrows.

"N-no," Dan stammered and felt his face flush.

"G-good," said Arman, and laid his arm across the back of Dan's neck.

Dan sat, paralyzed with self-consciousness, as the group dissected European political views in light of the Gulf War. Now and again someone would look up at the pair, with disappointment or envy, Dan wasn't sure. After that, Dan attended the talks as much on the chance of seeing Arman's honey-coloured skin and deep-set eyes as to hear the artist talk. Arman gave spirited debate on any subject under discussion, mesmerizing them with his accent and clear voice, receiving as much attention as the porter.

At midnight, the painter made it clear his studio time had arrived. The group broke up reluctantly, lingering in the hall to protract the discussions, this taste of the larger world. If neither of them had an early class, Arman might return to Dan's room, where the conversation resumed with Arman sprawled across Dan's bed in his scanty attire. Dan secretly hoped something would throw them together, but if Arman harboured any desire for his new friend, he never showed it. He seemed content being admired from the far side of the room. For Dan, to have Arman's exclusive company nightly had been enough at first.

On weekends the residence emptied, the students going home or out of town. Dan stayed behind, having no place to visit and no invitations to take up. One Saturday, Arman arrived at his door with a slighter version of himself. He introduced his sister, Kendra, who was studying fashion at another institution. They were off to Chinatown for a bit of shopping and invited him to join. Dan hadn't known Arman had a sister, let alone family in Toronto. He got the feeling she was a black sheep of sorts, which Arman later confirmed with various off-hand remarks letting Dan know he was ashamed of Kendra's whole-hearted embrace of North American life.

Like her brother, Kendra was keen-spirited and attractive. She made a habit of teasing Arman and quickly transferred that to Dan. That same day, over coffee, Dan asked her out, perhaps hoping to impress Arman or maybe to make him jealous — he wasn't sure.

They began to date. Dan didn't fall in love with her and he was sure she wasn't in love with him, but he was drawn to something behind the velvety eyes that looked purple in the right light. The first time they kissed — on the subway steps outside the Royal Ontario Museum — he imagined for a moment it was Arman he held in his arms and wondered if that was why he was attracted to her. Perhaps that was when he made up his mind to find out. If he couldn't have Arman directly, maybe he could have him through Kendra.

One evening, after too many pints at a local pub, he brought Kendra to his bedroom and, with her guidance, experienced the first and only heterosexual event of his adult life. Then she disappeared.

Arman was vague when Dan inquired: his sister was busy, she'd been out of town, and no, he hadn't seen her. As far as Dan could tell, Arman had no idea what had occurred between them. He continued to join Dan for their nightly

"UN Conferences," as they jokingly referred to them. Dan wasn't sure how Arman would react if he knew how far his relations with Kendra had gone. When it came to family matters, Arman was surprisingly conservative. While he tolerated Dan's interest in Kendra, he made light of it — the question of a future for them would never be in the picture.

After another week, Dan began to wonder if he'd done something to offend her. Finally she called. She was fine but couldn't see him, claiming an agonizing schedule. He pressured her, bewildered by her avoidance. Since their lovemaking, he'd spent the past few weeks imagining a future for them — marriage, a home. It never assumed a definite shape. He was even beginning to convince himself he was in love with her.

When she called next, a month had passed. Kendra was all seriousness — she was pretty sure she was pregnant. Dan panicked. There was a flutter in his voice. How sure? Very — a girl didn't say these things lightly.

Dan froze. He wondered if she were making a pitch for marriage, trying to snag him or at the very least a quick citizenship. He didn't voice these thoughts. After all, he'd been considering marriage himself. She reluctantly agreed to meet for coffee the following day.

It was a gloomy afternoon, sleet pelting the campus. Kendra stirred her mint tea, looking out the window from time to time. Yes, she'd had the results. Yes, she was definitely pregnant. Dan saw his future going up like the little wisps of steam rising from the greenish tea and vanishing between them.

"I'm sorry," he said.

A look of concern passed over her face. "It's not your fault," she said. "I can't believe I've screwed up like this. I've always been so careful."

She felt conflicted, regretting the situation she'd dragged him into and stricken with guilt over her neglect. Her bravado, the North American hubris she draped herself in, had fled.

Dan wanted to know what she was going to do. She shrugged. There was no question of telling her parents. They would cut her off financially — and who knew what else. "At least they don't do honour killings any more," she said darkly.

Dan grimaced. He didn't know what honour killings were, but he could guess. Had she told Arman? She looked aghast. *No!* Arman would be furious — he might even tell her family. Didn't Dan know her brother well enough by now? Anyway, she'd already decided to have an abortion.

Dan's stomach spasmed. It sounded worse than the spectre of marriage. He haltingly suggested an arrangement between them, wondering yet again if she were trying to snag a citizenship.

She turned her mocking eyes on him, reminding him even more of Arman. "You've got to be kidding," she said.

"Why?"

She saw his hesitation and reached out a hand to him. "I didn't expect you'd be emotional about this," she said.

"Am I?"

She nodded vigorously. "Oh yes, clearly you are. No offence, but I have ambitions to be more than a housewife, and I think you may realize one day that you're gay."

Dan's eyes flickered away.

"Besides," she continued, "no one in my family has ever married outside our culture. It would be a disaster."

The double slap came as a shock. "I'd keep it," he blurted out. "I'll raise the child." He had no idea what that entailed, and years later he often wondered at his outburst, but somehow the thought of saving the baby was foremost in his thinking.

"You'd do what?"

"I'll look after it. I'll raise it." The idea had taken control of him, driving his impulses.

Somehow it was imperative to make her understand this baby meant more to him than anything in his life so far. He rambled on, spinning himself deeper and deeper into his daydreams, his improvised fables of fatherhood. He thought she'd refuse, but her whimsical side won out. To his surprise, she agreed to consider it.

She began to scheme. She had an aunt, rumoured to be a lesbian and considered even more of a renegade, who lived in California with a bunch of crazy artists. The aunt could take her in for the final months of the pregnancy, which, she calculated, would coincide with the end of school and summer holidays. If all went well, she wouldn't be showing before then.

Her light-hearted smile returned. It was an adventure. Suddenly she was Holly Golightly making an impromptu appearance at the Go-Go-A-La-Mode, clearing everything up for him where he thought he'd come to rescue her. Afterwards, Dan was never sure if he'd made up his mind or if she'd made it up for him.

"Let me think about it," she told him.

Years later he related the story to Donny, who sat quietly through the tale of youthful courtship and terror.

"So you fucked her to be with her brother?"

Dan looked sourly at him. "No — I fucked her because I was drunk."

"Ah! That's different. I've always said we're all just one beer away from being straight." Donny winked. "I think it's cool that the kid owes his life to a pint of Heineken. You should have named him after it."

The prospect of a child to look after made a huge change in Dan's life, far greater than he could have imagined. He suddenly found himself willing to do anything as long as it would bring in money. Anything but hustling — that part of his life was over. There'd be no lonely middle-aged men this time to take him in and provide. Providing was what Dan would be doing.

It was agreed that Kendra would return to school in the fall, after the baby's birth. In the meantime, Dan would do whatever he could to bring in money. She would remain independent and they would live apart. Custody agreements could be drawn up later, but she already knew she didn't want to raise a child.

Dan had signed up for a third year at university, but even before his acceptance came through he realized he wouldn't be able to afford the tuition. Somewhere along the line, practicality won out.

He bought a newspaper and dug out the classifieds. With his limited experience and incomplete degree, there was little he was qualified for that would support a family.

The smiling man who answered his call and greeted him an hour later made him feel he'd been waiting for someone like Dan forever. That probably wasn't far off. The sort of people who tracked insurance scammers were little short of sociopathic misfits, Dan learned. While there was no short- age of those in the city, few were capable of holding down jobs, and the ones who were seemed even more dubious specimens of humanity than the supposed criminals they were tracking. If they were good at exposing scammers, it was because cheating was in their blood, low-life losers who thought, pissed, and shat scams till they became experts at them.

Dan accepted the comedown in expectations — from stalking bones in the Sahara to stalking flesh-and-blood rats in the gutters of the city — with equanimity. At least he was making money. He reported to the townhouse on Queen East near Logan each morning at seven a.m. before hitting the road with his assignments. This meant tracking a wide range of people who were in some way disabled — from those who'd lost the use of limbs, through those claiming whiplash and soft tissue injuries, to people with repetitive motion syndrome. Some had found themselves dismissed from their jobs outright. Others were luckier, having had the relative good fortune to have their mishaps occur at the workplace, making it harder for their employers to get rid of them. All became targets for insurance companies looking for an excuse to opt out of paying benefits.

While waiting for lawsuits to be settled, some disap- peared and were last heard from at Tijuana addresses or luxury chateaus up north. Others were luckier in having spouses support them for the duration. Still others, having lost their income, got swallowed up by welfare rolls or were glad-handed from relative to relative while waiting out the endless doctor reports and psychiatric assessments — the company doctors always finding reasons why the claimant should be working and the lawyers' doctors finding equally valid reasons why they should not. It was all a matter of perspective, unless you happened to be the sufferer.

This was where Dan came in. He was there to challenge the perspective. He became adept at disguising himself outside claimants' homes, snooping through their garbage, and making discreet enquiries of the people next door who were sometimes only too eager to divulge their neighbours' secrets. "He operates a business in his basement, customers come and go at all hours." Or, "I see her working down at the pub on the corner on Sundays." Many of those Dan caught in lies later expressed shock that the young man on their corner had been able to keep invisible till it was too late. After a handful of incriminating pictures, the potential lawsuits and hoped-for insurance payments became history.

His first month on the job, he located ten claimants who'd been impossible for others to find. He got incriminating pictures of seven. His supervisors were impressed and commended him every chance they got. He'd had misgivings about a couple of the ones he'd shadowed, wondering if they really were scamming or just making do the best they could. A guy who claimed to have a bad leg and got caught playing football was one thing, but several claimants he'd photographed doing everyday things that had to be done, like it or not. The pictures didn't show whether it had been easy for them to perform those tasks or how costly it had been in terms of pain and suffering.

He expressed his concerns to a supervisor. She gave him a wormy smile, the veins of a chronic drinker mapping her nose. "We know," she said. "It's a tough call. Just get the pictures and don't worry about it. Let the courts decide who's lying."

"Luck of the draw," a co-worker told him with a shrug. "Hey! It's not up to us to judge."

The more he got to know his colleagues, the more Dan realized he was working with people who'd rubbed themselves sideways against the law more than the norm. Confessions of impaired driving, assault, tax evasion, drug possession, and fraud were commonplace amongst his co-workers. Most of them talked freely about their pasts. Some bragged about the things they got away with. One admitted he was working off the payments of a paternity suit. Dan began to feel he'd been drafted into the city's virtually unemployable fringe set.

One cold April afternoon, he watched an older woman hobbling around her front walk with a shovel. She wore oversized rubber boots and a ragged overcoat. With a record snowfall blanketing the city, her movements hardly made a dent in the drifts thrown up by a street plough. According to the report, a fall had left her unable to fill her duties at a stationery factory where she'd worked for the past twenty-seven years. She was widowed, the mother of a thirty-year-old. If she'd been Dan's mother, he thought, she wouldn't be out there shovelling for herself.

He rolled down the windows and took a couple of pictures then sat watching, his breath hanging on the air. The woman stopped every few seconds to draw a lungful of oxygen and stretch her left arm. Dan saw the pain in her face. He put the camera down and stepped out of the car.

She looked up when he approached.

"Do you need some help?" he asked.

She leaned on the shovel and regarded him. "I hurt my arm."

"I can see that."

He took the shovel and cleared her sidewalk with a dozen brisk motions.

"Thank you, sir," she said.

"It's no problem."

She stood there watching him. "They told me I'd better watch out for anyone with a camera. They said the insurance company would take pictures of me and show the court."

He smiled. She'd known he was there. "What did you say?"

"I said I'd tell the court the insurance company didn't pay me my money for six months now, so I didn't have no choice but to shovel my own snow. Otherwise somebody's goin' to get hurt like I did and then they'll sue me!"

"You live all alone?"

She nodded. "My husband died. My son got married and went back to Jamaica. I ast the neighbour's boy would he shovel for me. He said he couldn't be bothered for no five dollars. I'll give it to you, if you want it."

She held out a bill.

Dan shook his head. "You keep it," he said, jabbing the shovel into a drift.

Back in his car, he yanked the film from the camera and returned to work to hand in his resignation. The baby was four months away.

A week later, another ad held out hope. If he could locate insurance scammers, Dan felt, surely he could locate other missing people. The office might be a dismal shade of grey that reflected in the faces of everyone who worked there, but it seemed a long step up from what he'd been doing. His colleagues were an interesting mix of former police officers and private investigators. What the walls lacked in colour his co-workers made up for in personality.

Somehow he talked himself into the job, beginning with a research position. Dan found he had the right stuff to find people who went missing for more compelling reasons than avoiding insurance investigators. He still suffered qualms over tracking down someone who might not want to be found, but he no longer felt he was enabling insurance companies to punish innocent people for doing what others did: living their lives as best they could.

A personal tape recorder, a high-speed camera, and a flashlight became his stock-in-trade. He wrote down all the relevant facts on a thick notepad, then memorized them and looked for ways to connect the dots. Theories without facts were useless, he soon learned, but facts that didn't stand up to testing were a waste of time.

Somehow he made it through the first year, then a second, with most of his personal beliefs intact and Ked growing like an errant weed he'd planted on a whim and was surprised to find waiting for him each morning when he woke.

He hired a nanny and trundled off to work and back again each day, spending his evenings alone with this bundle of living, breathing flesh that seemed as much a part of him as his own arm.

At times, the boy was his only companion apart from the TV. He tried to juggle Ked on his knee and watch the jabbering shows about raising kids and having a rewarding life at the same time. The ones where privileged women argued about epidurals and hiring midwives. In truth, the task was lonely and demanding and he seldom seemed to get outside of an insular world that had shrunk to almost nothing. There were days when he still wished he had a career that was impressive-sounding, but that thought died when he celebrated his twenty-fourth birthday alone.

SIX

Anger Management

THE MORNING PASSED with little excitement. The bottle
of Scotch did not put in an appearance. Just before one
o'clock Dan went off to the coroner's office on Grosvenor
Street, but the body of the missing person 55 Division
claimed to have a possible match for turned out to be
someone else. Someone who didn't even vaguely resem-
ble the persn in Dan's file, apart from being human and
male. There were doubts even about the latter, considering the raised mammaries that appeared to have been a
botched home job injecting silicone under the skin with
a hypodermic. Another victim of do-it-yourself beauty
school etiquette. All went well for these home-style
girly-boys until they misjudged the position of an artery
and sent the polymer mainlining into their hearts and
lungs. By then it was too late. Death came grisly but swift,
and the rictus masks left for their discoverers weren't
too pretty either.

At least the Serbian boy would be going home soon. When he'd left, it had probably been a merry send-off — women in babushkas and kerchiefs smiling and sipping Turkish coffee, bristle-faced men offering their worldly wisdom and passing the *šljivovica* from hand to hand while the children romped around the room, not understanding why they were celebrating their older cousin's leave-taking, but glad for the sweet rolls. Dan didn't want to think about the bumpy coffin ride back in the bottom of a cargo plane, the seven-hour flight to repatriate him, the teary return that awaited him in his homeland two years too late.

The sky threatened drizzle as he walked north on Yonge Street, keeping his distance from passersby who seemed to have nothing better to do than throng the intersections looking fashionable. He stopped for lunch at Spring Rolls. The downstairs was filled with a noisy young crowd who seemed to think it a glamorous social event rather than simply a quick, cheap eat. He bypassed the clamorous lunchers and went upstairs, where it was only slightly less crowded. A waiter waved him curtly to a window table. The man's face betrayed annoyance at having one customer take up a spot for two. Dan could remember when the place barely got half full. Whenever he found a convenient location to eat, it turned trendy in a couple of months. Then the wait time increased, the food went downhill, and the service got snarly. So much for Toronto's exalted dining experience.

He ordered a drink before he was seated. One beer to take the edge off. It wasn't that he needed it, he reassured himself. Just holding the tumbler in his hand made him feel better.

Two tables over, a rugged-looking guy in denim caught Dan's eye. Black T-shirt, chiselled cheekbones, thick moustache. Face like a motorcycle cop from the backend of a seventies porn catalogue. He looked familiar. Dan wondered if he was undercover, possibly someone he'd worked with before. He kept catching Dan's glance. The third time it happened the man smiled unexpectedly. Dan blushed and turned away.

He sipped his beer and kept his gaze averted, wondering how long the guy would keep at it before he gave up.

The waiter returned for his order. Dan stumbled over the name of one of the Asian fusion dishes. The waiter corrected his pronunciation and regarded him gravely, as though he'd asked for a side order of blowfish.

His meal had just arrived when the denim-clad mannequin laid a bill on the table. Dan kept his head turned as he walked past and dropped a slip of paper beside Dan's fork. Out of the corner of his eye, Dan watched him disappear down the stairs before turning it over — the name *Chuck* and a phone number. He finished his lunch and left the number on the table. Maybe his hurried waiter would think it was for him. The two of them could work it out.

Outside, the day had turned bright. The sun made a sudden appearance as Dan crossed through Allan Gardens, noting the unusually large number of addicts looking up uncertainly at the light, like seals left stranded by a retreating tide. He thought over the early morning meeting with his former neighbour at the donut shop, and wondered again why Steve had given Glenda the house, especially since she made more money than him. Is that what straight men did?

There was no reply from Bill when he reached the office. He tossed his coat over a chair then made a few calls about the young runaway, Richard Philips. At four o'clock he signed off on the file of a woman missing for five years who'd recently turned up — schizophrenic and amnesiac — on a Hawaiian island. She'd been living in an abandoned milk truck. Her appearance had altered so radically, it had taken a DNA test to convince her relatives she was the same woman. Sometimes that was as good as it got.

He opened another file and read over his notes without taking anything in. A fourth cup of coffee failed to revive his concentration. He'd been staring at his computer for some time without registering a thing. Just before six, he closed his laptop and left the office.

His counselling was an hour off. It seemed to be a day for wasting time. On a lark, he left his car in the underground garage and walked west on Wellesley Street through the downtown core. He ducked into a video arcade burgeoning with teens and pre-teens — kids who liked to hang out on the strip. He watched them in the half-light, silhouetted like an army of overactive gnomes labouring underground. A crazy quilt of sound came at him, the jabbering voices of boys and machines. The variety of games boggled his mind, newer versions at the front, older ones farther along the warren of blinking lights. Shooting games, driving games, even a fast-paced step-dancing game. Movie themes dominated: *Lord of the Rings* followed by *Star Wars* and *The Matrix*. Near the far end stood Roger Moore, as dashing as ever — James Bond is immortal, after all. Closer up, a perennial favourite: a Playboy Bunny with a waggling set of ears. Elsewhere, Nancy Reagan's much-quoted plea hung over a flaming bridge: *Just say no to drugs*. But what if they said yes to you?

Dan kept his eyes peeled for Richard Philips. He'd seen a million boys like the ones here today, all variations on a theme. He was the kid next door with the Popsicle smile or the ten-cent grin, a skateboard beneath his feet, a baseball cap on a crow's nest of hair, and a comic book tucked beneath his arm. You know him. He's the boy who got all As, or sometimes Bs or even Fs. The future baccalaureate or the wearer of the dunce's crown, the one who stupefied his teachers or failed miserably at his studies. He's the boy who cheered others on in their endeavours and threw matches at cats. Who won or lost at aggies, who skipped classes and lobbed crusts at other boys in the lunchroom. You know every variation of him. And every now and again one little thing went wrong, one screw fell out of place, and he was no longer that charming boy you thought you knew but a conniving criminal, a survival-minded sharp waiting on the other side of the lamppost, on the far side of midnight, leaning against the doorframe and taking your measure. But you know him. Because somewhere deep down inside, he is you or your son or your brother or maybe even your future father. You know him.

Dan watched the kids jockeying for place, aiming guns in the air, at the screens, at each other. *Blam!* He listened to the sharp yells as the boys won or lost, then started new games that took them to the far reaches of space, the depths of the ocean, or the deepest jungles. Losing themselves as successfully as they could.

Apart from Dan and the arcade manager, there was only one other adult in the room. At first Dan didn't recognize him. He was a bag of bones, an old haunt Dan hadn't seen in years. At forty he'd been a chronic predator; at sixty he was a fright. Dan watched him move among the boys like an aged shopper browsing the aisle of some fancy specialty shop, hands trembling with hunger. The boys all seemed to know him too — Wicked Uncle Ernie with his bag of magic tricks, all for kicks. Come home with me, kiddies. We'll watch some television, snort a little blow. Smoke some crack. Aren't I a charm? We'll have fun. Whatever turns up. And P.S. *Don't tell Mom.* The voice paced, the tone measured: here was sincerity, surprise, and now and then a little calculated enthusiasm. *Great shot, Tim! What a score. Keep it up, Bennie!* Whatever was required came tripping off his tongue in calculated increments, plotted to the needs of the moment. Now smile for the camera because: these premises are monitored 24-hours. Let the means determine the ends. Each according to his need. And now and then a gentle laugh, nicely modulated. Every syllable a sure step, one foot placed squarely in front of the other.

Dan caught the predator's eyes, tossed him a knowing nod to unsettle his dreams, and let him know he'd been noticed — who knows, maybe the former hustler had gone undercover after all these years — then left, heading for his counselling session.

Dan's work offered the weekly sessions to help employees deal with the supposed stress of their jobs. His employer was considered progressive. Words like "wellness" and "holistic" were floated freely around the office. Currently, however, Dan's counselling had also become "compulsory" after he dented a filing cabinet with his fist.

Two days before that incident, he'd successfully tracked down the spouse of a client who warned him that her husband, a manic-depressive, had left home without his meds. Twelve hours after being freed from a rehab centre, the man turned up a suicide in a west end back alley. It came as a complete shock to himself and everyone else when Dan spun around and slugged the cabinet.

A superior with fifties hair, a Father-Knows-Best attitude, and a pro-counselling bias decided to make Dan an example. "You're letting this get to you," he said from the far side of the room where Dan stood nursing his knuckles.

Dan was livid. "You're goddamn right I'm letting it get to me! This should never have happened. Who ordered this man released?"

"Calm down, Daniel."

"Fucking hell I'll calm down!" This time he kicked the cabinet, caving in one of the lower drawer fronts as though it had been to blame.

The others moved away, leaving him alone to carve out his self-destruction.

"It's unfortunate, I agree. But these things happen." The supervisor moved in on Dan as though he were a dangerous psychopath he intended to disarm.

"That's bullshit! Anyone with a history of mental illness is a critical case. This is a fucking tragedy. He should never have been let go without someone telling me or his wife!"

All his years of service would not buy his way out. The die had been cast, the hammer set to fall with a resounding crash. The incident got him six months' mandatory counselling and replacement costs for the cabinet. He'd resisted the counselling but, faced with the alternative of suspension, he relented. At least they were paying for the sessions. Reluctantly, he attended the weekly meetings, though it was seldom his work Dan wanted to talk about.

He approached Queen's Park, a miniature forest in the city's heart. A mounted statue of Edward VII towered over crisscrossing paths, transported from Delhi when India left the Commonwealth, like the prize in a prolonged custody dispute from a messy divorce settlement.

It was here that Dan had slept on the hard benches his first night in the city, while crepuscular figures flitted like moths in the dark. It wasn't till later he'd learned the intent of the men prowling the darkened pathways like vampires, but in search of a different kind of life-giving fluid.

Through the trees the sky was a honed blue, a nice ending to the day if you had nothing troubling you, but Dan knew by the time he finished his counselling session it would be dark, in keeping with his mood. After his hour with Martin, he'd walk back across Wellesley to the bars on Church Street and show them the picture of the young runaway. After an hour with Martin, he'd need to spend time in a bar.

He passed the brown brick residence at Whitney Hall where he'd met Arman and Kendra. After all this time the apple tree outside the porter's office still flourished in the back courtyard. A few crabbed globes clung to its scaly branches. It felt strange to look up at the corner window and know his son had been conceived there out of his own macho drunkenness.

Arman was currently in Dubai. A brilliant IT worker, he was shipped from port to port at great expense. He'd slipped out of Dan's world completely and married a woman chosen by his family, though by all accounts they were happy. Unlike his renegade sister, Arman had no compunction about doing what tradition expected of him. If things had been different in a very different world, Dan wondered, would Arman have been just as happy in an arranged marriage with a man if tradition ordained it?

Kendra lived a few blocks north on a tree-lined street in a hundred-year-old stone house. She'd become a success too, living life on her own terms and alone, as Dan knew she would. They may have been alike in looks and upbringing, but Kendra was a very different creature from her tradition-upholding brother.

He crossed through the heart of the university, past St. George and Spadina with their popular student pizzerias, to the euphemistically named Harbord Centre for Well Being, which was actually located on Brunswick Avenue. Like Edward VII, it too had been displaced, but kept its name after being transplanted to this little backwater street, like a deposed royal living out its life in an anonymous hamlet far from the cultural centres of its heyday.

Dan walked up to the decrepit building that showed at least three colours peeling through a brown topcoat like a bad tan. Someone had made a stab at beautifying the outside by placing pots of geraniums along the windowsills, but these had failed to bloom in the absence of direct sunlight. In fact, Dan wondered if anything could blossom along this rundown stretch of street. The scraggly, light-starved stems presented a pathetic welcome to anyone looking up from the sidewalk.

He checked his watch: he was twenty-three minutes early. He didn't want Martin to think he was anxious to see him. On the other hand, there was nowhere else to go in this neighbourhood of shabby student-chic housing. He spent the next ten minutes perusing the walls papered in notices for used textbooks, political rallies, flats to let, roommates wanted (and unwanted), descriptions of missing items with hopeful phone numbers beside them, as well as a plethora of numbers and email addresses of arcane purpose, the relevant notices having faded or been cut off or covered over by others clamouring for attention and demanding to be heard above all else.

The building's elevator was perpetually out of service. He took the three flights of wheezing, complaining stairs that announced visitors by their tread. Dan imagined the long queue of clients — timid or brave, world-weary or hopeful — who passed over this threshold and down the hall to the large oak panels behind which the eminent Martin Sanger and his dry, probing intellect waited. Dan had experienced moments of both hope and resignation as he approached these doors, but today he was what he usually was: irritable and angry at having to be there.

He reached the office and let himself in. The receptionist listened, blank-faced, as he stated his name. He wondered if she really didn't remember him when he walked through these doors every week at this time, or if this was part of his training to help him learn to be patient with what Martin had labelled his "perceived stupidity of others." Dan waited while she looked down at her appointment book, nodded as she discovered his name and asked him to take a seat.

He watched through the glass as she bent to speak into the intercom to relay notice of his arrival to Martin's office. She always struck Dan as nervous and unhappy. He wondered if she was also a patient here. Maybe reception work was how she paid for her therapy. This was the only time Dan saw her. She was gone by the time his sessions ended, and he emerged to a semi-darkened waiting room, as though she'd been compelled to take the light with her wherever she went.

Dan settled into what he'd determined was the most comfortable of three waiting room seats: a faded green club chair. Or in this case the least uncomfortable. The room was silent, with that surprising mixture of stillness and anticipation. From one floor above, he heard a sharp humourless laugh followed by a thump. A car passed outside the window and then, after a pause, another. He wondered why there was no music to provide comfort or distraction. Maybe this was part of his therapy too, his little wait in limbo while he was observed through a spy hole in the opposite wall.

He went over the list of topics he had lined up, imagining Martin's reactions. The tale of Steve and Glenda would elicit an anticipatory glance; it might also earn him a point for compassion at having met with Steve at four a.m. to talk over his troubles. He could follow this up with his annoyance at Bill's unreturned calls. No point in mentioning the lousy drivers he encountered daily in the city. They were par for the course; no one was exempt. He could also mention

Ked's new friend Ephraim, the ruffian. Or would Martin think he was being racist? He could simply not mention the boy's colour, if it came to that. But wasn't this session supposed to be a safe place for Dan to unburden himself? Didn't he have the right to express concern over his son's future?

If that failed to feed Martin's interest, he could delve into his childhood, that old stand-by. Martin seemed to like it when he did. During their initial session, the awkward getting-to-know-you of pre-interrogation invasiveness, Martin had asked him what triggered his anger as a child. Dan couldn't remember being angry as a child and Martin seemed to think that in itself was unusual. How could anyone get through childhood without experiencing anger? It spelled repression. Try being the child of a violent alcoholic and you'd probably repress your anger too, Dan said.

"Then why do you think you're so angry now?" Martin had asked.

"It beats depression."

Martin pencilled furiously on the sheet in his lap. After that, he brought up Dan's early years till Dan was sick of rehashing his childhood, as though the key to who he was now lay in some mysterious past time that had had the door closed on it forever and could only be viewed by coming to this man's office and peering inside its cage like visitors to the zoo.

In fact, Dan seldom thought about his childhood. He'd come a long way from his past and he intended to keep on going as far as he could. The best thing you could do with the past, he told himself, was forget it. Though if everyone thought like that, he'd be out of business. His job depended on other people wanting him to dig up the past and conjure it before their eyes: the young wife who hadn't returned from a trip to the bank; the father who left work and was never seen again; the sixth-grader who ventured out between Algebra and French and dropped off the face of the earth.

It wasn't till his third session that Martin asked him about his mother's death when he was four years old. Dan replied truthfully that he recalled little apart from a gathering of relatives in his apartment and the hush around them whenever he came into the room. He remembered briefly being shipped off to a neighbour's, and later being given Popsicles before returning to live with his father.

When she died, what little connection Dan had had with his father died along with her. His father seemed to have frozen over, ice covering the distance between them. It had stayed that way till his death ten years ago, though the ice was all on Dan's part by then. Even Kedrick's birth hadn't changed things. There'd been just one family visit, a brief, guilt-tinged appearance supervised by Dan's Aunt Marge, made at her request. Dan had watched, wary, as his father took the boy in his hands and sat him on his knee. The scar on Dan's right temple throbbed, the one he'd gotten when his father threw him against a doorjamb returning home late from school not long after his tenth birthday.

Since then he'd successfully covered the past with a shroud, convincing himself it had few holds on him apart from the ones dictated by genetics. As far as he was concerned, the legacy was unremarkable on both sides of the family. He was the son of a miner who was also the son of a miner. His father's relatives had lived in Sudbury for more than three generations. His mother had migrated there from Manitoba, no one seemed to recall why or when, and had been variously a waitress, a beautician, and a cashier at Woolworth's until her early death from pneumonia one Christmas.

As far as Dan knew, he was the only one in the family who had attended a post-secondary institution. He'd never been in trouble at school or with the law. Until he left home, he'd never lived anywhere but Sudbury. The only home he recalled had been the second floor of a rundown walk-up in the Flourmill District, an area uniquely devoid of distinctive features apart from the six squat cement cylinders that had lain unused for decades before being turned into a museum of dubious distinction not long after Dan was born.

"Do you have any nice memories of your father?" Martin asked unexpectedly one day.

Dan thought about it. After a moment, he nodded. "My father was sometimes nice to me when he drank. That and Christmas. Usually the two coincided. I guess he was sentimental about certain things."

"Did it change after your mother died?"

"That was when he stopped drinking." Dan paused. "You'd think it would be the opposite, wouldn't you? You might expect that he'd drink more when she died."

"Would you?"

"Yes, a normal person would."

Martin ignored the jibe, if he noticed it.

"My father didn't drink for a long time after she died, but he started up again during a mining strike in the late seventies. The strike went on for nearly a year. That's when I realized he resented me. Otherwise, I suppose he could have sat around getting drunk instead of working to support me."

Of his parents together, he had one small memory that might have been nothing more than a dream. A Christmas tree filled with lights and tinselly ornaments figured prominently. A glittery green and red bird with a shiny fibreglass tail caught his attention. He recalled reaching up and stroking it, only to have his hand slapped. From there, the memory shifted to an argument between his parents that seemed to go on a long time while he cried. He recalled his father's angry outburst as a hush overtook the house. Outside, snow was falling. Later, a worried knocking had come at the door, followed by a strange pathetic scratching. The details were hazy. There might have been more crying. Somewhere in there was the knowledge that his mother was not coming back. Then later, definitely more crying, this time from his aunt. Whatever else was there faded out of memory. He'd dreamed the event many times and took it as being symbolic of the death of his mother rather than any sort of reality.

How did he feel after having the dream? Martin asked. Terrible, of course. Dan wondered why Martin had to ask. What child wouldn't feel terrible on losing a mother? He wanted to ask if Martin had been glad to lose his.

Remembering his parents' arguing wasn't surprising, since that was the hallmark of their relationship, according to his Aunt Marge. She and her daughter Leyla were his only remaining relatives. He remembered the matronly Marge with fondness as the aunt who snuck him into the Empire Theatre for Saturday matinees and as the woman who raised him after his mother died. He thought guiltily of her now — she'd been in poor health for several years and he hadn't seen her in some time. His cousin Leyla he recalled as the first person in his sexual landscape, a dimly lit mural of touch-and-feel one night when they were forced to share a bed. He'd been impressed by the size of her breasts. In the family, it had been touted that "Leyla failed grade eight because she went boy crazy." He always smiled to think of it. He'd carried on the tradition, he supposed.

The receptionist stirred in her glass cubicle and glanced nervously about as though she sensed a seismic tremor coming down the hall. Dan looked at his watch. It was exactly seven. Martin opened the door and nodded.

"Come in, please, Daniel," Martin said in the same spiritless tone he always used.

Dan followed Martin to an office almost obsessively devoid of personality. Eggshell walls and off-white trim enclosed a cream-coloured carpet with a glass table placed precisely in the centre. On a desk in the corner, a whirling screen-saver offered glimpses of what outer space might look like from the POV of someone heading resolutely away from earth. Not drowning — waving goodbye. A narrow window looked out onto the pitch of other rooflines. A Piet Mondrian reproduction — a quilt-like abstraction of cross-hatches — offered the only colour in an otherwise almost obsessively bland room. It floated on the wall above Martin's head like a cartoon image of the contents of his mind.

The client chair seemed purposely set at a lower angle than Martin's. Dan sat and studied the thin face he couldn't quite bring to mind outside this unremarkable room. "Invisible" didn't begin to cover it. Even Martin's wardrobe seemed designed for camouflage. An oatmeal vest covered an ecru shirt tucked into light-brown trousers with immaculate creases. Half the time in these sessions Dan spent wondering what made this man so indistinct he could disappear right before your eyes. The shrink who shrank. Maybe if Martin lost his temper or betrayed an emotion, he might give off some vital signs.

After the formality of offering Dan a glass of water, which he always refused, Martin sat back with his hands tented and eyed Dan over his fingers.

"So what brings you here today?"

As always, Dan was tempted to say it was a choice between seeing Martin and losing his job, and that he almost hadn't come. Instead, he went into his preamble about his late-night talk with Steve Jenkins and his uncharitable neighbour, Glenda. Before he could get far, Martin cut him off.

"How do you feel about that?"

Dan wanted to say, "I think she's a selfish cunt. The kind who makes living in this city even more unbearable." Instead he said, "It's not fair. Here's this poor schmuck who loves his wife more than anything and she's taking advantage of the situation."

"So you feel a sense of injustice," Martin said, with a flash that might have been interest kindling behind his eyes.

Dan nodded.

"Do you see how you've removed yourself from the emotion and put yourself at a distance?"

"How is that?" Dan said. He was unsure whether agreeing with Martin's assessment might be a good thing. Surely feeling an emotion was better than observing it?

Thankfully, Martin was willing to enlighten him. "It's a rational judgment you're making about the situation. You've separated yourself from the emotion to view it with detachment. Whereas you might normally feel anger over a perceived injustice, you've distanced yourself. I think that's good."

Dan tried to look pleased.

"How are you feeling about life in general these days?" Martin said.

"Good. Fine. A little less irritable than usual."

"Why is that?"

Dan reflected. "Bill and I are going away for the weekend. We're going to a gay wedding."

Dan had stopped hypothesizing on Martin's sexuality and simply assumed he had none, though Martin always showed a keen interest in anything to do with Dan's sex life. Sometimes Dan went on at length when Martin showed curiosity, feeding him tidbits of information to see how he would react, though he'd tired of the game quickly.

"This will be the first time we'll be together for an entire weekend," Dan continued.

"And you feel positive about this?"

"Yes," Dan said, surprising himself.

"Is it a matter of feeling you have more control over the relationship?"

"Not really. Bill's always been in control of the relationship — when we see each other, for how long, et cetera."

Martin inclined his head. "I seem to recall you once said he was in control of every aspect of the relationship except for the bedroom...."

Dan leaned in. "Well, he calls the shots there too, more or less. What I meant was, he lets me be in control when we have sex."

"How do you feel about that?"

"Obviously I'm willing to go along with it or I wouldn't be with him."

Martin waited.

Dan cleared his throat. "I'm learning to be patient," he said.

"That's good. Very good." Martin nodded encouragingly, like a grade school teacher rewarding a student for a correct answer. "Have you had any difficult moments since you were here last?"

"Not really."

"Not really or no?"

"No."

Martin made a mark in his notebook. "Good," he said. "No banging with your fists or yelling?"

Dan remembered the incident with the dog. It seemed funny in hindsight. Surely it was a sign he could laugh at himself. "I got a bit upset with the dog, but it was just the excitement. I didn't mean to yell."

Martin looked up from his notebook. "Isn't that how you described the incident at work when you hit the filing cabinet? You said you yelled at your superior without meaning to."

Dan shrugged. "Okay."

"Would you say this is a common response you have in tense situations?"

"This wasn't a tense situation. I was walking in my front door."

Martin was rapt. "Tell me what happened. Does the dog have a name?"

Of course the fucking dog has a name, Dan thought. "It's Ralph," he said slowly.

"Ralph," Martin repeated, making it sound like a foreign word. "Is Ralph a male? May I refer to Ralph as 'he'?"

"Sure."

Dan rubbed his temples. A nice fat glass of Scotch would drown out how much he detested sitting here with this emotionally repressed insect dissecting his every thought and word, as though using the wrong adjective to describe a reaction or labelling a dog by the incorrect gender might be a crime.

Martin pondered his words as Dan explained how he'd yelled at the dog.

"When you think about what Ralph did now, in this moment, how do you feel?"

"I don't feel anything now. At the time I was pretty pissed off," Dan said. "I'm sure he does it on purpose."

Martin made an elaborate note in his book. He looked up. "Of course you realize a dog isn't conscious of its actions the same way humans are?"

Dan shrugged. "Actually, I'm convinced he does it to annoy me. It's a big 'Fuck You' when he does it at the front door. When it's an accident, he tries to hide it in the basement."

The pencil jogged around the page. Martin looked up. "Do you know that for a fact or do you just imagine you know what the dog's motivations are?"

"He's a smart dog and he's been through obedience training. He knows what he's doing."

"Can we talk about how Ralph might feel in these circumstances?"

Martin looked over his shoulder as though conferring with the Mondrian. Maybe it talked to him, Dan thought. Maybe it prompted him on what train of thought to follow.

"How would I know what the dog feels? Do dogs even feel?"

Martin tented his fingers again and leaned back. "Try to imagine what it might be like for Ralph. You said he does it to annoy you. Why do you think that is? Was he feeling neglected? Had he been left alone without access to a place to defecate?"

Dan tried to imagine Martin bending and scooping up Ralph's big turd with a teaspoon, balancing it as he made his way across the office to a wastebasket.

"My son said that even dogs need love."

"Good!" Martin said decisively. "And do you agree?"

"He's probably right."

"So how did Ralph respond when he perceived himself to be neglected? When you didn't give him the love and attention he wanted?"

"You just said dogs weren't conscious in the way humans are. How could he 'perceive' anything?"

"Unconscious perception can be even stronger than conscious perception. If you believe the dog was 'acting out,' then clearly the dog perceives when it's been neglected. Do you see?"

In Dan's mind, he saw Martin's hand tremble and drop the turd. It landed with a soft thud and rolled across the carpet, leaving a faint brown trail. "This is really stupid."

Martin untented his fingers. "Is it stupid, Daniel — or do you perceive it to be stupid?"

"Either — both — Martin."

"And why does stupidity, perceived or otherwise, justify your anger?"

Dan felt his face flush. "Because it just does."

"Was your father a stupid man?"

"Maybe. I don't know. Can we change the subject?"

Martin stared like a man watching something squirm at the end of a hook. "Don't you think we should explore what made you so angry about the dog's disobedience?"

"No. Let's change the subject."

Martin made a few more scribbles in his book. "Fine," he said. "I understand that you don't feel like being challenged on this issue today."

Dan's teeth were clenched, but he kept his voice low. "Look, Martin, you don't have to tell me that you understand or that you don't understand. I don't care. I just don't want to talk about the fucking dog."

Martin paused then said, "All right. Can you tell me at least why you don't want to talk about it?"

Dan looked out the window over the rows of roofs. The clouds folding into one another. The oncoming darkness. "No."

Martin scribbled another note. "Okay. Let's talk about something else. Have you felt violently angry at any time in the past week?"

Dan turned his gaze to him. "Other than right now?"

Martin eyed him warily. "Yes. Other than right now."

SEVEN

Now Auditioning

DAN FELT A PROFOUND AMBIVALENCE for the gay ghetto at Church and Wellesley. On the one hand, it was where he'd first been accepted when he came to Toronto; for that, he felt a loyalty verging on heartfelt gratitude. Then the other hand rose up and, with it, his disillusionment came into focus: it lacked pride. The kind of pride he felt a gay ghetto ought to have, though maybe the primary word here was "ghetto" and not "gay." He'd been to other gay neighbourhoods; few of those had impressed him either. They struck him as being caught between lacking self-respect and not trying hard enough. *We can do better,* he thought.

Maybe it was the city encroaching on the ghetto that stopped it from being more remarkable. You couldn't make people respect invisible boundaries, lines drawn in sand, but Church Street always felt unnecessarily tawdry and sad, with its dilapidated awnings and faded storefronts, like a dyspeptic drunk. As though it would rather be something else, but couldn't decide what. Nor could Dan. He'd taken his time coming out, not because he was ashamed of being gay but because he couldn't identify with so many gay men and women. It baffled him why they accepted second-hand treatment at the hands of others. It was as though they derived their identity from the fact that they'd been denied by the rest of the world.

And so with the ghetto. He'd never choose to live there. It wasn't the urge to band together that bothered him so much as their willingness to accept this small bit of turf as all they could have. He often felt sold out by his own kind. Coming to Church Street only exacerbated the feeling.

He headed south along the east side of the street, past a roving pack of club kids, tattooed, coiffed, and spouting song lyrics. Cocky with their twenty-something-ness. The darkened glass of Byzantium superimposed Dan's reflection over a pair of diners, an Asian kid and a white kid sharing a jocular moment with their waiter. The Asian boy speared Dan's stomach with a fondue prong and leaned in for a bite. Further along, the windows at This Ain't The Rosedale Library shouted with book titles and magazines he'd never heard of because being hip took too much energy. If he needed to know anything current, Donny or Ked usually filled him in.

The Black Eagle wasn't known for being a hustler haven. It was primarily a leather bar, a netherworld of S&M accoutrements catering to a clientele that identified with a vaguely threatening, power-oriented sexuality. Skinhead and biker looks were popular. Dan's ruggedness fit right in. He'd once gone home with a man he'd met on the upstairs patio, only to discover his apartment decorated with Nazi paraphernalia. He hadn't stayed long enough to find out if it was a joke.

The out-of-work bodybuilder planted outside the front entrance threw Dan a smile. Steroids had given him pectorals a drag queen would envy, while anti-virals had finished off the effect by reinventing his face. Dan always felt he'd passed some sort of mutation test by coming here. He pulled out the picture of the runaway.

The man looked it over and smacked one fist into the other. "Kid like that comes in here and we'd kick his ass out in a second," he said. "Don't need that kind of trouble — those kids have their own places to go to anyway."

"What about in the daytime when no one's on the door?"

The bouncer tilted his head toward the entrance. "Ask Charlie. He's on the main floor."

Dan went in. The interior carried an aroma of stale beer and body odour while suggesting scenes of torture and imprisonment rather than anything overtly erotic. In fact, a little sex appeal would have cheered the place up, but the premises evoked an aura of pain inflicted in lieu of pleasure. Dan considered physical abuse the dull side of the sexual imagination. He'd stopped going there when one too many pickups expressed disappointment at his gentle touch.

"Do you want to strangle me a bit?" one suggested, after a few minutes of foreplay. "It might make it more exciting. Besides, you look the type."

"I'm outta here," Dan said, the door slamming behind him before the man could even protest.

"How come a big hunk like you is so sweet?" another asked, clearly disappointed at not having his endurance limits tested. "I was hoping for a little abuse."

Dan flexed his biceps. "Who said abuse was free? Usually I get paid to hurt guys like you."

The man pulled a face. "I'm only thirty-three. You're crazy if you think I'm going to pay for sex!"

Dan retrieved his underwear and pulled it on. "Ever been to a bathhouse?"

The man gave him an odd look. "Of course."

"Then you've paid for sex."

In the bar on the main floor, heavy metal music ground through the speakers. The place was empty apart from a shirtless bartender who looked like a double for Jim Morrison right before his drunken downward spiral. He looked Dan over approvingly.

"Hi there."

"Evening," Dan said, to put things on a formal level. "You Charlie?"

"Yep. That's me."

Dan pulled the picture from his case and laid it on the bar. "Ever see this kid in here?"

Dan could see him calculating whether he was a cop. The bartender shrugged — it wouldn't matter either way so long as the kid wasn't in there now. "He looks pretty young. I doubt I've seen anyone under twenty in here yet."

A few doors up the street an early crowd had gathered in Woody's. Heads turned at his approach. Woody's was an upscale pub, a preppy bar for kids with clean good looks. Dan seldom rated more than a passing nod from this crowd. From experience he knew he looked like one of two things: rough trade or a hustler on the make.

Inside, he almost ran into a drag queen. Bricklayer hands and Maybelline eyes. Forget-me-not blue. She was

Anybody's Girl. She looked at Dan and flashed a smile: *Our Little Secret*. Dan smiled back. Why be unfriendly?

Cosy and comfortable, Woody's favoured décor over theme. Drag routines on slow nights and amateur strip shows mid-week, the bar managed to keep its clients happy without leaving them awash in Gwen Stefani and Britney Spears videos. For a while it was known as the bar in the American *Queer As Folk* series. Woody's also held a record for selling more beer than any other bar its size in the city. Despite this, breweries were reluctant to make a showing at Pride in the years before it became a sell-out and everybody wanted in on the advertising opportunities. Woody's stood up and got counted. "No Pride, no beer." It became a mantra repeated cheerfully to every brew-master within hearing. Next Pride Day, all but the most uncooperative contributed to Woody's float. You might not wring respect from a bigot, far less a corporation, but money had a way of leaping over personal qualms and setting its own rules. That move had earned the bar Dan's everlasting respect.

By light of day, the glamour faded and Woody's became just another dingy pub with a surprisingly small stage considering the number of drag queens who managed to crowd onto it any given Sunday. The interior was always dim, as though the aura of false twilight it carried was a prize feature. Dan padded through the wood-lined interior to see who or what lay inside.

A bartender called out hopefully. "Hey, sexy dude." It was probably the same name he had for half the guys who came into the place. He was short, twenty-two-ish, and filled his Baby Gap T-shirt in a way that left few questions unanswered, at least about his top half. "Good to see you again!"

Dan walked up to the bar and sat, knowing the last time he'd set foot in the place this particular bartender probably hadn't even applied for a position or slept with the right someone to get it. Or maybe even graduated from high school. "A pint of Rickard's Red," he said.

The boy pulled the tap, watched disinterestedly as the glass filled, flicked off the head, and pulled the tap again. He slid the glass forward. Dan slapped a ten on the counter, Sir John A. side up. There he was, father of the country with his steadfast stare, snowy curls, and not a hint of the alcoholic about him. Dan pushed the change back and took the top off his drink.

"I'd like some information," he said, retrieving the photograph from his briefcase. He flashed it at the bartender. "This kid ever come in here?"

The boy picked it up and looked it over carefully. He shook his head. "I don't think so. But I go for blondes, so I may not have noticed him even if he was right under my nose." He grinned. "Sorry."

Dan tried two other bartenders. No one gave him a positive ID. The tattooed bald-headed guy at the front bar just shrugged. "I see fifty variations on this kid every time I work a Saturday night," he said, looking back at Dan. "Now *you* I would remember. In fact, I do, though you haven't been in for a while. You're a Scotch drinker."

Dan smiled. "Only on a rough night," he said.

"Best kind of night there is. I didn't know you were a cop." His face suggested he might be willing to be handcuffed and frisked at a moment's notice.

"I'm not. Sorry to disappoint you."

The man's expression hovered between mirth and skepticism. "I doubt you'd disappoint anyone." He waited a beat, but Dan didn't pick up his cue. "Come back in sometime when you're looking for someone a little older — say, my age. I'll be willing to help in any way I can."

Dan laughed. "I'll keep it in mind, thanks."

He ran into the same story all up and down the strip. Either no one recalled the kid or they recalled a hundred just like him. He was about to give up when he saw a slim figure up ahead. For a second, Dan thought it might be Richard Philips. The boy sauntered past Starbucks and stopped to check his reflection in the storefront of Eyes On Church.

He had the same wary eyes and disappointed mouth as Richard. His scrawny build and jerky walk cut a swath ahead of him, while his hands busily defined the air. Even at a distance Dan could see the wear and tear he'd picked up on the streets. But it wasn't Richard. Just another street kid with ill-fitting jeans and a growing attitude. At fifteen, he'd be considered desirable by a certain crowd. That had probably been enough to make him head full-tilt down the wrong road. From the looks of him, he was now seventeen or eighteen. By twenty he'd be too disease-ridden to sell for over-ripe fruit, though there'd always be some fetishist willing to use him as a human ashtray in exchange for a place to stay when no one else wanted him. Still, he wasn't Richard. But give it a few years and he would be.

The boy had seen Dan. He turned and headed over. If Dan had been as forward during his time on the street, who knows where he'd be now?

"Hi, sir," the boy said. "Have you got the time?"

"Sure, I've got time," Dan said.

The boy's eyes darted up and down the sidewalk while he talked, as though afraid he might miss something. The jerky mannerisms continued. His pupils were so black, Dan felt it was like looking into a void. He had that intense sexual vibe street kids seemed to exude effortlessly, their inner antenna always attuned to someone else's desire.

"Let's go somewhere," the kid said, cocky now, as though he'd just lucked into a good thing.

"Not that kind of time."

The eyes turned suspicious. "What do you want then?"

"I'd like to talk."

"What about?"

"You legal?" Dan asked.

"I got ID," the kid said, puffing up his scrawny frame.

Dan resisted the urge to laugh. "I just wondered if we could go into a bar to talk."

The boy's eyes narrowed. "You a cop?"

"No."

"Then let's go." The boy led the way.

They wandered into Zelda's — probably the only trailer park–themed restaurant in the country. At the door, Loretta Lynn's transsexual cousin met them in a red-and-white gingham dress with a large bow on the back. She showed them to a table before flouncing away to feed her flock.

The boy eyed Dan. "What'd you want to talk about?"

"What's your name?"

The eyes narrowed. "Grady."

"Hi, Grady. Mine's Dan."

They shook. The boy smiled. This might be going somewhere after all.

"What are you drinking, Grady?"

The boy cocked his head as though it were an odd question. "Whatever."

Dan handed him a ten-dollar bill. "Go get yourself a whatever and keep the change. But make sure you come back and talk to me, right?"

The boy walked off to the bar. Dan didn't bother to watch. He knew the kid would be back. He was the only source of available cash at the moment.

Grady came back with a local beer, bill still in hand. "You said I could keep the change, right?"

Dan nodded. *Smart boy,* he thought. "It's yours."

The boy sat next to him and leaned in close enough for Dan to smell his body odour. Pungent, but it had an appeal. He rubbed his knee against Dan's. "So what do you wanna know?"

Dan fished out the photograph of Richard Philips. "I'm looking for this kid," he said.

The boy took the photograph and scrutinized it. Dan saw something in his face when he looked up. "He in trouble?" Grady said.

"He's not in trouble for anything he's done, but he might be in trouble wherever he's headed. I'm trying to find him to see if he needs help. I'm not asking you to rat on him."

The boy nodded and looked back at the photograph, running his tongue over his lower lip.

"His name's Richard," Dan said. "If that helps."

"Uh-huh. Maybe it was. His name's Lester now." The boy grinned. "If that helps."

Dan handed over another ten. "It helps a lot. Do you know where he is or where he might work?"

Grady pocketed the bill. "You sure you're not a cop?" he said, eying Dan squarely.

"No. I'm not a cop. And the boy's not in trouble, as I said."

"'Kay," the kid said. "I don't wanna rat on anybody. So yeah, I know a bit about Lester."

"How do you know him?" Dan asked.

Grady took a long drink and set the bottle down with a satisfied sigh. He looked around the bar as though afraid of being overheard, but his volume increased rather than diminished. It was probably how he advertised, Dan realized.

"We worked together — not long ago."

Dan nodded. "On the street?"

The boy shook his head impatiently, anxious to disabuse the idea. "We did a flick. A porno. All good-looking young guys," he said, as though to distinguish it from the ignominy of being in a film with old trolls. He took another long swig from the beer. It was two-thirds empty now.

This time Dan held out a twenty. "Where?"

The boy clutched the bill and drew it slowly through Dan's fingers. "Place out on Danforth."

"Name? Address?"

"I really don't remember the number," the boy said. "But it's across from the Canadian Tire. Moonlight Cinema or some shit like that on the door."

"Thank you," Dan said. "You've been very helpful."

The boy was watching him carefully. "There's more," he said.

Dan waited. "I'm out of cash," he said.

"Why don't we go to your place? No charge." He rubbed Dan's thigh, letting his fingers slide up to his crotch. "You look tough, but I can tell you wouldn't hurt me. I know guys."

"I've got a son at home who's not much younger than you."

The kid withdrew his hand. "You're not straight though," he said, shaking his head. "I can tell."

Dan shook his head. "No, I'm not."

"But you think it would be weird to sleep with someone who reminds you of your son?"

"Something like that," Dan said. The kid was sharp.

"Too bad," the boy said, pushing back his chair. "Even soft I can tell you got a nice dick."

"So what else do you know?"

Grady nodded and looked around, as though taking stock of his prospects for later. The bar was dismal. He turned back to Dan. "They called me for a sequel," he said. "For a couple weeks from now."

"You going to be in it?" Dan asked.

The boy cocked his head. "Can't," he said. "I've got a date with this rich guy from Montreal. He's taking me to Cuba."

Lucky you, Dan thought. *Turning down a starring role in a film for a private performance.* He wrote down the details, wondering if Lester was really the boy he was looking for or if Grady had told him anything remotely like the truth. His gut said yes. They shook hands again and Dan wished him luck.

Outside, the street was filling with the usual mid-week crowd. Cars slid past. The air was fine. It would be busy soon, another prime evening on the strip. Dan wouldn't be sorry to miss it.

On the way home, he swung by the place Grady mentioned. He found the production house above a fruit and vegetable shop in a row of dreary two-storey buildings across from the inverted orange carrot of the Canadian Tire logo. An arc of light beamed above the door, a lone moth drawn to its promised glitter, the fool's gold of the insect world.

From outside, Moonlight Cinemas looked like a regular business: a place that videotaped weddings and bar mitzvahs and put its trash out on the street along with the other businesses. There was even a plastic plaque over the door. Then again, Dan thought, why shouldn't it be? Unless someone nabbed them for using underage models.

He got out of the car, trying to be casual as he strolled past. All the second-floor lights were off. Or, more likely, the windows were permanently blacked out. Above the mail slot, a smaller handwritten sign with letters in faded marker read, "Now auditioning. Call back during business hours."

EIGHT

Do You Have a Dress Code?

THE HOUSE WAS DARK AND STILL with the sound that empty houses make. Dan looked for the telltale blink of the answering machine from the end of the hall, but found none. He flicked on a light and set his laptop down with the mail. In the kitchen, Ralph's tail wagged a hesitant welcome, as though waiting to see what kind of mood Dan had arrived in before going all out. At least there were no messy presents, despite his having been gone most of the day. Usually the dog behaved for a few days after being yelled at. More proof he knew what he was doing.

"Good boy," Dan said.

The tail thumped harder, but Ralph stayed put.

"We talked about you today," Dan said. "Martin and I, I mean. I assured him you were a very smart guy. He's not so sure about me."

He draped his coat over the back of a chair. With Ked at his mother's, he could afford to be lax. These days Kendra had him almost as much as Dan did. Maybe she was afraid he'd grow up thinking she didn't care about him. It wasn't true. She loved Ked as much as Dan did but with a detached edge, the way she loved all things. It was as though he'd never really been a part of her body, whereas Dan felt Ked had always been inside him, waiting to emerge.

So far Ked hadn't shown any signs of troubled behaviour that children of divorced parents exhibited, perhaps because his parents had never been together, either in memory or before. He was a happy accident rather than the spoils of war. And since his parents got along, Ked seemed to think it fine that he had two homes to go to, two bedrooms to mess. No one fought over Christmas or other holidays. Double birthday celebrations at two different addresses guaranteed double gifts and two cakes. No complaints there.

Dan cast his eyes around. The house was in reasonable shape. When Bill got around to returning his call, Dan would entice him over with a promised romp. A few softly murmured dirty words were usually all it took. Dan didn't mind if Ked was home when Bill came by for his infrequent visits, but he preferred he wasn't. At first he'd fooled himself into thinking he didn't want Ked to overhear the crescendos of their sweaty sex romps — and Bill certainly liked to vocalize his pleasure — but in fact Dan didn't want Ked there because Ked looked down on him for dating Bill. He should have found that amusing, but it made him uncomfortable knowing his son thought less of him for his choice of romantic partners. Though admittedly there was really nothing romantic about Bill.

He went upstairs with his laptop and emptied his inbox with a few quick replies. Done, he tossed some ice in a glass and poured a tumblerful of Scotch, priding himself on having waited that long. When Ked was around he stuck to beer, but tonight he was alone. He sat in the living room and looked out at the street. The birch in the front yard hid the window from view but allowed a bird's eye view of anyone passing. He flicked on Jazz FM and caught something dark and rhythmically complex. He had no idea who it was. Donny would, of course.

His second glass had less ice, more Scotch. He returned to the chair. Outside, the street was empty apart from an occasional car stirring up leaves before passing from view. The program switched over to Jeff Healey's *My Kind of Jazz* and his archive of treasures from the twenties and thirties. The old, growly blues records — wonderful stuff — bringing to life voices and musicians from nearly a century ago. And then it was time for another drink.

In the kitchen, the dog stared as Dan cracked the ice tray and filled his glass. He tried to recall if he'd let Ralph out when he came home. He rubbed his eyes and blinked. The room turned blurry for a moment then cleared again.

He remembered Ked's injunction on speaking to Ralph. "What do you want?" he said, opening his arms wide the way Ked had done.

The dog whimpered but didn't move.

"What do you want? Show me what you want." *I'm talking to a dog,* Dan thought. "Do you understand what I'm saying, Ralphie?" he said in exaggerated tones.

The dog scampered up, racing to the front door.

"I guess you do."

Ralph whimpered worriedly as Dan fumbled with the leash and struggled with his windbreaker. Outside, it was a cloudy, moonless night. Leaves littered the sidewalks. The dog lunged down the walk. Caught off guard, Dan lurched into the fence. He heard a loud crack as his knee connected with a fencepost.

"Goddamn it!" he bellowed.

The dog looked back, straining to keep as far from Dan as he could. "Stop pulling!" Dan yelled.

He felt around with his fingers. No pain. It had been the fence post rather than his leg he'd heard cracking. They continued to the street, Ralph dragging him along.

"Stop it!" he commanded. The dog stopped and waited, then sprang forward as soon as Dan moved. Dan yanked on the leash and Ralph yelped. He cowered as Dan came toward him. "No, it's okay," Dan said gently. "Just stop pulling."

They continued at a slower pace. Ralph seemed to like to lead, so Dan gave him some distance. He trotted proudly, looking back once in a while as though checking in or encouraging Dan to walk faster. *You can do this*, Dan told himself. *You can walk the dog without getting angry*.

They reached Danforth Avenue and turned left. Outside various halal shops, bearded men in white thobe robes sat looking otherworldly, smoking mysterious-smelling herbs and muttering strange syllables, as though they knew secrets they shared only among themselves. In a Greek butcher's window, trussed lamb and goat carcasses hung down, skinned and venous. Ralph sniffed at the doorstep, a biblical angel checking for smeared lambs' blood, and lapped at a dark spot on the sidewalk.

Dan's head was losing its fuzziness. He thought of the drink he'd poured and forgotten. They turned back at the borders of Riverdale and headed south again. Arriving back at the house, Ralph trotted up the walk and curled up on the rug in the living room.

The ice had melted in Dan's glass where it sat perched on the arm of the chair. He had no idea why he'd placed it there. Maybe the idea of balancing it on the arm had appealed to him. In any case, Scotch was for drinking, not for balancing on chair arms.

He took a slug, waiting for the slow burn in his throat. His father had been an angry, frustrated man most of his life. The irony was he was nicest when he drank, as though alcohol allowed him a bit of headroom on the tight leash on which he kept his emotions. But nothing ever brought his father closer. Dan had filled the mantle with athletic trophies from school, but his father hadn't cared. He'd done the housework, but his father seldom noticed. Even when his Aunt Marge pointed it out, praising Dan in front of him, his father only grunted in his usual incoherent manner, as though it made no difference to him whether dishes got washed and beds made, whether the garbage was put out on the curb or left to stink up the house.

Dan took another swallow and felt the warm release, wondering if this was what his father had felt when he drank. And this was always, always when he thought about Bill. The images jutted like a loose floorboard he'd tripped over and couldn't resist pulling up to see what lay beneath. Only with Bill there was never really much there.

They'd met at Sailor's on a Saturday night when the bar was crammed. Dan seldom went out to bars and, if he did, almost never on a Saturday. Crowds made him claustro-phobic, but mostly he disliked being jostled and touched. There were also too many slight, pimple-faced youngsters who reminded him not a little of Ked a few years on — boys who tried too hard to be desirable when in truth they were simply awkward, thin and insecure.

Dan knew boys like that. They wanted Jake Gyllenhaal, but they'd settle for a guy like Dan who could make their hormones twitch with a glance. Especially once the bar lights came up and they found themselves alone again. But those boys required work once you got them home, made them feel safe, fucked them till they grinned, and then hoped they'd leave so you could get some sleep and forget you'd just bedded another twenty-year-old who had pleaded for your number but would never call. The next time they saw him in a club, they turned their heads and pretended not to notice him for fear he'd assume there was anything between them.

That particular Saturday, he'd been about to leave when a nicely built guy in jeans and a sweat-top caught his eye. The man pushed himself off the railing, tumbler in hand, and lurched in Dan's direction. Blue eyes and brown hair. Toothy gash for a mouth. Casual and assured. He might have been handsome except for the squat nose that brought out the petulant teenager in him, the one who always yelled "It sucks!" louder than anyone else.

His new acquaintance was quick to be physical, run-ning a hand over Dan's chest and sizing up his biceps with a practiced grip. Another guy wanting a weekend rough-up, Dan thought. The more they talked the more Dan expected him to lose interest, but in fact the opposite was true. If the guy thought he'd met trouble, he was pleased to discover it had a mind.

They exchanged names. Talk came around to work.

"I cut out hearts for a living," Bill said.

"I can beat that," Dan boasted. "I resurrect the dead."

Explanations ensued: Heart Surgeon meet Missing Persons Investigator. They clinked brews right there, leaning against the railing over the john. It never occurred to Dan there was a reason Bill had planted himself there.

Bill leaned in for a kiss wreathed in alcohol. Dan let it happen, playful at first. A hand reached out, massaging his nascent erection. Bill pulled back. His face said "impressed."

On-stage, a drag queen pantomimed giving head to some lucky eighteen-year-old. The boy looked anything but amused, though his expression fell short of frightened. Even the suburban kids were jaded these days.

"Why don't we get out of here?" Bill suggested.

In another minute they were outside and on the way to Bill's car. When Dan mentioned his address, Bill gave him a toothy grin.

"Really? You live in Leslieville? We'd better go to my place then."

"Why? Are you closer?"

"No. That's just a bit low-rent for me. I don't have a visa to go past Riverdale."

Dan stopped. "Since when is it acceptable to insult someone's neighbourhood?"

Bill's mood shifted to surprised innocence. "Sorry — I wasn't insulting you."

"No? What were you doing?"

Bill grabbed Dan's arm. "I was trying to be funny. C'mon."

Dan stood there, not moving.

"C'mon," Bill urged in pacifying tones. "I'm a little drunk. Forget what I said. Here — this is me." He pointed to an Audi R8. He dangled the keys. "You know you want to."

Dan relented. "All right, but I'm driving." He snatched Bill's keys and slid behind the wheel.

"I'm sorry, I didn't mean to insult your neighbourhood," Bill said, leaning against the headrest.

"I live in Leslieville by choice," Dan said. "Chances are I wouldn't like your neighbourhood either."

"I live in an expensive part of town…."

"Case closed," Dan snapped. "I generally don't like rich people."

Bill made a face. "Okay, I get your point."

They drove in silence for a while. Bill put a hand on Dan's chest, tweaking his nipple through the soft cotton. "Do you like your neighbourhood? I've heard good things about it."

Dan turned his head toward him. "Drop it, okay?"

They slid up Mount Pleasant and along St. Clair to a four-storey townhouse complex that made Dan think of ornate birdcages. He wanted to ask if they had a dress code but realized he'd be the one forcing the issue. The car slid underground and inside the building.

Bill took Dan on a tour of his house. In the living room, the skyline stretched before them like a giant mural. Bill waited a beat before turning on the lights to give Dan the full effect. A Persian carpet rolled across the floor like a minia-ture sea, dotted here and there by chic aluminum furniture with translucent frames and rare wood finishings. They were the kind of pieces people bought to impress others as much as themselves. Bill suddenly seemed a lot less drunk than he had in the bar as he related tales of buying sprees and exorbitant prices. He tossed designer names casually about — Paola Lenti, Herman Miller, Breuer Wassily — as though he knew them personally, and gave the impression he did. Dan was clearly supposed to be impressed by the show, so he purposely kept his face impassive.

Dan followed him to a bedroom where a four-poster bed took centre stage. A water feature trickled in a corner. The walls were hung with pictures arranged to catch the viewer's eye from every angle. Bill had obviously paid a great deal for his taste.

Bill had them both undressed in seconds, pushing pillows and linens onto the floor. Dan had been right: Bill liked it rough. He was all slither and slink, posing in positions that suggested submissiveness-to-order copied from the best porn videos.

"Get you rich boys out of your clothes and you're all the same underneath," Dan said.

For the most part, he went along with Bill's fantasy, though he refused to bareback when Bill asked.

"C'mon — I can tell you're healthy," Bill pleaded.

"Uh-uh," Dan said, his cock see-sawing between Bill's legs. "This little traveller doesn't go underground without a protection suit."

"That's no 'little' traveller," Bill said, wriggling into position. "Please! I want to feel you in me."

There were condoms on the bedside table. Dan picked one up. "You'll feel me. I promise."

Bill grabbed his hand. "Just put it inside me for a second," he said. "Just one second!"

Dan gave what he hoped was a reprehensible stare. "What kind of attitude is that for a doctor? Besides, I'm a responsible dad. I can't get sick — I've got a kid to take care of."

"What?" Bill's mouth was agape. "You mean your sperm has fathered a child?"

"That's right."

"A real live daddy? Now I *really* want you inside me!" Bill exclaimed, gripping Dan's erection.

Dan slapped the hand aside and unpeeled the condom over his cock. "If you want this to happen, you'd better behave. And I need extra large next time."

Bill gasped as Dan wedged himself in with no niceties. "Oh, yeah!" he exclaimed. "You wonderful beast!"

It was over the top, but at least Bill hadn't made him feel like a mercy fuck for being the victim of a radiation leak, the way others had. The sex always went fine, but usually that was the end of it. Dan could tell by the looks on their faces. The more satisfied they were during, the sooner they hoped he'd pack up and leave afterwards. Somehow, covering up his prizefighter's body always brought attention back to that face.

It's not that it was ugly, and it's not that it wasn't. In school, Dan had been taunted by the other kids. A cruel scrawl on a washroom wall claimed he'd been the victim of a nuclear attack, conjuring images of holocausts and radiation mutation. He had a brooding quality, an intensity that scared people. The eyes were what held you — grey-blue, ghostly. Like they'd seen too much. There were fine features

— the broad cheekbones, sharp brow, and long lashes — but the overall effect didn't add up to a pretty picture. The broken nose and red scallop racing from his right cheek up to his eye told part of the story. It begged wariness on the viewer's part. So did the rough skin that bore the traces of a memorable battle with acne, the permanent outline of a beard and the jaw that was rugged at one angle but menacing at another. It was the face of a man you might enjoy being roughed up by — a well-aimed slap, a welt or two — and then escape before one or both of you took the fantasy too far. It was a face you might expect to see inset in the tabloid coverage of sex crimes, with an earnest police report warning area residents to lock their doors at night and to be on the lookout for any suspicious activity. It was a face your mother would tell you to stay away from.

Bill's mother must have been an exception.

Dan sat up and reached for his jeans. Bill lay against the pillows, running a hand over his belly. "Where are you going?"

"Home," Dan said without looking over. "It's late. I'll let you get some rest."

"Oh no, you're not!" Bill rolled over, wrapping his arms around Dan, his fingers toying with the cum-smeared, sweat-matted hair on his chest. "More, please," he whispered, pulling Dan's face down for a kiss that was unexpectedly genuine.

Even more unexpectedly, Dan stayed.

Dan woke to a still house. He was sprawled in the living room chair next to the fireplace, his feet extended, an empty tumbler on the floor beside him. He dragged his tongue across his teeth and felt the resinous coating. He stumbled to the kitchen for a drink of water. It was five thirty. Ralph lay in the corner on his bed, a paw tucked over his eyes.

Ked's shoes were on the front mat. Obviously he'd returned at some point and gone off to bed without waking him. On the way back to the living room Dan saw the red flash.

"Hey, lover boy! Guess I missed you." There were party noises in the background. "We'll figure out the driving thing, don't worry. I'll call you at work tomorrow."

The time on the message was 4:43. It was Donny who'd suggested that Bill's almost inhuman ability to go without sleep was pharmaceutically related. Dan had never seen any trace of it other than the drugs Bill preferred to beer at parties, but it would be easy for a doctor to disguise such things.

The message ended. Dan stood and waited, as if expecting more. Ralph raised his head and whimpered a question. Dan played the tape a second time then pressed erase. He waited while the machine made its satisfied clicking noises as it ate up the recording before continuing up to bed.

NINE

Death by Haunting

THEY WERE SURROUNDED BY MIST. The monochromatic outline of trees and barns drifted by like ghosts on either side of the road. Rain had dogged them all the way from Toronto, only now giving way to something finer, a damp chill that got right inside their clothing. Passing cars fanned plumy sprays across the windshield, making the wipers do double time.

"How much farther?" Bill said, staring out at the passing landscape.

"Not much."

They were in Bill's car. Dan drove, despite a hangover. He'd barely made it through the morning at work. When Bill arrived to pick him up, he tossed his canvas bag into the trunk alongside Bill's leather ones, climbed into the driver's seat, and headed for the Don Valley Parkway. An hour out of Toronto, they left the 401 to join the stretch of coastal highway running south through Hillier and Bloomfield and on to Picton. The mist thinned momentarily as a forlorn strip of trees appeared on their right, water in front and behind it like a film backdrop, one-dimensional, floating in the middle of a never-ending lake.

"This is boring," Bill declared. "Where are we?"

"We're in Prince Edward County on the Loyalist Parkway," Dan said. "It's a considerable bit of Canadian history."

"Do people actually live out here?"

Dan glanced over. "Not everyone wants to live in Forest Hill."

Bill was looking worn. He had the beginnings of a bald patch, shadows beneath his eyes, and a paunch he self-consciously sucked in. Still, he had an undeniable charm, like a jock dad gone to seed. Despite his impatience and shifting moods, there was a boyish eagerness about him that held Dan. Even Bill's casual cruelties — like when he ignored Dan's calls for days — only sank the hook in deeper.

Other than an ecstasy habit and a fondness for dancing in dimly lit after-hours clubs, there was nothing noticeably gay about Bill. Dan suspected he was making up for a missed adolescence. He seemed overly fond of the kind of clubs where you climbed into darkened rooms via fire escapes or sat on rooftops while thrash music blared and incomprehensible films were projected on the walls of neighbouring buildings. Once, he brought them to a party that got shut down by axe-wielding police as guests escaped down back alleys or onto neighbouring balconies. Another had featured a live sex show. Dan watched as a black substance was poured over the participants, becoming more and more of an adherent as the bodies, both male and female, grappled and copulated in various permutations on a makeshift stage. Still, it was nothing as artful as a good porn flick, Dan thought as he went off to get a beer.

Bill twiddled with the FM dial as the mist closed over the shoreline again. Sounds faded in and out, white noise, the burps and farts of radio emissions. A ragged voice shot through for a second then disappeared in a snarl of static.

"Hey — that's Shaggy!" Bill exclaimed. "I love Shaggy." His hands twisted frantically. "Gone," he announced mournfully, as though Shaggy had vanished forever.

"We'll find you another one," Dan said. "You want Shaggy, we'll get you Shaggy."

"I love all kinds of music," Bill said in a proprietary way.

Bill was proprietary about many things. His taste in clothes always seemed an advertisement for the latest trends, coming straight out of one catalogue or another — J.Crew, Harley-Davidson, Hugo Boss. He always had the newest CDs and DVDs. Style filled his cupboards — he could well afford it. It was Donny who'd pointed out Bill's pretensions as they left his rooftop patio one evening after a catered meal and some pricey wine shared by a gathering of Bill's overly loud, fawning friends.

"Ghetto fags," Donny sniffed. "I've never seen them north of Bloor before."

He was working out an irritation. There'd be no stopping him till he was done.

"Nice place, though," Dan said.

"That man thinks he invented 'cool,'" Donny said. "Did you catch the reference to 'Coal Train'?"

Dan shook his head.

Donny rocked with barely suppressed laughter. "When Roger asked what music was playing, Bill said it was 'Coal Train' by the Africa Brass." Donny looked at him. "Ring any bells?"

"Not really." Dan shook his head. "Wait! Not John Coltrane? Surely not!"

Donny rolled his eyes and laughed. "Yes! It was Coltrane's *Africa Brass Sessions*. He hadn't a clue what it was. The pretentious twat!"

"Hey! That's not fair — Bill's a brilliant surgeon. He can't know everything."

Donny made a face. "Oh, right! Excuse me whilst I slag your current *amour*, since you don't have the good sense to do it yourself."

At the time, Dan hadn't expected Bill to last beyond the summer, but here they were a year later driving Bill's car along the Loyalist Parkway. Picton swept past, a colonial town in miniature. Ten minutes later the highway came to an end, turning abruptly down to the Bay of Quinte. Apart from the brewery and a former gristmill that housed the current Ministry of Natural Resources, there was little to see.

"What's this place?" Bill grumbled.

"This is the Glenora ferry crossing. John A. Macdonald used to live here."

"Who?"

"Our first prime minister? Sir John A. Macdonald?"

"Oh, him." Bill grunted.

"You know, sometimes you worry me," Dan said.

"I'm distracted," Bill snarled. "I didn't sleep much."

Dan reached over and squeezed his knee. "I was kidding. Don't worry."

"I work hard, you know," Bill said petulantly. "Thom better have champagne waiting for us when we get there."

They joined the line of vehicles waiting to be transported across the tenuous link connecting the two counties. Bill craned his head to make out the far shore. It was draped in fog. "This place is eerie."

"But beautiful," Dan said. "I like the feeling of isolation...."

"I don't. It creeps me out. I don't like to be this far from the city."

Dan cocked an eyebrow at him. "Aren't you the one who always wants to go camping?"

Bill snorted. "Sure — as long as I get to sleep in a five-star hotel."

The line-up advanced, braking and inching forward again in little shimmy movements. The gate swung closed on a full load and the boat surged into the bay. Fifteen minutes later they rolled onto the opposite shore. The fog was denser, hanging in soft folds in the trees. Dan drove slowly, alert for road signs and wary of oncoming cars shooting out of the grey gauze in an anxious rush to catch the return ferry. He skidded past the arrow pointing down a country road, then reversed and headed for the north shore.

The house was visible from a distance where it sat framed by pines. Once the mist cleared, it promised a breathtaking view of the bay. A whimsical third-floor tower with curved glass windows and a wrap-around porch softened the otherwise sober exterior. Red creeper curled over grey stone. Flowerbeds surrounded the drive in fizzy, mist-muted bands of yellow and a late-season patch of bright azure blue. Dan turned up the cobblestone half-circle. The house seemed to be watching them. Its windows winked in and out of the fog.

"Leave the car here," Bill commanded, craning his head to look at the upper stories.

"I can't leave it in the middle of the driveway."

"Don't worry about it. Park it over there, then." He waved to the side.

Dan hefted their bags from the trunk and turned to find Bill staring at him. "What? Am I dressed wrong for this set?" he joked, glancing down at his plaid jacket, navy T and khaki pants.

"Thom's going to love you," Bill said apprehensively.

"What? How do you mean?"

Bill gave him a pained look. "I know Thom's type. And you're essentially it. I just hope he doesn't try to steal you from me."

Dan made a face. "I thought he was getting married this weekend."

"That wouldn't stop Thom."

"Well, I'll stop him if he tries. I'm here with you."

"You don't know Thom," Bill said. "Besides, the rich make their own rules."

"You're rich, aren't you?"

"Not that rich."

A knocker resounded deep inside, as though the house went on for miles. After a few seconds, Bill grabbed the handle. The door opened onto a panelled foyer bright with flowers. A note awaited them on the hall table.

Welcome Billy and Daniel!

Your love nest is the first room on the left up the stairs. Make yourselves at home. (Food, drink, pool boys, etc.)

Seb and I will be back around 2.

XO Thom.

It was well past two now. Dan followed Bill up the stairs. Their room had an en suite bath and a fireplace. He set their bags down and looked around. A bay window overlooked a green swath that disappeared in mist before it reached the water. Dan walked over to the mantle and picked up a framed photo of a young man in a rowing scull. Big smile, bigger arms. The blond, blue-eyed looks of a matinee idol. Pretty enough for daytime soaps, though possibly not serious enough for prime time.

"That's Thom," Bill said, almost reluctantly.

"He's rich *and* good looking?" Dan exclaimed. "How unfair!"

"He was an Olympic rower the year the team won a silver medal. Thom's got it all," Bill said with what sounded like disdain. "In fact, he's even better looking in person."

Dan thought it over. It wasn't disdain; it was resentment. He heard it clearly now.

Bill pulled a rose from a bud vase, sniffed it, then laid it aside on the runner. "Come on," he said, turning. "I want a shower."

In the bathroom, Bill yanked at Dan's T-shirt, then left off to unzip his fly. Fingers snaked inside his pants. "You have the most perfect cock."

Dan slipped off his trousers and stepped into the shower. Bill knelt and looked up at him through the stream. "Who am I?" he demanded.

"You're a dirty little hitchhiker I picked up on the Trans-Canada," Dan said. This was Bill's game, though for the most part Dan went along with it. "Who am I?"

"You're a big sweaty trucker and you're taking me to a place off the highway to make me suck your big dick."

Dan ran a hand through Bill's hair.

"Oh yeah!" Bill exclaimed. "Hit me … slap me around."

Dan tapped Bill gently on the cheek.

"Harder!"

Dan gave his hair a tug. "I told you — I don't mind make-believe, but I won't hit you for real."

Bill leered up through the pouring water. "What if I deserve it?"

"Then you'll have to find someone else to give you what you deserve."

"What if I told you I already have?"

Dan felt himself stiffen.

"You like the thought of someone else fucking me, don't you? It turns you on."

"Shut up," Dan said.

"Yeah! Call me names. Tell me what to do!"

Dan thrust until he heard Bill gag. He felt slightly used, the unwilling participant in a porn video aware the camera is on him but closing his eyes and thinking of the money he needs to buy medication for his infant son.

Bill milked him until he stopped throbbing. "Sweet! You are so fucking hot!"

"And you are a very bad doctor," Dan said. He towelled off and returned to the bedroom to dress.

Bill followed him. "Got you going there, didn't I? It gets you hot to think about me getting off with other guys, doesn't it?"

"Does it?" Dan said, adjusting his shirt.

Bill stood beside him. He turned and regarded his reflection with a frown. "I'm getting fat."

Dan wrapped his arms around Bill from behind. "More to love?"

Bill reached behind, impatiently tugging at Dan's zipper again. "More," he commanded.

"Later," Dan said, doing up his fly. "We have to be downstairs to meet your friends" — he checked his watch — "forty minutes ago."

Bill made a disapproving face. "Friend," he corrected. "I've never even met this other guy." He stood. "All right, then. Mr. and Mrs. Thom Killingworth await."

A picture window gave way onto an unbroken view of the harbour. Idyllic, grand. For a moment, the sun broke through the clouds like a promise of better things to come. The light reflecting on the waves lent the room a solemn stillness, mysterious and exotic, like something hidden in plain view, all the more startling when you finally notice it.

Bill looked around the empty room and shrugged. "Told you," he said. "There was plenty of time. We could have done it again."

Oil paintings hugged the walls. Even someone unversed in art would know it for a serious collection. The intricate filigrees and whorls of the frames spoke of cultured tastes and leisurely times when the art of woodcarving was a commonplace but necessary attribute. Still lifes predominated — apples and pears in bowls, flowers in vases, slabs of butter, and loaves of bread on tables. There were also landscapes — glowering forests, rugged mountains, stormy lakes, and open-throated skies — in cartoon-dreamy colours. There were no portraits. Impressionism favoured the inanimate.

"Thom's a collector," Bill said, looking them over as though considering a purchase. "What do you think this room is worth?"

Dan glanced over the walls. "I have no idea. I don't know much about art, except that it's usually bought by rich collectors for a lot of money after the artists are dead."

He recalled the impressive jade tiger dominating Bill's living room. On their second date, Bill had tossed a silk shirt over it as though it were a hitching post. The garment sizzled and slipped to the floor. Bill had left it lying there as he went for Dan's belt.

"Do you know anything about Canadian Impressionism?" Bill asked.

"Not really."

"That's what this is. It's pretty pricey stuff. I'd say this room is worth at least three or four million."

"I didn't know there was anything other than Group of Seven." Dan looked over the nameplates at the bottom of the frames — Mary Wrinch, Clarence Gagnon, and a few others. He'd never heard of any of them, apart from an A.Y. Jackson over the fireplace.

"Well, there is," Bill declared. "This is it. Most people don't know about this stuff. Thom collects it. Paintings and sports — that's Thom." A photograph frame sat on the mantle. "Here, just look at this."

It was a triptych of Thom manning a sailboat on the left then in his scull on the right. In the middle, a much younger Thom sat on a black horse, an alert-looking hound by his side. The mantle thronged with trophies and awards.

Footsteps approached. Dan turned to see a slightly older version of the rower in the flesh. Keenly cut hair hugged the sides of his head, giving him a distinguished look, like an ad for business executives flying first class on British Airways. His deep tan and billowy shirt exuded a casual sportiness.

"Billy!"

Bill's face lit up. "Thomas, old man! How are you?"

Dan listened with amusement to the good old boy affectations. He knew the private school system and its presumption that money and social worth went hand-in-hand. He'd have plenty to fill Donny in on later.

"Let me introduce you — Thom Killingworth, this is Dan Sharp."

Thom turned to Dan with an appraising stare. "Wow. You're pure sex," he said as they shook.

"I don't know about the 'pure' part, I'm afraid," Dan said.

"Don't believe him! He's all that and more," Bill said, in much the same way as he'd declared the value of the paintings.

Thom flashed his matinee idol smile. "I'm intrigued. Does Bill lend you out? Oops! Forget I said that — it's my wedding day, after all!"

"I'll forget it," Dan said.

Thom shot Bill a look. "You didn't mention he was cocky. I might just have to steal this one away from you, Billy."

"Go ahead and try," said Bill, glancing at Dan. "If you think you can. This one has staying power."

They were interrupted by the arrival of a young man with an impressive physique and a chiselled face that looked far more serious than might have been intended. He was twenty-one or twenty-two at most, dressed in tight-fitting jeans and a sleeveless T-shirt over a gym-sculpted body. Mother Nature at her most appealing. The shirt emphasized the boy's chest and squared triceps. The jeans packaged bulging thighs and a spring-form butt. On a catwalk he would have been a one-name supermodel — Tyrone or Ché or Lars. In an escort service, he'd be top-dollar flesh rented by the minute. Here, in the living room of the Killingworth estate, he radiated a mercurial sexual appeal few could equal.

"My *husband*," Thom said, with an ironic inflection.

"Isn't that husband-to-be?" Bill said.

"We've had the pre-nups already," Thom said. "The test drive was awesome!"

The boy stood uncertainly in the middle of the room. His permanent scowl wasn't eased by a row of pearly whites bared into a grimace like a child's approximation of happiness.

"Does he have a name?" Bill said.

"This is Sebastiano Ballancourt," Thom replied.

Dan offered his hand. "Dan Sharp."

"I am very pleased to meet you," the boy said with an articulation straight from a translation phrasebook.

"Sebastiano's from Brazil," Thom said, as though anxious to explain away the single flaw in an otherwise priceless commodity.

"How did you meet?" Bill asked, savouring the boy like an after dinner mint.

"We meet … I mean, we *met*," Sebastiano corrected himself, "on the site for gays on the computer."

"We met on *sex4men.com*." Thom looked at Dan. "I'm sure you've heard of it."

"Actually, I've never been on a chat site," Dan said, annoyed by Thom's presumption yet feeling strangely prim, like somebody's maiden aunt discovering a skin magazine stashed under a mattress.

"Really? How queer." Thom's tone was ironic again, though whether out of disbelief or disdain wasn't clear. "Seb's a mail-order husband. We had a brief chat the first night and I flew him up from Sao Paolo the next day."

Sebastiano bared his crooked smile. "Thom likes everything so fast," he said, as though recounting a particularly funny moment from his day.

"And it was lust at first sight!" Thom laid an arm over the boy's shoulders, giving him a peck on the cheek. "Love came a bit later. I proposed the following month." Sebastiano beamed. "Of course, I made sure we both got tested. So now we know."

"Know what?" Dan said.

Thom looked surprised by the question. "That we're both HIV-negative, of course."

"Oh." Dan looked at Sebastiano. "Congratulations."

"Thank you," the boy said solemnly, as though he'd just accomplished a particularly harrowing feat.

"Of course it was no surprise," Thom said, grinning at Sebastiano. "No one's ever tupped this Brazilian bull."

Sebastiano laughed long and hard, shaking his head at the remark.

"And now we're about to embark on a lifetime of commitment till death us do part." Thom turned to Dan and winked. "Starting tomorrow. Tonight, anything goes."

"Yes," Sebastiano echoed happily. "It's true."

Bill leaned against the fireplace. "Now that Thom's getting married, he's going to inherit a fortune."

"Oh, shut up, Billy," Thom said irritably.

"Well, it's true!" Bill turned to Dan. "Thom's grandfather left an inheritance to whichever of his grandchildren married first. That was to make sure the queers got cut out of the will."

"The silly old fuck," Thom said, nibbling Sebastiano's ear. "Fortunately, the laws have changed to help me accommodate grandfather's wishes my way. And what's more, I've found the love of my life. He's beautiful, sexy, and disease-free. And best of all, he's all mine!"

Sebastiano leaned his head on Thom's shoulders with such an overt expression of affection, Dan knew immediately it was false. The boy was marrying for money, of course. And Thom was clearly marrying for sex.

Sebastiano smiled at Dan. "Tonight you will meet Daniella!" he said enthusiastically, like a child holding out hope for a long-promised event. For a moment, Dan thought he might even clap his hands in glee.

"Sebastiano's sister," Thom explained.

"I love her so much — more than anything on earth!" Sebastiano stopped and looked cautiously at Thom. "Except for Thom, of course. Because now I love him even more." He gave Thom a hug. "My beautiful husband!" he exclaimed.

Thom looked out the picture window. "It's clearing up," he said. "We should go for a drive." He turned to Dan. "Have you ever been to Lake on the Mountain?"

Dan shook his head. "Actually, no — though a friend of mine was telling me about it."

Thom nodded. "We'll go. You have to see it."

†

They disembarked from the ferry, headed past the families waiting with faces expectant or bored, and veered left onto County Road 7. Lake on the Mountain was a minute's climb up the hill. Near the top, they passed half a dozen weather-worn houses, an old church, and an inn set back from the road. Dan angled the car into a lot and sat facing a wooden rail overlooking the bay. Far below, the *MV Quinte Loyalist* and *MV Glenora* headed toward one another in the after-noon sun. The far hills were a blanket of colour. There was no trace of mist now. It had turned out to be a handsome day, unusually warm for September.

"Quite the view," Dan said as they gathered at the rail. "And so peaceful up here."

"That's what the United Empire Loyalists thought when they fled the American Revolution," Thom said. "They trekked through four hundred miles of wilderness to call this place home." He looked over his shoulder where a small lake glittered in the distance. "But it's the other side of this place that makes it famous — or infamous."

Under a bank of trees, the shallow water rippled in the breeze. On the far side, a red canoe eased silently along, paddlers and canoe replicated perfectly on the lake's placid surface. The wind gusted suddenly and the water danced a blue-grey jitterbug.

Dan looked back at the Bay of Quinte where miniatur-ized sailboats flashed like butterflies in the sun. Something tugged at him. He couldn't name it at first. It was an unset-tled feeling, the barest of hints at the back of his brain like a nagging intuition. In this place where breezes played on the water and wind stirred in the branches overhead, something was wrong. It was a sigh heard in an empty room or ghostly fingers straying across your cheek while you dreamed.

Thom was watching him. "Do you feel it?"

"Something's odd here," Dan said, almost apologetically. His brows knit. "I'm not given to ghosts and the like, but there's something strange about this place." He looked to Bill. "Do you know what I mean?"

"I know exactly what you mean!" Bill exclaimed. "There's no bar!"

Their laughter died over the surface of the lake. Dan tried to recall what Donny had said about the place. "It's the water, isn't it? It shouldn't be this high." His gaze returned to the bay. "It should level off with the water below." He turned again and looked across the lake. "And behind those trees is Lake Ontario, also quite a bit farther below...."

"... and yet here we are, hundreds of metres above the bay and the lake, and the water level up here never drops," Thom continued. "That's it. That's the mystery of this place."

Dan drew a breath. "It's freakish. It's as if it's breaking a law of nature."

Bill shook his head. "I don't feel anything. Besides, they say that about us."

"They say that about doctors?" Thom joked.

Sebastiano, who had been quiet till then, spoke up. "What do they say about doctors? Are you a doctor?"

Bill turned. "So they tell me."

"Never mind, Seb," Thom said. "It was just a joke."

Thom stepped onto a flat rock offshore and turned to them. "Forbidden love," he declaimed. "Legend has it a Mohawk brave and his Ojibwa lover committed suicide here when their tribes tried to prevent them from running away together." He pointed to the right of the parking lot. "There used to be a waterfall here that was once compared with Niagara. The settlers used it to power the gristmills."

Thom looked over his shoulder. The canoe had reached the end of the lake and was headed back, sliding silently along like an image in a dream. "No motor boats. They don't allow them." He stepped nimbly back onto shore and took Dan's arm, pulling him aside. "I just want to say how happy I am for you and Billy. He's my closest friend and I love him to death. And anyone who loves Bill is a friend of mine."

Dan nodded his thanks, but Thom had already moved ahead, as though uttering heartfelt sentiments was a casual thing for him. They caught up with Bill and Sebastiano on a walkway overshooting the water. A few yards out, a black stain spread under the water's surface. Another mystery, Dan thought, until he realized it was where the lake plummeted.

"If you were in a canoe," Thom said, "you'd see it's a sheer drop. It just plunges and gives you a little chill. The early settlers claimed the lake was bottomless."

"Any idea how deep it is?" Dan asked.

"Actually, I know exactly how deep it is," Thom said. "Thirty-seven metres. As a comparison, the Bay of Quinte where we ferried across is only seventeen metres at its deepest point."

"Where does the water come from?"

"It's speculative," Thom said, "but they think it might come from Lake Superior."

"But that's hundreds of kilometres away."

Thom nodded. "Scientists did some experiments releasing radioactive isotopes in the water, and that's what they've determined."

"It really is a mystery then."

Sebastiano was glancing around. A panicked look had taken hold of him. "I don't like this place. Bad spirits live here." He shivered. "I feel it is haunted."

Thom placed an arm across his shoulders. "Don't worry, Seb. I won't let them get you."

Bill eyed them. "I think it's boring," he said. "Let's go to town and find a drink."

Dan rested a bronzed arm on the windowsill, hair bristling in the breeze, as the car wound away from Glenora toward Picton. All four looked ahead expectantly, following the route the Loyalists once used. There would barely have been a track back then as they hacked their way through trees and dense growth, alert for Native attacks. Anticipating their new homeland, far from the tyranny of mob rule in the newly emancipated republic to the south, four hundred men and women loyal to King George III were setting the stage for the then-unnamed country's own tenuous path to independence.

Bill and Thom carried on a desultory conversation in the back. Sebastiano sat silently up front with Dan. He'd been spooked by the lake. Thom was used to its mystery and Bill hadn't felt a thing, but Dan thought it odd how strongly the boy had reacted.

Up ahead, a steeple beckoned. A mast-filled harbour flashed by with a collection of tilting crosses, and suddenly they were there. They roared over a bridge just as the town opened up. One block further along a pub hailed them from the first floor of a grand hotel that had survived the times. It stood there, a displaced duchess keeping up her artifices and routines in a world that no longer sustained a belief in royalty. The black and gold frame above the door dated the premises to 1881, a bit past John A.'s tenancy, but significant nonetheless in a land where anything old was seldom encouraged to hang around.

The Black Swan, known to regulars as the Murky Turkey, was an old-world fade-into-the-woodworks establishment replete with stained glass, stained menus, and a permanent ethos of beer and cigarettes that repulsed the lively but enticed the world-weary in for more.

Where the Scots pioneer went, drink was sure to follow. A mutinous-looking collection of malts and mashes lined the darkly mirrored bar, sixteen taps at hand for the discerning drinker. For better or worse, tradition demanded fish and chips on every menu, with a selection of fine eats. This one eschewed such old-world delicacies as haggis and blood pudding, but made up for it with offerings of fatty fried foods and dishes featuring animal entrails. Steak-and-kidney pie topped the list. For an added touch, sausages and mash were on offer, wisely located near the bottom of the menu owing to the fact that most Canadians would never have heard of it.

Heads notched toward them as they entered — a cast of regulars whose sluggish responses and leaden pallor suggested they hadn't moved or seen daylight in recent memory. The newcomers slid into chairs, their youthful voices and quick movements at odds with the room, bending their elbows against a table scarred with cigarette burns and the sweat rings from countless rounds of cheer. The look said vintage, though the exact period would have proved hard to determine.

Sebastiano had cheered up considerably since leaving Lake on the Mountain. He barely stopped talking as they doffed coats and settled in. "This is a good place," he said, looking around. "I like it here."

"It almost looks as though it might date from Loyalist times," Dan said.

"So does the waitress," Bill said, as a stooped spectre approached wearing a hesitant smile. He looked at her nametag. "Hello, Erma," he said.

Her smile blossomed into an unkempt garden of teeth. "Hear the specials, love?" she asked hopefully.

Thom shook his head. "Just drinks."

Erma's smile faded. She took their order and soon returned balancing a tray that threatened to topple her. "Just passing through?" she asked, marking them with their glasses.

"We're here for a wedding," Bill chimed in.

"Oh? That's nice. Whose?"

"His," Bill said, pointing at Thom. "And his." The finger went round to Sebastiano.

Erma nodded solemnly, as though unsure whether to take this news in jest. "That's nice," she said again. "Are youse from around here?"

"He's a Killingworth," Bill said, nodding at Thom before taking a slug of his drink.

Erma fixed her stare on Thom, as if imagining him in another setting. "From the other side of the harbour then."

She nodded to the far wall, as though looking directly through the brick and wooden beams.

"Yes," Thom said quietly.

"I know the family," Erma said, voice cautious. "Which one are you, love?" More than a tad interested now.

"Thom."

"Thom. Thomas." She mulled this over. "And was it your father who disappeared?"

Thom's eyes betrayed annoyance. "Yes," he said curtly.

"That was a long time ago, wasn't it? Did he ever turn up?"

"No. No, he didn't."

Dan tried to recall if Bill had mentioned Thom's missing father. It seemed odd given Dan's occupation, though maybe people with bad hearts sat through entire meals with Bill without broaching the subject. It wasn't the strange things that necessarily got talked about in people's pasts. In fact, they were usually spoken of only on long nights over tall glasses of whiskey, with cigarette ash burning down to the knuckles, before anyone thought to mention them.

"I'm sorry for your loss," Erma said, as though he'd been recently bereaved. She picked up the tray and shifted her weight. Her eyes grew shrewd again. "You had a brother too, I think."

"Still have," Thom said, not looking at her. "He's around."

"Oh?" She looked vaguely disappointed, as though a missing father required a missing son as a complement. "Well, have a lovely wedding," she said. "It's supposed to be a nice weekend."

"Thank you," Thom said, still not smiling.

Erma left, tray at her side.

Bill held up his lager and looked across at Thom and Sebastiano. "Here's to a lovely wedding," he said, tipping his glass.

For a moment, Dan thought Bill's smile betrayed some sort of amusement at Thom's discomfiture.

The young woman in the drawing room looked up from her book as they entered. She reminded Dan of Sebastiano, only a feminized version of the ardent Brazilian. They had the same strong features. Her hair was cut short, like his. Her face centred on a sleek nose and pouting rosebud mouth. Her eyes, however, were black where Sebastiano's were blue. With a bit of work and the right clothes, she might be truly beautiful.

Sebastiano called out in Portuguese and she responded with a laugh. She put the book down and stood, her graceful hands smoothing out a black knit dress. She was tall and willowy, with a gymnast's breasts. She came toward them and offered her hand. "Hello," she said. "I am Daniella — Sebastiano's sister."

Dan took the hand and held it. "I'm Dan. It's very nice to meet you, Daniella. Your brother's a charming fellow."

She smiled graciously, shook hands with Bill in turn, and then threw her arms around Sebastiano, pulling him close and breathing in his scent.

"My baby sister, you come back to me!" Sebastiano exclaimed over her shoulder to the others.

"I always come back to you." Daniella released him and opened her arms to Thom. "And beautiful, sexy Thomas," she said with a giggle.

"What were you reading just now, Daniella?" Thom said.

She shrugged. "It's nothing — just a Brazilian novel. A stupid thing." Her boyish, animated features reminded Dan of Kendra.

"Who's for a drink?" Thom exclaimed, despite the fact they'd just returned from the Black Swan. Bill and Sebastiano accepted. Dan and Daniella declined. "Not a drinker, Danny?" Thom's eyebrows rose mockingly. "Bill said you could knock back your share of rye with no problem."

Bill smirked. "He's a drinker, all right. He just prefers it after dark. Along with other things."

Dan ignored him. "I try not to drink during the day — even on vacation."

"Sensible," Thom said. "Pop? Juice? Anything?"

"I'm fine, thanks."

"Daniella?"

Her hair bobbed a response. "No, Thomas. *Obrigado.*"

Thom went to a sideboard and splashed drinks into glasses. He handed them around then sat with a satisfied sigh, arms raised on the back of the sofa. "So-o-o," he said, smiling. "Here we are." He looked over at Sebastiano. "My darling husband-to-be." He turned to Bill and Daniella. "And our two lovely best men!"

Daniella smiled and curled into the chair like a cat. "I am your 'best man,' Sebastiano," she cooed at her brother.

"You are my best everything," he replied and then shot a look at Thom. "And you too, my beautiful Thomas."

Thom turned to Dan. "Did Bill tell you we've got two best men?"

"No, he didn't."

"Well, we do — Bill and Daniella. I figured there was no need for a bridesmaid, since neither of us is a blushing bride." He nodded at Sebastiano. "Him least of all, but I don't think I'd feel right wearing a dress." He turned to Daniella. "And Daniella's offered to dress up in a tuxedo for us, haven't you, sweetie?"

"Of course," she said. "For my beautiful best men!"

Dan stood and went to the window, pushing aside his irritation at how everything seemed to be a great joke. The day was still bright, but the shadows had crept over the hills on the far shore. He turned to the room. "I think I'll take a walk," he said.

No one spoke. The others were so absorbed in their little charades, they seemed to have forgotten about him.

TEN

Knox and Calvin

THE KILLINGWORTH GROUNDS WERE EXTENSIVE, reaching from the road down to the water, and stretching for more than an acre in either direction. Along with the main house, they included a six-car garage, a boathouse and launch, as well as a small barn and stables beside a disused garden showing the remnants of winter-hardy herbs and self-seeding perennials. Dan noticed more of the azure blue flower he'd seen outside the window of the main house. He thought he recognized it as something he'd once been warned against picking, but couldn't put a name to it. The outer gardens clearly hadn't felt a gardener's touch in a long time. The boathouse held a sixteen-foot racing cat and two canoes strapped against the upper beams alongside a collection of lifejackets flung haphazardly overhead. Like the garden, the stables too were abandoned. There were stalls for six horses, and the barn held the remnants of hay bales. A rusted can of rat poison perched on an unpainted window ledge, its ancient emblem warning against improper usage barely visible. The drafty interior had become home for field mice and jittery swallows zooming about in the shadows and through the shafts of light penetrating the beams.

Dan crossed a deep carpet of pine needles and set off along the shore. Algae-covered rocks and logs extended under the waves, spectral ladders reaching down into another world. He stayed away long enough to dispel the irritation and gloominess that had dogged him since arriving. It was Bill's weekend, after all; he wouldn't spoil it.

By the time he returned, the company had broken up in the living room. Charged by the hour, the room reflected an expectant stillness as light settled over the carpets and caught on the backs of the sofa and chairs.

Dan went upstairs to look for Bill; the room was empty. Further along the hallway hung a realist portrait, an anomaly in the house. The artist's name meant nothing to Dan. A tag labelled its subject as *N.M.* The man's eyes carried a foreboding look while his placid features masked a dark spirit. Dan felt he wouldn't have wanted to be alone with him, whoever he was.

He turned and almost collided with someone coming along the hall.

"Sorry," Dan said, surprised by the man's sudden appearance.

For a moment he thought it was Thom. He had the same northern good looks — wavy hair, tidy sideburns, smooth skin — but with rounder features and none of the razzle-dazzle.

"Hello there," said the stranger in a voice that suggested competence, sincerity. "Another guest shanghaied in service of the wedding party?"

Dan laughed. "Just a casual hanger-on, I'm afraid," he said. He held out a hand. "Dan Sharp. I'm with Bill McFarland."

"Ah! Thom's old school chum." A brilliant smile geared down to something gentler. They shook. "Trevor James. Thom's disreputable cousin from the west coast. I've just arrived."

"You don't look so disreputable to me," Dan said. "Though I know appearances can deceive."

"In this family, disreputable means 'not rich enough.' They introduce me with caution."

"Then I guess I'm disreputable too," Dan said, feeling the gratification of an instant liking.

"We should form a club. I was just about to head downstairs to find cousin Thom. What about you?"

"Same," Dan said. "I've been out wandering. I should let them know I'm back."

"Let's search together."

Downstairs was empty. From outside came a shriek. Trevor glanced outside. "Looks like everyone's down at the boathouse."

They found a back door and crossed an expanse of lawn, past birdbaths and torches set along a flagstone path. In another month it would be unthinkable to have a party out here, but the evening was surprisingly warm and humid, as though it were still the middle of August.

Others had arrived. Bill was talking animatedly to a couple down by the boathouse, gesturing grandly over the water as though describing a plot of land he intended to build on for future generations, or perhaps asking them to guess how much the bay was worth.

Thom turned as they approached. "Daniel, there you are. Bill's been quite worried." He made a face at Trevor. "And so should I, now that I see your company. What has my dreaded cousin been telling you about me?"

"Nothing, actually," Trevor said. "I've been talking about myself for once."

"How gauche! Didn't you tell Daniel I was the first person you had sex with?"

Trevor smiled indulgently. "No, I thought I'd leave that little mishap unspoken for once."

Thom turned and pointed to the stables. "It was right over there. I sucked Trev's cock when he was only nine years old and I was — what…?"

"Ninety?" Trevor said.

Thom made a slightly drunken bow. "Thank you kindly."

Trevor turned to Dan. "Apparently the blame fell on me when I was seduced by Thom. Another reason I'm considered disreputable."

"You're nothing of the sort," Thom insisted. "But only because you don't try hard enough."

"The first person I had sex with was my cousin, too," Dan said.

"Really? How big was he?" Thom demanded. "Tell us all about it. What was his name?"

"Leyla," Dan said, and Trevor laughed out loud.

Thom pretended disgust. "A woman? I'm disappointed. I thought you were a purebred!"

"No," Dan said. "I already told you — there's nothing pure about me."

"So I'm learning."

"Go on," Trevor said. "Tell us about Leyla."

"I'd heard a rumour that Leyla had the best tits in junior high school, so one night when I slept over I pretended to be asleep while my hands did a bit of exploring...."

Thom feigned a gasp. "And was she asleep too?"

"Apparently not. She let me feel her up for a while, then she grabbed my winkie dink and gave it a squeeze."

"Smart girl...."

"I let out a scream. Her mother came running in and separated us. She thought we were fighting. That was the end of it."

Trevor was laughing.

"Not exactly a tussle over your lost virginity," Thom concluded. "One day I'd like to hear that story. And maybe even watch a re-enactment."

A voice hailed Thom. They turned and saw someone heading toward them from the house. The newcomer was small and slightly stooped, as though aged, but dressed in striped cords, paisley shirt, and rock star shades.

"Speaking of lost virgins ..." Thom murmured.

"I heard that," the man said.

"Good — I intended you to," Thom said.

"Cousin!" the newcomer said to Trevor. "You look splendid!"

"It's been a long time," Trevor said. "How are you?"

"Fine. Very fine. It's good to see you again."

"My brother," Thom said apologetically, leaning in to Dan.

"Richard the Lost," said the man, shaking hands with Dan.

"Is that who you are now?" Thom asked.

"Yes, it is. I've changed my name again."

"Don't believe him," Thom said to Dan. "This is my brother Teddy," he insisted. "Teddy is a filmmaker."

"Ted, please...." Ted's shades glittered in the fading light, reflecting the oncoming sunset as though a movie were playing inside his head.

"And Dan's a missing persons investigator with a lurid past. He was just telling us about it."

Ted gave him an appraising look. "How intriguing! Maybe you could sell me your story. How lurid is it?"

Dan shook his head. "Not very, I'm afraid."

A woman with high cheekbones and ringletted hair stood on the periphery of the group, sipping from a martini glass. She smiled shyly. It was, Dan thought, the smile of someone uncertain who she was.

"Ah! And here's Jezebel observing everyone," Ted said. "My leading lady."

Jezebel laughed a high-pitched laugh for no reason anyone could discern. They turned to watch and her expression transformed: shyness to modesty betrayed. Now she was Julia Roberts spotted buying tampons and toothpaste in a common pharmacy. She tipped her glass at them and her expression changed again, as though she were trying out for the role of a character suffering multiple personality disorder.

"Isn't this place wonderful?" she cried.

†

The guests seemed perfectly placed in an artist's rendition of an autumn lawn party. Others were still arriving, singly and in pairs. Dan watched as a rather shockingly well-endowed young man crossed the yard wearing only a leather jacket with a blue Speedo underneath. Someone else turned cartwheels across the grass. The sticky end-of-summer heat thinned as the light died out behind the hills.

Loudspeakers blared down by the boathouse. At one point nearly everyone seemed to be dancing. Thom and Sebastiano gyrated at the centre of the action. Dan stood at the edge of the lawn looking on. He felt someone standing near him and turned. Daniella was watching her brother and Thom.

"Tell him not to marry," she said, her words barely audible.

For a moment, Dan wondered if she meant Thom or her brother. "You don't want your brother to marry?"

Daniella's look was flint. "If I wanted to, I could stop it like that!" She snapped her fingers.

"Why would you do that?" Dan said. "They seem happy."

Her mouth hardened. She looked as though she would answer, but Sebastiano's voice cut through the air.

"Daniella!" He waved to her to join him and Thom.

Daniella turned and walked past her brother down to the lake. Sebastiano called after her, though she refused to acknowledge him. He gave up and turned to Thom with a shrug.

"Trouble in Paradise?" Dan turned to see Trevor beside him. He'd come up soundlessly behind him again.

"I gather there is not total consent among the Brazilians about this marriage."

"Really? I wonder if Thom knows about it."

Dan shrugged. "I guess it can't be easy for them to accept, coming from a Catholic country."

Trevor pursed his lips. "Well, they've got to learn sometime. They don't own the world," he said softly. "Or morality either, for that matter."

"Cheers to that," Dan said, finishing his drink. He looked over. "Can I get you a refill?"

"No, I'm good, thanks."

Trevor's voice made Dan think of a particular breed of man — confident and content without needing to show it. Men who knew when they needed drinks and when they didn't. Men who smiled and made others around them feel at ease without giving the least suggestion it was at their behest that they felt so.

In the kitchen, Ted leaned against the range. He still wore his shades, even indoors. "Ah — the sleuth!" He lifted his glass as Dan entered. "Guard your secrets, everyone," he called out to the empty room.

Dan thought he seemed buzzed, though maybe it was just party energy. Ted followed Dan's movements as he retrieved a beer and popped the top off, a painter examining a subject for a study or a director blocking moves for a scene.

"So what has my brother told you about our illustrious family?"

He was being ironic, Dan knew. It amused him that both brothers seemed to think themselves important enough to be talked about. "Nothing, really."

"What?" Ted feigned surprise. "You mean you haven't heard about the family crest with six emasculated dragons, the silverware rotting in the cupboards, the skeletons in the basement…?"

"I did hear something about your father having disappeared."

"Oh." Ted waved a disparaging hand. "Oh, that. Yes, it's true. The old man up and left us one night, never to be heard from again. It's old news. It would be a comfort to know he's actually dead, but what can you do?"

"Well, there are a number of avenues you can follow," Dan said. "If you're seriously asking."

Ted eyed him keenly. "That's right! You would know. What can you do to find a son-of-a-bitch who upped and left his family? You would know these things, wouldn't you? Tell me."

"What have you tried?" Dan said.

Boredom returned to Ted's face. "The police, of course. The local ones first, then later the Toronto force and even the RCMP, because you can never get what you want from small town cops, can you?" He smiled as though he'd said something amusing then looked at Dan with exaggerated chagrin. "Sorry! Are you a cop? I didn't mean to offend you."

Dan shook his head. "I'm not a cop. I'm a missing persons investigator."

Ted looked confused. "But it's the same thing, yeah? I mean, you're practically a cop or something."

"We're a totally different breed."

"Well, good — that's good," Ted insisted, without specifying why it was good.

The door opened and Thom came through. He looked from Ted to Dan. "Am I interrupting?"

"Not at all, dear brother," Ted replied.

"We were just discussing your father," Dan said.

"Ah!" Thom removed a beer from the fridge. He kissed Ted's cheek and patted his shoulder. "My good brother," he said patronizingly. "Please stay out of trouble, just for this weekend."

"Of course, dear brother of mine." Ted snaked an arm around Thom's shoulder, grinning. One small and dark, the other broad and blond. Seeing them together, Dan would never have suspected they were siblings.

Thom looked at Dan and shrugged. "Brothers — you have to look after them. What can you do?"

Ted nuzzled Thom's neck. "I am deeply indebted to my brother Thom for … everything. If it weren't for him, why I'd have nothing at all." He looked around, taking in the kitchen. "Though by rights this place should be mine. I am the oldest." He nodded to Dan. "It's been in the family for about a hundred years. Did you know that?"

"No," Dan said. "I didn't."

Thom shot Ted a hard glance. "Just be careful you don't end up in the lake again, all right, Teddy?"

Ted laughed. "Never fear, I won't do anything to embarrass you on your wedding weekend."

"Thank you."

Ted left. Thom waited a beat and said, "Excuse my brother's atrocious behaviour."

"Not at all. He's been quite amusing. What's he done, by the way?"

"To embarrass me?"

"No." Dan laughed. "I meant, what films has he made?"

"Oh, that! He made a few little films — nothing important. He went to some prestigious film school in New York years ago, but he hasn't really done anything. He starts things but never finishes them." He paused and sipped his beer meditatively. "My brother's a drug addict, in case you haven't figured that out yet."

Which explained the buzz and the shades, Dan thought.

"I suppose since I give him his money it's up to me to make him stop. There's nothing like a junkie with money to burn." He looked off in the distance, a pained expression on his face. "My poor, poor mother — a drug addict and a homosexual for sons, and a philandering husband who ran off with another woman. Bad luck for her. She should have stayed a virgin."

Thom laughed softly and took a long pull on his beer. Dan's gaze lingered on his profile, the perfectly formed chin and brow. Thom had rolled his sleeves up, exposing his rower's biceps. It was impossible not to find this man attractive. Dan felt sweat gathering between his pectorals, the skin beneath his shirt. He lifted his beer and went out.

A hazy sunset had accrued by the time Dan returned to the gathering by the lake. Over the mountain, the underbellies of clouds were flecked with pink. He looked up at the house framed against the dying light. He couldn't recall ever having been in a house owned by the same family for a hundred years. All along the reach were similar places with intricate histories, family secrets — homes with the names and birthdates of forebears embedded in family bibles going back generations. Dan knew its legacy of Protestant indus-triousness: the women in long dresses with their hair in tidy buns as they worked in the kitchens, the men in black serge over stiff collars, diligent clerks and tradesmen and day labourers, and the children, seen but not heard, and unset-tled by looks that discouraged frivolity. All living life in a way that precluded any indulgence in pleasure, straining after the little that might be allowed them, and looking for salvation in all that was hard-hearted and plain of manner.

It was this same Presbyterian industriousness that had carved a nation out of wood and stone and given thanks to God, grateful for the newfound flag of freedom as they set up gristmills and established schools and churches across the continent, spreading their long-suffering humanity like the walnuts and oranges left in children's stockings at Christmastime.

In some of the nearby houses, there would be remnants of that life still: the polished walnut tables and stiff-backed chairs so you wouldn't forget yourself and get too comfy, portraits of men with dour glances and whiskers down to their chests echoing words voiced in stoic endurance, their wary glances and harsh whispers directed toward anything that constituted strangeness in their worlds. It was not a charmed existence, this life led by the followers of Knox and Calvin, but it had a certain magisterial appeal, the very essence of morality and probity, a life where men raised themselves up by hard work and right-minded adherence to the Word of God. Hallowed be thy name.

No communal joyfulness or fervent lifting of voices of the evangelical Baptists, or the hand-wringing Puritanism of the Seventh Day Adventists with one eye on the

Second Coming and the other on the ever-present wrath of God. Not the hand-clapping, tambourine-bashing, candle-burning witchery of the Catholics or the Old World, left-behind-for-the-Messiah-already-came-and-wentness, and the one-day-off-the-weekly-calendar Sabbath of misguided Jewry, but the Real Faith, the One True Faith of the new Promised Land. This was the dour, grey-skied heart of Protestant Reform. Johns Knox and Calvin, lead us forward out of sin.

It was a life where good deeds were done quietly and acknowledged humbly, where praise was rare, and roast beef and Yorkshire pudding were served on the Lord's Day. Where the axe and plough were put away as vests and topcoats were donned for Sunday dinners with abundant echoes of "We praise thee, O Lord," followed by a murmured chorus of amens as silverware tinkled and dishes were passed with smiles of appreciation and drink was frowned on till the following evening. All this, followed by a brief respite of merry-making as "God Save the King" was sung in the more prominent homes or banged out on the parlour upright by someone's elderly aunt, followed by fond memories of — how many decades was it now? So hard to recall! — when it had been "God Save the Queen." May she forever rest in peace!

Dan knew the breed well. His childhood had been a late-twentieth century blossoming of this Calvinist faith with its hard-hearted virtuousness. As he walked across the grass, the light sent up its final rays, the eaves returning to shadow as the day retreated. The house looked like a castle from some far-off shore, replete with memories of *lochs* and *bairns* and foreign sounding words like *bonnie* and *didnae* and *wee nyaff*, while the glittering descendants of those hard-hearted, well-intentioned settlers twirled and gyrated on the lawn.

Now and then someone would stop briefly to listen to the hooting of a ferry making a tenuous link between distant worlds as twilight came on, settling over the Bay of Quinte and fading up on the mountain over a lake whose depths and deepest origins remained an unsolved mystery.

ELEVEN

Till Death Do Us Part

THE KITCHEN WAS TRANSFORMED. The beer bottles had been cleared out and the room stood bathed in a perky yellow light, steeped in the aroma of fresh coffee. Daniella was reading when Dan walked in. She glanced up, perturbation written on her face.

"Good morning," he said.

She looked out the window as if she hadn't considered it. "Yes," she said, after a moment. "It's a beautiful day."

"Anyone else around yet?"

"No, it's just me. Sebastiano and Thom are still in bed. Together."

Dan wasn't sure if the last word had been added for emphasis or clarity. He watched her gaze sulkily out the window, her dark eyes fixed on something that might have been over on the far shore or possibly much farther away.

"What's the order of events this afternoon?" Dan asked.

She turned a gloomy gaze on him. "What does this mean?" she said abruptly.

"The order of events," Dan repeated. "What's happening before the wedding?"

"Ah!" She brightened. "We are having brunch at eleven then some of us are going to get ready to go on the boat. Nobody told you?" She looked at him with something like pity.

"No," he said. "Thank you for telling me."

Dan had just sat down with his coffee when Ted slipped into the room, still wearing his shades, his skin the colour of cold porridge. The giggling Jezebel followed, only slightly subdued from the night before.

"Good morning all!" Ted called out.

There was a bit of silliness at the coffee maker. Jezebel poured herself a cup and Ted attempted to withhold the sugar from her. She grabbed his wrist and wrested it from him, leaving a red mark on his arm. Their laughter sounded competitive. Dan found himself disliking them. If he'd been in public, he would have found another place to sit.

"The happy couple not up yet?" Ted said, squinting at the brightness outside the window.

"Not yet," Daniella said with a forced smile as she tucked a strand of hair behind her ear.

Ted snorted. "I'm not surprised. I think he and Sebastiano had a three-way with the best man last night." Jezebel nudged him and he turned to look at Dan. "Oh, sorry — is he with you?" He grinned. "I was kidding, of course."

"You're quite a kidder," Dan said, exiting with his cup, their ghostly laughter following him.

†

It was almost noon when Bill finally showed. Dan had never known him to sleep in. He'd missed brunch but declared in a jaunty voice that all he needed was coffee. Dan looked outside and saw Thom stepping into a car.

"Shouldn't you be going with Thom?"

Bill shook his head. "Nothing so formal," he said. "Thom and Sebastiano are driving down together." They looked out in time to see Sebastiano in tails, his hair neatly coiffed, following Thom. "It's not like it's a real wedding, anyway."

Dan gave him a look.

"You don't know Thom," Bill said defensively.

"No, you're right — I don't."

A crowd of well-heeled men and women hovered by the dock, with a few children and at least one Pekinese. A man with a headset was attempting to direct them onto the boat, but no one seemed to be listening. They resisted his directives like teenagers set on being difficult, yet without knowing what they were rebelling against.

Bill introduced Dan to a thin young man with shoulder length hair standing with a grey-haired older man who was his partner. The younger man, a dentist, seemed particularly giddy. He wore a mock turtleneck with a chain of glittering stones on his chest.

"Another one! Can you believe it? It's like the whole world's getting married! I keep swearing to myself, no more gay weddings! But whenever they ask me, I say yes. I always say yes!" he shrieked, his actions seemingly inexplicable even to himself. He turned to the older man.

"Why do you let me, Freddy? Why do you always let me say yes?"

Freddy's eyes twinkled, as though he found his partner's antics infinitely amusing. "But you wouldn't say yes if you didn't want to, Derek. I know you. You just wouldn't do it!"

Bill turned to Dan and said, *sotto voce,* "My god! He's daring. I can't believe he wore the diamonds!"

Dan turned to take in the garish necklace. "Are they real?"

Bill nodded. "You're staring at half a million dollars."

The hilarity seemed to be spreading as all around them people began to say giddy things that seemed to imply their attendance was largely a matter of whim. "I can't believe I'm even here," said a matronly woman in furs, without stopping to explain why she found it hard to believe in her physical proximity at that moment.

The man with the headset went by, his face set to *concern.* "Please board the ship everybody. The ship is sailing in ten minutes. We need everyone on board."

Freddy seemed to find this particularly amusing and broke into giggles. It was only when a blast went off from the boat that the crowd relented, turning in their fabulous finery of furs and diamonds and high-heels like a strange species boarding an ark.

Bill caught Dan's eye. "Shall we?"

Dan nodded and felt Bill clutch his arm. For a moment, he thought of Ted's insinuations at breakfast. Then he dismissed them, filled with a sudden glow at being Bill's chosen partner in a very public ceremony.

"You look terrific," Dan said.

Bill had transformed by putting on a tuxedo. What had seemed dowdy in street clothes had taken on a regal tone. He had broader shoulders and suddenly the paunch was gone. The prince replacing the frog.

"Thank you, kind sir. You're pretty damn hot yourself."

On board, Bill excused himself to perform his obligations as best man. "Thom needs me," he said, giving Dan a kiss before going off to attend his duties.

Dan looked around. On one side of the room was the same fashionable crowd he might see at Woody's on a Saturday night. Well-dressed, attractive, they included an assemblage of real estate agents whose trendy clothes, pricey haircuts, and bone-white smiles proclaimed them one step away from being famous, and who seemed to be enjoying the lifestyle as though they already were. Off in another corner, Dan recognized a couple of design-show hosts noted for their popular lifestyle series. One had a face and the other a body, Donny said. If you found a third with a brain and put them together, they might almost make a whole person. Dan wondered if the stories about their sex lives were true. Where could they possibly have found the time?

On the opposite side of the room huddled the straights, the divide between the two groups unimpeachable except for one attractive man in a camel-hair coat who seemed to be observing it all with detached amusement. His expression, coupled with his position between both worlds, defied any effort to place him within a geo-sexual context.

The women were either severe or deferential. Many had never been lookers but they had the money and nerve to dress as though they were, with pushed-up bosoms and low-cut fronts. They made it clear they traded in social status and husbands almost interchangeably, leaving the financial concerns to the men. Of the men, the younger ones invariably wore flashy ties and smart suits, while the older ones seemed largely the type who drank whiskey and soda and bought out competitors with a nod of the head.

Occasionally, an oblivious heterosexual male would find himself chatting with someone on the other side, only to realize that an all-male gathering here meant something quite different than at the club. Inevitably, he'd try to make a good show of it, chat a little longer before disengaging himself to rejoin his own side with a nervous backward glance and a forced laugh, so his friends and associates would know he'd been mistaken and was now coming back to the fold. No matter how tolerant and open-minded you were, in a male dominated world where win-or-lose was written over everything, winners still didn't associate with queers.

Dan was unsure where he'd stand should he be forced to choose. Perhaps with the ambiguous presence in camel-hair in the middle of the room. A large, sweaty man came up and saved him the bother of having to decide.

"What school did you go to?" the man asked, wiping his brow with a napkin.

"Sudbury High."

"Sudbury what?" the man exclaimed with a shocked look. "Is that a private school?"

"No," Dan said.

"I thought everybody here went to a private school!" He eyed Dan as though he might be an impostor. "Did you have a choice?"

Dan shook his head. "No."

The man looked around, sucked the ice at the bottom of his glass and said, "Neither did I. I never went to private school." He made it sound like the greatest loss he'd ever had to endure.

"We're probably better off for it," Dan said.

"Oh, no!" the man exclaimed. "Don't fool yourself." He whirled abruptly and extended an arm that took in the entire room. "These are the people who run our country — or who will be running our country in a few years. Look at them." Dan obliged the man by turning to look at the crowd. "Amazing, isn't it?"

Dan wasn't sure what he found so amazing. "Politicians are anything but amazing when you get down to it...."

"I'm not talking about politics!" the man exclaimed. "I'm talking about who really runs things — the entrepreneurs, the business class. This is it, gathered in this room." He shook his head. "Just imagine! If this boat sank, the country would lose half of its ruling elite."

"Do you think they'd be missed?" Dan said.

The man thought about this. "Maybe not," he conceded.

A band started up in another room. An assured voice crooned a line from a forties tune. Trevor caught Dan's eye and came over. Dan introduced him to the other man, who said a few words before leaving to join the ranks on the far side of the room.

"I guess he thought I was straight," Dan said with a bemused grin. "How's it going? The social register keeping you busy?"

Trevor laughed. "You know, there are some things that are a given in life. I know, for instance, that I'll never be half as rich as most of the people in this room, just as I know I could never dedicate myself to the kind of work that would make me that wealthy. And just as I also know," he glanced toward the room where the music came from, "that I will never like Michael Bublé."

"You're not a jazz fan?"

"*Au contraire*," Trevor said. "I *am* a jazz fan. But let's not slag the local talent — it's beneath us. Besides," he took a good look around, "there are far more deserving targets right here in the room. Look at these people. Most of them have suits instead of personalities."

Bill suddenly reappeared clutching a glass. He looked around with a frown and headed toward Dan. He saw Trevor and paused.

"Here comes the boyfriend," Trevor said with a smile. "I'm going to mingle with the lions and tigers. Wish me luck."

Bill nodded curtly at Trevor as he left. "Am I interrupting something?"

"Not at all. Finished your best man duties already?" Dan asked.

Bill shook his head impatiently. "Apparently I wasn't needed."

"Oh?"

"I gather I was keeping Thom from getting in one last fuck before the wedding." He took a gulp of his drink and looked around the gathering. "Quite the dog and pony show, isn't it?"

"Who are all the suits?" Dan asked, glancing across the room.

"Business associates. Thom's mother made them come." Bill smiled grimly, his voice louder than necessary.

"Interesting woman, Lucille Killingworth. It seems money can buy quite a bit of loyalty in her world. It can even make your colleagues attend the wedding of your gay son and his Latin Lothario."

"You're getting drunk," Dan said, trying to keep out a note of disapproval.

Bill looked at the glass in his hand. "Not drunk enough," he said, tipping the glass back to empty it. He reached out and grabbed Dan's crotch. "I want you to fuck me silly tonight."

A few feet over, an older couple turned their heads then quickly looked away.

Bill tinkled the ice in his glass, oblivious to the attention he was getting. "I can't believe he's marrying that mail-order gigolo." His voice carried across the room.

A strained look passed over Dan's face. "Do you need to be so loud?"

"Why? Getting touchy?"

Dan shook his head. "Just sensitive."

"Right. I forgot you were bought and paid for once."

Dan's shoulders sagged. "That's really uncalled for…."

"Don't mind me," Bill mumbled. He looked toward the bar. "I need a refill." He glanced at Dan, contrition covering his face. "I'm sorry. You have no idea how difficult this is for me."

Folding chairs had been set up around the upper deck. A tarp stood nearby in case of rain. The guests filled the rows until the entire deck was occupied. At the last moment, Bill took his place beside Thom while Daniella stood next to Sebastiano. As promised, she'd donned a tux and gelled her hair back in sophisticated lesbian attire, though Dan doubted she was one. With the change of wardrobe, her mood had reverted to her casual laughing self. To Dan, she was nearly as handsome as her nervous, elegant brother.

The minister, a stout, dark-haired woman in a cleric's outfit with a bosom like a shelf, exuded a stern no-nonsense-on-the-job demeanour, though Dan suspected she was probably a lark in her off-hours. Her carefully inflected reading of the ceremony carried an air of respectfulness that many traditional weddings lacked. Her jokes, though few, were appropriate and her solemnity solemn enough without being too serious. If he and Bill were ever to marry, Dan thought, he'd look her up.

The couple exchanged vows, looking elated as they leaned together to seal them with a kiss. Their blue eyes seemed the connecting thread between the light-haired Thom and the dark-haired Sebastiano. Bill, whatever his hidden sorrows, more than looked the part of supportive best man to his best friend.

They stayed on the upper deck for pictures as the boat headed through the Adolphustown Reach and on toward Lake Ontario. Other vessels passed, exchanging greetings and horn tootings as they recognized the nature of the ceremony, though a face or two looked perplexed at not being able to locate the blushing bride in her fancy meringue outfit alongside all the handsome men in black and white.

After the reception line, the guests filed below deck to a dining room. Dan found himself seated with three straight couples who all seemed to know one another. Once past the introductions, they ignored him in favour of exchanging gossip about people he'd never heard of. They endured the various speeches made by and to both grooms. Dan carefully measured his intake of wine. Bill was drinking enough for the two of them. Thom and Sebastiano mingled with the guests. At one point, Thom plunked himself down beside Dan with a satisfied smile. "All good?"

"Very nice. Congratulations — it was a terrific ceremony."

Bill drifted over and sat, placing his hand on Dan's knee. Had he thought Thom was making a move on Dan? Was that what Bill's difficulty had been earlier? Surely he knew Dan better.

Thom playfully squeezed his best man's shoulder. "Thank you for loaning me Billy for the day," he said to Dan.

"My pleasure."

"Not a bad turnout," Thom continued, looking over the assembled guests.

"Where is Sebastiano's family?" Dan asked.

Thom pointed out a small dark-haired woman seated near to the bar. "There. That's his Aunt Naida. His mother's sister."

"That's it?"

Thom shrugged. "That and Daniella. The other side hasn't really accepted it yet."

Bill rolled his eyes. "You've got the bull and you own the barn. Who cares if you've got the pedigree or not?" He stood for a refill, pausing to look over the room. "They sound like a dreary lot anyway. They should be grateful you're rescuing their son from his squalid life."

Across the room, a woman in a yellow dress with a light green scarf threw Thom a smile. Had Catherine Deneuve's younger sister been kidnapped as a child, this woman would have made a good candidate for the title of foundling. Her laughter carried to them from the group she was addressing.

Thom followed Dan's gaze. "My mother," he said.

Where some women faded with age, others grew into it with vigour and self-assurance. Not as the result of chemicals and operations, but through inner discipline and will. Lucille Killingworth was one of these.

"She's beautiful," Dan said.

"And deadly." Thom smirked. "Don't be fooled. Her approval is necessary, so I try hard to stay on her good side."

"And keeping your brother in check is part of that?"

Thom gave Dan an appraising stare. "Bill never told me you were so perceptive," he said.

"I don't think he's noticed yet. But I do my best to please."

Thom's eyes narrowed. "I like a guy who likes to please."

"I take it Sebastiano's a pleaser."

"In every way. And I'm always happy to reward the men who please me." He glanced sideways, chipping the ball back at Dan. "I don't suppose it would be wise of me to make a pass at you?"

Dan couldn't help smiling at the smoothness with which Thom had done just that. "No."

"I didn't think so. You're not the type, are you? Or maybe I'm not your type."

Before Dan could answer, the clinking of silver against crystal caught them off-guard. Ted stood, drink in hand.

Ted had removed his sunglasses. His eyes glittered weirdly in the light. "I'd like to propose a toast to the men in my illustrious family," he said.

A strained look came over Thom's face.

"First, to my loving brother Thom, to whom I owe everything I am today." Ted looked at Thom and raised the glass high. "Yes, dear brother — everything." The comment was met with applause. "And here's to our grandfather, Nate Macaulay, the old son-of-a-bitch." Dan flashed on the portrait of the malevolent N.M. "You could say a lot about the old bastard, but you have to admit he made a hell of a lot of money!"

"You tell it, Teddy boy!" someone called out.

"For fuck's sake," Thom mumbled.

Over at the head table, Lucille Killingworth maintained an expression of bemused tolerance.

"And of course," Ted continued, "we shouldn't forget our dear father who loved us so much he spared us his miserable company for the last twenty years." The room had gone silent, mesmerized by the matador's sword raised over the dying bull. "I'd like to see the look on his face if he saw his baby boy getting married to another man. I'd give anything to get him in here and watch his expression."

Thom raised his glass. "Amen to that, brother," he said loudly and downed his drink, inviting the others to follow.

Ted looked around with a silly grin, as though he'd just pulled off a very amusing joke.

"My undying thanks to my brother Teddy for his marvellous toast," Thom said before Ted could start up again. "I think it's time to adjourn to the other room for some music and mayhem of a different sort."

The scraping of chairs filled the air as people stood and headed for the ballroom.

"I'll fucking kill him," Thom mumbled.

The band played a gleeful concoction of trills and well-heeled themes. Rock transformed to rumba. The dancers twirled on, oblivious to the sea change as light glittered on women's gowns and the dandruff-flecked shoulders of middle-aged men anxious to show they still had it, or perhaps just hoping they did.

Daniella came through the doors, still in her Dietrich drag. She stood watching the dancers, a martini glass held breast high. Her eyes lit on Thom and Sebastiano gyrating and grinding together at the floor's centre. Her mouth formed a hard line. Still blue, but less than an angel. Then she spied Dan. Her expression changed as she swept across the floor to him.

"Danny! You're so sexy!" she cried. She had a way of eliding her consonants, making one liquid syllable flow smoothly into the next, as though they'd been written just for her. "Come dance with me!"

He obliged her, but just as they reached the floor the music changed from a samba to a slow motion wave. She wrapped herself around him, glass aloft, and drank over his shoulder. Fingers slid between the buttons of his shirt, caressing his chest. She bent her head back and extended a trousered leg, the young Martha Graham impersonating a Joshua Tree. Dan felt more like a piece of sculpture than a dancer.

"Daniella!" Sebastiano gave her a disapproving look.

Her eyes flashed rebellion. She continued to dance only slightly less wildly, then downed her drink and went off for a refill. Dan watched her flit between the tables, a pale drunken butterfly, with everyone's eyes on her. She seemed to be flirting with the entire room. At one point she nearly stumbled into a table. If not for the quick reflexes of a man standing nearby, she would have fallen. A trio of men became instantly solicitous, but she brushed off their concern.

"You ought not to drink so much," Dan heard one of the men say. "Especially if you can't stay on your feet."

She glared. "I'm not drunk," she declared then turned away indignantly.

Sebastiano broke off his dance with Thom and went over to her. They exchanged a few heated words in Portuguese. Daniella tossed her head angrily and looked away, but Sebastiano was insistent as he pulled her protesting onto the floor. The music turned from a wave to a shimmer. He tore off his jacket and tossed it aside. His slicked-back hair, sheer cotton shirt, and tightly drawn trousers lent him the contours of a matador. He stood, chest extended, the young Valentino regarding his hermaphroditic self-portrait: Rudy and Judy. They might have been twins. Dan felt a tingling of lust.

Sebastiano came alive, hands whirling overhead. He glowed, a dark angel taking flight. Inspired by the dancers, the band launched into a fiery tango. Daniella unclasped her heels and threw them beneath a chair. The music grew feverish as she moved back and forth, mirroring her brother. Sweat hung in the air. He pulled her so close they seemed to be one body.

The crowd warmed to the tempo, arching themselves into the music, though none could match the Brazilians for ardour and grace. The room broke into spontaneous applause time and again. Even Thom watched them admiringly.

It was midnight. The band had moved on to a more northerly clime, the tempo chilled to the formal rhythms of a Viennese waltz, a confection that might have been popular in Hitler's time. Older couples dominated the floor, feet shuffling, heels lifting gently as though nostalgia demanded a softer tread. Someone had coaxed Lucille Killingworth up onto the floor. The mother of the groom moved gracefully, scarf twisted lightly about her throat. She danced with a white-haired man who smiled a lot, though he seemed in deadly earnest. He looked down frequently, either worried about stepping on his partner's feet or following some imaginary numbered dance steps on the tiles. Dan noticed his expression — admiration laced with desire seen through the eyes of a barracuda. This man had designs on the Merry Widow.

Bill and Thom had disappeared in the melee. The minister was chatting with another dykish type over in a corner. Dan saw he'd been right — she laughed and held her drink like a trucker bedding down at a pub for the night, clearly no longer discussing ecumenical concerns.

Sebastiano and Daniella had retrieved their discarded clothing and sat cooing at one of the tables. He pushed her hair from her face with his fingers. Whatever their argument, they seemed to have made up. A candle basked in the glow of Daniella's pale skin, making her look sad and fragile.

Dan toyed with getting another drink, but decided against it. He felt flushed. He descended to the lower deck for a breath of cool night air. A couple huddled against the railing. It was the giddy dentist with the diamonds and his older boyfriend. They looked up at his approach.

"Cheers!" said the older man, raising a champagne glass and sipping from it before placing it on the railing.

Dan gave a friendly nod and leaned into the opposite corner where the rail curved against the back of the boat. They'd started their return. From above, music and laughter floated out over the water. On either shore, lights from passing houses gleamed like earthbound stars. Now and then, they swept past other vessels manoeuvring their way home.

The boat made a marked shift to the right, following the channel. The forgotten champagne glass inched toward the rail's outer edge. Dan was about to say something when the boat shifted again. The crystal fell in slow motion, an arc of whiteness hitting the waves with a silent splash before disappearing in the blackness.

Dan left the amorous couple and made his way upstairs. A squadron of servers hoisted trays of hors d'oeuvres, passing him on the way to the ballroom. He felt cooler but his head throbbed. He stopped in the corridor and leaned against a doorway.

A voice came through the wall, the tones low and serious. He couldn't make out the words. He stood there, not really intending to listen.

"You've got to pull yourself together." It was Thom's voice, followed by what might have been a stifled sob. "Look, it doesn't mean anything. Not really."

"But you're *married!*" Bill's voice rose in pitch, like a child whining about not being given a promised treat.

"It's only a ceremony, Billy," Dan heard Thom say in consoling tones. There was a long silence. Dan's blood jumped with adrenaline as he waited.

"You're the only one I've ever loved," he heard Bill say. "In my entire fucking life!"

You have no idea how difficult this is for me. Dan felt sickened, torn between leaving and staying to hear more. Curiosity won out.

"It's okay, Billy. It's okay," Thom said soothingly. The talking died to a murmur. Then he heard Bill ask, "Who am I?"

"You're my hot little cabin boy," Thom answered.

Dan felt a flash of rage that had preceded some of the stupidest acts he'd ever perpetrated. His fist raised itself of its own accord. He wanted to pound on the door and demand the lovers emerge red-faced, *in flagrante*. In his mind, he saw himself denting the filing cabinet and remembered how good it had felt. He fought the rage, sucking in air even as his fist resisted.

There are mirrors in junk shops, silvered over with age and mildew, reflecting whatever lies before them pressed against a mottled, timeworn backdrop. Without breaking the glass, they shatter the illusion by giving an image of the outer world while simultaneously revealing the thin edge of reality beneath. This was what Dan felt he was looking at. His hand recoiled with a shiver of recognition; his stomach rebelled.

He lurched down the passage in search of a washroom, barging past startled guests. A changeroom presented itself, the door half open. Inside, Sebastiano stood before a full-length mirror. Dan's anger bobbed, shifted, and found a new focus. He toed the door open with his foot. The boy looked up.

"Need some help?" Dan said.

Sebastiano watched curiously as Dan tugged at the ends of his bowtie. Next, Dan straightened the suspender straps, smoothing them over Sebastiano's shoulders as though dressing a child. The boy leaned back with an expression of trust. Muscles strained his shirtfront. Dan knew there'd be no struggle.

"You and your sister dance well together."

Sebastiano's chin rose and fell in what might have been agreement. Dan's move was smooth, unhurried. He knew the hypnotic effect gentleness had on boys like Sebastiano, even the experienced ones. His fingers reached around the back of his neck. He waited till the boy looked him in the eye then pulled their faces together. They kissed more deeply and intimately than Sebastiano had kissed Thom after their vows. The sensation was wet and soft; their teeth clicked together a few times before they got the rhythm. After that, it was simply a matter of closing the door and getting down to business. Sebastiano's pants slid off easily, as clothes do when worn by men whose bodies fit the cut, with no excess flesh to consider. Dan unzipped his own trousers and let them slide to the floor, pulling his underwear taut across his thighs. Sebastiano turned his broad back to Dan and braced himself against the mirror.

Dan knelt and breathed in the smell of funk. His tongue twitched and darted. He felt the short sharp bristles and heard Sebastiano moan. He slid a glistening finger, then a second, deftly up into moist warm flesh. Sebastiano made what passed for welcoming noises. Dan stood. Quickly, before Sebastiano could protest, he plunged in. He felt warmth, wet, goo. It felt good. Familiar, yet not. He hadn't fucked without a condom in years, not since a drunken fling in a garage that had been left open on Hayden Street when he'd been followed down the lane at four a.m. after a night of dancing. It had taken an excess of alcohol for him to be reckless that time. This time all it had taken was rage.

There were no protests as he rode the Brazilian stud. The boy arched himself at the mirror, face pressed against the glass. Dan gripped the boy's abdominals, straining and forcing himself all the way in. There were no protests about that, either, only murmurs of pleasure and a few encouraging words in Portuguese. A drop of sweat glistened and fell from the tip of Dan's nose. It landed on the small of the boy's back, rolling down to where Dan's cock joined Sebastiano's body in slithery, piston-like motions. He came quickly, discharging completely before pulling out with a solitary plop. Sebastiano let out a groan and came in jerks and spasms onto the mirror, his spunk whiter than any Dan could recall. It hung there, almost muscular in its clinging, not running down. Dan grunted, as if in reply. His cock swung sloppily between his legs, a telltale smudge on the head. A pungent smell filled the air.

Dan picked the boy's underwear up from the floor and wiped himself off with it. For good measure, he wiped the mirror too. The boy turned to face him. "Good fuck?" Dan said.

"Yeah — good fuck." The boy grinned.

Dan smiled, but his anger was still intact. *Good, yes — but I bet you won't be too quick to brag about it. Maybe I'll spread the word myself.*

"I have to go," Sebastiano said without a trace of sheepishness.

"Me too."

Dan handed over the boy's underwear with the stain smeared across the bottom.

The boy's smile vanished. "I cannot wear this," he said.

Dan looked around, as if perplexed. He brightened. "Here," he said, handing over his own silk boxers. "You can have mine. A little something to remember me by when you have your honeymoon fuck."

The boy looked at them dubiously then shrugged. "Why not?" He pulled them up over his legs. They fit.

Why not, indeed?

"They look good on you," Dan said. "Keep them. It's the least I can do."

Gentle arabesques of light fanned over the ballroom and across the dancers, glittering diamonds creating a fantasy landscape, the happy ending to some fairy tale. Trevor stood just inside the ballroom door. His face lit up when he saw Dan.

"Hey! I've been looking for you. How's it going?"

Dan had to fight to make eye contact with him. He was suddenly and utterly consumed by shame. Whatever had possessed him only minutes ago had begun to slacken like a balloon losing altitude. The blood urge for revenge was gone, leaving only the afterglow of remorse.

"I think I just did something very stupid," he said.

Trevor watched him curiously. "Anything to do with your boyfriend?"

Dan nodded. "My boyfriend and your cousin. It seems they've been a good deal more than best friends. My stupidity, I guess."

Trevor put a hand on Dan's shoulder. "I'm sorry," he said in that calming voice. "They're not a nice crowd — my cousin and his friends. They're awful people. Selfish and insincere. I shouldn't be saying this, but you seem like a nice guy. I wouldn't want to see you get hurt."

Dan shrugged, his face a portrait of self-reproach. "Too late."

Trevor attempted a consoling smile. "Is there anything I can do? Anything I can say?"

"No, but thanks."

A clamour broke out in the hallway behind them. It grew in volume as a small crowd rushed into the ballroom with Thom at its head. Thom seized on Trevor and Dan. "Where's Sebastiano?" he demanded.

Dan felt a sickening sense of oncoming retribution. He'd expected there might be a scene over what he'd done, but he hadn't expected it to happen so fast. And certainly not here, in front of the wedding guests.

Without waiting for a reply, Thom turned and looked over the crowd. "Has anybody seen Sebastiano?" he yelled over the music.

Faces turned to regard him with a mixture of amusement and consternation, unsure of the intent of this impromptu game. Several people shook their heads.

"I did," Dan said. "I saw him just now."

Thom whirled to face him. "Where? How long ago?"

"A few minutes ago. Four or five. He was in a change-room off the lower deck."

Before Dan could say more, Sebastiano came through the door like a spirited horse approaching the pack.

"Thank god!" Thom exclaimed. His voice held an edge of panic. "Someone said you fell over the railing into the water."

"No." Sebastiano shook his head, bewildered. "I am here."

"They said you fell over," Thom insisted, his face set with concern. "They said your jacket was on the railing."

Behind them the band went through a change of pitch, moving southerly again, notching the rhythm up to a jerky reggae beat. Outside the windows, the darkness suddenly seemed immense.

"My jacket? My jacket is on the chair — over there." Sebastiano pointed to where he'd been sitting half an hour earlier. His unclaimed jacket sat waiting. Confusion passed over his face, followed by fear as the impossible suggested itself. "Where is Daniella?" He looked around in a panic. He grabbed Thom's arm. "Where is she? Where is Daniella?"

"I don't know," Thom said, shaking his head. "I haven't seen her." He turned to the others. "Has anyone seen Daniella?"

Murmurs broke out around the room, but no one replied. The band continued, oblivious. The dancers stopped one by one as realization settled in that the mood in the room had changed. Sober faces regarded them. Dan saw Bill enter from the opposite side of the room.

"Anyone?" Thom repeated, his voice tense. "We're looking for Daniella."

"I saw her about twenty minutes ago," said a bald man with a concerned face. "She was on the upstairs deck. I think she had on a jacket like Sebastiano's."

Sebastiano let out a moan.

"Look," Dan said decisively. "Let's find out for sure what's happened. Who said they saw someone fall overboard?"

"We did," came a voice near the back of the room.

They turned to see an older man in black tie standing with a woman in a mauve dress, their faces pale with concern. "My wife and I definitely saw someone fall from the upper deck."

"We thought it was that young man." His wife pointed at Sebastiano.

"Where was this?" Dan said.

"We were on the back lower deck when someone toppled from above. Whoever it was fell right past us."

Sebastiano looked around in terror. He latched onto Bill. "You're a doctor. Do something!"

"Okay, let's not panic," Thom commanded. "We'll notify the captain to turn the boat around." He turned to Sebastiano. "We'll find her — don't worry." His eyes stopped at Dan. "Would you please organize a search on board for Daniella? She's got to be here somewhere."

Dan nodded. "I'll start upstairs."

"I'll go with you," Trevor said.

TWELVE

This Terrible Place

THE LIGHTS OF GLENORA APPEARED up ahead like a cord pulling them onward to a terrible fate. The band had stopped playing as the ballroom filled with grave faces. Most of the guests stood silently by or talked among themselves in concerned whispers. It was clear Daniella was nowhere on board. The outside decks were abandoned after a quick search failed to reveal anything. Bathrooms and anterooms had also been checked. Authorities were notified of the disappearance, and a search-and-rescue team from Trenton was called out. Within fifteen minutes a helicopter could be heard sweeping overhead, its searchlight mapping the waves. A local volunteer crew had already formed. A dozen small craft operators were patrolling the darkened waters of the bay, looking for signs of struggle or movement.

The ship docked at Glenora and the guests filed off in a light drizzle. Officers from the Picton OPP detachment met them onshore. They listened as Thom explained how Daniella had fallen from an upper deck.

Sebastiano stood to one side, rocking and shivering. "Why did we come to this awful country?" he moaned. Dan thought of the Serbian boy who'd come to Canada and ended up in a ravine with gunshot wounds to his head.

An EMS vehicle stood onshore, its lights flashing silently while figures moved about in the rain. Dan's name rang a bell with one of the questioning officers. "We never met, but we worked together on a case once," the man said, squinting at him in the lantern light. "You helped us locate a woman named Sarah McNeill. I'm Detective Constable Peter Saylor."

They shook. The officer looked at Sebastiano and motioned Dan over for a private word. "Do you think she's done a runner? You weren't far from shore. She's a visitor, right? Some guy's sister? Maybe she wanted to stay."

Dan shook his head. "I doubt it. She came for her brother's wedding. They're from Brazil, not Cuba. I overheard him say she couldn't swim."

The officer took a deep breath. "That's rough," he said. "I guess if she's out there, we'll find her." He let Dan through and nodded to the next in line.

Bill was waiting in the car. He stared straight ahead. Dan got into the driver's seat without a word. The silence stretched taut between them.

"I'm sorry about what I said earlier," Bill said finally.

Dan shook his head. "It's not important."

Bill nodded. "I spoke to Thom. He'd like us to stay at the house tonight. If you don't mind, we'll go back there."

"Of course. Whatever he needs."

Trevor opened the door for them. He looked at Dan. "I persuaded Aunt Lucille to go to bed," he said. "She didn't want to, but she was quite shaken. I've just been sitting here feeling useless. Is there anything I can do?"

"Not that I know of," Dan said. "Ted took Jezebel home. She was pretty shaken too. I don't know when Thom and Sebastiano will be back. They wanted to stay to see if the patrol boats turned anything up."

They spoke in subdued voices. It seemed possible that if they were gentle and kind enough, the night's events might unfold in a more optimistic manner, that the outcome might not be as dark and dire as it seemed at that moment.

Without waiting to be asked, Bill poured everyone a drink. They made desultory conversation for another hour. At three o'clock, Trevor went up to his room. Thom and Sebastiano arrived looking grim-faced an hour later. Sebastiano resisted all efforts to console him.

"Bloody awful business," Thom murmured, his hand on Sebastiano's shoulder.

"Give him these," Bill said, placing something in Thom's hand. Thom looked down at the pink pills. "I've got more, if you want any yourself."

Thom took Sebastiano upstairs and returned twenty minutes later. "He's asleep," he said.

"How was he?" Dan said.

"As you saw — a mess. The only thing I could get out of him is that he wants to go back to Brazil immediately. I can't talk him out of it."

Bill nodded knowingly. "Leave it for now. He'll be calmer tomorrow."

Thom lit a fire to distract himself. Bill poured him a drink. Thom sat on the sofa, his hand playing absently with the polished curve of the arm. Bill tried to reassure him that Daniella would turn up. Thom nodded distractedly, only half-listening. Eventually they turned the conversation away from the events of the evening, anxious for the consolation news of things that had nothing to do with them might bring. Thom assured them there was nothing they could do for him. They said goodnight.

"I'll be fine," he said, waving them away.

Upstairs, Dan lay on the bed fully dressed, staring at the blackness outside. The shimmering urgency of fear had drained away, leaving an empty calm, the bone white shock of lightning that reveals the world in negative for an instant before snapping off again. He dropped off to sleep just before five. He wasn't sure when Bill slept or if he did.

Morning brought a return of the mist, a dull grey haze settling over everything. The call came just past seven. An officer from the Picton OPP told Thom they'd recovered the body of a young woman just before six thirty that morning. He asked them to come to the morgue as soon as as possible.

Someone had made coffee. Dan grabbed a cup and went out to bring the car around. Bill got in the front with him. Thom emerged with Sebastiano, and the pair slid silently into the back. The boy's face was grey, his eyes glassy. Even his cheeks seemed sunken. Dan glanced in the mirror. He recognized the look. He'd seen bereaved clients with that haunted glaze compounded of sickness and misery.

They endured the ferry crossing in silence. The blue water took on an ugly sheen; distant sails raised in joyous furls seemed an insult to them. The ride to town took forever. At the hospital, Thom got out first and went around to help his husband, but Sebastiano refused to leave the car. He sat with his arms wrapped tightly around his chest. "I don't want to go," he said, his voice hoarse.

"You have to come," Thom insisted. "They'll need you to identify her."

The boy shook his head. "I can't."

Thom looked grim. "They need you, Seb."

Sebastiano glared. "I hate you!" He pounded his fist against the door. "I hate you! How could you do this to us?"

Thom shook him by the shoulders. "I didn't do anything. I told you not to bring her." He looked around at the others. "I didn't want her here."

Sebastiano turned away, sobbing against the seat.

"Thom," Bill said. "Leave him." Thom jerked his head around at the sound of Bill's voice. "Let's go in. It might not even be her."

Thom nodded. "You're right."

The hospital was small, red-brick efficient. It had been erected in the eighties and outfitted with hanging plants to allay the severity of the exterior. They were joined by Constable Saylor, the officer who'd recognized Dan's name the night before. Still fresh-faced and earnest. Eager and correct. They followed an assistant to an alcove lit by a rack of fluorescence where all the warmth had been sucked out of the room. A burnt smell hung in the air.

A modest shape lay beneath a sheet, a bulge concealed beneath a mound of fresh snow. It scarcely seemed possible that something as momentous as death lay before them. Dan thought of the lamb and goat corpses in the butcher's window on the Danforth. Even they had seemed more imposing, more noteworthy somehow. The officer pulled the sheet down to reveal first the head — lips blue, skin grey, as though she'd been embalmed already — then further down. It seemed needlessly cruel to expose her like this under the harsh glare.

For a moment, Dan doubted it was Daniella. The body was so bloated, it seemed as though it might have been someone else, one of the countless nameless faces in the Doe files. Dan stepped forward in disbelief, ready to proclaim it a case of mistaken identity. Looking closely, however, he realized he was staring at Sebastiano's sister. That was clearly her hair, now damp and dishevelled, those the fingers that had pawed his chest only hours ago.

Thom made a small choking noise. He reached out and touched a wall, as though he might faint. Bill and Dan were used to seeing bodies in various states of decomposition. Still, Dan felt a surge of nausea followed by something like grief, even though he'd hardly known her.

Thom rubbed his chin between his thumb and forefinger like a man trying to decipher a difficult problem. "It's her. It's really her. Fuck." He turned away.

Something on Daniella's right temple, an irregularity near the hairline, caught Dan's eye. He pointed out the dull purple bruise mostly hidden by hair. "Did anyone notice this?"

"Yes, we did," Saylor replied. "I noted it in the report." He looked at Dan. "Is anybody here related to her?"

"Jesus," said Thom. He looked up. "Sorry, no. The person you want is out in the car. I don't know if it's a good idea to bring him in here yet." His hands moved in small circles, warding off an unpleasant event. He wanted to be out of there, away from the swollen body with the telltale bruise on her forehead. "He's not in a proper state of mind."

Saylor assumed a look of professional sympathy without seeming insincere. "I understand, sir. Perhaps you could get him to come in when he's ready?"

Thom nodded. "I will. I'll bring him back."

They emerged blinking into the daylight. The sky was pastel with soft clouds scudding overhead. Apart from a few passersby, the town looked deserted. For a moment Dan wondered if everyone was in church, just another small town Sunday.

Thom paced, walking himself through his dilemma. He turned to Dan and Bill. "Stay here. Let me do this," he said, glancing back at the parking lot.

He went to the car and got in beside Sebastiano. He sat there looking forward and spoke a few words. At first there was no reaction, then Sebastiano turned and hit him with his fists. Thom took the punishment until Sebastiano finally stopped and leaned his head against Thom's chest. Thom's hand reached up and smoothed his hair. It was another five minutes before they got out of the car and came haltingly to the door.

"I told you it was haunted," Sebastiano said softly. "It was a bad place!"

Thom looked at Bill and Dan in confusion. "I don't know what he's talking about."

"I think he means Lake on the Mountain," Dan said. "He seemed pretty spooked by it the other day."

Thom shook his head in bewilderment, not comprehending how one thing related to the other. He turned to Sebastiano. "Are you ready? You'll have to go in some time. If not now, then later."

"Then it is Daniella? For positive?"

Thom nodded and Sebastiano crumpled on the steps. His grey pallor was succeeded by bright red. The veins on his forehead seemed about to burst. He ran a hand through his hair, the gesture becoming obsessive in its repetitiveness. "I told you I didn't want her to come. I told you ..." he broke off, choking on his sobs.

Thom shook his head impatiently. "You *did* say you wanted her to come. It's not my fault."

"No, I never wanted this!" Sebastiano moaned, as though denial could change the outcome. "I never wanted her to come to this terrible place!"

"Look — pull yourself together. I'm sorry, but you have to pull yourself together."

Pulling himself together looked to be the last thing he would be able to do, Dan thought. Fury, exhaustion, rage — these seemed more reasonable responses to expect. His own father had been practically catatonic in the years following his mother's death, till he liberated himself by drinking himself to an early grave. Why was it so hard for some people to express their grief and so hard for others not to?

"My god!" Sebastiano wailed. "Why did we have to come here? Why?" He switched to Portuguese, rocking and moaning.

With Bill's help, Thom lifted him to his feet and guided him to the door, arms linked like any married couple going for a stroll. Dan held the door to let them pass.

When Sebastiano came out again, he seemed to have undergone a profound change. His posture was erect, stiff, where before he'd been a rag doll. His eyes were hard, his expression tight. Thom came up and held him in his arms, though it seemed to be Thom who needed reassurance.

The door opened and Saylor emerged. He approached Sebastiano and said gently, "Sir, thank you for coming in to identify your sister. I know how difficult it was for you to do."

For a moment, Sebastiano appeared not to have heard. A look of silent menace spread over his face as Thom put a comforting hand on his shoulder.

Sebastiano shook off the hand in a fury. "No!" he cried. "She is not my sister. She is my *wife!*"

The others looked around in confusion. "He said she was his sister," Thom insisted forlornly.

"Sir?" Saylor said. "Are you telling us this woman was married to you?"

Sebastiano nodded, head in his hands. "In Brazil, yes. She is my wife for two years!"

THIRTEEN

Circumstantial Evidence

THE DRIZZLE THAT HAD BEGUN the eve of the wedding returned by afternoon and seemed to follow them home. The two-plus hours it took to return to Toronto was endured mostly in silence. Dan dropped Bill off at his townhouse and cabbed it back to Leslieville. He was at his desk Monday morning. Donny had called three times before Dan got there to say he'd heard about the drowning on the news. The event had been made to sound even more lurid and colourful when magnified by the immigration angle and the novelty of a gay wedding. Dan spoke with him briefly then pleaded work commitments.

It wasn't till the following day that he heard anything further. Just before noon he looked up to see his office assistant standing in his doorway.

"Hello, Sally."

"They're calling it suspicious," she said, waving a file in front of her. "I thought you'd want to see it immediately."

Sally normally had no compunction about barging in unannounced; today, she hovered in the doorway decked out in an orange blouse and burgundy skirt. She seemed dressed for some occasion Dan wouldn't be privy to: a U2 concert or the arrival of the Dalai Lama. Or possibly a protest at the American Embassy, though that would have required different colours, say, just the right shade of black on black — somewhere between polished charcoal and Death — with militant-looking armbands.

Dan knew little about her personal life. She was one of the restless MTV tribe that crowded shopping malls and dance clubs, sporting their quirky fashions, celebrity obsessions, and shortened attention spans, and who took time to record their innermost thoughts at Speakers' Corners and graduated from mid-size universities with vague degrees, hoping for careers in anything arts-related before settling for something less spectacular but more lucrative.

"Come in, Sally."

She took a tentative step forward and stopped, looking around as though she'd never been there before. "Thank god somebody's got a design sense," she said, noting the reproductions of abstract art on the walls. "Everybody else's office is just …"

Dan waved her forward abruptly. Startled, she nearly dropped the file.

"Everybody else's office is just what?" he said, smiling to show he wasn't being unfriendly.

Her eyes went around the room again, comparing what Dan's office was with what the others weren't. "It's like they're colourless or something. Nothing but beige and grey." She shook her head over the incomprehensibility of it all.

"Thank you. You're the only other one who's noticed."

Sally nodded. "That's because you and I come from the same planet," she said conspiratorially.

Dan leaned forward. "And to what do you attribute all this colourlessness? Our alien nature?"

Sally cocked her head. "I think it comes from being Canadian," she said. "We're raised to be bland and agreeable. Even the immigrants who come here eventually fade into some sort of creeping beigeness. There's something wrong with that."

Dan nodded at the file in her hand. "You said they were calling it suspicious?"

Sally nodded vigorously as she handed it over. "Big bump on her head. They think someone bashed her and dumped her overboard. You saw the body. What do you think?"

Dan looked down at the report, thumbed open the cover. "I noticed the bump," he said. She waited. Dan looked up. "I'll need some time to look this over," he said, smiling patiently again.

"Oh right — of course! It's all yours." She turned to leave then stopped and turned back. "One other thing. You probably already knew this too. She was pregnant."

Dan looked up in surprise.

Sally smiled. "Well, you do now."

The pregnancy wasn't the only item of interest in the report. Daniella's blood-alcohol level showed she hadn't been drinking. Not a drop. Dan recalled the martini glass he'd watched her empty and how pale she'd looked. And, later, how she stumbled as though she'd been drunk. But she hadn't. Obviously she'd known she was pregnant.

He'd just finished the report when the phone buzzed. The display identified the call as coming from the Prince Edward Country OPP. Dan picked up.

"Hi, Dan, Pete Saylor here."

"Pete! How are you?" Dan pictured the neatly dressed officer from Picton, wondering to what he owed the call.

"Have you got a minute?" Saylor asked.

"For you, I do — shoot."

"I guess you've heard we're calling it a suspicious death."

"I just finished the report."

"So what do you think?" Saylor asked, launching in without preamble. "You were there. Would anybody want her dead for any obvious reason?"

Dan hesitated. He'd already considered the question and come up with a few plausible if conjectured answers. "I haven't really had time to think this through," he said.

What he was really thinking was that small-town cops were known for taking things out of context and hanging on like pit bulls when they smelled blood. Bored by years of putting out grass fires, dragging drunks out of bars, and handing out tickets to careless cottagers for polluting rivers and lakes, they exaggerated harmless circumstantial evidence into something much larger when the chance came to seize on a moment of glory. More than one man's reputation had been destroyed because somebody had had what at the time seemed like a good idea, but which later proved false, the victims of small town zealotry. David Milgaard, Steven Truscott, Guy Paul Morin — those were just a few names that came easily to mind. There had been others, men and women whose names weren't as familiar, who had spent time in jail for other people's crimes. And there were probably many more besides who never had the opportunity to have their names cleared.

"Completely off the record," Saylor said. "Just between you and me."

Dan tried to imagine Saylor in the larger picture: more than competent at his job, boxed in by life but devoted to a wife and kids living just outside the town limits, possibly in a grand version of a log home, something unique and half-hidden by a copse of trees off a busy highway. He'd watch sports, follow *Hockey Night In Canada* assiduously, but maintain an avid interest in the news, curl up with his honey over reruns of *Sex and the City* or possibly even *Will and Grace* for a lark after the kids had gone to bed when there was nothing better on. Sophisticated and good-natured, but under-challenged. The thought of cracking a case like this, if case it turned out to be, would have a strong appeal for him, something that would continue to glitter and twist in the back of his mind long after his shift was over.

"Pete, I really have to think about it before I open my mouth and get some poor innocent schmuck in trouble."

"All right. I thought you might say that." Pete laughed lightly. "Want to hear my theories?"

"Can't hurt," Dan said.

"Good man. I need to try them out on somebody — in confidence, of course."

"Understood."

"First there's the gay aspect. It was a gay wedding." He shifted gears here. "By the way — are you gay? It's cool if you are, my younger brother's gay."

Dan frowned and wondered if it was true, but he let it pass. "Yes, I am," he said. "And I was an invited guest."

"Hey, no hang-ups here. We're a new breed of cop," Saylor said breezily. "So anyway, there's that aspect. And we already know the dead girl was his wife, not his sister, as he'd claimed."

"Actually, they'd both claimed that. I think they fooled everyone."

"Right. Well, we had a few eyewitnesses who testified that the girl and her husband seemed to be arguing after the wedding, maybe half an hour before she disappeared. Apparently she hadn't wanted him to go through with it, though my sense is he was bucking for citizenship...."

"I know all this," Dan interrupted, trying not to sound impatient.

"Right. So it's possible he killed her to stop her from ruining his plans," Saylor said.

"I see what you're getting at. That's very interesting." *Except,* Dan thought, *I was fucking her husband around the same time you have him tossing her overboard.*

Saylor sounded pleased. "The other possibility is that the guy he married — Thom Killingworth — quite the name, huh? Anyway, it's possible he didn't want her messing things up for them, so he killed her."

Which is also a reasonable guess, Dan thought, *except that Thom was busy fucking my boyfriend when it happened.* On the other hand, he couldn't confirm that Thom and Bill were still together when Daniella disappeared. Bill had arrived at the ballroom a minute or two after Thom. They could have gone their separate ways earlier, while Dan was tupping the Brazilian bull.

"What about family?" Dan blurted out before he could stop himself. He was thinking of Ted Killingworth. How far could you trust a junkie? But maybe Ted was exactly the sort of person who got caught in the crossfire of these things, innocent yet unable to clear his name.

"I've definitely thought of that one," Saylor said. "Did you ever wonder what the parents thought about their son marrying another man?"

"I wonder about things like that all the time," Dan said. "And wish I didn't have to."

"Point taken."

"But in Thom's case his mother paid for the wedding, so presumably she approved of it. I heard the father's been missing for twenty years, so it's not likely he had anything to do with it unless you assume he returned in time to murder the woman everyone presumed was his son's sister-in-law."

Dan heard Saylor chewing that one over. Maybe he was one of these cops who hated to be shown up. "Actually," Saylor said. "I meant the other guy's family. The Brazilian side."

"Oh. Well, I think it's fair to say they would have disapproved of the event, had they known the real story, which I now doubt they did. Still, doesn't it seem more likely that they would try to kill the boy rather than his wife?"

"I'm getting to that," Saylor said. "What if I told you I think the girl was targeted by accident and that it was really her husband that was supposed to die?"

This gave Dan pause. "What makes you say that?" he said slowly.

past decade. Or maybe not so begrudgingly — there were just so many old money families left in Toronto, and not all of them wanted to live on a hill in an enchanted forest. Especially not now, with the newcomers changing the tone of everything.

Dan drove south, noting the declining numbers. He was momentarily stunned when he saw the one he wanted. The Killingworths' in-town residence made their country home look like a summer cottage. Someone in the family had a preference for imposing structures. One of the grande dames of a bygone age, this was Bayreuth and Klingsor's magic castle rolled into one.

Dan parked curbside and climbed the stone walk past a rose garden and the trunks of a dozen century-old trees. A servant answered his ring, a bent and withered ancient whose presence seemed to have been wrested from the earth. He stood there, grim in a hair-shirt, guarding the ancestral realms.

The walk-in foyer was lined with oak panels and over-hung by the polished links of an eight-tiered chandelier. Terra cotta angels danced on the perimeter above the entrance. It might have been the first sight glimpsed by the dead entering Valhalla. Dan's coat was hung in a closet the size of most people's living rooms. A staircase twisted up and out of view. Dan recognized the glowering features of Nathaniel Macaulay — another oil portrait. This one clearly predated the one in Adolphustown. Still, the family forebear looked no friendlier at thirty-something than his aged self had. "Malevolent" was the word that came to mind. Dan wondered if they made portrait subjects sit on tacks back then.

He was shown into a sitting room and left alone, half-expecting to be given an admonishment not to touch the valuables. A damask weave sofa and two armchairs commanded centre stage; a vase of blossoms, gigantic and pale-pink, languished on an oval table. A fireplace with a cavity large enough to stand upright in filled the north wall. In medieval times, it might have served to feed the king and his men as they passed through on their way to the crusades. In the front window, lid cocked, a full-size grand piano waited expectantly, keys glittering like freshly minted teeth beside a gold-framed harp and standing cello. Dan wouldn't have been surprised to see a circus troupe waiting in readiness, with a couple of prancing ponies and a small corps de ballet to complete the set. Was it Thom or his world that Bill was in love with? Dan mused.

After a moment's wait, Thom entered with his mother. He was dressed in jeans and a white shirt and seemed to have recovered from his ordeal. He took Dan's hand, greeting him with an earnest sobriety, like old comrades who'd been fighting the same battle for years. Lucille, somewhat more subdued, wore a chaste beige sweater over a long black knitted dress, possibly her attempt at mourning. In the room's autumnal light she appeared more severe than Dan recalled, her face pinked with syllables of exhaustion or worry. He could see the family resemblance now, the wide, intelligent brow, the long, full cheekbones, the gold under-toned hair.

She offered him a hand. "Thank you for taking time out of your busy day to come all this way to see us," she began, her voice suggesting fragility. She gestured toward the sofa. "Please, sit."

Dan sat on the end near the fireplace. Thom sank into one of the wide chairs across from him. Lucille remained standing. Nervousness, Dan thought. Or maybe she intended to keep things brief.

She clasped her hands and addressed him directly. "As you know, we're anxious to learn as much as we can about this terrible situation," she began, her voice quickly regaining its equipoise. "Naturally, we're shaken by this poor girl's death. I can only imagine how her family must feel." She stopped and looked at Thom. "My son and I thought — in light of what's occurred — that it would be best if we were prepared for whatever might happen next. Bill McFarland felt you might be able to help...."

Dan saw this as his cue to jump in with words of reassurance, possibly wisdom, though he doubted that what he had to say would fall into either category. "I might have a bit of information that will help," he said. "I've been in touch with a constable at the Picton OPP detachment. I believe you already know they're treating Daniella's death as suspicious."

"Yes," Lucille said with a shiver. "That's what's so worrisome. It seems ghastly to think anyone could suspect that one of our guests might have had something to do with this. Have they considered that it might simply have been an accident?"

"I'm sure they have. It's routine to treat a death as suspicious unless it was clearly the result of an accident. Without any witnesses, they have to consider other possibilities."

Lucille absently fingered one of the pink blossoms. Begonia, Dan thought. Or maybe peony. He thought of tissue-paper pompoms used to decorate wedding cars. Not funeral flowers.

Lucille continued. "But several people have said she was quite inebriated before she fell overboard. A number of people saw her drinking heavily that evening. Surely they must realize it was a case of a tragic, drunken fall?"

"The autopsy revealed there was no alcohol in her system," Dan said. "In fact, she hadn't been drinking at all."

"Is that possible?" Lucille's face resumed its pensive look. "Even so, what makes them think it could be anything but an accident?"

"There was a large bruise on her forehead just under the hairline above her right temple. Thom saw it."

Lucille looked to her son, who nodded. "And ... that's why they think she may have been murdered?"

"I don't think the police would use the word 'murder' at this point. The bruise is one reason they're treating the death as suspicious," Dan said.

"Will we need alibis?" Thom said suddenly.

"They'll probably ask people to state where they were once they determine when Daniella fell overboard," Dan said. "The window of time in which it could have occurred is small. Can either of you say with accuracy where you were right before you heard of her disappearance? Or rather, Sebastiano's disappearance, since that's who people seemed to think had fallen overboard. If it comes to that, we may all have to prove where we were at the time."

"I was with Bill," Thom said, running a hand through his hair. "We went off for a little drink and a private chat. He was ... concerned about something."

"And I was in the stateroom with my guests the entire time," Lucille said. "But still, do you think it will come to that?"

"I hope not," Dan said. "In fact, I rather doubt it. The only people who might have to worry about providing alibis will be anyone who was wandering alone on the upper decks at the time Daniella disappeared."

Lucille wrapped her arms around herself and looked over at Thom. "I guess it's time to call Larry," she said softly.

"Our family attorney," Thom said, to Dan's inquisitive glance.

Dan wondered why they'd hesitated to call him before now. His thought was interrupted by Lucille.

"I was hoping to keep this out of the papers," she said grimly. "But it's already been all over the news. The 'troubled Killingworth family.' They've even dragged up my husband's disappearance."

"I'm sorry to hear," Dan said. "I hope things are resolved as quickly as possible."

"Thank you." She gave him a resigned smile, the gracious hostess whose concern is first and foremost for the comfort of her guest.

"Where is Sebastiano? If I may ask?"

Thom answered. "We've arranged for him to stay at a hotel downtown until the body is released. Then he'll go home with Daniella. Under the circumstances, we thought it best that he was somewhere else."

"Of course. It would be difficult to have him around. There is one other thing you might want to know," Dan said, looking from mother to son. "Daniella was pregnant when she died."

Thom's face flushed. "You've got to be kidding."

"How awful," Lucille said quietly.

"My god," Thom said, anger overtaking the shock. He turned to the fireplace. "These people were unbelievable!" His mother put a hand on his shoulder. Thom turned to face Dan again. "We had no idea. None!"

"It is quite incredible," said Lucille. "To think that Thom was so thoroughly deceived by these people. Is there anything else we should know?"

"Not at the moment," Dan said. "But I'll let you know anything I find out — provided I have a legal right to do so."

"I understand," said Lucille. "We wouldn't ask you to do anything that might compromise yourself." She took his hand and squeezed it warmly. "You've done a great deal to ease our minds, Daniel. Thank you. Is there anything we can do for you?"

Dan's eyes met hers. For a moment he wondered again why he was here. He couldn't see that he'd done or said anything that might be of use. "Not at all. I'm happy you feel I've been helpful."

"Then we won't keep you," Lucille said. "Thank you again. My son will see you to the door." She swept out of the room with more assurance than when she'd entered, her conscience eased, her heels making small clicking sounds.

Thom sat shaking his head and looking down at the floor. "Fucking hell," he said at last. "This is really awful."

"I'm sorry things have turned out so badly," Dan said.

"I can't believe I trusted that guy. I mean, I'm not naïve. I knew I was helping him, but obviously he was just waiting to get his citizenship, then he would have dumped me and brought her in as his wife."

"I doubt they would have got away with it," Dan said.

"And the pregnancy! I guess I can tell you why I — why my mother and I — were shocked when you mentioned it. A good portion of my grandfather's money is held in trust for the first great-grandchild."

A clock chimed three. It had been less than half an hour since he arrived, but Dan felt he'd been there for ages. "Did Sebastiano know?"

"He knew." Thom made a sound of disgust. "And I agreed to it. They duped me completely. The plan was for her to have a child with help from a fertility clinic after the wedding. But it was supposed to be *my* child! I might never have known!"

He looked tormented, as he had the morning they'd gone to identify Daniella's body, as though truth had a demoralizing rather than an edifying effect on him. Thom was one of the ones who got no relief from the knowing, Dan saw.

Thom straightened suddenly and laid a hand on Dan's knee. There was nothing lascivious in the gesture, his expression set beyond all that. "Thank you," he said. "You've really been great about everything. I'll tell Bill how helpful you've been."

"I was happy to help."

Thom stood. In the hallway, Dan said, "I thought Bill was going to be here. His message gave me that impression."

"No, I don't think Bill intended to be here this afternoon. At least not that I was aware of."

Something in Thom's expression suggested otherwise. Dan ignored it. He busied himself with his leave-taking. The putting on of his jacket, followed by a patting of pockets and the double-checking — *Ah, here they are!* — for his keys. They both pretended to be taken in by this dumbshow.

Thom's self-assurance had returned. He shook his head sympathetically. "Maybe Bill changed his mind."

"I must have misunderstood," Dan said.

Thom opened the door and Dan stepped through into what was, all things considered, just another ordinary day. The world beyond seemed a little less dazzling than the one he was leaving. He hadn't wanted to be there. Now that he was, he didn't want to leave.

"I'll be in touch," he said.

The drive across St. Clair and down Bayview delivered him to his driveway in less than twenty minutes. He could have returned to the office, but he wouldn't have been able to concentrate. On the way home, he mulled over his visit to the Killingworths. He hadn't helped them in any way he could see. Had they simply wanted hand-holding? He pulled out his cell and left a message for Bill saying how the meeting went.

Ralph did an anxious little dance at the back door, wanting to be let out. Then he came back in and settled on his bed in the corner. Ked wasn't due for another two hours. There was nothing further demanding Dan's attention. *Me Time,* he told himself. It had been weeks since he'd been jogging. His leg muscles ached with anticipation.

He stood on the rise over Riverdale Park with its view of the downtown skyline. The city spread out like a medical cadaver, the skin peeled back to reveal the working organs, muscles, and nervous system. It seemed incredible to think he'd lived here for twenty years. He padded across the metal footbridge, down the stairs, and turned north. His run took him through a drainage tunnel echoing with the chirps of mechanical frogs — some civil servant's idea of an ecological joke — under the arches of the Bloor Viaduct. Above, subway trains and rush hour traffic raced along as the 905-ers abandoned the city for another day.

His feet pounded the trail as his mind melded with the green space whizzing past. He climbed a gradient running headlong with the Don Valley Parkway — more cars escaping the city. Here the path headed toward Pottery Road and the supposed haven of leafy suburbs or, if you turned right instead of left, on to Scarborough, where it was said that bad Torontonians went when they died. (The good ones, presumably, going to Vancouver.)

A helicopter hovered overhead, stuck in the loop of rush-hour traffic reports. A posse of bikers passed in the other direction, heading for the lakeshore trail, always crowded with roller-bladers and dog walkers these days. Dan preferred the quiet of the valley where passersby were less frequently encountered.

Now and again, the Don River appeared through the trees in patches of brown flecked with yellow foam. Toronto was probably the only major city in the world to relinquish the chance to commercialize a river running through its centre. While that might have seemed an ecologically sound choice, in reality the river had been slowly poisoned by surreptitious chemical dumps and garbage spills, and left to fill instead with abandoned shopping carts, stolen bicycles, and cast-off tires. Merchants would have shown more concern for its appearance and welfare. Dan thought of Ked's enthusiasm for the decrepit world of *Blade Runner*. Perhaps some enterprising young dreamer would one day populate the Don's turgid depths with robotic fish to accompany the chirping of the mechanical frogs.

He came to the top of the rise. He'd meant to take this time to think about Bill, but instead he was worrying about water pollution. A chorus of images from the weekend jarred his thinking. He remembered the rush of betrayal he'd felt hearing Bill confess his love for Thom. It went a long way toward explaining why Bill found intimacy so hard. Dan, on the other hand, had no such difficulties. It had been easy to devote himself to Bill, though common sense told him his lover wasn't as dedicated in return. Did it ultimately matter? Was the cool affection Bill showed him enough? Maybe the other would grow with time. Or maybe he just needed to recognize when he'd been kicked in the balls.

With a sudden swoop, the helicopter turned away from the valley, disappearing in the clouds. He'd just topped the hill, his breathing nicely measured, when he saw the biker in full riding gear racing toward him. The guy braked a few feet off — the near-collision hadn't really been that near, all things considered.

The biker flipped up his sun visor and smiled. Two travellers meeting on a lonely road. He leaned down to unstrap a water bottle from the bike frame. "Is this the way to Pottery Road?" he asked, taking several long gulps.

"No," Dan said, breaking his pace. "This way heads down to the lake. You probably just passed Pottery Road. Didn't you cross a roadway a few minutes back?"

The biker laughed softly and admitted he had.

"That was Pottery Road. If you head back and turn right under the bridge, you'll hit Broadview. A left would take you to the Bayview Extension."

The man nodded. He seemed to be checking Dan out. "Are you Dan Sharp?"

"Yes," Dan said, perplexed. He usually had great recall for faces. Maybe it was the helmet. "Have we met?"

"Oh, you don't know me," the man said. "But I've heard of you. You date Bill McFarland, don't you?"

Dan cocked his head curiously. "Yes."

The man gave him a thorough once-over. "I saw you in a video. You're pretty sizeable."

Dan shook his head. "Who showed you a video of me?"

The man laughed like it was a private joke. "Bill did."

The path extended in both directions, giving a good vantage to oncoming traffic. They were alone on a windy hill.

"Would you like a blow job?" the cyclist asked. "There's no one around."

Dan clenched his teeth. "No, I don't want a blow job."

The cyclist persisted. "I'd love to get my lips on it."

Dan's hands went out palms-first, pushing him up against the wire fence. If he could, he would have pushed him and his bicycle down the hill and into the bramble. *Fucking Bill,* he thought. *How fucking dare he?* Dan held a fist in the man's terrified face. "How would you like your lips on this?"

"You're a fucking madman!" the cyclist choked out.

Dan relaxed his grip and the man slid down the fence to the pavement. "Pottery Road is that way," Dan said, pointing. He took off at a trot.

†

211

Dan heard a match being struck on the other end of the phone as he tossed a shoe into a corner. Sweat ran down his chest under his nylon trainer where he lay sprawled in the living room chair. The dampness in his crotch was making his balls cling to his shorts. He'd started by recounting the incident on the trail, followed with a review of the events of the weekend, and ended with a full confession about his bare-backing tryst with Sebastiano. He tossed the other shoe into the corner and waited.

"Tell me you didn't just say that," Donny said.

He'd sympathized with the story about the lustful biker and listened respectfully as Dan detailed the events leading to Daniella's death, but now he was angry. Quietly angry. "Okay, I really don't want to know any of this, but it's too late because you've already told me." All this in a calm, cool voice. "That is the stupidest thing I've ever heard come out of your mouth." He took a drag on the cigarette. "Do I have to list all the men we know who are no longer alive because they did something like that — just once — and paid for it with their lives?"

"I know. I know how stupid it was."

"Good. Glad to hear it. But what I'm wondering, what I'm dying to know, is what you're going to do about it. And by 'it' I mean that piece of shit you've been dating for the past year."

"Let's not get — okay, okay — I suggested counselling a couple times, but he's not interested."

Donny made a strangled sound. His tone was pure exasperation. "Of course he's not interested! It's a perfect arrangement — for him. He gets all the sex he wants and keeps you hanging on hoping for more. But the man is not capable of more. Meanwhile, he makes videotapes of the two of you having sex without your knowledge to show to his locker room buddies and god knows who else. And just so you know, those counselling things never work. Jamie and I tried it just before we broke up...."

"I didn't know that. What happened?"

"We ended up sleeping with our counsellor. Then we broke up."

Dan pressed a forearm across his eyes, shutting out the light. His post-jog endorphin high was fading and the fatigue setting in. "So what are you suggesting?"

He heard another drag followed by a quick exhalation — important things needed to be said. "I've given you my opinion on that one a dozen times already. Get rid of him. Bill treats you like a rent boy because you let him. Ask yourself this: with all his wonderful bedroom acrobatics and his classy townhouse and rich friends and artfully dyed but rapidly thinning hair — does he feel anything for you?"

"Even if he doesn't, how does that make me a rent boy? I always pay my own way."

Donny harrumphed. "It makes you a rent boy because he's interested only in one piece of your anatomy ... and it isn't your heart."

"How do I know what he feels for me? Maybe Bill doesn't even know what he really feels."

"Does he know your middle name? Has he memorized lines from your favourite movie? Does he make camp references to your mother's side of the family in public or whisper your secret nickname in stirring undertones during sex?"

"Well, the latter, at least."

Donny paused. "Really?"

"I'll never tell you what it is, so don't ask."

Donny snorted. "As if I need to ask."

"You might be surprised."

"If it's not 'Beercan,' I will be." The cigarette noises started in earnest again. "Remind me — how long have you two been dating?"

"A little over a year."

Donny whistled. "A little over a year! And how many times has he slept over at your place in that time?"

"You know Bill doesn't sleep over...."

"So therefore none." The tone said it would brook no opposition. "And in that time you've slept over at his place, what ... twenty-five, maybe thirty times?"

"Something like that. Maybe less. It's only on the weekends when Ked stays at Kendra's place...."

"There are fifty-two weekends in a year ... you see what I'm saying?"

"No, I don't actually."

"I'm saying that out of consideration for you he could have split the difference and stayed at your place some of those nights."

"It's not important to me."

"Apparently not. Out of curiosity, how long was your last relationship?"

"With David Bonner?"

"You tell me. I don't keep track of your boyfriends."

"Three ... maybe four months."

"Right. I seem to recall he was CEO of some import firm. Very successful, too. What happened to him?"

Dan lifted his arm from his face and looked out. Rain clouds had gathered. "David was insecure. Apparently my size bothered him, because he felt I was out of his league. I told him size didn't matter but …"

"The second gay lie!"

"What's the first?"

"Take your pick: I'll love you forever or I won't put this on the Internet. Ba-dump. What happened to him?"

"I got tired of telling him it was all right. It was such a drama just to get him into the bedroom. I eventually stopped returning his calls."

Donny made a flushing sound. "What about before that? Who came before David?"

"Perry Donaldson. That only lasted a month."

"I remember him — the accountant. Also very successful. Nice guy, but a terrible pianist. What happened there?"

"Perry had a huge hang-up about his mother. He could never see me on Fridays because that was their night to speak on the phone. She hated that her only son was gay and he was tormented by guilt over it. I told him if he wanted to see me then either he had to set his mother straight or stop complaining about her to me."

"And he didn't?"

"No and no."

"So he got the big flush too?"

"Yeah … I guess so."

"And what about Gordon, that nice banker in Rosedale?"

"I never dated him."

"No, but you were friends. Good friends, in fact. Why haven't I heard you talk about him in a dog's age?"

Dan hesitated. "We don't really … talk anymore."

Donny jumped on this. "Why?"

"It got too difficult. He was always too busy to do anything."

"I think you said you saw him flirting with Bill."

"That too. It pissed me off. I don't think that's acceptable behaviour from a friend, no matter what anybody says about the gay moral code."

"And I say you're right. No one should flirt with your man in front of you. Behind your back's another story, but I'm not telling that one right now. Are you seeing a pattern here, Danny Boy?"

"No — should I?"

Donny sighed. "I'll say. You date these highly successful guys or become friends with them till they piss you off, then they all get the royal flush and you withdraw your affection. It's how you punish people who get close to you."

"I don't think that's — am I really that complex?"

"No, you're that simple."

Dan felt the sting. "Well, what would you suggest?"

"Get some loyal friends and a lover without hang-ups? I don't know." Donny exhaled impatiently. "Did you ever get close to any of them? Close enough that you thought you might have been in love?"

"Not really. But I was fond of them."

"Ah! The big revelation — you were *fond* of them. How sweet." Donny was silent for a moment. The cigarette started up again. "Just out of curiosity, will you tell your therapist about your Brazilian weekend adventure?"

"No! Are you crazy? I tell him I dream of cuddly bunnies, not urges to kill myself. I want out of those fucking sessions."

cheerleader at Wawa Senior High. Dressed in a Hallelujah Pink sweater with matching lipstick and nails, plunging neckline, and thigh-high skirt, she'd toned down the look with a black nylon windbreaker, placing her one solitary rung above her husband on the evolutionary ladder.

Dan thought he detected an odour — it might have been two — of something faintly melony covering the scent of fried fish. A moment passed before he could distinguish that the fruity smell was coming from her and the fried smell from her husband. He wished he'd eaten. The combination was going to be difficult on an empty stomach.

He asked for their version of events the night Richard disappeared. He listened with considered solemnity as Gloria Philips retold the story, tapping her pink nails on his desk for emphasis. It all sounded familiar except for one detail: Richard had been getting money from somewhere. Dan nodded as Gloria told of a series of unexpected electronic gadgets — cell phones, iPods — and overnight trips to Toronto that her son had explained as being a friend's invitation to concerts.

Gloria's account ended. She eyed her husband. "His version's the same as mine." The human grunt nodded as Gloria looked Dan in the eye. "But I didn't come here to hear myself talk," she said, tapping the file. "I want you to tell me what's being done to find my son."

Dan closed the file and sat back. "The reason I asked you to repeat the story is because there's often a detail that gets overlooked, and sometimes it comes out when people talk it through. The detail that stands out here is that Richard seems to have been getting money from somewhere. Do you have any idea where it came from?"

Gloria looked at Paul then back at Dan. "No. Maybe he was stealing it from somewhere, but not from me. I always know what's in my purse."

"What do you know about the place where the police picked up your son twice in the weeks before he ran away?"

She shook her head. "It was some place queers went to prey on young boys."

And yet somehow those boys always managed to find themselves in those places by accident or were inexplicably drawn to them against their will time and again, Dan finished silently, thinking of the shadows beneath the trestle that had shaped his own adolescent sex life. "Do you think that's where your son got the money?"

The look of disgust on Gloria's face could have wiped the rust off a nail. "Are you telling me someone was paying my son for sex? Is that what I'm hearing you say?"

"I'm trying to determine where he got his money."

Gloria's voice was hard as flint. "He was fourteen years old! He's too young for sex."

"That's the legal age for sex. Prostitution is another matter."

"Who the hell made it legal for some pervert to fuck my kid up the ass at the age of fourteen?"

Her husband squirmed in his seat. Gloria reached out and clutched his forearm, driving five pink nails into his skin, either to pacify or restrain him.

"He's not old enough to engage in anal sex, just oral," Dan said.

"Nice distinction!"

"I'll be honest with you," Dan said. "We have reason to believe your son has been involved in prostitution and possibly in the pornography industry here in Toronto."

Her husband interrupted. "Let's get out of here." He looked over at Dan. "You don't know what you're talking about!"

"Shut up, Paul. He's my kid and I want him back."

"Yeah? Cry me a fucking river. He'll come back with some faggot disease. And I don't want him in my house if he does!" Her husband stood and went out, having a moment of indecision whether to slam the door with its glass plates and risk breakage or just close it loudly on his way out. His cuff caught on the knob and he effected what was, all things considered, a very prissy exit for a very large man.

Gloria Philips leaned over the desk. She stabbed at the file with a buffed fingernail. "Find my kid. You find my kid and bring him home or I'll have you taken off this case!"

Dan sat rigid. "You're welcome to request another investigator at any time, Mrs. Philips. Just as I'm free to pass the file along to somebody else."

"I don't like being told off," she said icily.

"Neither do I. But I probably know more about finding missing teenagers than anybody else in this town. I've already made some progress on Richard's case and I may make some more. If I do, I'll let you know what I turn up."

"You do that, buster." She stood and walked out of the office.

Scary, Dan thought, wondering what reasonable chance any kid with those parents would have to grow up to be anything other than fucked up.

Sally opened his door and peeked in. "Are they gone?"

"It's safe."

"Thank goddess!"

"What were you saying about people not being colourful anymore?"

"Sometimes white trash is too colourful." She slapped something down on his desk. "Sorry to spoil your afternoon, but the fun's over," she said.

Dan saw the name Daniella Ballancourt in capital letters. He opened the file. Her death was no longer being considered suspicious. The coroner had determined the bump on her head was caused during her fall from the boat. The skin around it contained traces of paint consistent with samples taken from a lifeboat strapped directly below the upper deck where she was believed to have fallen. More importantly, a couple had come forward and testified they'd observed Daniella alone on deck moments before she disappeared. She'd been bent over the rail, vomiting. When asked if she needed help, she'd turned them away. The account had been given by a respected judge and his wife. Dan recalled the older couple who'd seemed annoyed by the fright they'd had. He thought they'd said they were on the lower deck when she fell, but perhaps that was another couple. He was on the phone with Saylor again.

"It just showed up on my desk, too," Saylor said. "Damn!"

"Why did it take so long for them to come forward?" Dan asked.

"I've got the inside scoop on that. From what I heard, they didn't want to be associated with the whole event, from the gay wedding right on down."

"Then what were they doing there in the first place?"

"They were Lucille Killingworth's business associates. Apparently she pressured half the Canadian establishment into going to the wedding."

"I heard that, too."

"Anyway, it looks like the case is closed. I guess that's that."

"So it would seem," Dan said. He paused. "Did you bring up the fact that Lucille Killingworth had paid for the girl's abortion?"

There was a hum on the line. "I did," Saylor said. "It wasn't well-received. Everyone here was eager to accept the verdict of accidental death. Say no more."

"Seems odd," Dan said.

"That's what I thought." Saylor seemed anxious to be off the phone. "Well, better luck next time. If you're out this way, drop in and see me."

"Will do."

For once, Dan was on time to pick Ked up. His friend the "ruffian" was nowhere to be seen. Perhaps they'd had a falling out, though Ked didn't really fight with other kids. Maybe he'd decided the boy wasn't friendship material. Probably better than finding out the hard way. They made it home without hitting any traffic snarls. No annoying neighbours or dog turds on the step. The universe had stopped targeting him with booby traps. Dan was a little surprised, but grateful nonetheless. He plucked a bundle of mail from the box as he entered. Bills, flyers, restaurant menus, lists of services available, items for sale, requests for donations to build a water filtration plant in Namibia, feed the hungry in Libya, stop the proliferation of landmines, and put an end to the seal hunt. A thousand plans for saving the world. None asking whether it was worth saving.

An envelope caught his eye — parchment yellow, good quality paper. He flipped it over and caught the name: L. Killingworth. Surely it wasn't a thank-you note for his presence at the wedding. He opened it and a cheque for $10,000 dropped into his hands. On the memo line were the words "For services rendered" next to Lucille Killingworth's signature.

He carried the envelope and cheque upstairs to his office and laid them on his desk. His first instinct was to call Bill, but he knew there'd be no response. He picked up the cheque and dialled the number under the address. To his surprise, Lucille answered. Her voice remained unchanged when he identified himself. Dan thanked her for the cheque and explained that he wouldn't be able to accept it.

Her voice expressed concern, with a tone of annoyance shaded in. "But you did some valuable work for me — important work. I simply wished to express my gratitude for your loyalty to my family."

"Actually, Lucille, I never considered it work. As for loyalty, I simply did a favour on Bill's behalf."

"Yes, I understand that."

"I can't accept it. It would look bad."

"Nevertheless, I am grateful," she said with quiet insistence.

"And I accept your gratitude," Dan said. "But there's no need to pay me for what I did."

"Well, then I guess I will have to respect your wishes," Lucille replied with reluctance. "Though it seems silly you won't accept it." She gave pause. "What about a charity? I could donate it to some cause of your choice."

"Thank you — it's not necessary. I'm happy to know the case turned out all right."

"Yes, it has, hasn't it?"

And all so very neatly, Dan thought. He wondered for a moment if the judge and his wife had received a cheque in nice yellow parchment paper as well. "I'm just wondering, though…."

"Yes?"

"When we spoke the other day, I told you Daniella was pregnant."

"Yes. A dreadful thing."

"You seemed surprised."

"I was — shocked."

"But you didn't mention you'd paid for her to have an abortion." The pause was long enough. "So I take it your shock was actually on learning that she was *still* pregnant."

The voice remained unchanged. Dan admired her cool. "It was between me and the girl. It had nothing to do with what happened afterwards."

"How did you learn she was pregnant? Did she come to you for help?"

"A woman knows these things." There was another slight pause, and Dan wondered if she was considering calling "Larry" again. "I think I had best not say any more," she said with hostess perfection, the unassailable "thank you for your kindness" to someone whose name meant not the slightest thing to her. Though the voice remained unchanged, the tone of conversation had altered imperceptibly. "Thank you again, you've been most helpful."

231

Yes, I'm sure I have, Dan thought, as the call clicked to a close. *Though I'm still not sure what purpose I just served.*

He and Ked ate supper together. Afterwards, they watched some mindless TV about a Chicken Man that Ked seemed to comprehend far better than Dan did. Ked walked Ralph and went to bed. Dan was still putting away the dishes and mulling over his conversation with Lucille Killingworth when the phone rang. Bill's home number showed on the display. He grabbed it.

"It's Bill," came the edgy voice.

"Nice to hear from you," Dan said. "I was hoping you'd be in touch earlier."

"I've been busy."

"I gather you've heard the news about Daniella. They've decided it was an accident."

"Yes, thankfully. Look — I'm not calling to chitchat. I'm calling to say that I know what happened between you and Sebastiano on the boat. He claims you initiated it and that you practically raped him." Bill went on before Dan could speak, his voice hard. "You're a bloody hypocrite, you know. How many times did you tell me you don't bareback, but then you practically rape this boy?"

Dan was stunned. "I…."

"Anyway, I have no interest in ever seeing you again. You can go back to the gutter where I found you."

Dan found his voice. "Where we met was Woody's. And you were the one in the gutter that night." He expected Bill to hang up, but the silence hung on between them. "I can't believe you're jealous after what's been going on between you and Thom."

"Don't try to turn this around!" Bill shouted. "Thom is my closest friend!"

"Far more than a friend, from the sounds of it."

"You don't even know Sebastiano!" Bill sounded nearly hysterical.

"Let me get this straight — you're saying it's all right for you to fuck Thom on his wedding night because you're his friend, but it's not all right for me to fuck Sebastiano because I'd just met him?"

The question was met with silence.

"Bill?"

"I'm hanging up," Bill said.

And he did.

Dan smashed the receiver down. "Fucking hell!" He picked up the receiver and smashed it down again. "You cowardly fucking prick!"

He listened for stirring sounds from Ked's bedroom. He unclenched his fists and tried a breathing exercise — *in*-two-three-four, *hold*-six-seven-eight — one that Martin had recommended. It didn't help. Dan doubted whether Martin had ever felt true rage in his life.

He went over all the things he should have said to Bill, going back to the night they'd met when Bill insulted Dan's neighbourhood and later asked Dan to have unsafe sex with him. What Dan should have said was, *Get lost, you loser!* Why hadn't he? Because Bill had been nice to him. Because Bill had accepted him and his sordid background and his cheap little world and his awkward ugliness, and let him drive his expensive car and make love to him in his tasteful townhouse and dirty his expensive satin sheets. Because he, Dan, was the real loser for taking whatever he was handed instead of demanding better. And because deep inside Dan knew he was to blame for this, just as he'd been to blame for his mother's death and his father's drinking. It was his fault — every loss and degradation he'd suffered, beginning with his mother's demise and his father's disgust with his only son.

Thinking of his father made him want a drink. He poured a Scotch and waited till the warmth in his gut muddled his affections. He began to feel bad for everyone — not just himself, but for Daniella and Sebastiano, whose quest for a new life had failed utterly, for Thom and Lucille, whose world had been rocked by the tragedy, and even for Bill, who he missed already despite everything, and for his best friend Donny who'd been forced to make Dan face reality. Which he now saw was something Donny had never wanted to do.

By the second drink Dan was thinking of Bob Greene, remembering the stability they'd had during those three short years in Leaside. Was that all the happiness you were allotted in life? As strange and ill-fitting as the relationship had been, the love was real. In fact, it was one of the best things that ever happened to him. At the time, he hadn't realized he'd lucked into an archetypal gay relationship: the patient older man and the confused unlovable kid who needed to belong. He had been happy with Bob, but he couldn't bring to mind now the last time he'd felt anything remotely like happiness.

He picked up the bottle and peered through it. The world appeared more pleasant coloured by the amber liquor. One more drink, he knew, and the cynicism would creep in beside the self-pity. He wouldn't be thinking of the love that had worked between him and Bob, but of the older man with money and the kid with the sizeable cock. So why not skip the drink and go straight for oblivion? Go right from the Sermon on the Mount to the Crucifixion. The way he ruined everything by going too far.

For a fleeting second, he saw the repulsed faces of the men and women he'd asked for spare change on his arrival in Toronto. Their expressions had said it all. They'd known him for what he was: a piece of shit who got nothing because he deserved nothing, and never would. That was why bleakness had followed him all the days of his life. Except for Kedrick.

Except for Ked.

This thought radiated against the darkness and lifted him up. He remembered the first time he'd been handed the bundle of warmth wrapped in blankets and looked down at his son's wrinkly red features. The tiny miracle he'd participated in. All the things he and Ked shared that belonged to no one else: comforting words whispered in the dark before bed, hands held climbing stairs, moments of anticipation and worry as Dan watched him grow and learn. He recalled the first time his son had asked his advice and the wondrous trust creeping across Ked's face as Dan helped solve his problem. The glow he'd felt knowing his son looked up to him. All the good that had been and would always be. So who had judged it otherwise, and why? Dan had, of course. Whatever others said about him or did to him, it was he who'd accepted it. No one had made him what he was but himself.

The phone rang and his heart zigzagged. It would be Bill calling to apologize, to say he loved Dan, always had, and just wanted to talk things out. Dan picked up and listened to the mechanical whir of a line being transferred. Only an 800 number. He hung up before some desperate telemarketer came on the line.

He walked to the door and fingered his jacket. He could go over to Bill's and try to talk to him. But what was the sense? Bill might change his mind tomorrow, but Dan wouldn't be able to push him into anything tonight. He stood there fighting the feeling. Wanting to give in, but not give in. He was doing exactly what he'd done as a kid when anything upset or troubled him. Holding it in and pushing it down till he'd conquered his feelings. Till they no longer scared him, a dangerous reef lying blackly below the surface of the water, the boat's vulnerable bottom skimming only inches above.

He breathed out, pushing hard against his diaphragm to empty everything. He wanted to shrink, get smaller and smaller, till he disappeared. He stood in the hallway, looking from his coat to the door. His eyes fixed on a wall calendar, a bucolic scene in a country lane with children and chickens and a nurturing mother watching over her brood. It had always seemed full of life's complex mysteries, promising all that and more every time he looked at it. But now it had changed. Now it was just a picture in the same way his coat was just a coat and the door just a door. Empty. In some way he couldn't define, things had lost their meaning, their substance slipping away without his recognizing it. He stood there among the lifeless objects and realized they were just that: lifeless.

Maybe it was better that Bill had barely spent any time here. Otherwise Dan might spend years remembering where Bill had stood, the things he'd touched and the expressions on his face. The ghost of memories past. He'd be haunted by Bill long after he was gone.

Dan shook his head. What was he doing? Bill had dumped *him*, when Bill was the one to blame. Fucking hell! *I am a loser,* he thought. He slumped in his chair and looked at the void surrounding him. He poured another glass and left it sitting on the arm of the chair. He felt a little better just knowing it had been poured. He stared at it for a long time, then lifted it to his mouth and drank.

He felt calmer. He was in control again — the inner him that knew how to avoid life's obstacles. He could put himself on automatic pilot and wait for the soft immolation that came in the aftermath of these emotional implosions. He fingered the glass. If he stopped now, he'd be fine. He picked up the phone and dialled.

"I just wanted you to know that Bill and I are through."

There was a brief pause then, "Congratulations! That's the smartest thing you've done in years."

"I didn't do it," Dan said. "He dumped me."

There was another second of silence as Donny absorbed this. "You're kidding! He dumped you? That's priceless! Aren't you glad now you're still talking to me?"

"Why? So you can mock me in the midst of my misery?"

"Ah! Baby — don't think of it like that. It's the beginning of your freedom, a newfound period of emotional sanity. Tomorrow you will rise up like the phoenix from the ashes. Tonight I want you to go out and conquer somebody. Anybody!"

"Listen, I don't really feel like staying on the line right now."

Donny's voice became soothing, sensing the seriousness of Dan's mood. "I can come over, if you'd like."

"No, don't do that."

"Are you sure? Tell me you're okay about this."

"I'm okay," Dan said. "Actually, I was thinking I'd stay home and get drunk."

"I'm sorry if I'm making light of things. Is this going to be a big crash?"

"Maybe."

"Shall I call you later to make sure you're all right?"

"If you like."

He hung up, brought the bottle to the living room, and sat in the chair facing the window. He needed to find the dullness and slip into it till everything that bothered him had moved far, far away from where he sat in the gloomy interior of the room, of his life.

He put his hand on the bottle and uncorked it. He lifted it and watched a long, thin stream spill down and pool in the bottom of his glass.

SIXTEEN

The Dog Days of Autumn

THE DREAMS WERE CRUEL, but the reality crueller. Dan woke to a vile taste, an acid finger probing his throat. Someone had a hand over his face, smothering him and holding him down. He fought wildly against the nothingness surrounding him, the unseen appendage holding him prisoner. He lurched to the kitchen sink and gagged till the residue spewed from his mouth. Heart pounding, he gasped for breath and sank to his knees. When he could breathe freely again, he poured a glass of water and ran the tap to wash the sickness away.

Ralph watched him with curiosity. His tail thumped briefly and stopped. Humans were unpredictable. Outside, a dazzling greyness had taken over the sky, another gloomy morning just around the corner. Dan went back to the living room to survey the scene of his recent debauch. The chair still bore the impressions of his body. An empty bottle sat upright on the floor, a lone sentinel standing guard. Apparently he'd lost the battle not to drink it all. It had poured an awful lot of drink before it quit on him. Just like a good friend.

He was still wearing yesterday's clothes. He obviously hadn't thought of going upstairs to bed. The acid-etched neurons of his brain fired in fits and starts as he remembered his conversation with Bill. It hadn't been long, but it felt final. Strangely, he felt good about it. There was no emotional hangover, just a good solid physical one coming on full gallop. Better that way then.

He also remembered talking to Donny and the promise to call back. He went to the front hall. Sure enough, the answer machine flashed its little red message of hope. A pungent whiff hit his nose — something unpleasant, like old garbage. He turned to the front door. There were two dark elongated shapes like a stain on the floor. The anger rose inside him. Dan felt himself choking again, only this time on his rage.

"Son-of-a-bitch!" He heard Ralph rise off his bed in the kitchen and scurry out of the room. Dan was after him in a flash.

"Fucking dog!"

Ralph snarled as Dan grabbed at his collar. He felt the flesh on his hand tear and well up with pain.

"You son-of-a-bitch! Don't you fucking bite me!" He kicked out at the dog's back legs. Ralph was thrown off balance, toppling and skidding as he tried to scramble through the door.

"Dad!"

Ked's voice came from behind him. Dan whirled to see his son standing in the doorway in his underwear.

"Your fucking dog bit me!"

Ked ran across the room and crouched beside Ralph, wrapping him in his arms. "Dad, he's just a dog!"

"He bit me and he shit on the floor again!"

"I'm sorry!" Ked wailed. "I didn't let him out this morning. Please, Dad! Don't hit him. He bit you because he's afraid of you!"

Dan felt the anger subside, the fury loosening its grip. He was yelling at his son, for god's sake. What was wrong with him? "I'm sorry," he said, suddenly ashamed.

Ked broke into sobs. "Don't you see everyone's afraid of you?"

"I'm sorry," Dan said again quietly, filled with remorse and self-contempt.

Still sobbing, Ked turned to look at his father. "Dad, why do you hate everyone?"

"I don't, Ked." Dan shook his head. "I don't hate everyone." He knelt and tried to wrap his arms around Ked, who was still clinging to Ralph. Ked wiped his face with the back of his hand. "I don't hate anyone," Dan said quietly.

"Then why do you try to hurt everyone?"

Dan pushed the hair off his son's forehead then reached slowly down to pat Ralph, carefully, so the dog wouldn't flinch. Ralph's yellow eyes watched him warily.

"I'm sorry," Dan said. "I have no excuse for what I just did. None."

He stood and went to the bathroom and bandaged his hand. He got out the mop and bucket and cleaned up the mess at the front door. When he finished, he returned to the kitchen. Ked lay in the doorway with Ralph, playing with his ears and stroking his fur. Dan came over and crouched, holding out his hand to let the dog sniff the bandage.

"Bill and I broke up last night," Dan said softly.

Ked looked up. "I'm sorry, Dad."

Dan shook his head. "Don't be sorry. It was time."

"Is that why you were upset?" Ked asked.

"I don't know." Dan shook his head. "I just don't know." He stared at Ked. "Are you afraid of me?"

Ked sobbed and looked away, sniffling into Ralph's fur.

"Oh, Ked." Dan wrapped his son in his arms. "I'm so sorry."

Dan hugged his son so hard he feared he might hurt the boy. Ralph looked over and licked his hand. Dan squinted away a tear and reached out a hand to pat the furry head.

"Good old Ralphie," he said.

"It must be hard for you to have to look after me all by yourself," Ked said through his sniffles.

"No, it's not hard. Having you for a son is the thing I love most about my life. Sometimes I think it's the only thing."

"Really?"

"Really."

Finally, Ked said, "Okay."

Withrow Park was a blizzard of leaves wreathing mothers with strollers, dog walkers, and skateboarders in a profusion of energized calm. The yellow on the ground mirrored the leaves above. The annuals were still fringing the edges of the paths in laser colours, despite temperatures that skirted down each night toward some impassable limit. Ked let Ralph off the leash and watched him bound away. He ran right up to the edge of the park before he came to some invisible dog boundary then turned to look back.

"Good boy, Ralph!" Ked called out as Ralph rolled on his back in the grass. "He loves it here," Ked said.

Dan stood watching for a moment. "Do you remember when we first got him and you wanted to call him Suzie?"

Ked laughed. "Yeah. Poor Ralph."

"I wondered about you for a while after that."

Ked was listening to his iPod, his chest looped with wires linking head and body. "Wanna hear something cool?"

He offered the earphones to his father. Dan held them to his ears and heard a thin boyish treble singing against a violin in a cloud of reverb.

"Nice. Who's this?"

"Owen Pallett. He calls himself Final Fantasy, but he's mostly just a solo guy who accompanies himself on violin with a feedback loop."

Dan tried to look impressed.

"He's gay and he lives in Toronto...."

Was this Ked's subtle hint that Dan should track down Owen Pallett and ask him out? Maybe he should let Ked filter his dates from now on. He couldn't do any worse than he'd done on his own.

"And," Ked continued, "he gives money to Doctors Without Borders."

Dan took that in. "That's cool, I guess. As long as he looks after himself and his loved ones first, of course."

Ked rolled his eyes. "Can't you ever just relax, Dad?"

Dan looked surprised. "What do you mean?"

Ked sighed. "Everyone knows you've done all the right things for me. So just relax, okay?"

"I can relax," Dan said.

Ked looked at him skeptically. "Yeah? Then let's see you."

Ked took off toward the skating rink where roller-bladers whirled in soft circles and kids played hacky-sack. Dan caught up with him.

"Hey, Dad — that guy just checked out your ass!"

Dan turned. Sure enough, a jock type flushed when he saw Dan looking back. On top of a rise they watched an obese dad playing baseball with his son. The man's saggy tits jiggled as he tried to keep up with the energetic teenager.

"That'll be me in a few years," Dan observed.

"Not if you renew your Y membership!"

Dan smiled. "How's the book going?"

"*Blade Runner*?"

"Yeah. Finish it yet?"

"No." Ked shook his head. "I'm at the part where Jake realizes he lives in a city full of androids. Even some of the other bounty hunters are androids, only they don't know it. Almost all the real people have left Earth because of the nuclear fallout, so only the freaks and androids remain. Even the pets are robots, because no one can afford a real one."

They watched Ralph run past them and stop to wait for them to catch up.

"Sounds more and more like the real future," Dan said, wondering if he should be contributing to Ked's cynicism.

Ked's eyes were alight. "What if they just keep replacing everybody till there's nobody real left on Earth?"

"Who would notice?" Dan said.

"Exactly!" Ked said. "That'd be so cool! These androids could be living among us right now. Nothing real any more. They can even pre-set their emotions!"

"That's called Prozac," Dan said, then felt bad again.

"But what I don't get," Ked said, "is that it's not just good moods. Sometimes they pre-set depression and despair. If you can choose your mood, why would you choose a bad one?"

The city opened before them, the towers of the financial district stern and upright. The CN Tower dominated the horizon, venerating the twin altars of media and finance. Sleepy green boroughs spread outward, filled with thousands of houses. Dan wondered about the personal arrangements, the tentative lives each contained. He'd never felt at home here. How had he ever thought he could belong in this city of giants, let alone thrive and prosper? Though on some level he'd done just that.

"Just a guess," he said. "But maybe what they want is to experience the whole range of emotions."

Ked looked at his father. "Is that why you stay in Toronto?"

"Is that supposed to be funny?"

Ked shook his head. "No. I know you hate it here. I heard you tell Uncle Donny it was a 'soul sucking hellhole.'"

Dan snorted. "Don't listen to everything I say. Or to your Uncle Donny. Some days I like it here just fine."

"Oh." Ked thought about this apparent contradiction. "But then other days there are too many androids, right?"

Dan smiled. "Something like that."

In the distance, Ralph stirred up a flock of pigeons that flew off over the trees. Ked watched for a moment then turned back to his father. "Mom says you like to be miserable."

Dan looked at Ked. "Do you think telling me that is going to make me think better of your mother?"

Ked shrugged. "I guess not."

A very determined-looking boy of two or three went past dragging a reluctant stroller, seemingly already aware of the great responsibilities life held in store.

"So why are you telling me? Do you want me to move away?"

"No, but it might make you think about what's bothering you so much."

Dan stopped to consider his son for a moment. "Should I be paying you for this advice?"

Ked smiled. "Nah. You couldn't afford me anyway."

"Smart-ass." He gave Ked a loose punch on the shoulder. "So how am I doing with this father-son heart-to-heart thing?"

"Pretty good."

"What else does your mother say about me?"

Ked paused. Dan could see the lightning flashes of thought flitting over his face, wanting to say whatever it was and wanting not to hurt him at the same time. "She says you're unforgiving."

Dan considered how to answer. Was it true? All that came to mind was a question: "Do you think I am?"

Ked looked away. He took so long to speak that Dan thought he might not answer. "I'm just afraid that one day I'll piss you off and you'll stop loving me, too."

Dan placed a hand gently on the back of his son's neck and pulled him closer. "That will never happen."

Ked looked up. "Promise?"

Dan nodded. "That's one thing I promise. It will never happen."

"Okay," Ked said uncertainly.

SEVENTEEN

Meet John Doe

THE BLINDS IN MARTIN'S OFFICE were drawn, the desk lamps pointed down in little penumbras of shade and brightness, as though he'd a developed a light sensitivity. Dan waited for an explanation, though none was forthcoming. He turned down the offer of water and proceeded to describe his break-up with Bill, weaving in strands of the conversation with Donny in which he'd nearly ended their friendship.

As always, he was leery of how much to tell Martin. Was it just paranoia that whispered in his ear and said Martin might label him a psychopath or a menace to society? As Dan's psychiatrist, he'd been granted the authority to judge Dan's ability to function at his work. Maybe that extended to other areas in his life, like his suitability as a father. He imagined Martin standing at the gates of Auschwitz, pointing to various doorways: a set of twins directed to the left for experimentation, others to the right for a more succinct end. Though maybe that wasn't fair. Perhaps Martin wasn't the monster Dan believed him to be, but he wasn't willing to take the chance. That he exhibited not a single sign of having emotions while isolating and observing emotions in others made him suspect. It was people like Martin who inspired books like *Blade Runner*.

Dan brought up his concern for Bill, explaining how he'd struggled to understand what Bill was going through being in love with his best friend while attempting to maintain a relationship with Dan. He thought Martin might award him a gold star for his efforts, as he had when he tried to get Dan to understand Ralph's needs.

For once, Martin didn't ask Dan how he felt about the situation. Instead, he said, "That's a lot of responsibility you place on your shoulders — anticipating other people's needs as well as your reaction to them. Are you trying to be perfect?"

Hardly, thought Dan. *No one going for a good behaviour award would have done what I did afterwards.* "No, I'm far from perfect. I have no illusions there. I bashed in a filing cabinet, remember."

Martin scribbled something in his book. Was he marking the reference to the incident as mocking or simply noting that Dan had a sense of humour about it? He looked up. "Do you think you might be trying to make up for your perceived lack of perfection?"

"How is that?"

"You said Bill was particularly hard to please, ergo, you were never able to function to his satisfaction. You probably saw yourself as imperfect in Bill's eyes...."

Dan interrupted. "I think Bill saw everyone as imperfect in Bill's eyes. I never thought that was my fault."

Martin smiled his patient smile, the one he wore when he wanted to coax Dan toward a conclusion of some sort. "Was there another relationship in your past where you tried to please a man who couldn't or wouldn't be pleased by anything you did?"

"I tried to make my father love me."

"But you failed, didn't you?"

"Miserably."

"Because — as far as you believe — your father never loved you."

Dan nodded.

"But you won't accept that perhaps your father was incapable of love. You prefer to take on the responsibility for his lack of affection toward you."

"Maybe. Does it matter now?"

Martin's pencil poised over the pad. "It might help if you saw that Bill is another version of your father: a man impossible to please."

Dan looked at the clock — twenty-five minutes left — then glanced at the framed diploma in psychiatry awarded to Martin Sanger. Googling his therapist in the early days of their sessions, along with a list of publication titles to his credit, Dan had come across the German translation for Martin's last name: *pincer*. He envisioned a giant set of pliers tugging at the neurons in his brain. "Yes, I can see the connection," he said.

Martin leaned forward. "Do you think that might be why you get angry with Ralph when he messes the floor or why you dent filing cabinets with your fists when something goes wrong at work? Is that why you want to cut off your closest friend when he tells you the truth about yourself?

You want everyone around you to be perfect, because otherwise you feel you can't love them."

With a chill, Dan remembered his son's words in the park: *I'm just afraid that one day I'll piss you off and you'll stop loving me, too.*

Martin looked pleased, as though he'd just inserted the last tile in a ten-thousand-piece jigsaw puzzle, completing the image of a damaged man unable to express love. Dan wouldn't give him that satisfaction.

"Is that what you think, Martin?"

Martin's eye blinked, a lizard sunning itself on a rock. "I'm asking you."

Dan swallowed. "I don't have an opinion," he lied.

He wanted to say, *Don't think you know me,* to this grotesque impersonation of a man bent over his notepad beneath his Mondrian reproduction. Wasn't it Mondrian who despised nature? Hated trees?

Dan wondered about the others who sat in this chair revealing or hiding themselves from this man and his bloodless, probing intellect — a collection of damaged beings going through the motions of expressing their desires and fears, before letting themselves out the big doors to stand deflated in the hallway beside the elevator that never came. Before returning to the other world — the real world — where theories did nothing to piece together the shattered bits of themselves. The depressed, the despairing, and the broken: women whose spouses beat them, adult children of alcoholics who went through life feeling unworthy and unloved, the emotionally distraught. How did sitting here for this hour do anything to help? When they left, their time up, did they leave a residue of pain and disappointment, an invisible trail leading all the way from this chair down the hall? Did any of them think it a virtue to sit and suffer over all this? Perhaps Martin gave out badges after it was all over, and they'd divulged all there was to divulge. A little something to say, "I suffered." Maybe, Dan thought, he could ask for a bumper sticker instead. What would Martin scribble in his little binder if he said that?

In the daytime, Bill had begun to revert to a bad memory, a sour taste on the tongue. Yet each morning on awakening, Dan's first thoughts were of loss. He found it difficult to drag himself out of bed and suspected he was fighting a lingering depression over the split. He knew nothing would help get him through it but time — preferably time spent alone.

Ked was long past needing Dan's help to get ready for school. Dan found the signs of his son's passing each morning: the dog leash hung over the banister, a cereal bowl and spoon washed and left in the dish rack, the newspaper dropped on the side table in the hall. These were Ked's morning footprints. For such a big kid, he took up relatively little space.

The days went by in a whirl of strategy meetings and negotiations with despairing or difficult clients. Dan hadn't expected to hear from either Bill or Thom, so he was surprised to find on his desk an application bearing the name Killingworth. Not Lucille, Thom, or Ted, but Craig. Someone wanted him to make an inquiry into the disappearance of Lucille Killingworth's missing husband.

The name of a solicitor was prominent, but there was no client named, nothing to say who'd requested the search. Dan flipped through the file. Was this Lucille Killingworth's way of getting the better of him, by hiring him publicly after he'd turned her down privately? Could she be that stubborn or foolish to think he could be bought? If so, he was happy to show her otherwise.

He read over the letter — not yellow parchment this time — and pressed the intercom. His boss came on the line. Ed Burch was a straight-talking, no-nonsense retired cop who never took no for an answer. "What are the chances?" That's all Ed ever asked. And then you were off on your own. He'd been the first to congratulate Dan for becoming a single gay dad. To Ed, the word "limitation" didn't exist.

"It came through a solicitor," was Ed's reply. "That's all I can tell you. Why?"

"I know these people," Dan said. "I don't like them. I don't want to take this one on."

"It has your name on it, Danny. The client specifically asked for you."

"Well, tell them I'm not avail —"

His boss cut him off. "I can't do that. You start things in motion and I'll look into it once you've got it going. If I can, I'll put someone else on it then."

"And if not?"

"If not, we'll see."

Dan knew his options were limited. He was still doing penance for denting the filing cabinet. He felt like a schoolboy who'd been caught writing naughty words on the blackboard. He'd have to keep his fingers clean until someone else did something worse and his little indiscretion faded from memory.

He buzzed Sally, who came in wearing a sky blue sundress, orange loafers, and a violet kerchief. Not colourless.

She stood waiting for orders. Dan wasn't sure where to start. Most of his cases involved searches for people who'd disappeared within recent memory. Cases where he could start by asking the client about the last time they'd seen the misper. What did anyone expect him to find after more than twenty years?

"Check with the Picton OPP. They should still have the original files. You can tell Detective Constable Peter Saylor I requested this."

Sally was scribbling on her pad.

"Also check with Toronto police. Tell them I want to look at their John Doe files from the time. Canada-wide. Especially anything that's not online. You can give them the specs, but tell them not to narrow things down too far. They can leave that to me. I'm sure the report must have been filed in both places, even if he disappeared in Prince Edward County."

Sally went off, pen in hand, a rainbow in motion, leaving his door open.

Two days later he had Saylor's transcript of the original missing persons report on Craig Killingworth on his desk. The photograph showed an attractivex man in his late thirties or early forties: curly brown hair, a strong jaw, and intelligent eyes with a serious set. The kind of man you wouldn't hesitate to ask directions of or maybe even buy a used car from, if the price was right. A charmer. Thom had obviously inherited his good looks from both sides of the family.

Some of the facts about the case seemed unremarkable; others merited a second look. Dan was intrigued to learn that at the time of his disappearance Lucille Killingworth had had a restraining order imposed against her husband for assault and uttering a death threat. On her testimony, Killingworth had been suspended from his job as principal of a local high school after spending a night in jail. He'd also been ordered not to make contact with his sons on the grounds that he posed a potential threat to his boys. He'd disappeared before the case made it to court.

It was a heady read. The file gave an address in nearby Bloomfield, ten minutes out of Picton, as Craig Killingworth's last known residence. He'd lived there for two months estranged from his family until his disappearance, the exact day of which was unclear. It had eventually been narrowed down to the weekend of November 1–2, right after his appearance on the Friday at the Picton Courthouse when a date had been set for his trial. At that hearing, Killingworth tried unsuccessfully to have visiting rights to his sons reinstated. On his wife's testimony, the court upheld the original order.

The report compiled by Picton OPP in the weeks following his disappearance created a portrait of a methodical man. All his bills had been paid, including his rent in advance, for the next two months. His pre-furnished residence had been orderly and recently cleaned. The bed was made, dishes washed, and an empty travel case tucked behind a door.

Apart from a photograph of his sons and a handful of books stacked carefully on a shelf, there'd been few personal items. There were no signs of trouble or a break-in. The only thing missing was a bicycle; it had disappeared the same weekend Killingworth was believed to have vanished. The report confirmed that a number of locals had seen him cycling on the highway between Bloomfield and Picton on several occasions in the weeks prior to his disappearance.

Dan wondered why a wealthy man would be riding a bicycle. He read on. The Glenora ferryboat captain, Terry Piers, stated that Craig Killingworth had made the trip over to Adolphustown on his bicycle on the afternoon of Saturday, November 1. He hadn't returned. Because of the sighting, and the court restriction against seeing his family, the report concluded that Craig Killingworth had headed past Adolphustown and cycled east to Kingston. Whether he'd disappeared by choice or by chance was anybody's guess.

Several additional sightings of Craig Killingworth were made in the weeks and months following his disappearance. None turned up any substantial leads. A month later, a second report looked briefly into the suggestion that Killingworth's disappearance might have been the result of foul play. Mention was made of a gardener employed at the Killingworth home a few months before Killingworth's disappearance, not long before charges were laid against him by his wife. According to the report, Craig Killingworth had fired the gardener on suspicion of theft. An anonymous writer suggested in bold script that Killingworth's disappearance might have been the result of an act of revenge by the gardener. A subsequent note, appended in a different hand, argued that Killingworth had more likely given up on his efforts to clear his reputation, abandoning home and family to start over elsewhere.

A statement by family members included a plea by Craig's sister, Clare, that he get in touch with his family, as well as a tersely worded comment from fifteen-year-old

Theodore Killingworth to the effect that his father was "a liar." The table of contents listed a third document noted only as M.H. Dan looked through all the papers, but it seemed to have gone missing or never to have made it into the larger file. Nor was there anything to suggest who or what M.H. might be.

He buzzed Sally. She entered clutching a large manila envelope. Dan pointed at the paragraph mentioning the fired gardener.

"Find a name for that person — that's who I want to talk to."

Sally squinted at the file and took note of the reference.

"And this one here." He pointed at the name of the ferryboat captain. "See if you can locate either of them."

"Will do. Now my turn," she said, tapping the thick envelope in her arms. "Here are the John Does from that time." She dropped it on his desk and smiled. "Have fun."

The Doe files were the saddest, most dismal collection of human relics Dan could ever have imagined. If there was anything more degrading than to end up strangled in an industrial park, stabbed beneath a bridge or fished from a river wearing concrete shoes, it was to find that no one was interested in claiming your remains or learning who you'd been. Not one thing in your life stood out enough for anyone to want to trace your steps and reconnect you with your past, with the people who had given birth to you, reared and loved you. Not one.

Dan was familiar enough with the Doe files. What struck him was how generic most of the facial reconstructions were or how unlikely it was that anyone, even those who'd known the dead person intimately, might actually find a resemblance between the faces drawn, sculpted and recreated by computers, or sense a sliver of recognition between these humanoid images and the people they were supposed to represent. On the other hand, a few were so sharply portrayed and with so much circumstantial evidence noted — rare blood types, unusual scars, and dental records, even handmade clothing — it seemed improbable that they hadn't been recognized: the buck-toothed boy with a bowl-shaped haircut found wearing a cap available from only one store in the county, or the young woman buried beneath a construction site and mummified so that her remains had barely altered in twenty years, with severe scarring to her left hip, probably from a car accident. How was it they had never been identified?

The only probable reason was that someone didn't want them found. In all likelihood, the reports had never been filed and the searches never begun. But if so, where were the grandmothers missing grandchildren, the husbands missing wives, and sisters missing brothers? Only a concerted conspiracy of silence by friends and family could have left them unnamed and unclaimed. For every one who vanished, Dan reasoned, there had to be between four and forty people who would notice sooner or later.

He could never shake off a sense of futility when he went through those files, thinking of all the faces that might never be identified, all the lives that would never be reconnected with their pasts. Some had wanted to vanish, true enough, and that's exactly what they'd done. But had they really meant it to be forever?

New technology and improved networking between agencies sharing databases sometimes made identification possible decades later. The DNA retrieved when the bodies were first recovered might no longer be usable, but if the remains were exhumed then experts could take fresh samples that would respond to modern testing. Sometimes it was just a matter of diligence and old-fashioned stick-to-it-ness. Other times, it seemed a wasted effort. You never knew. Often families didn't come forward for years then suddenly, for one reason or another, they did. Files were crosschecked with other files and it became a simple matter of matching a name to a photograph. It could be surprisingly simple.

It kept Dan up nights wondering why families waited so long to report a missing relative. The reasons varied. Sometimes the misper had a habit of disappearing and it was assumed they wanted to stay lost. Others had a criminal record and the family believed they would only make things worse by looking for them. Then years went by without word, and it began to dawn on them that perhaps their son or daughter was no longer alive. Still others turned up alive years later — sometimes decades — and at last spoke about threats of violence or the trauma of an unwanted child. You just never knew.

But there was one thing Dan knew: once asked, the questions didn't go away just because they went unanswered. They hung around and festered, especially when you looked at them too closely. It was easy to obsess over unsolved clues, like the faded handwriting on a piece of paper that refused to yield up its secrets or a lake on a mountain that obscured its origins.

No reply, no return. These were words Dan found unacceptable. Because they meant that somewhere someone wasn't trying hard enough.

"The gardener's name was Magnus Ferguson. He showed up on one other report…."

"Unusual name, Magnus."

"… so it shouldn't be too hard to find." Sally smiled. "It wasn't. Last known address: Surrey, B.C., about five years ago." She stood before his desk, pad in hand, waiting.

Dan felt that tingle of excitement that came when something suddenly appeared within reach. Sometimes things took years to budge then suddenly the floodgates opened and it seemed as though they'd always been there, just waiting to be discovered. A single piece of thread that had seemed innocuous at the time might turn out to be a special material manufactured by only one company and sold in just a handful of locations. And suddenly you had a piece of a puzzle that unlocked a significant clue.

"Did you phone to verify that it's the same person?"

Sally shook her head. "There's no Magnus Ferguson listed in all of B.C. I didn't have time to check the rest of the country…."

"But you will."

She groaned.

"And you'll have it for me by when?"

She grinned. "Probably by the time you get back from seeing the ferryboat captain in Picton. I've booked you an appointment for tomorrow."

"Sweet," Dan said. "When and where?"

"Two p.m." She looked down at her pad. "It's got an unusual name," she said. "Ever hear of the Murky Turkey?"

Dan smiled. "Sally, I'm promoting you. You can stop cleaning chamber pots and start sharpening pencils effective immediately."

He drove along the same route he and Bill had taken to the wedding. The ghostly forms that had been obscured by mist then were revealed now, innocent and unprepossessing in the fresh light of day. A simple fall landscape, seemingly devoid of mystery.

He was early. He reached Picton at noon. He thought over his plan again and continued on to Lake on the Mountain. He parked in the same lot and sat looking out over the water before walking to the resort.

"I'd like to rent a boat," Dan said to the man puttering around in the garden shoring up trellises.

The man gave him a sharp look. "What sort of boat would that be?"

"A boat to explore the lake," Dan said.

The man grinned. "Well, that should be simple then. We've only got one kind. It's a rowboat. You looking for a good workout for your arms?"

Dan smiled. "A little exercise never hurt."

The man left his trellises and went inside. Five minutes later, standing beside the boat, the man sized Dan up and offered him an orange life vest. "Keep this thing on at all times when you're in the boat — it's the law."

Dan placed it over his head and secured it around his chest.

"Can you swim?"

"Yes, I can."

"All right, then I won't worry about you." The man held up an orange plastic capsule. "There's a nylon rope and a whistle in here. You run into any trouble, you blow it as loud as she can blow. I usually rent them for an hour," he glanced over at the parking lot, empty but for Dan's car, "though I suppose you can take your time. I'll tell the crowds to wait till you get back."

Dan did a wonky duck waddle getting in, then settled in his seat and pressed an oar against the shore. The boat shifted off the rocky bottom. After a few tentative strokes, he found his rhythm and the craft surged forward.

He scanned the caramel-coloured rock passing underneath him. Without warning, darkness opened wide under the boat. Dan had the sensation that he'd jumped off a cliff, his fall arrested by the placid green surface of the water. The darkness went straight down with no sign of anything below. He peered into the depths, adjusting his vision, but saw nothing. It looked bottomless.

He turned his head and glanced up at the passing clouds then shifted in his seat and resumed rowing toward the middle of the lake. He couldn't shake the sensation that the world had fallen away beneath him.

The Black Swan winked at him as he approached. It looked no different than it had a month earlier. Not surprising — it probably hadn't changed much in the last hundred-and-twenty-five-odd years. Dan spotted Terry Piers right off, a grey-haired man in a heavy grey-and-orange sweater, sitting upright at the bar and talking non-stop. A wrinkled smile and periwinkle eyes greeted him. Dan felt the strength in his grip, heard the thunder in his tone. Captain Bligh on shore leave. An eye patch and a tri-cornered hat were all he needed to complete the picture. Hale and hearty at seventy or more, he'd probably see a hundred before he was done, without giving up either smoke or drink. In fact, they probably fortified him.

Dan ordered a pint of Glenora. The former captain pooh-poohed him for buying that "local crap" before lifting his glass to a portrait of Elizabeth II on the wall behind him. It was the young queen, very glam, around the time of her coronation: glowing, radiant. Long before she was side-swiped by her *annus horribilis* and her star-struck wretch of a daughter-in-law. Dan let Terry regale him with talk of the "old days" on the ferry watch before launching into the subject of his inquiry.

When he spoke Craig Killingworth's name, Terry grew thoughtful. "Oh, yes, I remember him," he said softly.

"In the report on his disappearance you said he went over to Adolphustown on his bike that weekend but didn't return."

"That's right."

"And you were sure it was him?"

"Aye. Not a doubt."

"And was he carrying anything — luggage, or any sort of baggage?"

"I don't believe so."

"But you said you thought he was heading for Kingston?"

"Well, not exactly." Terry scratched his head and looked off into the distance of time, as if to remember what it was he had said. "You see, if you were heading to Toronto or anywheres west of here, you'd head north up to the 401. If you were to take the ferry across to Adolphustown, well, from there you'd be travelling east to Kingston and the like. But only if you wanted to go that far. What I said was that if he didn't come back, then he was probably headed that way or farther."

Dan considered this. "Could he not have come back across in a car?" he asked. "He might not have been on his bicycle. Perhaps you didn't see him in the back of a car?"

"No sir, that is not likely. Have you been on the ferry?"

Dan recalled the outdoor deck with its three short lanes and twenty-one-car capacity. "Yes."

"Then you know it's small and everything's in the open. For one thing, I could see anyone inside those vehicles. For another, I knew him well enough by sight. If he came across on the ferry without me seeing him, well then he'd have to be tied up in a trunk."

"And you're sure of the date you said you saw him crossing on?"

"Absolutely sure. You see, we were keeping a log to chart the sort of traffic that came across. There was only one other bicycle that weekend, come across from Adolphustown later that evening, and it wasn't him."

"You're sure it wasn't him?"

"Absolutely."

"I don't mean to doubt you, but why are you so sure? I mean, if it was nighttime — a hood or a cap, the darkness. It might be hard to be certain."

"But I was certain. For two reasons," Terry began. "As I said, I knew Craig Killingworth on sight. Well enough, you'd say, though I couldn't have called him a friend. But his face was known around town. And at that time he'd lived here many years. It's a small enough place, and you know who you know real well."

And a wealthy man would always be known, Dan thought, though he didn't voice his assumption.

"He was a very friendly man," Terry continued. "He'd always call out to you on the street, say hello, ask about the weather, that sort of thing. You know how it is in small towns — or I'm sure you can guess, if you don't."

Funny, Dan thought, *how the rich and the dead are always exalted in their eulogies.* Men who assaulted their wives and abandoned their families were remembered for a friendly greeting on the street, while for the most part the abuse and threats went unrecorded. He smiled. "So if he'd gone across on the ferry, you'd have no doubt he would have greeted you."

"As I said…."

"But you said there was a second reason you were sure it wasn't him you saw returning with the bicycle."

"And I was coming around to that." Terry winked. "In my own fashion, of course."

Dan waited as Terry took a quaff of his beer and set the glass down.

"The other reason I am sure it wasn't Craig Killingworth I saw with the bicycle that night was because it wasn't a man. It was a youngster. Last run over on the ferry but one." Terry looked triumphant.

Dan thought it over. "Did you recognize the kid?" he said at last.

Terry shook his head. "Afraid not."

†

He had one final stop. He drove back along the parkway to the OPP detachment on Schoharie Road. Inside the long grey bowling alley, flanked on either side by an empty parking lot, Dan's name elicited an immediate response. Saylor came through the door, pressed smartly into his uniform, greeting him as though he were a long-lost friend.

He ushered Dan into a spacious office the colour of unfired pottery. A policeman's sanctuary. He'd covered his walls with posters, handwritten notices of crimes, some recent and others from long ago, alongside the Xeroxed faces of people wanted in connection with any number of incidents. Some of the reprobates scowled at the camera while others smiled, seeming to enjoy their little moment of notoriety. The usual detritus of police station life.

Saylor was clearly glad for the interruption in his routine, where Dan might find himself pressed to make even a fifteen-minute opening in his day. Small town-big town, he mused. That was the difference. In smaller places you had time for people, even if they were casual acquaintances.

"Good to see you, buddy. What brings you out here?"

"Just passing by," Dan said. "I thought I'd drop in and say hello."

"You got the file I sent you?" Saylor asked.

"Yes, I did," Dan said. "Thanks for being so prompt. I'm looking into it now." He paused. "I take it there's been nothing further on the Ballancourt case?"

Saylor looked at Dan curiously. "No. It's still closed. Were you expecting a change of direction on it?"

Dan affected an in-confidence tone. "Am I the only one to think it was awfully convenient for Lucille Killingworth to have a judge around to back up the claim of death by misadventure?"

Saylor shrugged. "The thought occurred to me." His expression brightened. "I still think my theory was pretty ingenious."

A knock came at Saylor's door. A head poked in, white-haired, intense. Dan recognized him immediately. It was the serious-looking man who'd danced with Lucille Killingworth on the boat the night of the wedding. The man with barracuda eyes.

"Oh, my apologies," he said. He didn't seem to recognize Dan. "I'll come back later, Pete."

Before Saylor could introduce them, he'd vanished around the door. Dan waited a beat then tried for casual. "Who was that?"

"That's Commissioner Burgess," Saylor said, grinning. "The big shiny brass in this small town."

"I think he was at the wedding," Dan said nonchalantly.

"Yeah." Saylor kept his voice low. "He's a friend of Lucille Killingworth's."

Dan nodded. "Can we step out for a coffee somewhere?"

The Royal Café in downtown Picton was another holdover from Victorian times. A tin ceiling held onto its silver paint, but only barely. Large flaps hung down here and there, as though the sky had given way.

"Shoot," said Saylor. "It's free to talk in here." He turned his head to the back of the café, where an older woman stood wiping cake crumbs off a table. "Maggie's deaf," he said with a wink.

"That file you sent me — did you check to see if it was intact before it went to the courier?"

Saylor looked at him. "I never even thought to look," he said. "Wasn't it all there?"

Dan shook his head. "Most of it, but there was one document missing."

"Any idea what was in it?"

"It was labelled M.H. Possibly someone's initials. Maybe a clerk's. My guess is it had something to do with the assault charges Lucille Killingworth filed against her husband. I was hoping you could take a second look for me."

Saylor looked perplexed. "I'll try," he said, "but I sent everything there was. I can get one of the junior officers to look around and see if it was misfiled, but I wouldn't hold out much hope. It was in a bunch of boxes that got shuffled off to a storage unit more than ten years ago. I had to get special permission to open it." He shrugged again. "I don't know what to tell you."

Dan was silent for a moment. He looked up at Saylor. "Did you ever meet Craig Killingworth?"

"No," Saylor said. "But my brother went to the high school where Craig was principal. I remember there was some scandal and he disappeared for a few months in the middle of a school year. Then came the assault charges and he lost his job. Suspended, actually. It shocked a lot of people." His tone became reflective. "You never know about people — the secrets they hide."

"I guess not," Dan said.

"Last month I got called to a place just outside town. A mechanic, one of the toughest guys around, hanged himself in his barn. Of all the people you might expect to commit suicide, he wouldn't be anywhere near the top of my list."

"You're right," Dan said. "You never know. I'm curious though, why was a rich guy like Killingworth working as a school principal?"

Saylor's face frowned in concentration. "I guess because it was her money," he said. "I think she expected him to earn his keep." He stopped and looked over at the counter. "Maggie!" he called in a loud voice.

The old woman looked up. "Yes, Pete? Did you call?"

"I did, Maggie. I'm just wondering if you remember the Killingworths."

"Who?"

"Killingworths," he said, even louder. "The husband disappeared about twenty years ago. He was the school principal."

"Oh, yes!" she said, her face suddenly transformed by memory. "Other side of the reach."

"Rich family, weren't they?" Saylor asked.

The woman nodded slowly. "Oh, yes," she concurred. "It was her father's money. Nathaniel Macaulay. I don't think you'd remember him. It was Nate's great-great-great-grandfather who founded Picton. The Reverend William Macaulay. With a Crown grant of four hundred acres. I'm surprised you don't remember your local history, Pete. Nathaniel must have died twelve, fifteen years ago. Something like that. You could check on the gravestone if you wanted. He's buried up the road at St. Mary Magdalene."

"Thanks, Maggie."

She turned back to her work.

"There you have it," Saylor said. He checked his watch. "I'd better be getting back before I'm missed."

Out on the street, he shook hands with Dan. "Are you single, by the way?" He winked. "I could set you up with my brother."

Dan grinned in embarrassment. "Thanks, but I'm not on the market at present."

"Too bad," Saylor said. "For him, anyway." He nodded to a young couple passing on the sidewalk before turning back to Dan. "Just a word of warning," he said. "It's a small town here. Watch your back while you're snooping around. Especially with Commissioner Burgess a friend of Mrs. Killingworth."

"Warning noted," Dan said. "Thanks for everything. I'll be in touch."

"And thanks for coming by," Saylor said, as though it was Dan who had done him the favour.

Sally gave him a glum look on his return the following morning. She'd retired the blue, orange, and violet for an all-black outfit. She was a veritable Queen of the Night, with a stroke of magenta eye shadow. Mourning or colour fatigue, it was hard to say. She sighed and plunked her notebook onto his desk. Dan glanced up, trying not to look amused by this expression of exasperation.

"I can't find him anywhere," she said.

"Who?" Dan said, playing dumb.

"Oh, great! You don't even remember what you asked me to find for you."

"Fill me in," Dan said.

"I can tell you without doubt there is not a single Magnus Ferguson listed with any public telephone directory in the entire country," she said. "I have now checked the records dating back ten years." Dan whistled. "Not only that, I've also called all one hundred and fifty of the 'M. Fergusons' listed and not one of them claims to be or to know a 'Magnus.' And now, if you don't mind, I'd prefer to go back to cleaning chamber pots."

He laughed as she flounced out of his room and then turned right back around. "Oh yeah — and this very creepy guy has been trying to get hold of you since yesterday. He refuses to leave a message." She placed a name and number on his desk and left.

Larry Fiske. Dan didn't recognize the name. He dialled the number and reached the reception desk at the firm of Fiske and Travis. Dan was put through immediately. Fiske identified himself as a lawyer representing the Killingworth family. Of course, this was the mysterious "Larry" that Thom and his mother had discussed during their meeting with Dan. Finally, Dan thought, he was going to be told Lucille had hired him to find her missing husband. He had more than a few questions, and was still undecided whether or not he'd willingly continue with the request to find Craig Killingworth.

"Mr. Sharp, I'm told you have been very loyal to the Killingworth family."

That had been Lucille Killingworth's phrase, Dan recalled. He needed to make clear his position once and for all. "Mr. Fiske, I would not describe my actions as being loyal to the Killingworths," he said slowly. "When I met with Lucille and Thom last month I was simply doing them a favour. In a personal capacity."

"I'm very glad to hear that," Larry went on. "So are you taking on the case?"

"I'm considering it, yes."

"Then I have to advise you that the Killingworth family would take exception to your decision if you choose to take on that request. Craig Killingworth's disappearance twenty years ago caused his family considerable grief, which they have since managed to get over. They would not want all that stirred up again. They would also not take kindly to having you turn against them now."

Dan was completely thrown. If they didn't want him to take on the case, then who did? His tongue suddenly got stuck to the roof of his mouth. "In what capacity are you advising me, Mr. Fiske?"

"In a personal one."

He oozed unctuousness. Dan decided he would hate this guy if he ever met him.

"Perhaps it's a good time to mention that it has come to my attention there's some question of attempted rape in connection with you and a guest of the Killingworths...."

Dan exploded. "What?"

Larry went on as though he hadn't been interrupted. "... as well as a question of intent to spread the HIV virus. I'm sure you know what I'm talking about. If a test shows you to be HIV-positive, you could be up on charges of attempted murder."

"Who's going to order me to take an HIV-test?"

"You know very well that it's within the jurisdiction of any court, should the matter come to that."

There was silence on the other end. Dan felt his heart galloping a path through his stomach, but he wasn't going to let a lawyer get the better of him. "Don't try to bully me, Mr. Fiske. And don't insult my intelligence. I'm obviously smarter than you."

"Really?" Fiske's voice dripped disdain. "How do you figure that?"

"Simple — because I'm not a lawyer. And if anything, I'm the one who should be worried about catching something."

"Yes, Mr. Sharp. You probably should be very worried. I'll leave you with those thoughts."

The call clicked off.

"Son-of-a-fucking bitch!" Dan snarled. His hand shook as he forced himself not to bang the receiver down. His mouth was dry. He tried to marshal his thoughts. Things were definitely getting out of hand. And worse, what he'd assumed about being hired to find Craig Killingworth was totally false. The mystery was spreading, with no sign of who wanted Killingworth found.

Dan thought back to the report. Craig Killingworth had disgraced himself in his hometown and in the eyes of his family, then got on his bicycle and — what? Been hit by a car and died? Committed a crime and scrammed? Or simply started a new life for himself without looking back? All of these were possible. Sometimes locating a missing person seemed like taking a multiple-choice exam. Other times it felt like digging through the rubble to find something you only suspected was there, if it wasn't in one of a thousand other places.

Sometimes, with a few known facts, it was like a recipe. Put in all the ingredients, including a few conjectured ones, stir round and round, and *voila!* — a cake — though in this case a particularly inedible one. Dan smiled at his analogy. He'd try it out on his boss one day. When he'd cleared himself of the filing cabinet incident. When his boss regained a sense of humour. Okay, maybe not. And — oh yes! — don't forget the missing ingredient: *I have to advise you that the Killingworth family would take exception to your decision if you choose to take on that request.* That was the icing on the cake. Maybe Lucille Killingworth did not want her husband found. Why? Did she have something to hide?

Dan looked over the information Sally had left on his desk. He turned to his computer and checked flight schedules then pressed the intercom button. His boss answered. "Good morning, Daniel."

"Good morning, Ed. It's about the Killingworth case.…"

"I haven't had time to think about who I might be able to spare."

"It's okay," Dan cut him off. "I don't want you to replace me. I've decided to stay on with it. If that's all right."

He heard his boss give a confused chuckle. "Yes — by all means. It's fine with me. More than fine."

"Good," Dan said. "In fact," he checked his watch, "I'm off in about three hours to catch a plane to B.C. to follow up on a lead there."

"Fascinating. Enjoy the weather."

"I'll be sure to do that."

EIGHTEEN

Islands in the Strait

FROM THE WINDOWS OF THE PLANE, the green span of Lion's Gate Bridge glinted in the sunlight. Below, the city was a quilt of urban crosshatches rolled up against the mountains and edged down to the sea. For the first time in weeks, Dan felt a sense of relief. Maybe it was just the rush of flying, the release of escape. Flight brought a sense of endless possibility, of life lived elsewhere than the city he'd planned and failed to leave every year for the last ten years. (Then again, he reminded himself, it always felt a little like failure to think he might actually leave it for good.) Or it may have been his proximity to Trevor, the Mayne Island Hermit, whom he hadn't yet made up his mind to see. It wouldn't do to get Trevor's hopes up if things were suddenly to take him elsewhere. The vicissitudes of fate did not smile favourably upon chance love affairs in strange cities. The gardener he'd come to find might prove not to be here after all, putting an abrupt end to his trip. Still, a call at least was in order: *Hello, I'm here. Goodbye again.* But what was the point?

Beneath them, the Earth turned while the plane resisted gravity. For the moment he was a pirate, an Old World explorer circling the new one, with endless opportunities stretched out below. And in those limitless seconds of suspension, right up until the moment the wheels touched ground and life resumed its expected course, it seemed as though anything could happen.

They were over the Strait of Georgia. Below, the Earth lay fractured in a myriad broken pieces. Mayne Island was one of them, a soft bed to land in. The dying light gave the islands a magical cast, their dismembered outlines surrounded by silvery moats and darkening shorelines.

Surrey, on the other hand, was anything but magical. It was tawdry and squalid, though unlike other urban disasters this one wore its squalor with a sort of hometown pride. B.C.'s moderate climate and reputation as a haven for drug users had created an underclass of addicts and an attendant criminal fringe element. The push to ready Vancouver for the Olympics had unsettled its transient population, and many had migrated to the tidal plains to the south.

Picking up his rental car at the airport, Dan watched a wreck of a man scouring the asphalt for cigarette butts. The ride got grimmer the closer he got. Surrey made the unseemly parts of Toronto look like a picnic basket on a checkered tablecloth. He stopped for directions at a 7-Eleven. A Native woman approached him holding a can of Schlitz, tab clicked open. She held it out, her expression childlike. "Drink?"

"No thanks."

"What's your story, honey?" she asked.

"No story — just looking for directions."

She smiled hopefully. "You want directions to my place?"

Dan shook his head.

"I got beer," she said.

"I can see that. Thanks anyway."

His hotel lobby was bright and cheerful, but the effect ended there. A doughy young man handed Dan his keys and pointed down a dim hallway with a carpet one shade away from dog vomit. It bulged when he stepped on it, as though he were walking on something alive. Irregular stains indicated either an errant house pet or water leakage. He looked up. Sure enough, the ceiling bore telltale signs of dripping.

At first glance his room appeared fine, apart from a faint odour of wet fur that permeated everything. Dan opened his suitcase and hung up his clothes. Jet lag was hitting him in the back of the neck. At home it was already past midnight. He stripped off his shirt and pants and lay on the bed in his underwear. He looked up at a sudden sound. Ten feet outside his window, a very large woman appeared on a balcony and began to pull laundry from a line. She was backlit, dressed in a shift that emphasized her shapelessness. Dan crept sheepishly over and drew the curtains.

He thought of Bill and laughed, imagining his distaste at being stuck in such a place. Then he thought of Trevor again — so near, yet so far. He toyed with the idea of calling but decided against it. He watched part of a movie and a bit of news, then turned off the television and slept.

†

The neighbourhood would have been hard put to say it had seen better days. Nor did it look like it ever would. It was a shameless, almost desperate mismatching of poorly constructed warehouses, chemical plants, and odd-fitting homes with yards buried under debris that seemed like they'd never had the temerity to hope for anything better. Nor, in all likelihood, had its denizens.

Dan approached a row of townhouses that appeared to have survived a bombing blitz, but only barely, one of which bore the number listed as the last known address for Magnus Ferguson. The fenced-in front yard resembled a dustbin and suggested the wrecker's ball would not be far off. *To each his own,* Dan thought. He knocked, but no one answered. The stillness that came back might have been the stillness of a mausoleum.

A window lifted on the second floor of an attached house. A scruffy head poked out, little more than a skull with a wisp of grey fleece stretched over it. "Who is there?" called down a gap-toothed East Indian, a smile shifting his unshaven jowls.

"I'm looking for Magnus Ferguson," Dan said. "Do you know if he still lives here?"

The man chuckled. "Maggie? No, sir — he doesn't live here no more. I haven't seen him in years." He stopped to scratch his head. "He could be dead, for all I know." He smiled, as if the thought brought him some small comfort.

"Is there anyone else around who might know where he went?"

The man shook his head. "No, sir. If I don't know it, no one does. I see everything around here. Whatever goes on, I hear about it. I'm in the wheelchair, you see?" He lifted himself up by the arms and pressed closer to the sill, as if willing Dan to see the chair he claimed lay under him. His head and torso slumped back down.

Dan pulled a card from his pocket and held it up for the man to see. "My name's Sharp," he said. "Dan Sharp. I'm going to stick this under your door. I'll write my hotel number on it. If anything comes to mind, please call me."

"Sir, excuse me for asking, but does it pay?"

Dan looked up from where he'd knelt to insert the card. "It could," he said. "If it leads to anything, it could."

"I'll see, sir, if I can turn anything up for you." The man poked his head with a finger. "I am all the time having ideas."

"I'd be much obliged."

The second address turned out to be only blocks away, though Magnus Ferguson's tenancy there predated the other by more than a decade. A pair of raggedly dressed men lay on the steps, their legs barring the doorway. One was an older man, small and wiry. He looked like he'd lived a long time on the streets. The younger appeared to have a few years to go before he caught up with his companion.

Dan stopped in front of them. The younger man eyed him warily and motioned to his companion to let Dan pass.

"You a cop?" said the older man, making a half-hearted attempt to move out of Dan's way.

"No," said Dan.

"See," said the older man to the other. "He ain't gonna hurt ya." He put a hand out to touch Dan's leg. Dan stepped out of his reach.

"Don't touch him, man!" his companion said, spooked.

"I'm just being friendly," said the other.

"Okay, but don't touch him, man. He doesn't want to be touched."

"You two live here?" Dan asked, breaking up the pathetic charade.

The pair looked at one another, as though to get their story straight before answering. "Nah," said the young man, shaking his head. "We don't live around here."

Dan mentioned Magnus Ferguson, but the name drew a blank. "Thanks, then."

He took the stairs to the third floor. The hallway reeked of urine and years of accumulated neglect. There'd once been carpet laid down, but that had been ripped out and remnants of an adhesive left stuck to the concrete floor. He knocked on a faded blue door that opened almost immediately. A thin woman in a pink sweater stared at him. Stringy hair hung down past her shoulders. Dan would have been hard put to say if she were young or old. The smell of something meaty and slightly sour caught his nose.

She looked at him uncertainly. "Oh, I thought you were Mary," she said, tucking a brown strand behind one ear. Then, "Can I help you?"

"I'm looking for a former tenant, Mr. Magnus Ferguson," Dan said. "I believe he lived here a number of years ago."

She scrunched her brow and appeared to be thinking. "Doesn't sound familiar," she said, turning back to the room. "Mom? Do you remember a Magnus Ferguson used to live here?"

"Oh, yes," came the feeble reply. "He used to live down the hall when we first moved here. You were still a kid, though, so you wouldn't remember him likely."

"You're right, I don't," the woman called out over her shoulder. She turned back to Dan. "I don't remember him," she said with a shrug.

"Who's asking?" came the mother's voice.

"My name's Dan Sharp," he called over the pink shoulder. "I'm a missing persons investigator. Would you by any chance know where Mr. Ferguson moved to?"

"Let me think. I seem to recall he moved just a few streets away from here. I saw him once or twice after he moved."

Dan read out the address he'd just visited. "Would that be where he moved?"

"That sounds right," came the disembodied voice.

"He's not there now, but thank you." He wrote Magnus's name on the back of a card and gave it to the woman in the doorway. "Call me, please, if you or your mother think of anything else."

She scrutinized it then looked up. "Uh-huh. Okay. Will do." She smiled sadly and watched till he reached the end of the hallway before closing the door.

On the ground floor, the two derelicts were still lying on the doorstep. They looked up with glazed eyes at Dan's approach. He seemed to register with them briefly before they turned away again.

The doughy hotel clerk recognized him as he crossed the lobby. He hailed Dan and handed him a note. "I didn't want to miss you, sir," he said, as though he'd been waiting anxiously all afternoon for Dan's return.

"Thank you for being watchful," Dan said, tipping him.

He looked at the note: *Call Ahmed Rathnam ("guy in wheelchair"),* followed by a phone number.

"Hello, Ahmed, this is Dan Sharp. I got your message."

"Hello, sir. Good to hear from you. Mr. Sharp, I think I may have some information for you, sir."

"About Magnus Ferguson?"

"I have indeed, Mr. Sharp. I think you will be pleased. I have an address for you."

Dan's ears picked up at that. "Is it recent?"

The man laughed again. "Sir, I know it is recent."

"I'll be right over," Dan said.

He was at the man's door in fifteen minutes. Ahmed waved at him from the same window. He turned back to the room and Dan heard him call out. A moment later, a small boy opened the door and looked up with wide brown eyes.

"Come in, please."

Ahmed appeared at the top of the stairs in his wheelchair. "Sir, I think you will be pleased with what I have found for you. It is an address. A current address." He called out to the boy, who ran nimbly up the stairs and snatched a paper from his hand and back down again, handing it to Dan.

Dan read it over and looked up. "I'm grateful. Will fifty dollars compensate you for your troubles?"

The man bowed his head. "I humbly thank you."

"If you don't mind my asking — where did you get this?"

The man laughed. His index finger touched his forehead and pointed up. "I told you, sir, I am all the time having ideas. This woman comes to collect the mail once or twice a month. I sent my grandson Naveen out to find her and he came back with this."

"And this is where she sends his mail?"

Dan read the rural route and postal box number on Vancouver Island. There was no guarantee Magnus Ferguson would be there, but it merited a try. He might be seeing Trevor sooner rather than later.

"It is, sir. It is."

Dan handed the boy the reddish bill.

The boy grinned as he held it out before him. "Five-zero. Fifty. That's a lots of money!" he exclaimed.

"Yes, it is," Dan said. "Make sure your grandfather buys you something nice with it."

The boy nodded, smiling. "Oh, yes," he said. "Oh, yes! No more kurta pyjama. I want Game Boy!"

Out on deck, the engine's hum filled the air. A blurry moon burned a bone-white path along the darkened strait. Mountains loomed black on either side of the boat, deceptively close. Mayne Island was somewhere ahead. If Trevor sounded welcoming, Victoria could wait a day or two.

He flipped open his cell phone and dialled. Trevor's reassuring voice answered.

"Hi there, sexy guy."

There was a pause. "Dan?" The voice was hesitant.

"Correct. How are you?"

"Great! I'm really well, thanks! How are you?"

"I'm doing all right, too. I thought I'd call and say hi."

"Well, I'm glad you did. It's good to hear from you. It sounds really windy, by the way. Where are you?"

"Outside on my cell phone."

"It's nice to hear your voice."

"And yours. I've been thinking about you a lot lately."

Trevor laughed softly. "That's sweet. Though it would be nicer to hear you say it in person. I was serious when I said you could visit any time."

"I know. I've been thinking about that."

"So?" Trevor's tone was jocular, half-taunting. "When are you coming?"

Dan pretended to mull this over. "How does now sound?"

He heard Trevor laugh. "Now what?"

"How does right now sound for a visit?"

There was a pause. Dan waited. "Um, explain?"

"I'm on the ferry. I'll be berthing at Village Bay in fifteen minutes."

"*What?*"

"….and I sure hope there's a hotel on your island if you're too busy to see me."

"Is this for real?" The ferry's three-toned wail sounded over the engine's roar. "Oh my god!" Trevor exclaimed. "Are you really here?"

"How far are you from the terminal?"

"Ten minutes by foot, if I start now." He paused. "You're not kidding, are you? I mean, I hope you're not, you bastard."

"I never kid. See you soon." Dan clicked off and went back inside.

Dan couldn't remember ever having driven in such utter darkness. It could have been the blackness of death, deep and irrevocable. Here and there cottage windows glowed like fireflies, winking in and out between trees. Trevor talked excitedly all the way, pausing briefly to announce an upcoming turn Dan could barely make out. A long, narrow drive elbowed into the forest, turning perpendicularly before lurching upwards over rocks and weeds. High above, a roof jutted from a hilltop like a misplaced runway. Lights sheared off from the windows and into the trees.

"Even in the dark I can tell this is quite a piece of architecture," Dan said.

"Thanks. I designed it myself," Trevor said. "We have to park here and walk up."

The headlights died and everything disappeared outside the car.

"Sorry it's so dark," Trevor said, swinging the flashlight back and forth on the path ahead. "My garden lights stopped working last month."

They navigated the stone steps studding the hill. The climb brought them to a metal walkway spanning a gully and leading to the front door.

"In the daytime this gives a great view of the harbour," Trevor said. "You can stand here and see clear across to Pender Island."

At the door Dan waited for Trevor to step forward with the keys. "Go ahead — it's unlocked," Trevor said with a laugh. "It's always unlocked."

Dan put his bag down inside the entryway. Trevor scooped it up and trotted off with it. "I only have one bedroom, and you're sleeping in here with me," he said, "so don't get any ideas!"

"I wouldn't dream of it," Dan replied. "I didn't come all this way to sleep on a couch."

Three walls of windows flanked an open space whose ceiling sloped up at the far end. The blackness outside seemed to press in on them. Sleek lines and clean surfaces lent the interior a modern tone, but the old-fashioned feel of wood and tile kept it comfy and warm. Dan suspected it mirrored its owner's personality.

"You've done well," he said.

Trevor shrugged. "Back when I had a real job.…" He removed a bottle of wine from the fridge and held it up. "White okay?"

"Sounds great."

Trevor uncorked the bottle and set it on the counter. He looked at Dan with an odd smile. "I can't believe it."

"What can't you believe?"

"You. That you're here!"

Dan stood in the middle of the room. Trevor came over to him. The kiss started as a question but quickly turned insistent, the flat of Trevor's hand on his back urging Dan closer. Trevor broke it off with a sigh.

"Please — have a seat," he said, running around the cottage, switching off lights and pulling down shades.

Dan sat as Trevor stepped onto a back porch and returned with an armful of logs, stacking them in the fireplace. Flames reached up from rolled newspaper and kindling to the logs. Trevor's nervous energy seemed to be running down. He slid onto the couch beside Dan.

"I'm afraid to look too closely," he said. "I'm afraid this will turn out to be a dream and I'll wake up lonely again." His hand on Dan's neck drew them closer. "Kiss me again. If it's a dream, this will wake me."

Their lips met and withdrew. Trevor smiled. "Mmm … not a dream."

"You feel pretty real, too, I'm glad to say."

"Okay. What are you doing here? Have you come to live snuggly ever after with me or what?"

"Actually, I'm here on a case."

"You're searching for someone? How exciting! But if it's me, your search is over. I promise not to resist."

Dan smiled. "You're number one on my list, but there is someone else I'm here to find."

"Wait!" Trevor exclaimed and shot up from the seat. "This calls for a drink." He returned with the bottle and a pair of glasses. "I hope you like Viognier."

Dan's eyebrows rose comically. "I adore caviar."

"Ha!"

They toasted and Trevor sat back on the couch. "Shoot," he said, glancing over to check that the fire was burning properly.

"I've got a lead on a misper that's taking me to Vancouver Island," Dan said.

Trevor's face was a blank. "You've got a lead on a what?"

Dan smiled. "Sorry. A 'misper.' A missing person."

Trevor searched Dan's face, eyes focusing on his lips. He inched closer. "On second thought, let's save business for later," he murmured, running a hand over Dan's chest. "If I wait any longer to touch you I might explode."

Dan woke to a window full of stars. Fingers reached down his belly and began to stroke him. Dan wrapped his fingers around the hand and squeezed, filling his cock with warmth. He searched in the dark for Trevor's mouth and kissed him long and hard.

"I'm jealous of every man you've ever slept with," Trevor murmured. "Are you always that fantastic in bed?"

"Generally speaking, I'm not even mildly interesting, so no."

"Liar," Trevor said, his fingers continuing their work. "You are hot hot *hot*!"

When they lay back again twenty minutes later, the stars had dimmed, the treetops beginning to lighten.

"If we get up now we can have breakfast and watch the sunrise," Trevor said.

"Are you always this romantic?"

"Always."

Outside the sky was cool and grey. The chill felt good against Dan's skin. Sounds filled the air — branches rustling, birds calling, the far-off rush of water — noisy in their way, but different from the city's restless pulse.

His impressions of splendour in the dark had been right. The house sat perched on an incline, surrounded by soft fernlike branches of green and rust. From the walkway he could see the harbour between the trees and catch an occasional glimpse of Pender Island's dark cliffs through the mist.

He crouched along the steps leading to the drive, his fingers trailing the wires that connected the garden lights. By the time Trevor called him for breakfast, he'd repaired the short.

"Anything else need fixing?"

Trevor's eyebrows rose comically. "Besides me?" He smiled. "Seriously, can you build a wood shed? My firewood gets wet out on the porch, even with the tarp. The damp gets into everything here."

"No problem," Dan said, glancing around. "It looks like there's no shortage of lumber."

The mist stubbornly clung on all morning and refused to part for the sun while they ate and put the dishes aside.

"Come on," Trevor said. "I want to take you someplace special."

"More special than this?" Dan said, looking through the windows at the canopy of trees dropping to the ocean in the distance.

After twenty minutes of walking they reached a turnoff. Trevor stopped to look over the backdrop of Western Redcedar. It was the clothes, Dan thought. And the uncombed hair — a little windswept. Trevor wasn't exactly dressed in full-lumberjack garb, but he had an outdoorsy look, different from how he'd looked in the city. In a good way. Not a J.Crew posed-for-effect way. Then again, he was a man who would look good in almost anything.

Trevor turned, as if he'd heard Dan's thoughts. "Want to stay here with me and grow old together?"

"You make a compelling case for it."

"It's paradise here. Or it would be. But every Adam needs his Steve." Trevor smiled. "Just a suggestion."

A family of deer crossed the road and stopped to regard them with big liquid eyes.

"Pretty fearless, aren't they?" Dan said.

"No natural predators," Trevor said. "That's the best thing about living on the island. There was a wolf once. It used to swim from island to island and eat its fill of deer, but it was shot over on Pender when it attacked a dog."

"Any bears?"

"None that I've heard about. There are a lot of cougars, but only the human variety." Dan looked at him curiously. Trevor was grinning. "Single, middle-aged women hunting for men."

"Oh!" Dan laughed. "I'm out of practice with straight humour." He paused and looked around. "Speaking of, is there much gay life on the island?"

"I know a few couples. No single men that I've come across. There's not much gay life here, but then there's not a lot of anything other than retired straight couples and me."

"Must get lonely."

"All the time."

A car passed. "Wave," Trevor commanded.

Dan waved and someone honked. "Who was that?"

Trevor shrugged. "Just people. Doesn't matter. Everyone's friendly here."

The sign pointed down the path: *Japanese Memorial Garden*.

"We're here," said Trevor.

The garden had been built to honour the Japanese-Canadians who settled the islands and were incarcerated during the Second World War. The scant quarter acre surrounded by forest was inventively landscaped. Unobtrusive signs identified shrubs and trees planted strategically throughout the space, gingko living beside yews and plums and flowering cherries. Everything centred around a green-encrusted pond. At the far end, a giant rhubarb with leaves the size of small satellite dishes drooped gently down to the water.

"I'm still amazed that I live here," Trevor said. "I guess I'm not convinced I deserve it. I've always lived in cities — Calgary, Edmonton, and before that in Vancouver for a number of years. That was a long time ago, in another life."

"How did you end up here?"

Trevor stepped carefully over a patch of emerald moss. "The truth?" he said.

"If it's appropriate."

Trevor smiled. "Very diplomatic — but I don't mind saying. I had a breakdown." He shrugged, as though to say it was over and there was no use going through it again. "Afterwards, when I realized I was going to live — and that I might one day even *want* to live — I knew I needed to disappear."

"So you came here…."

"For years I had a job that paid me a lot of money but gave me absolutely no joy. My life — what I called a life — was spent in a box in the sky that smelled like Febreze. I had a nice view and all the right friends and everyone said I was a success, but the truth was I got no pleasure from anything. I wasn't even alive." He smiled ruefully. "So I gave it all up and moved here. It's lonely but much easier on the nerves."

"You can be lonely surrounded by millions of people. Cities aren't what they seem," Dan said. "Most days I can barely stand Toronto. It's become so greedy and aggressive and uncaring."

Trevor laughed. "Isn't that what people always say when you tell them that? Cities aren't supposed to care — they're too busy being cities."

"I've never known what to do about it."

"You can do whatever you want — including nothing. I think that's what most people do. They just live with it and never figure out that it's killing them."

The *Queen of Nanaimo* edged into view, a giant white swan against the green-black of the water. They watched the boat manoeuvre the coastline and head into harbour.

"So here I am," Trevor said. "Alone on my island retreat, lonely as hell, but with my peace of mind intact." He paused. "Come on, I want you to meet someone."

They made their way around the pond to a fence where dozens of small brass plaques had been affixed at regular intervals.

"Joe meet Dan. Dan meet Joseph."

Dan bent closer to read the inscription: *Joe Wilkinson 1968–1999*. He looked to Trevor for an explanation.

"My ex. The one thing I couldn't leave behind when I moved here. I scattered his ashes in the forest over there." Trevor pointed past the far side of the gate. "And some in the water over there."

"I'm sorry," Dan said.

"Don't be sorry, he's happy here." Trevor smiled and looked along the length of the fence. "Here with all the others who nobody really remembers except the ones who put up the plaques." He shrugged philosophically. "And a hundred years from now, no one will even remember who we were."

A curved metal plate hung between two trees, an exotic bronze art piece catching the sun, with a clapper strung next to it. Dan struck it and the gong reverberated through the forest, rich and low, holding its tone long after they'd passed through the gate.

Trevor scrambled down a rocky ledge to the shore. Tidepool sculpin darted in the pooling water while birds with flecked wings flitted in the branches above. He jumped up onto a rock and crouched there like a garden gnome. "I never heard the rest of your story. You mentioned you're here on business."

"Yes. Thanks for reminding me."

"So I shouldn't hold out hope that you've come to live with me forever?"

Dan sighed. "You're welcome to try to convince me. But no, I've come on business. And I can't forget I've got a family back home." He paused. "Actually, I'm in B.C. to look for Thom's father."

Trevor looked at him with a quirky smile. "Thom Killingworth? You're looking for my Uncle Craig? I didn't know he was in B.C."

"I'm not sure he is, but the trail leads here."

"So, why…?"

"Someone hired me to look into his disappearance."

"Who? If I can ask."

Dan shrugged. "It's odd, but I don't know who the client is."

Trevor licked his lips and nodded. "Is that why you came to see me? You think I can tell you something?" Dan started to speak, but Trevor cut him off. "It's all right — I understand if you did. I'm still grateful that you're here."

"I said that's why I came to B.C. I came to Mayne Island to see you."

Trevor admitted a slight smile.

†

293

They stood on the upper deck of the ferry heading to Vancouver Island. It had rained for an hour that morning, as it had nearly every morning since Dan's arrival, then the sky cleared and turned blue by the time they reached the terminal. Dan left Trevor outside the public gardens in Victoria.

"You sure you'll be all right? You won't get bored?"

"It's my favourite place to shop," Trevor said. "I might even have High Tea at the Empress Hotel."

"I'll see you back here at three then."

"Say hi to my uncle if you find him."

Dan followed the highway north out of town. At an intersection outside Ladysmith a dirt road hesitantly joined the highway. Dan found the bank of mailboxes just past a ridge. He looked down the rows of numbers till he came across 37 and the name Magnus Ferguson in a tight script. It had been that easy. Then he reminded himself that he'd found a man's name on a mailbox, not the man himself.

Dan's eyes followed the dirt road where it disappeared around a line of trees half a kilometre ahead. He looked back at the mailbox that held upwards of fifty names. How many of these places would he have to investigate? How many were even down this stretch of road ahead? There were probably a half-dozen others nearby.

He got his answer at the fourth place he tried. Three German Shepherds ran alongside his car, barking insanely as he drove up the drive. He stopped outside the squat bungalow and waited. Lacy curtains parted and a face appeared in the window. The door opened and a man approached wearing a T-shirt, jeans, and rubber boots. Dark eyes followed him as Dan rolled down the window. "Sorry for the intrusion. I'm looking for Magnus Ferguson."

The man scratched his chin and grew pensive. "You'll find his trailer three, maybe four drives down on the right," he said. "But I don't think you'll find Magnus."

Dan's eyebrows rose.

"You family?" the man asked.

"Distant."

The man looked concerned. "Well, I don't think he's alive any more, I'm sorry to tell you. He went off to the hospital in Vancouver a couple years back. He was looking pretty poorly at the time. The wife heard some time later that he died. Lung cancer, I think it was."

Dan nodded. "Can you tell me who looks after the trailer now?"

The man slumped. "I did for a while, but I stopped about a year ago. I figured he wasn't coming back."

"Do you know who collects his mail? His name's still on the box out by the road."

"Sorry, I don't. I'd be surprised it he even got any now."

Dan looked away. All this way to hit a dead end. Somehow it didn't seem right. For a moment, he wanted to thank this man for looking after the trailer of a man he never knew.

"What was he like, if you don't mind my asking?"

"Nice guy. Kept to himself mostly, but friendly if you approached him. Always kept a neat garden. I imagine it's gone to pot now." The man smiled ruefully. "Not that kind of pot. He even stacked his firewood meticulously."

Dan thanked him and drove on to the white-framed twenty-four-footer. The power lines were still attached. The garden surrounding it looked like it had once been something, but now it was overgrown, disappearing into forest, the line between what had been kept in and what kept out impossible to distinguish. He stepped out of the car and knocked on the flimsy door. The sound reverberated through the woods and startled a murder of crows.

He waited a moment but knew there was no use. He stuck his card in the doorframe and went around back, where a pile of meticulously stacked firewood greeted him. It had grown green with moss around the edges. No one had removed any of the logs for some time.

He drove back to the main road and stopped beside the mailbox. He wrote a longer note and put it in an envelope, slipping it inside the box.

The fire burned low in the grate. Dan held Trevor's hand against his chest. The feeling was warm and richly layered. They might have been a couple, still together after many years, nourishing and measuring what lay between them, amazed by the continuance of life.

"You never told me what happened between you and Bill."

Dan stirred. "Didn't Thom fill you in?"

Trevor shook his head. "I'm not really in touch with Thom. In fact, I was surprised when I got the wedding invitation. I think that was Aunt Lucille's doing. I was always a little scared of cousin Thom, to tell the truth. He was older and knew how to get what he wanted."

"Like you?"

"Like me and a whole lot more. He was always pushy, but after his father left he became downright cruel, especially if you challenged him at anything. I guess he was just reacting to being abandoned. He eased up as he got older."

"What about Ted?"

"Ted was the soft one — self-indulgent, poetic by nature. Not as good-looking as Thom. He always seemed to fail where Thom succeeded."

"Has no one tried to stop his drug problem?"

"Apparently not. He's always had easy access to drugs, thanks to the family money."

Dan ran his fingers through Trevor's hair, letting them linger along his neck. "Do you remember your uncle at all?"

"A little. He was my mother's brother."

"Clare," Dan said.

Trevor looked at him. "Yes. How did you know?"

"It's in the police report."

Trevor nodded. "We used to visit when I was a kid, but then we moved out to the coast. There was a scandal before my uncle disappeared, though. My mother and father actually stopped talking to him."

"Was it because of the assault?"

Trevor shook his head. "No, it was before that. About a year before, I think. Uncle Craig moved out of the house for a while, but then he moved back in again briefly. Marital discord of some sort — nobody really talked about it. Then later he was suspended from his job as principal. The rumours just kept getting worse. I didn't get all the details, just assumed it was one of those adult things you weren't supposed to know about." His face was lost in thought for a moment. "There was something else — I barely remember it now, though it made a huge impact on me at the time. Not long after Uncle Craig disappeared — or maybe it was just before he left home the first time, I can't recall — all his horses died."

"His horses?"

"He kept horses. Six of them. They all died one night. They'd been poisoned, I think. I remember Thom wept. He loved those horses."

Dan recalled the photograph of Thom astride a large black horse on the mantle in the Adolphustown house.

Trevor looked up. "Now that you've reached a dead end, will you be leaving soon?"

Dan smiled. "Am I crowding you out already?"

"Not at all!" Trevor brought Dan's fingers to his lips. "Believe me, I'd love to keep you here forever."

"Except what would I do for a living?"

Trevor smiled. "I've already got that one figured. I've got a neighbour who'd kill to have your skills available for hire. She brought her husband over to see the shed you built. I could feel the envy burning a hole in my wood. In fact, there's probably not a person on the island who doesn't need something handy done. You could make a killing here."

Dan looked over at the window, the darkness pressing in against the glass. The other day he'd realized how easy it would be to disappear here. To vanish from your previous life and start over again. It would be that simple. No one but the trees to know of your defection from the real world. Though what could be more real than this, he couldn't say. "I can't say I haven't considered it," he admitted.

"I don't want you to leave thinking I don't desperately want you to stay. But you're not ready. I can see the signs. To some people living here is a retreat; to others it's a prison.

It's very different when you're here for an extended period of time."

The darkness outside the windows reflected in Trevor's eyes, those eyes that had moved away from the disasters of the past and looked forward to a more hopeful future. Dan scarcely dared think he could have any part of it.

NINETEEN

My iPod, Your iPod

Dan set his bags on the hallway tiles. Late afternoon shadows emerged from the corners. There was no Ralph peering at him from the kitchen, tail wagging expectantly, and presumably no Ked, which meant he was either at practice or still at his mother's. One day Dan would have this place all to himself, with Ked grown and living on his own, the dog wherever the dog ended up — either with Ked or out in some greater greener pasture that held a place of awe in animal lore.

His answer machine yielded three messages. The first wasn't entirely unexpected, the next two were. He hit play and his cousin Leyla's distinctive bleat filled the room, as though she was there with him and not four hundred kilometres north and two decades back in time. Here was the girl who had been almost like a sister to him, the girl whose "impressive" breasts were the subject of schoolyard lore, which he recalled now with amusement. Her voice took him a long way back.

He listened carefully to the message then dialled her number and played catch-up for a few minutes. Then she got around to the subject of her mother's latest test results — they hadn't been favourable. Dan felt a pang of guilt; it had been more than three years since his last visit. He'd sent birthday greetings, Christmas presents, anything to bridge the gap between trips, but there'd always been some excuse keeping him away. He hated to think they might believe they were no longer important to him.

"God, Leyla, I'm sorry. I don't know what to say."

"Three months — that's what the doctor said." She was matter-of-fact about it, though Dan had no doubt she loved the mother she was about to lose, if not sooner then later. She paused. "She was hoping ta see ya, Dan. Can ya come up?"

"I'll come up."

"Better make it quick, eh?"

"What about you, Leyla? You need anything?"

"No. I'm all right. Kurt pays the child support on time. One thing he's been good for, at least. He's stayed out of jail the last couple years, but we're through. Last time I marry a guy because he's got a nice motorcycle, know what I mean?"

"At least he never hit you."

"No, he never did or I mighta left him sooner. Too bad, eh? Wanted to hit him myself a few times, though." She laughed.

"I'm just back from a trip out west. Let me check in with work to see whether they can spare me this weekend. I'll give you a call."

"It'd be good to see you, Danny. Well, you know what I mean — despite the circumstances."

The second message was from Donny. He'd been fired from Holt Renfrew after fifteen years. He sounded shell-shocked. While Dan saw Donny as something of a Zen master who could maintain his equanimity in the middle of a war zone, he could tell his friend was having a hard time with this one.

Donny was in the midst of cooking when he answered on the second ring. "I was wondering why you hadn't bothered to return my calls," he said sulkily. "Anyway, I'm already over it. I'm not even angry any more. I think."

"So they just fired you? They just said get out?"

"More or less. I wasn't escorted to the front door, but there weren't any flowers either."

"But why?"

"I've been trying to sort that one out. I think it's the ooh-la-la factor. It's not chic right now to be buying per-fume from a black man."

"Are you saying they fired you for being black?"

"No. Not at all. They fired me for being out of fashion. Or maybe for not being Indian or Arabic. All the chi-chi jobs are going to Indians these days. It's the accent. The Rosedale ladies love it. I'm Yesterday's Girl."

Dan pondered this. "You'll get another job. You're not too old. Just be glad this isn't happening a decade from now." He tried to sound convincing, but he knew it was the verbal equivalent of a pat on the back, the way he talked to Ked sometimes. Cookies and milk would have been more of a comfort. "Why not take a vacation? Get away for a couple of months. You've got money."

"Thanks, but I wasn't planning on going anywhere just now."

"You'll be more relaxed and in the mood to look for a job when you get back."

"I'll also be older. I'm in an industry where youth suc-
ceeds far more than a relaxed attitude."

"Maybe it's time for a change of career," Dan said,
trying to sound hopeful. "There's always government."
In his mind's eye he saw corridors thronged by men and
women clutching briefs as they scurried about in search
of political patronage — a helping hand, a meaningful pat
on the back. The perks of civil servitude.

"I always said I'd kill myself before becoming a civil
servant."

"Well, then? What are you going to do?"

"I've got a nice gas stove here. I could stick my head in it."

Dan heard the sounds of clanking pots on the chrome
range in Donny's well-appointed Jarvis Street condo.

"Maybe you're right," Donny continued. "I need to get
out of the city. I'm currently looking from my prestigious
penthouse window down over the panorama of our beloved
Commonwealth of Gay. And it doesn't add up to very much
right at this moment. When did the world become so …
colourless?"

"You and my assistant should get together."

"I thought your assistant was a girl."

"Never mind." Dan cast around for something positive
to say. "Look — you'll find a new job. Maybe a better one.
This will pass."

"And this too shall pass."

Dan thought of Trevor and his island. "You could
always cash it all in and go live in the country where it's
green and smells at least halfway clean."

Donny snorted. "And where would I cruise on a
Saturday night?"

In the past twenty minutes the room had eased from late afternoon to an early twilight. A silvery light slipped through the partially opened kitchen door. Dan struggled for something to say. "Look, do you want me to come over?"

"No. Thank you." There was a long pause. Then, "Would you miss me if I died?" Donny said, his tone casual, as if he'd asked Dan to pick up a pack of cigarettes from the corner store.

"What a question!" Dan said.

"I'm serious. Can you answer it?"

"Of course I can. And, yes, I would miss you a great deal. Probably until the day I die. Don't do this to me!"

"I'm all right, really. I was just wondering."

Dan heard more cooking noises. "Of course I'd miss you. For one thing, I'd have no one to laugh with over those sentimental old movies we watch after your fabulous dinners."

"Well, that's good to hear," Donny said. "I was never sure if you realized we were *supposed* to be laughing at them. Anyway, I'm okay. I didn't mean to alarm you. If it's all right with you, I'm going to get on with my Nasi Goreng. I'll call you tomorrow."

The answer machine yielded its final message. Dan listened twice to be sure he got the gist of it while anger twisted its tendrils around him like a strangling vine. Kendra's voice cut through the stillness of the house as Dan imagined Ked's future lying shattered on the tile floor like the glittering pieces of some rare Etruscan vase. *This* was what came from not choosing your friends wisely.

He was about to call Kendra back when he heard the hollow thud of footsteps on the outside stairs followed by a key in the lock. Ked stepped in looking gloomy, but with a rebellious glint in his eyes. He put his backpack down and glanced warily at his father.

Dan said, "I got a call from your mother...."

"Yeah, and she didn't believe me either," Ked began.

Outside, a streetcar sizzled along the rails. Dan paused to take stock of the situation. "Let's not start there," he said. "I never said I don't believe you. I haven't even heard your side of things."

Ked slumped against the wall.

"Talk to me, Ked."

"Okay — I was listening to an iPod in the schoolyard...."

"Whose iPod?"

"Ephraim's."

"The kid I see you with sometimes after practice?"

Ked nodded without meeting his father's gaze. "Anyway, when the police came...."

"How did the police get involved?"

"I don't know, they just ... someone called them, all right? I don't know!"

His son was working himself up. Whatever he'd been through at school had taken its toll. "Take a breath," Dan said. "And just tell me what happened."

"They said they were going to charge me with possession of stolen property."

"The police said this?"

Ked nodded.

"And where was Ephraim?"

"I don't know."

"What do you mean you don't know? You had his iPod." Dan heard his voice getting louder. If Ked persisted in giving these two-second answers, he might explode. It could only disintegrate from here. He felt broken glass underfoot.

Ked's eyes narrowed in anger. "I don't know where Ephraim was. He loaned me his iPod and then he left."

"And you had it when the police got there?"

Ked nodded. "Look, why would I have stolen property when you buy me anything I want? I already have an iPod and a Game Boy and a million other things, so why would you even think I would steal? Have some faith, Dad."

Dan looked at his son slouching against the wall. He was torn between comforting him and wanting him to suffer a little — long enough that the humiliation would leave its mark. Deep enough that he would never do anything like this again — whatever it was he'd done. But more than anything, Dan thought, he wanted to protect Ked from the million ways a life could be ruined by the actions of a single unguarded moment. "It's not me you need to convince," he said.

Ked looked up. "Then who is it?"

"The police, your school principal — you need to convince the people who don't believe you. The people who don't know you as well as I do. I simply want you to tell me what happened. What were you doing with a second iPod, for instance?"

"Eph let me borrow it. He wanted me to hear something on his that isn't on mine. Is that such a strange concept?"

"No," Dan said. "Not at all. Except that you happened to borrow an iPod that was stolen. Let me ask you this — does this Ephraim sell stolen goods?"

Ked shot his father an angry look. The rebelliousness returned to his face. "No! He just bought it from some guy!"

"Would you calm down, please?"

"Why should I calm down? You're accusing my friends, Dad. I know Eph, and Eph would never purposely handle stolen goods."

"Then why did he have it?" The argument was turning circular.

"Who would turn down an iPod for thirty-five dollars?" Ked screamed.

"Didn't it occur to him that a thirty-five-dollar iPod might be stolen property?" Dan's voice sounded angrier than he'd intended.

"Apparently not," Ked said, his eyes misting over. "You don't believe me either. You don't trust me!" The hurt in his face was apparent. "I always tell you the truth and you don't trust me!"

He took the stairs three at a time. Dan heard his bedroom door slam.

Kendra was inclined to reserve judgment on the question of whether Ked had known the iPod was stolen property.

"I mean, think about it, Dan. He's always told us the truth, hasn't he?"

"Of course."

"Well, sometimes at that age you don't think about the consequences of things."

"That age, nothing! He can't afford not to think," Dan snapped. "I'm sorry," he said. "This is really rattling me."

"It's all right. I'm sure there are things here for both of us to learn."

That was Kendra — all about learning things when the world was falling apart. Still, Dan admitted, it was better than falling apart with it. "It's just that kids sometimes do stupid things. I'm not saying he was stealing, but maybe he simply turned a blind eye to what his friends do."

"Then this will be a lesson he won't soon forget," Kendra said softly. "Come on, it's not the end of the world."

"This could be on his record for a very long time — guilty or not, it doesn't matter."

"I know." Kendra sighed. "But we've gone this far without these troublesome parent-teenager issues, so I think we've done a pretty good job, all round." She paused. "No — *you've* done a good job. I've mostly been sitting on the sidelines reaping the rewards. So try to remember that before you beat yourself up over this."

The issue lingered like a dark cloud, with Ked suspended from school. His friend had quickly cleared him of all suspicion regarding ownership of the iPod, but the issue of stolen property remained. Then suddenly, the day turned bright again. The school principal called to apologize to Ked and his family, dismissing the terms of suspension and asking Ked to return to school. That same day Ephraim's mother produced a receipt from a pawnshop showing she'd bought the item legally, and all charges were dropped against the boys.

Dan was glad to have the issue resolved, but in that time his son remained edgy with him, tense and barely communicative, as though in Ked's mind Dan had gone beyond some sort of acceptable parent-son boundaries.

TWENTY

Sid and Nancy

KNOWN LOCALLY AS "THE 69," the highway to Sudbury does little to prepare you for the city itself. True, the farther north you go the more barren the terrain becomes as the Canadian Shield rises from the earth like a giantess spreading her apron to shelter a multitude of stunted children, the towns and cities marginalized and tethered on the periphery of the land. Offering boreal forests in the south and tundra to the north, the Shield is better known for its abundant mineral deposits and the mining communities that have exploited them for more than a century.

The landscape had changed greatly since Dan's time. Much of the change was positive in ecological terms, undoing years of bad. The International Nickel Company's much-vaunted Superstack, a 1,247-foot, concrete chimney, had been built not long after Dan was born, as if to commemorate his arrival. The poisons and pollutants that once blanketed the town were now sent spinning into the atmosphere at an altitude high enough to cut Sudbury's pollution by more than ninety percent. His aunt recalled days when she'd had a raw throat all summer long from the sulphur emissions, conjuring images of ash films that blackened the snow outside her basement apartment in winter.

For miles around, forests had strangled on the noxious by-products of mining, the conifers turning rust-red as their needles dropped and the plants slowly died. The region's pink-grey granite turned black with soot and the vegetation crawled farther and farther into the bush while lakes filled with acid and the fish population shrank and died. With the coming of the Superstack that suddenly stopped, as urban centres to the south began to report mysterious lines of yellow haze scrawling across the sky. Even Inco's reinvented Tower of Babel couldn't whitewash the filthy scud away forever. It had to come down somewhere.

To a child, Sudbury had seemed an intricate playground of things gone wonderfully awry: houses jutting from mountainsides, car-sized boulders in basements with washing machines and furnaces tucked around these incongruences. Buildings pitched and tilted to the sway of winding streets, as though the Crooked Man who'd built a Crooked House had returned with a vengeance to construct an entire derelict, lopsided town crowned by the searing gold spill of slag dumps, a magisterial ring of fire poured down nightly on the Earth.

Local legend saw the town nested in the crater of an extinct volcano, just waiting for the return of the fiery forces to extinguish it again. Geologists speculated it was the site of a giant meteor crash that gave the area its vast iron and nickel ore deposits. Years of annual spring floods led some to conjecture that the downtown was in actuality a giant swamp, as water rose over the streets with their smattering of English and French names that mingled New and Old World history: LaSalle, Elgin, Wellington, and the generic but obligatory catch-alls of King and Queen. Who the hell Frood was, no one seemed to know or care. At times the floods were so severe they seemed to be mocking the city planners until they put their heads together in the mid-sixties and devised a drainage system that dealt with the problem once and for all.

Despite its problems, Sudbury affected a sense of home-grown achievement. Schoolchildren recited proudly how prior to the first Apollo moon launch the flight crew trained in the terrain around the city because it resembled the lunar landscape closely enough to launch an astronaut's career in earnest.

But if Sudbury was the moon by proxy, then the Flourmill District was the dark side of that moon, an industrial, monochromatic soot-on-soot neighbourhood of the type that sprawled throughout England in Victorian times, finally slouching across the ocean to end up reborn as a living museum exiled in northern Ontario ever after. It made the gritty black-and-white misery of other industrial centres seem like a dove's cry.

Dan pictured the cold-water flat without a bathtub where for years he'd washed in a sink with a tap that never entirely turned off, and whose drips left a turquoise stain on the ceramic basin, just a few streets over from the colossal concrete towers that sat like a giant six-pack of dynamite behind his home. The nearest of the six bore an irregular hole the size of a small child just a few feet above the ground. Lore had it the flourmill had once been set for destruction. The hole, it was said, offered testimony to the fact that even explosives had failed to topple it. Children's fancy, of course. More likely the dimple had been caused by an errant bulldozer that limped off afterwards with a damaged shovel, having learned to pick on something closer to its own size. As a child, you never admitted you came from the Flourmill District. Not only was it the wrong side of the tracks, it had seemed the worst place to come from in the entire country.

Dan passed a tavern he hadn't thought of in years, a shallow trough where he'd been sent more than once in search of his father. "Get your father home for supper," his Aunt Marge instructed in her chirpy voice, though Dan knew supper would be long put away by the time he returned, with or without his father. Dan never had a problem getting into Sudbury's bars. The bartenders, if they guessed his age, simply turned a blind eye. Or perhaps they knew him for Stuart Sharp's son. More than one son or daughter had shown up to fetch their parents over the years. Many returned for a longer stay once they came of age. More likely, they assumed Dan was as old as his dark looks proclaimed, which was significantly older than his actual years.

Inside, he knew, was the latest generation of miners, the hard-working men who earned their living pulling precious metal out of the bowels of the Earth, a whole under-class who spent their hours toiling in darkness, not seeing the sun for weeks at a time, who woke one day wondering where their lives had gone and how they'd managed to miss out on them. Meanwhile, their children had grown up without them, their wives had become bored and discontented, and no one could tell them what it had all been for. Until his death, Dan's father had been one of these men, his personality stuck on edgy, his face so expressionless it had probably not exercised its muscles in years. Permanent immobility was written all over it.

He found the house on the hill at the top of Bloor Street, the same flowered curtains in the windows as when he was a child. Probably they weren't the same, but no doubt his aunt had replaced the originals with curtains of the same style and colour. He sometimes wondered if growing up surrounded by rock had convinced her that all things were more or less permanent, and that efforts should be taken to preserve them just as they were.

He stepped down the crumbling concrete steps and stopped for a moment where his four-year-old self had heard one of the neighbours say, "She's gone, poor thing." The woman had looked at him with such a pitiful gaze that it etched itself onto his heart forever. His mom was gone again, that much he understood. Where she'd gone or when she'd return, no one could say. Except that time she hadn't come back.

Leyla was waiting at the door with open arms and a ready smile. He wanted to say something like, "You haven't changed a bit," but it was such an obvious lie it would only have caused embarrassment. Pretty as a teenager, her looks had been fleeting, like her youth. Her skin sagged, her pallor the colour of oatmeal. She hadn't gotten stout, but her once impressive breasts were, he gathered, more of a hindrance now than an enticement. She seemed to have wrapped them in an old sweater to keep them from getting in the way. The one thing that hadn't changed was the glint of joy in her eyes. Dan gave her a peck on the cheek and squeezed her in his arms. She felt tiny.

"Mom's been so excited knowing you were coming," she said, in a way that told him his absence the past few years had been more marked than he cared to believe. "How's Ked?" she asked.

"He's good. He's really tall now. Almost as tall as me."

"They grow so fast you can't keep up with them. Geez, eh? It's funny. Mine are nearly grown too. I hardly see them any more."

She still talked like a high school majorette. Dan recalled her fondness for mohair sweaters, pleated skirts, and hair barrettes.

She put a hand on his shoulder and nodded to the bedroom door. "Go on in, Danny. She's been waiting for ya."

Gloom met his eyes, a half-drawn shade simply masking the fact that the light was permanently obscured by the house next door. The wallpaper was Sedona Rose on Pickle Green, some daft artist's rendering of happiness and cheer. Paper daisies in a snow-white vase sat atop a dresser. The room smelled of disinfectant covered with something homely. If he were to die of a wasting disease, he knew, he could do worse than come back here to be tended to by Leyla. Everything had been tidied up and put away, the room almost too clean to admit to any suffering. He imagined the dull days winding ahead for his aunt, but with a fixed value attached to their number.

On the mantle ranged the usual collection of cards: *Get Well Soon, Heard You Needed Some Cheering,* and *Hope You're Feeling Better* — his own hadn't reached them yet. All with the usual compulsory euphemisms that said everything but the truth: *Goodbye For All Time* or *Prepare To Meet Your Maker.* From behind one card peeked the corner of a photograph: himself as a dirty-faced kid of three or four, with a grin to break your heart. What had happened to that boy? Dan wondered.

His eyes adjusted. His aunt lay on the far side of the bed, as if avoiding the light. Flannel rose in soft swells around her sleeping head. A hearing aid curled around one ear like a pink foetus, her hair Marcel-waved into tiny seashells. As a boy he'd watched, fascinated, as she egg-whited the tips of curls and stuck them to her cheeks. Imagining herself glamorous, no doubt. Maybe she'd fancied herself a movie star: Joan Fontaine or Lana Turner. And why not? Life held few enough rewards for someone like her.

At one point she'd briefly turned Jehovah's Witness, driven for comfort by a husband's beatings and a brother's drinking. Eventually the husband vanished, though Leyla said for years afterwards her mother would turn a hopeful ear to the door if there were footsteps outside at night, still praying for his return. It never came. No one knew if he were still alive or, if dead, where he'd been buried. The consensus was that he'd come to a bad end somewhere and that it had been well deserved, whatever it was. Dan recalled her sweaters that always smelled of dampness. She would wait till his dad had gone to work and then start in on him, clutching him to her chest and making him promise he would never drink, smoke, or swear. Devil's work. His father did all three, Dan knew. He used to wonder if she'd asked him to make the same promise. He hadn't listened, if she had. But even religion hadn't lasted forever, like most things in her life.

He remembered her as a woman who spent much of her time planning diets of one sort or another: the grapefruit-only diet, the no-bread diet, the sugar-free diet, and various others with no particular name. All of them defined by a lack. She'd never been a great cook, but she always made sure there was food on the table for Dan and Leyla. Her specialty was peas in gravy on white bread, with greasy ground beef mixed in. Her version of a balanced meal, no doubt. Some days there might be mashed potatoes instead of the sliced bread with its tan leathery borders. Afterwards, orange fat lay congealed at the bottom of the electric frying pan — her one frivolity — until its rounded corners slid under the iridescent soap bubbles in the sink. Most of her days were spent in silence, which was just as well because when she spoke people looked in fright at the sound of her voice, like a whoopee cushion on Prozac. But more than anything, he remembered her as a woman who had taken in another woman's child to raise as her own.

Someone — probably Leyla — had propped a chair in the corner. He dragged it close and sat next to her. Here she was, his aunt who had always been kind, always accepting. His aunt, who had spent thirty years selling tickets at the movie theatre before retiring on a government pension. Goodbye and thanks for a job well done. When she was younger she'd dreamed of reinventing herself by opening the classifieds to see what fascinating job she could apply for that might just blow her horizons wide open and make all her dreams come true. What'll it be next: waitress at Kresge's Red Grill or counter help at Herb's Bowl-a-Rama? Another time it was a day cashier at Woolworth's followed by a stint as stock clerk at Zeller's. The options were stupefying. Maybe she thought they'd go on forever, but one day they ran out and she ended up where she began, dying of emphysema, her life and choices behind her forever.

Dan leaned over the bed, taking care not to bump the fat green cylinder that pumped itself out via the long thin tube attached over her head and feeding into her nostrils. Her skin was wrinkled and translucent, as if, oxygen-starved, her body had subsisted on a diet of light. Her hands were swollen like pudgy starfish.

Here, then, was the salt of the earth. It didn't get any better or purer.

Eyelids flickered open, eyes cornflower blue. "Hello, Danny," she said, as though she'd seen him only a short while before.

"Hello, Auntie."

"My goodness, you look awfully good. Handsome as ever. It's so nice to see you home again."

The sentence must have exceeded her lung capacity, because Dan heard the intake of breath, the sharp rasp behind the words.

"How are you feeling?" he asked. "Is Leyla doing a good job of looking after you?"

She spoke a little slower, pacing herself. "Oh, don't you worry — she's doing a good job. You know what she's like." She took a long pull on her oxygen.

There was a peaceful sound to her voice. Or maybe it was resignation — he'd never known her to be a fighter.

She would just as easily go along with whatever Death had in store for her as a request for supper to be made for visitors. Compliance — her greatest virtue — was one and the same with her.

They spoke for ten minutes before Dan felt her tiring. She wouldn't let him go, hanging onto him as long as she could. "I'll come back again tomorrow," he promised.

She shook her head. She needed more of him right now. "Will you go out to visit his grave while you're here?" she asked, squeezing his hand as though encouraging a small boy about to tackle a very big task.

"Sure." He turned his eyes to hers. He hadn't intended to go to the cemetery and knew he probably wouldn't keep his word, but she wanted him to say yes. "And maybe hers, too."

"You haven't been out for a long time," she said, heaping on the reasons to go now that she'd got him to say he would, just as she'd once made him promise never to drink, smoke, or swear.

"No," he said. "I haven't."

"You weren't so lucky when it came to parents," she said.

"I had you," Dan said, resting his hand on her arm.

"Still do." Her eyes teared up a little. "He loved you too, you know. Even though you thought he didn't." She took another pull on the oxygen.

Dan shook his head. "I don't know."

With all the presence she could summon, she gazed directly at him. "He did," she insisted.

Dan smiled indulgently. "Maybe I didn't understand him. It was a long time ago. It doesn't matter now."

"Doesn't it matter to you?" she asked. She was silent for a while. "I think you're right. Maybe you never understood your father." Her eyes carried a look of well-worn sorrow.

"You knew him better than I did," Dan managed. *Don't,* he told himself. *Don't argue with a dying woman.*

"It broke his heart when you left." She smiled pityingly, as though she knew she would hurt him by saying this. "You didn't know that, did you?"

Dan went on as though he hadn't heard her. "I had to go. He always seemed so angry. I never knew why. At the time, I thought he hated me."

"Yes," his aunt said, her eyes a long way off. "He was an angry man. But it wasn't you he hated." She sniffled. "She was no angel either. Your mum, I mean. She went out and drank and hung around with god knows who half the night. No, she was no angel herself. You wouldn't remember — you were just a little kid, Daniel."

Something boomed in the distance, a prelude to doom, that well-worn fiddler's march to the scaffold. There was a worn quality to her voice, water rushing against a shore. The memories were returning, like some half-forgotten love affair. Only the story ended in death — the first by pneumonia, the other through self-destruction.

"It broke my heart watching him drink himself to death. Though for a few years he tried hard not to — for you." Dan gave her a sharp look, but she caught him. "Yes, for you. Maybe to make it up to her, too," she allowed. "But you can't change the past. I just wish you'd known he loved you, no matter what he felt about himself. No — it wasn't you he hated. It was only himself."

Her voice had gone quiet. Dan leaned in to hear her better. He saw his father as a thoughtless man who destroyed the things he loved. Then he saw himself kicking at Ralph and screaming at Ked in his impatience, wondering again what drove him to do those things.

"They were arguing over you," she said. "He said, 'Christine, you shouldn't be going out with a small child in the house.' And him working till all hours, and it being Christmas too, but your mum was drunk and he couldn't stop her." She paused for a long time before she continued. "She went out somewhere — the bar probably — we never found out. But she went out. He locked the door, as he did every night, and went to bed. I guess he thought she had a key. Or maybe he thought he'd wake up and let her in, but he didn't hear her … if she knocked." She was looking off now, not talking to him but to the past, the people she saw there. "We found her nearly froze to death on the doorstep in the morning. He was never the same after she died. Never the same."

Dan could hardly breathe. The dream came back to him, the one with the Christmas ornament and the glittery tree and the strange scratching sound at the door. The door his father had locked when his mother left and not opened for her in time. He looked at his aunt folded into the covers, vanishing before his eyes, into sleep, into time. "He locked her out? In the cold?"

Her eyes turned to him. "He locked her out of the house. Maybe he thought she'd go and stay with her sister, but she didn't."

She finished her tale of old sorrow and lay back on the pillow, eyes pleading with him to let her be, as though she'd finally done her work and might now go to a much-deserved sleep, forever to forget what she had told him.

Dan glanced up at the dancing neon of girls kicking up their legs and waving top hats while a floating martini poured itself endlessly onto the sidewalk. He'd promised his aunt he'd visit his father's grave, and perhaps this was it. He caught his breath and ducked inside.

The interior smelled of litter and broken hearts. It was a commoner's pub, but the noise was an uncommon racket. As taverns went, the Colson lay between a back alley asylum for life's unwanted-unwashed and one of those annoying modern-day wonders bent on fusing good cheer, good times, and good friends by invoking the holy trinity of Darts, Karaoke, and Trivia, with quizzes about dead Motown artists and quick-time sports statistics that interested no one but the poor sods who surprised themselves silly by knowing the answers in real time: *Hey, Bernie! Next round's on me!*

This one was a simple watering hole for the working men and women looking for a chance to put up their feet, catch their breath, recount the day's troubles and have a cold one, two, four or more, to help shorten the hours as best they could. The camaraderie was cheap, and for the most part you got what you paid for. As for gizmos and gadgets, the condom dispenser outside the "Gents" took first prize over the ATM affixed to the "Ladies."

Jukeboxes had gone out of style long before the compact disc killed vinyl, but this one boasted an impressive relic, an antique by any standards, sitting over in the darkened corner behind an unused bar. Now and then, one of the faithful would walk over with a confident smile — *This one's for all the boys in shaft number 3!* — fish around in his pockets and toss in a slug, punching the litany of numbers like Moses transcribing the stone tablets for God's Chosen. Good old Sudbury, thirty years on and still happily awash in the cat-gut twang of Freddy Fender and Conway Twitty, second only to the power chords of Bachman Turner Overdrive. Three minutes and thirty-three seconds of pure golden oldie pleasure. Just another Sudbury Saturday night. Old Tom and his PEI stompers had it right: Inco, bingo, and getting stinko was pretty much all there was on the menu.

Dan took a seat in the shadows. He was too late for day prices, but that was probably just as well — he wasn't planning on staying long. A drink or two at most. He looked around the room where his father had spent so many hours. How many drinks had it taken him to reach that place where it all stopped mattering, and the wife he'd killed without meaning to appeared before him with a smile and a forgiving kiss?

The bartender stood behind his dispensary, a dry cloth over one shoulder, pouring drink with the tireless faith of a priest in the confessional keeping watch over his flock by night. On the countertop a tray overflowed with dimpled beer steins, gold up to here, white froth above the cut, and all for a tinker's dam. He added one to the count and pulled another.

Behind Dan, a fat blonde laughed a high glossy trill, her table covered in empty glasses. Her look said trash but her saucy eyes said she could see the cheque good at any bank. Her smile was a retina-blinding flash of good times

322

and fun company, and maybe more if you played your cards her way. She reached for a cigarette, lit up, and tossed the deadened stick into a tray overflowing with burnt match ends and bent stubs like charnel house bones. *What No Smoking sign was that, dearie?*

A grubby one-armed man looked over at the blonde, calculating the moves in her direction. He paused, Casanova on the steps of the Vatican considering coming out of retirement to try his hand at eternal beauty one last time. A maturer man now, holding back a moment where once he would have pounced.

And suddenly Dan saw her, floating between tables, tray raised in a silent blessing. The Angel of Mercy who never spilled a drop as she poured her beatitude from one vessel to another: Marilyn's cleavage, but with Maggie Smith's face, and aware to the penny how much every inch was worth. A smile extended long enough to hear his request and return to the bar. Time for niceties later, if required.

He could still recall his last visit: he'd been thirteen, not quite fourteen. The doorman loomed like a refugee from a disreputable sideshow, looking him up and down before pronouncing Dan invisible and turning away in boredom. The whole time he was inside Dan waited for someone to tell him to leave, if not to pick him up by his scruff and toss him freeform through the door, while he scoured the room for a sign of the old man.

This was after his father had taken to drink again following the years of uneasy sobriety — the effects of a strike that had gone on past being amusing, the pleasures of idle afternoons long since worn thin. In their place, a bone-wearying boredom had set in along with occasional flashes of rage at "the man" — sometimes elevated to "the fucking man" — exacerbated by the bottle he talked to day and night. It had taken Dan a while to understand that his father wasn't referring to a specific man, but a collective one composed of bosses and managers and mine owners who "day after frigging day" conspired to keep him from his rightful place of employment under the ground.

No matter that he cursed the very same man just as thoroughly when there was no strike on. What the young Dan suspected, and eventually understood, was that his father hated things as much when they went smoothly as when they didn't. And when it came down to it, he pretty much hated all things equally, no questions asked.

That night, he'd found his father sitting alone in a corner nursing a whiskey on a table that held three empty glasses and a plastic-framed menu boasting that *The Best Eat Here!* A morose man, weaned in silence and hard times, sipping at his drink without a word. Now that Dan thought about it, it might have been around the anniversary of his mother's death, probably why his aunt had been even more insistent than usual that he find his father and bring him home.

That night Dan found him wrapped in his all-weather coat, a no-colour garment that smelled of tar and fish, with rips along the seam where the insulation had fallen out, like something bludgeoned to death with a tire iron. Loneliness was never pretty, even when it dressed up for a Saturday night, and it was seldom inviting to anyone on the outside.

When Dan tried to coax him home, his father looked murder at him. To Stuart Sharp, home was never where the heart lay, no matter how dark and stormy the world outside. When Dan asked why he wanted to sit there drinking alone, his father replied with all the silence in the world. It was what he did best, after all.

Now Dan picked up his glass and took a sip. He had a few more to go before he caught up to the old man.

Even for alcoholics there is a hierarchy of drunkenness: drink, drank, drunk, and drunkard. The tag on the liquor doesn't count for much. You don't get there any faster on expensive cognac than on cheap red wine, or even dollar store cologne if you have the stomach for it, though the first goes down a bit nicer. Put a smelly aquarium in the corner, fill it with bloated carp, and the crowd appeal goes up for some reason known only to God and His Angels. Something to look at other than the waitress's titties and the busboy's bottom, maybe.

It was as if there were two worlds, one for the perfect, privileged people in film and on television, and another for the rest of us who are neither perfect nor privileged enough to matter. But it was when you crossed over the River Merry into the Land of Shame that you knew you'd taken a very wrong turn. Especially if you couldn't remember how you got there and forgot to leave a trail of breadcrumbs to plot your way back again. Drinking itself wasn't the problem. The problem, Dan knew, lay in the degree that it took hold of your life and ran you about without your knowing.

Still, at its best drink could make you soar above the crowd. When the mood hit and the vintage suited, there was nothing better. You felt it in your veins, the way it lifted you up like a gifted amateur at a karaoke rally, turning heads with the talent you knew you had in you all along. It was the bird that flew high and took you, grateful, along with it, tucked beneath its spreading wings, till you touched the golden ball in the sky. At its worst, it carried a sledge-hammer's swing like those games at the midway, as you downed one drink after another without ever ringing the bell, when you knew with agonizing certainty that with the right drink you could slam that bell all the way home. Only you can't do it, swing after swing, because the rhythm is always wrong, no matter how ballsy you get, how rotten with drink, and you sink without flying upwards, without singing the song in your veins, going down as fast as you'd lose a wager on a three-legged dog. Dan knew he was in for a night of lead boots.

The lack of a karaoke machine didn't stop the optimistic or the desperate. From a far corner came the ragged improvising of one fellow who looked not long for this world, or perhaps he'd stopped in from the next for a quick one, blessing the living with his rendition of "Jumpin' Jack Flash," a laryngeal howl, raw as a fresh sunburn, and joined by an unlikely back-up from old times. Mick Jagger hungry for the glory days and Grace Slick coming down off a month-long bender.

Him: a wizened little monkey face, lips screwed up, his rock & roll all pain and attitude. Her: hair fringed like a sixties hippie, eyes staring from some forgotten acid trip, like she's haunted by a memory fixed in her brain that won't let go. Still, she's neatly put together: white blouse belted on over tight black jeans, Nancy Sinatra boots, good cleavage even in the light. She's over fifty, but then he might be nearly twice that.

One of the sure signs of being an alcoholic is when your three best friends are bartenders. These two had friends in spades, while all around them sat the tired faces of the hard-working men and women who looked like little more than deflated balloons and empty overcoats draped over chairs. What they all had in common was the uncelebrated lot of the working man and woman.

The singer sent the notes skyward with a particularly inventive phrasing to his rendition. "Go, Georgie!" some die-hard rock & roller called out, with Grace cheering him on. Made for each other, the pair was. She put her hand on the inside of his thigh, let it creep upwards with a raucous laugh, like it was an old joke they were sharing. The tune turned and he began to crow like a rooster, quenching thirst and drowning troubles as one. A covering of chartreuse over iodine: "The Green, Green Grass of Home" had never sounded so agonizingly verdant.

Dan reeled into his pocket and pulled out a mash of bills, peeled two off and slapped them onto the table. Maggie Smith came over and snapped them up, teeth stained chromium yellow like unpolished silverware.

Over by the door, a stain seemed to be trying to ooze into the shag without much success. Dan sidestepped it and staggered from the bar to stand breathing in the night air. That good clean Sudbury air, bought and paid for by the generosity of Inco.

Mist hissed from the sewer grates where shadows huddled against the cold, home to the unlucky and unloved. The cityscape faded into grey over the disembodied forms of a pair of unhappy wraiths. They glanced up at his passing. Purple hair and nose rings. Where did they get the money? Nifty hair and piercings didn't come cheap.

Dan walked on, trying to imagine his life if he'd stayed. Where would he be now if he hadn't taken that first step onto the tarmac of the 69, never lifted his thumb, opened the cab of the truck and said with stunning alacrity as though he'd done the same thing a million times before, "I'm heading for TO"? Stacking empties at the LCBO, probably, or driving a cab or even working as a clerk at the gleaming new taxation centre. Or maybe he would have died, one fistfight too many, the blinding flash of a brain hemorrhage followed by everlasting blackness. A line on a tombstone to indicate his whereabouts underground. But he would never, ever be *working* underground. Not for Inco. Not for Falconbridge Mines. Not for anybody.

Maybe he'd be the older man groping the teenaged striplings with their nervous eyes and taut tummies, jeans sloping down to reveal, pinked and toned, those smooth, muted buttocks, watching with quiet patience, one hand on his rod, while the trestle trembled and a boy timed his ejaculations to spew over his fist at the shriek of a train passing overhead in the dull monotony of a summer's afternoon, as the brooding older man with the scar on his right temple tried to recollect the shape of the future. *His* future. While the dark, mutinous side of him tried, and failed, to imagine the rest of his life.

Dan shook off the image. Memory's way was perilous.

He hadn't gone a block before his bladder nagged him to stop and take care of business. He looked around and stepped inside a cul-de-sac, like ducking into a darkened church, standing a few feet out of sight from the road while he fumbled with his fly and relieved himself. He looked down and laughed: *You're pretty sizeable.* He thought of the shocked look on the cyclist's face as he pushed him against the fence. He sprayed a box labelled with a brand of tissue papers, the drops splattering back at him, managing to wet his fingers in the draw. This, he knew, was the prelude to sloppy drunk. He was halfway through his meditations when he heard the voices. He swayed toward the dark and hoped he'd finish before they appeared or else that they would pass quickly and not look into the alley's dim depths and see him at prayer.

Shadows appeared over his shoulder, thrown long by the street lamps. From the sound of their footsteps he knew they'd turned down the entrance to the alley. He still had the presence of mind to feel embarrassed at being caught. He shook himself and zipped up before turning, ready to smile and laugh at his predicament.

At first he took them for an older couple. They looked burnt-out wisps of human beings. She appeared to be arguing, stumbling while leaning against him as they moved closer. Then he recognized them as the forms huddled on the sewer grates.

She looked him up and down, sizing him up for something. A coffin, maybe. "What are you doing, fuckhead? You fucking pissing in the street?"

A part of his brain considered this: not the nicest of greetings. Certainly not words to cheer you at two in the morning in a back alley. They continued toward him with their jerky, spastic walk, propping each other up like badly conjoined twins. Purple hair glinted in the moonlight. She wore a tight clingy skirt and leopard print leotards. The boy was in jeans with a black T. A tattooed dragon clawed its way up his throat and wrapped itself around his neck. Both had on pricey leather jackets. Between them they had enough piercings to fill a small jewellery box. Must've been hell getting through airport security.

"Did you hear me? I said what are you doing?" She snarled like a Ringwraith. There should have been smoke wreathing from her lips. "I want money, you cocksucker!" Her arm clutched a purse in a ridiculous parody of a woman. "How much you got, fuckin' dickhead?"

"Yeah!" said the guy. "We want your money. How much you got?" He laughed and rattled a chain wrapped around his fist. They were close enough for Dan to see their faces. The flat-eyed, no-mind stare of heroin addicts doing their diddly dance. Sid and Nancy in *On The Town*.

"Scum," Dan mumbled.

The chain quivered in quick junkie twitches. "You talkin' to me?" the boy demanded. Make that Sid and Nancy in *Taxi Driver*. The perfect couple. She had a cunt for a mouth; he had an arsehole for a brain.

Behind him, a fire escape traced a route to the roof, but it was blocked above the first floor. The only way out of the alley lay behind this highly colourful odd couple. At least Sally would be impressed. Dan reasoned he could bluff his way out or, if it came to it, he could manage the two of them without much trouble. They weren't big and they were addicts. They were probably used to rolling drunks who couldn't put up much of a fight. Then again, he was drunk.

They moved faster than he expected. She swung the purse, clipping Dan on the bridge of the nose with a wallop. His hands went up to his face as his throat constricted in rage. The sky pitched, shrank, then resumed normal proportions above. The brick had found its mark.

Sid raised an arm to follow up with the chain. Fuelled by anger and pain, Dan booted him in the balls. The boy staggered and fell to the sidewalk, the slither of leather on concrete. Through his outraged howl, Dan heard the click. Something glinted. Metal. Longer and sharper than a piercing. Nancy came at him, blade in hand, suddenly looking more than capable as Sid writhed on the ground. She would have at him for her man. Adrenaline surged like lightning. With no time for niceties, Dan kicked her in the stomach and sent her and her purple hair reeling.

He watched, awed by the slow-motion trajectory as she flipped and rolled and landed against the curb. Her head hit, making an ugly, disturbing sound like the clack of false teeth. She lay still. Was she breathing? In that light, it was impossible to tell. If anyone came around the corner, they'd be calling him the assailant. The boy would claim he'd attacked them. That he'd been bigger and faster — maybe fast enough to kill a teenaged girl. Self-defence had brought out the knife.

Over by the curb. An arm moved. Reached up to feel the head. Thank. Fuck. He hadn't killed her after all. For a moment he wanted to go over and help, but quickly thought better of it. The head looked around, fixing him with a hateful stare. Hands planted themselves in the dirt. The body twitched, inching upwards. She was like the Evil Dead, already coming after him again.

He flashed on the pub. Remembered he'd paid in cash. No paper trail. No one knew his name. Wasn't a regular. And was very very grateful.

Time to go.

TWENTY-ONE

Drink and Resurrection

DAN HAD NEVER ENDANGERED anybody's life — his own included — by mixing driving with alcohol. Even this latest zigzag life had thrown him wasn't going to make him change that. There were some rules no amount of alcohol could waive, though if drinking encouraged a state in which you could convince yourself of almost anything, then that went a long way toward explaining why so many drinkers didn't consider themselves subject to those rules. He sobered up long enough to patch his face, say goodbye to his aunt and cousin and get safely back down the 69.

Somewhere between Parry Sound and Mactier his mind got stuck in a loop as he imagined his mother returning home to find herself locked out in the snow, knocking without getting an answer. And always, just out of reach, himself as a four-year-old, listening to a strange scratching sound that came intermittently before fading out for good. *You wouldn't remember — you were just a little kid, Daniel.*

His aunt's words. Try as he might, he couldn't erase the memory's sepia glow.

Despite what he'd learned about his mother's death, Dan was determined not to fall apart over it. At least not any more than he had already. She'd been dead for more than thirty years. That wasn't about to change. Knowledge stopped the hoping, he reminded himself, but it didn't make things better.

In his mind there were two women who occupied his memory and vied for the title of mother: one was light and feathery, a rustle of flowers in the morning air, a woman who made Eskimo villages out of discarded half-shells of eggs upended on drifts of cotton batten snow. The other was slovenly, weepy-eyed, didn't dress before three in the afternoon, and made promises she didn't keep or remember. Neither of them seemed real, just illusions he'd invented to fill in the shadows where a mother was supposed to be. He'd always felt that if he could know which version was true — or neither — then he could stop trying to remember her, stop trying to piece her together after all these years.

Just outside Barrie he pulled over to the side of the highway and leaned his forehead into the steering wheel. A squadron of eighteen-wheelers roared past, rocking him like a child as he choked back his sobs, tears staining his pant-legs. The only thing that revived him was the thought of more drink waiting at home. Normally a draft or two would have stood him in good stead at a local pub, but the thought that he might not be able to stop there, coupled with the fear of getting stranded in Barrie, held sway. So there was hope, was how he saw it. If he still had priorities on where he would and would not allow himself to get pissed-drunk, there was still a little humanity left.

By the time he turned in his driveway, his mind had re-focused on Craig Killingworth's disappearance. It was an excuse, he knew, to keep from thinking about his mother's death. He dropped his bag in the hall and went upstairs to wash his face, marvelling at the yellow and purple stain spreading beneath the skin on the right side. In the kitchen, he cracked the ice tray against the counter, splashed a healthy hit of Scotch into a glass, filled a plastic bag with the rest of the ice, and went to the living room. There, holding the bag to his face, he spread the file and photos on the floor like a mad haberdasher's shop. He had a case to finish.

The whiskey brought clarity to his thinking. It helped him concentrate as it dulled the ache in his head and the pain in his heart. As he drank, he contemplated the code that might or might not unlock the past: a missing bicycle, a ferry captain who said he saw Craig Killingworth crossing just one way. All this time Dan had imagined a clean break or, at worst, death by mishap somewhere down the highway. But the lost portion of the file and the missing bicycle had entwined in his mind. It seemed as though they'd been telling him something different. He just wished he knew what.

He picked up Craig Killingworth's photograph, trying to read into its depths. No smiles were always the hardest to interpret. Sadness or just a lack of expression? Cheese or no cheese? There was a shot of Killingworth with his sons, the dolphin-like Thom, already beautiful, and the darker, thought-ravaged features of the slightly older Theodore. Ted. Even here, Craig Killingworth's upturned mouth was hard to press into service as a smile. What lay hidden behind those eyes? What held back the joy he might have felt at being with his boys?

A final shot showed the interior of what looked a lot like the stables Dan had explored behind the summerhouse the day before the wedding. Killingworth's trim figure was outfitted in jodhpurs and sport-shirt, collar turned up. He held a grooming brush in one hand; his other lay on the waxy brown flank of a gelding. Here, at last, he exhibited what looked like the ghost of a smile.

"Where did you go?" Dan spoke to the empty room. "And why does your family not want you found?"

A man had disappeared, leaving behind a wife and two sons. How had he not cared enough to come back? Suicide was one possible answer. For a moment, Dan pictured himself up on Lake on the Mountain. He saw himself grasping the oars as the rowboat slid over the surface of the lake. *It just plunges,* Thom had said. Whatever was below lay so deep it might never be found.

He moved the pictures and file memos around, rearranging the pieces of the puzzle to make them fit. They stubbornly resisted interpretation. He reached for the bottle — empty. There was another in the kitchen, but when he tried to pour from it, it flew from his hands, smashing on the tiles. He picked up the larger pieces, cutting his fingers. Blood trailed across the floor. He cursed the perversity of inanimate objects and wiped his bloodied hand on a dishtowel.

Did he really prefer being drunk? What a pathetic statement that made. More important, what to do about it? Why did despair always look so much better through the prism of a filled glass? Drink went into the body, through the mouth and down the throat, then on to the underbelly and, eventually, it left in a wash of fine yellow spray. And that was it for all that alcohol, pricey or not. Time to refill your glass and get on with your life. But the despair stayed, seeming to need no entry or exit, no replenishing, like mercury or some other poison that sickened without killing. Ingested by accident or by design, once in and never to leave. To rot your guts and muddle your mind till you were long past having a mind. What was it about the barrel's bottom that looked so good from the inside? Because surely it was hell from the outside, judging by the looks others gave you when you were down there.

The expression on Ked's face was pure disgust. His son turned and went into the kitchen without a word. Dan glanced around. It was morning, but still early by the feel of it. He lay stretched on the living room floor like a schoolboy after pulling an all-nighter, the contents of Craig Killingworth's missing person report strewn around him. He sat up. His eyelids felt as though they'd been peeled back with a can opener. His reading glasses lay on the floor beneath him, road-kill written all over them. He coughed and gasped at the pain searing his lungs. Obviously it hadn't been an easy landing.

Dan picked his way out to the kitchen where Ked had begun cleaning up. Glass glittered in the morning light. A bloodied tea towel lay in the middle of the floor. He might have believed the place had been broken into if he hadn't recalled searching for the third bottle of Scotch in his upstairs office drawer.

"I would've cleaned up. I wasn't expecting you home till later," Dan offered.

"I live here too, you know."

It wasn't a question so much as a flat statement asserting some sort of right which Dan was having trouble figuring out at the moment.

"I know that. I've never questioned it."

Ked turned, his eyes hard. "You're always telling me how to behave and not to fuck up my life. Now it's my turn." He was trembling. "I don't want a drunk for a father."

Dan could see the fear in his son's face. But he saw something else — something he recognized. He'd felt it himself enough times facing his own father in moments that had bordered on hatred. He saw determination hidden behind those disapproving eyes.

"Is that what you think I am?" Dan said slowly.

Ked nodded, taking quick breaths through his nose.

"I know I drink a lot," Dan said. "But I'm not a drunk."

"So you say." Ked stood there staring at him. "So you say, Dad. But I've seen you passed out enough times to know you have a problem."

"I like to drink. I don't think I have a problem," Dan said, trying to smile despite the pain. For a moment, he wondered if he really did have a problem.

"Then prove it." Ked's eyes challenged him. "I'm asking you not to have another drink for the next six months."

Dan scratched behind one ear. "That's pretty drastic."

"Walk the talk, Dad. Isn't that what you're always telling me? So walk the talk."

Dan looked around at the mess on the floor then up at this son of his, half-grown, but maybe knowing better than he had at that age. He studied the features of the boy's face. Somehow what was awkward in Dan had come out strong in Ked. He was becoming a handsome young man.

"Did something happen while you were away visiting Aunt Marge?"

Dan nodded slowly, calling to mind the conversation with his aunt as she lay in bed pulling on her oxygen. He moistened his lips. "Yeah. I guess it did."

Ked wiped back a tear. "Is that what set you off drinking again?"

Dan hated the disapproval on his son's face. "I don't really feel up to discussing it, Ked. Maybe later."

"Six months, Dad."

Dan started to motion with his hands, but Ked cut him off. "If you don't agree, I'm going to move out of here and go live with Mom."

Dan paused to take stock of the situation. His son was a meltdown waiting to happen. "Is that what you want?" he said softly. "Do you want to live with your mother?"

"*No!* I want to live here with you!" he said. "But if you can't … can't just…." The tears started flowing, cutting off the sentence.

"All right," Dan said quietly. "All right. I agree."

Ked looked up and sniffled. "You agree not to drink for six months — starting today?"

"Yes. I agree not to drink for six months."

Ked's stance relaxed a little. "Okay."

Dan wanted to say something to lighten the situation. "But your Uncle Donny's going to kill me when I tell him I can't even have a beer with him…."

"No, he's not." Ked shook his head. "I already talked to him. He agrees with me. You've got to stop."

Six months. Surely there would be any number of valid reasons not to keep the promise. Like right now, Dan thought. A drink would have gone a long way toward making his hangover just a little more bearable. How was he going to concentrate at work when it got really stressful? Sometimes things brooded on the horizon for hours waiting for a trigger, lying there inert then overtaking him all at once, unleashing their fury like a sudden storm. The searing, sizzling, electric dazzle of it. A desert rock, a splash of water, high noon. The pressure could build for hours, but all it took was one flashpoint to unleash his desire for a drink, and it all came crashing down. Leaving him exhausted, deflated, defeated. Disgusted with having lost control over himself once again.

Obviously he was going to have plenty to do to redeem himself in Ked's eyes. How had the father-son equation got so turned around?

Dan went back out to the scramble of photographs and documents spread across his rug. He gathered up the pieces and left the file on the dining room table. He dialled Donny's number. Better to confront the beast sooner than later. Donny picked up.

"Et tu, Brute?" Dan said.

"Then fall, Caesar." Donny blew a well-considered breath across the line. "I'm sorry, but I agree with your son. Just be glad we spared you the video cameras and the weeping host and the public intervention on television.

But if you're thinking about not living up to your promise, I wouldn't do it."

"No?"

"You sure like to make 'em suffer, don't you?"

Dan said nothing.

"Word of advice, Danny? Don't disappoint your son. He's very vulnerable right now. It's bad enough you didn't believe his stories about nicking junk at school, but this might do some permanent damage to your relationship if you're not careful."

"You really think so?"

"I know so. And that's why I'm telling you myself."

"I hear you. Thanks."

Dan went upstairs to the bathroom. He stripped off his clothes and stood in the shower under the cold water until it hurt. Whatever good it might do to punish himself for what had happened to his mother and whatever had or had not happened in his life, unlike his own father, Dan didn't intend to hurt anyone else with it. Ked least of all. It was time to stop feeling sorry for himself and get on with things. If what he'd learned in Sudbury could give him anything, then it could give him that.

TWENTY-TWO

Now Playing

THE DAY FOR THE PLANNED PORN sequel had arrived. Hardly the final instalment of *Lord of the Rings* or even *The Godfather Part III*, but still, Dan wasn't about to miss the premiere of Richard Philips's latest. He walked along the eastern perimeters of the Danforth, silently studying the words raised a head above the sidewalk: Zam-Zam Beauty School, Pro-Tax Accounting, Yummy Delicious Good Food. Hand-painted signs on plywood with lights affixed bore the perennial optimism of the eternally down-at-heel. He paused when he came to the Islamic-Christian Friendship Society. Was there any cause more hopeless at the moment? What well-meaning but futile urge lay behind the establishment of such a thing?

High over the rundown storefronts, a militant billboard proclaimed to the faithful that "You Deserve A Better Life." A message of salvation from an organization claiming to be "Debt Counsellors Since 1966." Dan imagined the first hopefuls lining up for the offer of a better life all those years ago. Had they achieved a better life or anything remotely like it? Was there someone even now passing by and looking up, thankful that a similar moment had saved him from a life of perpetual misery all those years ago? Or had those first clients just bumped through life from one misery to another and died eventually, the only end to debt they'd ever had?

Dan chose Yummy Delicious Good Food for a vantage point — half because he felt sorry for the place and half because it looked a step or two up from the donut shop on the opposite corner. Besides, it had its own soundtrack: Hank Williams Jr.'s "Hey, Good Lookin'" blared from tinny loudspeakers with its invitation to cook something up together. For all intents and purposes, it was as though the fifties never ended. A quick glance around the brown-on-orange interior with its garish lime green tablecloths and the display of yesterday's tea biscuits and revamped muffins under fingerprint-marred glass sent a further message that no one cared about the food any more than they were concerned with interior design or current music trends.

A tiny man whose chin seemed glued to his chest pivoted to regard the newcomer. Dan tried not to stare before realizing he was the one being stared at. To the man's left sat a wreck with a bloated face and swollen nose. Her drink-inflamed skin looked as though it couldn't decide where to settle, a herd of nomadic goats roaming across her cheeks. Another poor thing sat wistfully in the window wearing a yellow cardigan with a rose scarf tied neatly around her throat. Her idea of a bit of bright or just a subconscious urge to leave it all behind, like Isadora, with a quick jaunt in a Bugatti? Dan felt himself a relative beauty here. Lonely, sad, and unwanted — he called them the Eleanor Rigbys, friendless by chance or maybe even by design. Then again, who needed the grief that friendship brought? They were the city's detritus, its social castaways.

While others his age were moving in droves to Parkdale, awed to find drunks and crack addicts huddled on their doorsteps as though that constituted a more resonant form of city life, Dan had moved to Leslieville. Parkdale was for the middle-class kids who'd never experienced life outside the suburbs. Con artists went there to practise scams that were old in the forties and left feeling sad and somehow ashamed — something about children and candy. At least the rich kids knew better. Some days it seemed the city was filled with a million voyeurs. All audience and no show. Yet compared to this 'hood, even Parkdale seemed a buggy ride in Chelsea. But Dan had begun in the east and in the east he would stay.

He sat and watched the entrance to Moonlight Videos. Daylight was beginning to fade. No one came or went by the front door. After a half-hour, he began to wonder if the shoot had been cancelled. Until that moment it hadn't occurred to him that even a minor operation like Moonlight Videos might have a stage door. A private entrance for the artistes. He finished his coffee — surprisingly good for the looks of the place — and left.

A halo of lamplights brought the sky down low, making the street look like the backdrop to a Victorian melodrama. Pigeons cooed restlessly in the twilight. He crossed the road, eyes peeled for anything showing in the upstairs window; there was no sign of life.

He turned into a back alley, trying to decide which of the broken down doorways hidden by cast-off sofas, disintegrating cardboard boxes, and bags of rotting garbage belonged to Moonlight Videos. He was in luck. A hand-written note beckoned over a buzzer that glowed faintly in the semi-dark. He pressed the buzzer and heard the automated click. He entered and climbed two flights of dimly lit stairs with a single entrance at the top. He knocked and opened the door.

A wiry man with a clipboard glanced up. "Hi — come on in." He looked Dan over, his face registering interest. "You're just in time. You're a top, right? I told them I needed a top."

Dan looked over the man's shoulder and spotted his prey in jeans and a tank-top among the handful of people in the room. Dan pointed him out. "Sorry to spoil your party, but I'm here to take that boy with me."

"Oh." The man's face tightened. "You his father?"

"No."

"Who are you then? I've got an ID card that says he's eighteen."

"And I've got a court order that says he's a juvenile. Want to see it?" Dan offered the paper to the man, whose face turned the colour of ash.

"What the fuck's going on here?" And in came the Man in the Moon himself: a short, smudge-faced gump puffing on a cigar, as pocked and cratered as the dead rock itself. "Who are you?" he demanded.

"Dan Sharp — private investigations. You own this place?"

The man's bravado faltered and died. "I'm Dave Henigar. Yes, this is my operation." He paused. "Are you a cop?"

Dan shook his head. "I said 'private.' But I've got a piece of paper saying I can take that boy" — he pointed at Richard — "with me when I leave."

The hard look on Henigar's face returned, a barely contained fury that proclaimed him a force to be reckoned with. Without the court document, Dan wouldn't want to be confronting this man. He waved the letter under his nose. The offer to peruse it was turned down again.

"Believe me," Dan said. "You're better off if I take him off your hands, but I'll call in help from the police if I have to."

The man looked over at Richard. Ash fell from his cigar. "He's just partying with us."

"He made a movie for you last month," Dan said.

The man's eyes flashed venom. He barked at Richard. "You — kid! Get over here. Now!"

Richard scrambled toward them and stood there nervously.

"This guy says you're underage. That true?"

The boy's eyes flickered at Dan. "No."

"Don't fuck with me," the man growled.

"I'm not — I'm eighteen. My name's Lester Higgins."

"His name is Richard Philips," Dan told the fat man. "He turned fifteen last month and he ran away from home in July." Dan waved the paper at Richard, and for once someone took it. "Is that you?"

The boy looked up from the photograph, his face scared. More than just interrupting a party, the boy's livelihood was being jeopardized. Dan looked around at the others. A mulatto kid stood watching from a corner. Definitely underage, Dan decided. "Hey! How about you? You got ID?"

Henigar stirred. "He's mine."

Dan turned to him. "Your what?"

"My son," he said with a snarl, despite the aura of fear he was giving off at that moment. "And he's working the camera."

"Really? Glad to know you're using homegrown instead of stealing other people's kids." Dan tried for a demonic grin, hoping he looked a little deranged. "I sure hope you haven't distributed that film yet." He looked at Richard. "Let's go."

The kid looked at Henigar. "Do I have to?"

"Get out of here!" came the surly reply.

Out on the street, Dan opened the car door and shoved the kid inside. He checked to see that no one was following or writing down the licence plate number then got in the driver's side. The boy sat with his arms wrapped around his chest, pouting. "I don't want to go."

"Too bad. You're coming with me. And don't try jumping out at the light," Dan said. "I'm a fast runner."

He started the car. Traffic was light on Danforth at that hour. It was a good two minutes before the boy spoke. "I don't want to go home. *Please!* Don't take me in."

"I have to — you're underage."

"Please! Don't make me go back."

Dan stopped the car and put it in neutral. He sat there silently considering.

A calculating look came over the boy's face. "I'll give you a blow job if you let me go."

Dan was surprised by the vehemence of his reaction. "Listen, you fucked up little asshole. What you're doing is illegal and stupid!"

The kid cringed in the same way Ralph had when Dan kicked at him. He softened when he saw Dan wasn't going to hit him.

"I don't give a flying fuck about those guys and their movies," Dan said, "but you could have sent them to jail for about a million years for lying to them about your age. Do you want to do that? Huh?"

Richard began to cry. "Don't take me back home. You have no idea what it's like…!"

"Then what should I do with you? Just let you go?"

"Please? I'll get a job," the kid sniffled.

Dan considered this. He thought about what might happen to this kid if he ended up back home. "Would you stick with it if I did?"

The kid eyed him sullenly. The rebellion returned. "Would you?"

Wrong answer, Dan thought. This kid definitely didn't know how to play his cards. "You'd probably have to, considering I just put you out of business. They won't touch you now they know your real age." He was right — the kid's life was going to be fucked up no matter what he did. "The only thing keeping me from sending you back right now is I met your mother and her charming husband."

"You met them?"

"Yes, I met them. And I wouldn't wish them on anyone, dead or alive. So you've got that going for you. What I want is a guarantee you're not going to end up dead on some street corner a month from now."

The boy's eyes narrowed. "Why would you care?"

Dan stared at him. What to tell this kid about what he'd seen and done? "Tell me — do you like what you're doing?"

"What? The films?"

"The films. Hooking. Hustling. Selling your body. Are you even gay?"

A spark of self-respect stole into Richard's face. "Yes, I'm gay," he said.

"Congratulations — at least you know that," Dan told him. "Do you like having sex with guys for money?"

The kid looked out the window. "Not really." His voice faltered. "I got raped once."

"Have an HIV test?"

"Yep. It came back clear."

"Bet it was scary waiting for the results, wasn't it?"

The defiance returned. "Yeah. So what?"

"So what? You're asking me 'so what?' Do you want to spend your life having sex with guys who might rape you and infect you with a disease so you can die painfully and early?"

A hesitant shrug was followed by a long pause. Then, "No. I don't want to die."

"Okay. Fair enough. Then I'll tell you why I care." Dan waited till the kid turned to look at him. "I care because twenty years ago, I was you."

Richard looked long and hard at Dan, his eyes suspicious but curious. "What do you mean?"

"Boys Town — Bay and Grosvenor. That was my corner."

Richard shot him another look, one of skepticism mixed with awe. "Really?"

"That's right. Only I met a guy who helped me out. Otherwise I might still be there. Or dead."

Richard sat back in the seat and stared out the windshield. He nodded, as if convincing himself of something. "Okay, so what then?"

†

"Ked, this is Lester."

"Hi, Lester."

Dan eyed his son. Was this too much to spring on him unannounced? "Lester needs a friend right now. You fit the bill."

Ked's face showed something like pride and pleasure all at once. "Cool."

Dan turned to Richard, who was now Lester. "You'll stay here with us. It's only temporary, until I figure out what I can do for you."

Lester nodded. His eyes expressed gratitude, but his tongue was clearly tied in knots at that moment.

"There's a spare bed in my room," Ked said. "Where's your stuff?"

Lester looked perplexed. "I, uh, don't have anything."

"That's okay."

A howling came from outside. Ked's head swivelled toward the window. "I forgot Ralph in the backyard!"

Ked ran to the door. The dog came bounding in, nearly knocking Lester over. The boy leaned down and wrapped his arms around Ralph's neck, hands plunged in the gingery fur. "Hey, boy!"

"Lester, meet Ralph," Dan said.

Lester looked up at Dan with the first real smile he'd given all evening. "He's gorgeous!"

Dan stole a look at his son. Ked winked back.

TWENTY-THREE

Stalking Cool Blue

THE BEDSIDE CLOCK read 3:13 a.m. He'd been lying awake for nearly an hour. It was no use — he wouldn't get back to sleep with all the thoughts pursuing him. How had Craig Killingworth vanished without leaving tracks? The poor could vanish without a trace, no banks to chase after them, no tax office to care about the millions in unpaid revenue receipts. Abducted children disappeared, grew up and changed appearance, even became someone else's child, perhaps without knowing it. The aged and infirm simply became invisible. But how could a well-known man of influence just leave the earth, never to be heard from again?

A man's life consisted of certain humdrum routines — getting up and going to work, socializing on weekends, having supper with friends and colleagues, and a million variations on the same themes. You didn't just drop out and vanish without leaving a trail or at least establishing a new routine elsewhere. The more Dan thought about it, the more he was convinced Craig Killingworth was dead. Wherever he'd gone after getting off the ferry, he probably hadn't lived long enough to tell anybody about it.

He went into his office and opened the file. Sometimes repeatedly going over the details of a case drummed something into his brain that he would otherwise have missed. The words here still told him nothing. If there was a clue, he lacked the key to unlock it. He turned to the photographs, scrutinizing them with his magnifying glass. The shot of the stables held his interest. Was it the light in Killingworth's eyes? The hand on the gelding? No, that wasn't it. He turned his attention to the background. With a jolt he recognized the container of rat poison on the window ledge — the one he'd seen on his tour of the barn last month, only twenty years younger in the photograph. If he blew it up large enough, he might even be able to read the poison warning. He recalled Trevor's story of the horses that had died after his Uncle Craig disappeared. Accident or eerie coincidence? Who would want six horses dead, and why?

Dan thought of Magnus Ferguson and wondered what the now-dead gardener would have had to say about it. Had Killingworth really fired the man for theft or had there been another reason? A love affair with his wife, perhaps? Maybe Craig had disappeared after a violent confrontation gone wrong. Or had Lucille arranged for the gardener to kill her husband, paying him a tidy sum in a yellow envelope? He wouldn't put it past her. In fact, she might even have done it herself.

Dan let his imagination wander. How would a woman like Lucille Killingworth kill? Surely not by force. With a gun if she had to, but that was always messy. There'd be traces left behind: blood on a floor, guts splattered on walls and curtains. Not her style. It would be even riskier outdoors where someone might hear or see. The acoustics over the bay would advertise the action for miles. Would rat poison be too gruesome or risky for a woman like Lucille Killingworth? It might explain why she didn't want her husband found — if he'd been poisoned, his body would still bear traces of it.

But the other question remained: why the horses?

When he went back to bed an hour later, the mystery of Craig Killingworth was very much alive in his mind.

He was only halfway through what was promising to be a long and tiresome day. The computer's pop-up window cheerfully reminded him that he had his weekly therapy session to look forward to that evening. At seven he closed up shop and walked over to the Harbord Centre, as he did every Thursday. As far as Dan was concerned, there was only one item on the menu today. Martin listened quietly as he described what he'd learned on his stopover in Sudbury.

"How are you handling it?" was Martin's non-committal response.

"Apart from the fact that it seems to have blown my entire world apart? Well enough, I suppose."

Martin clasped his hands under his chin. He seemed disposed to relate the revelation to Dan's buried anger. "Think of your anger as an attempt to shake off a sense of futility, the hopelessness you felt over your mother's death. Sometimes we blame our anger on the city or the traffic or on other people's inadequacy. It can even make us strike out at things and people that have no relation to what is really disturbing us. What we're talking about is an inability to function in the normal world."

Dan said nothing.

"I'd like to refer you to a depression specialist."

"I'm not depressed."

"You may simply be unaware of it," Martin persisted. "Perhaps this is the epiphany you need to alert you to that reality."

"'Epiphany.' You mean a realization?"

"Yes — when a light goes on and we make connections."

"I make connections for a living."

Martin stared at him blankly.

"I connect the dots to find people who go missing from their lives. That's what I call an epiphany."

"I see."

Martin reached for his pad. A nagging thought brought Dan full circle. He held up a finger, his brain still formulating the question.

"How would you know if you had an android for a patient?"

Martin's face registered intrigue. For a moment Dan thought he might even smile, but he stopped short of that. "I don't know. How would I know if I had an android for a patient?"

"That's the question," Dan said. "How do we know if people are really feeling something or if they're just mimicking an emotion? Can emotions be learned?"

"The responses can. A clever person might even be able to produce certain physiological reactions deemed appropriate to the circumstance. Tears maybe, or even an increase in blood pressure in a heightened situation. Some people can actually blush on command. But it's not the same as having a real emotion."

Dan's thoughts were racing. "If you did something you felt guilty about for years, even if it was never found out, how would it register on your subconscious mind?"

"Are you talking about what happened to you because of your mother's death?"

"No, I'm not. I can accept the fact that I was four years old and unaware of what was happening. I don't intend to spend the rest of my life beating myself up over that."

Martin's pen scribbled furiously. He looked up. "It's hard to say. Guilt has a funny way of disguising itself as other emotions — egotism, a sense of entitlement, anger. Even self-hatred. It's impossible to predict."

"What if you murdered someone?"

Martin stared. "I still say it's not possible to predetermine the answer, but my guess is that in the end, if you can't reconcile it, it would eventually destroy you."

Dan pictured Lucille Killingworth's frozen smile. "But what if you're incapable of feeling emotion? No remorse?"

"Then maybe nothing would come of it, except the person might retreat further into a lack of genuine emotional responses. There are adults who never mature emotionally. They look and act like other people, but on an affective level they're very childlike."

"Immaturity?"

"It's more like an emotional retardation. These are people who don't feel the same things the rest of us feel. Lacking empathy, for example. Usually they learn to hide their responses. They become adept at masking how they really feel, giving expression to what they think we want to see."

Dan thought of Lucille Killingworth's artificial manners and tempered speech, her convincingly feigned dismay when Dan told her of Daniella's pregnancy. Her reactions had seemed real, despite being manufactured. Everything cool and restrained. But what, he was thinking, if you pushed her over the edge? What would happen then? Would she do or say anything to give herself away? What would it take to see that side of her?

Out on the street, Dan tossed away Martin's script for the specialist and put in a call to Trevor. His voice mail answered. Dan left a greeting, saying he was doing well and asking Trevor to reply to his question when he had a moment. If he didn't answer his cell, Dan said, then he was in transit and the call would forward home. He apologized for the unusual question but said it was important. He felt odd about asking, though he was already sure he knew the answer.

Trevor's reply was waiting on the machine when he got home. He'd called his mother to make sure. The answer wasn't what Dan had expected, but it still fit his hypothesis. Maybe even better than he'd hoped. Dan dialled Donny's number. His friend sounded calm, proudly telling Dan how he'd decided not to panic. There was plenty of time to look for a job, he said, though a vacation still wasn't in the works, as far as he could see.

Dan listened politely before changing the subject. "Question," Dan said.

"Shoot."

"If you were a woman …"

"*If?*"

"Okay. If you were a very *wealthy* woman …"

"Ah!"

"And you wanted to get rid of an abusive bastard of a husband…."

"It's getting better — keep going."

"How would you kill him?"

There wasn't even a pause. "I'd hire a hit man: Tracey Ullman in *I Love You To Death*. Or maybe I'd get my lover to do it, like Barbara Stanwyck in *Double Indemnity*. Or better yet, we'd do it together and then I'd die in a car crash, ironically leaving my lover to be convicted of killing me: Lana Turner in *The Postman Always Rings Twice*."

"Okay, let's rethink this. You live in a small town where everyone knows you and there are no hit men, maybe even no lovers. Then how would you do it?"

Donny thought this over. "First of all, I'd never live there, if there is such a place. And if there is, it's got to be in Saskatchewan. Second, I'd probably poison him and make it look like an accident."

"Me, too. Okay, where would you hide the body?"

"I wouldn't. The death already looks accidental, right?"

"What if you killed him somewhere he wasn't supposed to be, so you had to get rid of the evidence?"

"That's too difficult. I'd need to know the area to find a place that would be fair game for anyone to go, and where he might just end up getting poisoned all by himself."

"Exactly!"

"What film is this?"

"The Craig Killingworth Story."

"I was afraid you might say that."

"Kisses. Gotta go."

Dan hung up and replayed Trevor's message. His uncle's horses had not died from rat poison, as he'd expected. They'd died from something far more interesting. He pictured the stone house in the woods under the pine trees, the red creeper vine along the wraparound porch, and the bright blue flowers in the Killingworth garden the day he and Bill had arrived for the wedding a month ago — he looked at the circled date on his calendar — tomorrow. He did a Google search for images and found what he was looking for.

Dan barely slept, rising in the dark before Ked and Lester were up. He left a note and some money for Ked, telling him to take Lester to the zoo for the day — he'd square it with school later. He stepped into his car, feeling exhilarated. His mind raced all along the 401, heading east in the pre-dawn darkness. Just before seven o'clock, gold spilled over the horizon, the sky cracking open.

It was past eight when he reached Picton and rolled up beside St. Mary Magdalene Church. The grass was overgrown, the stones cracked and leaning. The church had been turned into a museum at some point in the past twenty years. That wouldn't make any difference. It was the man he was looking for, not the church. He thought back to his first impression of the Poplar Plains house: Klingsor's castle. The realm of a magician who controlled everything from afar without ever appearing in person. The ultimate trick of the dead.

He walked along the rows of plots. A long rectangular tomb leaked along the edges, water seeping down and turning green at the base:

Nathaniel Macaulay

1914-1990

A God-fearing Christian

Dan looked up at the weeping angel set atop the monument. His voice cut through the air. "What were you thinking, you miserable old bastard? What's to fear if you've done nothing wrong? What do you know?"

A tractor started up somewhere in the distance.

"Speak up — now's the time to confess. Tell the court what you did."

The wind stirred in the grass.

"And don't give me that, 'Oh, poor me' stuff. I'm onto you. There'll be no peace for the dead if there's none for the living."

The house looked the same, as much a showcase as ever. An olive green Saab was stopped at one end of the drive's half-circle. An upstairs window angled the light. Dan placed it somewhere in the hallway outside the room where he and Bill had spent their final night together. He drew up beside the Saab. No need to hide. A few minutes would give him all the time he needed and maybe an answer or two.

In the morning sun, the gardens were popping with the bright blue flower he'd noticed on his previous visit. Monkshood. Blooming this late in the fall meant they were a particularly virulent variety known as *Aconitum Michaelii*. A minimal amount would be fatal if ingested. Even the leaves were poisonous to touch. Symptoms showed up as soon as five minutes after contact. Vomiting, sweating, blurred vision, and paralysis would follow soon after. Cause of death would appear to be heart and respiratory failure. There was no antidote.

He'd brought his gloves. He pulled up a bunch of the deadly flowers with their bright blue spines and their little blue caps. He heard the door open. Lucille Killingworth stared at him in disbelief. He quickly grabbed a stock of purple asters in the other hand, holding them behind his back as he confronted her with the noxious flower held in front of him.

She eyed him warily, as she might a crazy person. "What are you doing? Please leave my property!" *Please* leave. Ever the gracious hostess.

Whatever had happened to Craig Killingworth had happened a long time ago, Dan reasoned. He was risking a lot by being there and doing what he was doing. There was no justification for it, other than one — he needed to be certain.

"Would you hold these for me, Lucille?"

Her face in confusion, she opened her hands to accept the Monkshood. Dan whisked them away at the last moment, substituting the asters. "Sorry, not these ones," he said. "I forgot — the blue ones aren't safe. Are they?"

"What is going on here? What are you doing to my garden?" she demanded.

"Is this what you poisoned your husband with? Or did you have Magnus do it for you?"

Fury overtook her. Her body trembled. In that moment, Dan was sure she was capable of violence. And now he knew what it took for her to abandon her social graces.

"I've had enough. Leave now before I call the police!" She headed back to the house.

"Yes, I'm sure you've got Commissioner Burgess on speed dial for emergencies like this."

She turned back to him. Her eyes flashed venom. Dan held her gaze. "Where did you bury him? Somewhere in the garden? What if I came back with a warrant and dug up your entire estate?"

"Is that what you think you're doing? Looking for my husband's body? My god, you're a madman!" Dan saw the defiance. "Go ahead."

"Or how about if I have them drag the bottom of the drop-off on Lake on the Mountain?"

The defiance wavered, but only slightly. Twenty years later it would probably be impossible to determine cause of death from something like aconite.

"You want me to open up a twenty-year-old cold case on the grounds that a woman has a poisonous flower growing in her garden — even after you've told me she didn't know what it was when you tried to hand it to her?"

Saylor turned to face him in his smart-look casuals. A definite Mark's Work Warehouse man. Dan had caught him before he went on duty, surprised to learn he lived on this side of the reach.

"All it tells you is that the woman doesn't know shit from Monkshood. She could have got someone to do it for her. I told you that's how she killed his horses."

"Unless they thought they were radishes and ate them accidentally in the field." Saylor eyed him. "Horses are pretty stupid. It's happened before, you know." They were sitting in Saylor's car, parked a few hundred yards from where a ferry tugged its load into place, lining up with the dock to release its conscripts. Dan watched the doors open and the cars surge forward. "And even if I dredge Lake on the Mountain, what am I going to find?"

Dan considered this. He hadn't worked out the details. Something still wasn't sitting right. "I don't think you're going to find his body up there — I think he's buried somewhere on the Killingworths' grounds."

"Really!" It was more a statement of disbelief than surprise. "You actually think this woman is stupid or daring enough to murder her husband in her home and plant his body in her garden somewhere?"

"He got off the ferry on this side of the harbour on the afternoon of November first and was never seen again."

Saylor looked off in the distance. "See that road? It goes on to Kingston. And a hell of a lot more places after that. What makes you think he even stopped at home before leaving? He was under strict court order to avoid his family. It could only have made things worse for him. And why would she kill him and bury him in the garden even if he did disobey the order?"

"I don't know." Dan shook his head. "I guess it doesn't seem all that likely, does it?"

Saylor shook his head. "Not if you know small towns, it doesn't. There's hardly a secret that escapes somebody's notice. Though whether they're respected or revealed is anybody's guess, but no — she wouldn't bury her husband on the grounds. I can almost guarantee it."

"You said 'almost.'"

Saylor shot Dan a look. "Give me a break, buddy. She would never do it."

"Okay, what about the lake?"

Saylor still looked doubtful. "Let me get this straight. You think she poisoned her husband, then dumped him in the trunk of her car and drove his body across on the ferry up to Lake on the Mountain? And she then dragged him across the road and dropped him into a lake frequented by tourists...?" Saylor stared at him. "Do you see how flimsy this is?"

Dan sighed. He was right. It sounded crazy coming from Saylor's mouth.

"You can't file a murder charge against someone without a body or at least some major evidence pointing to murder. You don't have either, and you may never have." Saylor paused to listen to a radio report. When it was over, he looked at Dan again. "In the meantime, don't be surprised if I have to serve you with a restraining order. Burgess is going to be all over me the second he hears about this. You'll be lucky if she doesn't charge you with attempted murder if she figures out what those flowers were."

Dan started to protest. Pete wagged a stubby white finger under Dan's nose. "I don't want to hear you've gone back there again. I know you mean well, but I've got a job to do. Please — don't get in my way again."

TWENTY-FOUR

Terminal

"Mr. Dan Sharp?"

The voice tugged at him like a rusty razor blade.

"Yes?"

"This is Magnus Ferguson."

Dan felt a bottomless space open under him. He listened, ears glued to every inflection, as Magnus described how the note Dan tucked into his mailbox had been forwarded to his current address.

"Anyway," he said, finally getting around to the heart of the matter. "I understand you have some questions for me."

"Yes, I do. I'm looking into a disappearance that took place some years ago. Did you once work for a man named Craig Killingworth?"

Ten, fifteen seconds evaporated. Dan thought Magnus wasn't going to answer or was scouring the storeroom of memory to retrieve a lost file. Then he said, "That's a name I haven't heard in a very long time."

"Then you did work for him?"

"What is this about?" came Magnus's savaged rasp.

"I'm a missing persons investigator."

"So your card said."

"I've been hired to find Craig Killingworth."

"Who are you working for? Is it Lucille?" the man asked suspiciously.

"If I told you I don't know who I'm working for, you might find that difficult to believe or understand, but I can tell you I'm definitely not working for Lucille Killingworth. I had a rather unpleasant call from Lucille's lawyer last week warning me not to pursue the matter."

Dan heard Magnus chuckling on the other end. "Oh, she can be persuasive, all right!"

"Do you know where Mr. Killingworth is now, by any chance?"

Magnus snorted. "He's dead."

"Do you know that for a fact?"

"Oh, I know it all right."

"May I ask how you…?"

"No, sir — I will not discuss this over the phone. I don't trust the phone." Dan waited. "You come here and I'll give you proof."

Magnus agreed to meet with Dan on the island. "I haven't been back out to my trailer for a long time," he said. "I think it's time I paid a visit."

Anywhere else, and at the very least they would have been hookers. In some parts of the world their dress would have got them killed. Here, they were schoolgirls having a lark — fishnet stockings, high-heels, pert fresh-cut hair, trim buffed nails, and pretty, chirpy smiles.

Dan and Donny navigated the narrow aisle leading to the back of the Walnut Café. With its Korean décor and mostly Korean clientele, the place was known mainly for one thing: a menu consisting of walnut-shaped nuggets of nougat-filled delight, with side orders of sugar-coated berry or seaweed pancakes, and lacy, tongue-shrinkingly sweet cookies. Make that two things: it also had the worst coffee Dan had ever tasted. It was Donny's favourite café.

In the back room, they found a chipped table among the coat racks and stacked take-out boxes. Inflected Korean syllables filled the air. On TV and in newspapers, reporters bemoaned once-liberal Canada's growing racism, as evidenced in the polls and statistics revealing a negative attitude toward the country's burgeoning immigrant population. *Are we no longer the tolerant, accepting land we once were? I doubt it,* Dan thought, looking around him. The question was wrongly put. Canadians were what they'd always been, but they'd grown wary on realizing a noticeable number of the new arrivals crowding their shores and cities in search of a better life had come intolerant themselves, or had at least come ignorant of the ideals of liberal humanism that allowed them to be here.

He looked over at the table of teenage girls trembling with laughter as they ate their treats and gossiped in Korean. Chances were some of their fellow immigrants would have sent them packing rather than allow them access to these same shores, given half a chance. Dan also knew that men like him and Donny would quickly have been refused entry or denied their rights by many of these same new citizens. That is, if they weren't imprisoned or killed outright. You didn't overturn positive human values and replace them with weaker, intolerant ones. That was not the Canadian way.

Donny was nearly over his gloom-and-doom act about the lost job, no longer convinced his life was at an end if he never sniffed another vial of overpriced skunk gland reduction. He was even considering taking time off before embarking on a search for the next phase of his existence. Still, he'd come in reflective, on the down-turned side.

Dan turned his attention to what Donny'd been saying.

"… and you start to wonder, you know, are the good things still ahead of you or have they already passed you by? And did you even notice?"

Dan listened as a sailor might eye heavy, low-lying clouds in a rising wind — concerned, but not overly. And then it was his turn. He described his confrontation with Lucille Killingworth outside her estate.

Donny paused, walnut cake halfway to his mouth. "As if I don't have enough to worry about! First the incident on the boat with the Brazilian boy, and now attempted murder. Is there nothing you won't stop at? I think you're becoming unhinged. And nice shiner, by the way. I assume you'll let me in on that one eventually?"

"Nothing to tell — I got mugged in Sudbury."

Donny looked at Dan for a long while before speaking. "Why are you doing this?"

"Doing what?"

"This!" He waved his hands about, oblivious to the Korean family sitting next to them warily evading his reach. "All of this crazy man stuff."

"It's my job."

"Your job is not to run amok at weddings and attack rich heiresses whose families comprise the bedrock of the Canadian establishment."

"True."

Donny slowly shook his head and looked away, a monk contemplating life's greater mysteries. Finally, he turned back. "Who were your heroes, man? And don't give me some crap about Superman, 'cause he's not a real hero and you're not an American."

Dan shoved a bite of walnut cake into his mouth, savouring the sweet warmth. "What if he *was* my hero?"

"I detect insincerity."

"Okay, then maybe I don't have any larger-than-life heroes." Dan shrugged. "My heroes are the people who manage to get through the day without doing damage to themselves and others around them. The ones who do the best they can, without throwing the towel in and crying foul because they wanted more than life's meagre offerings allowed them. People like my Aunt Marge."

"Good one." Donny nodded, downed his coffee with a flourish. "Me? Angela Davis. She was my hero as a kid — and still is now. Black rights, human rights, women's rights, the struggle for truth and justice. She fought for what she believed in and she paid the price. All those years in jail and all those words written for the cause. That woman had more conscientiousness and compassion in her little finger than … I don't know what. But is it not the very *definition* of tragedy," here his eyes glinted mischief, "that this woman who did so much to further the cause of race and class struggles and fight for human dignity, should be reduced in our collective consciousness to a hairstyle?"

Dan grinned. "But a hairdo with attitude — or latitude. It was a pretty big 'fro, remember."

From self-pity and childhood heroes through to the shear absurdity of life. A trip across the universe over a cup of coffee. That's what he loved about Donny. You could never tell what would come out of him next: gloom or joy, kindness or anger. He was a jazz riff tossed from horn to bass to sax, used up and carried around and turned inside out till it was almost gone, only to return triumphant in another key. That was his genius.

"Compassion, huh?" Dan said.

"That's the word."

"So just how compassionate are you feeling these days?"

"I smell a leading question," Donny said, eyeing him with suspicion.

"Are you willing to do your part for the cause? To help further the struggle, given the opportunity — and I gather that you have time to do so, given the inclination."

"Now I'm really suspicious. Tell."

Dan took a sip of coffee, tried not to gag on the taste, and added another spoonful of sugar. "I only do this for you, you know," he said. And proceeded to fill Donny in on his adventures with Lester and his upcoming trip.

"Another chapter in the Craig Killingworth Saga?"

"Uh-huh. And what I need," he said, "is for you to take Lester for a few days while I'm in B.C. Because I still haven't found a place for him."

Donny's face was impassive. Dan felt the need for a sermon coming on, one of those "Here Are Ten Good

Reasons Why You Should Do This" manifestoes. The kind he'd invariably failed at with other kids at school. "Ked's going to stay with Kendra, of course. But I can't ask her to take in a stray."

"Okay," Donny said. "I'll do it."

"Okay? Just like that — okay?"

"Do you want me to say I'll think it over?"

"No, I want you to say okay."

"And then you say…?"

"Thank you."

Donny nodded. "You have a need. I have time and opportunity, as you put it. I'm out of work, feeling suicidal, and in need of distraction. Plus I am deeply concerned about you, so I will do this for you. A few days, you said? As in three or fewer?"

"Guaranteed."

"And then the Craig Killingworth Story will be over for good?"

"Absolutely."

"Done."

Dan watched the big boat manoeuvre the cliffs and head into the harbour, water dividing white and dark behind it. *The Queen of Nanaimo*. The wake rebounded off the island. He'd watched with a feeling of regret as they passed between Mayne and Pender Island, but there was nothing to be done about that. He'd sensed the unvoiced questions in Trevor's emails, heard the hopeful tone when he asked if Dan might be coming back that way for a visit. It wouldn't do to contact him if he had no intention of staying.

Once off the ferry terminal, he noted the wary faces that marked his progress up the coast. They seemed to sense his outsider status, the eternal other-ness about him that followed no matter where he went. He passed farms and homesteads. Here the roadside stops were less inviting, less intriguing to his eyes. He recalled the angry dogs running alongside his car on his last visit. Having retreated to an island in their minds, these people were relegated to one in time as well, cut off, isolated, and dwindling slowly to nothing. On Mayne Island he'd felt a sense of community. Here they were lost in the landscape and wanted nothing so much as to stay lost.

He was at the dirt road leading to Magnus Ferguson's trailer in less than half an hour. From a distance he saw the tall white-haired scarecrow tugging at the earth with a hoe. For a second, it seemed as though he were looking at a badly aged version of Craig Killingworth. He thought he'd found the missing man. A whole scenario flashed through his mind, how Killingworth had simply disappeared to escape his past and ended up in the woods of B.C., aged but alive, and mostly nuts.

Magnus leaned the hoe up against the trailer and came over to meet him with a mixture of suspicion and curiosity, the way the Natives must have regarded the first white men to land on their shores right before it all went wrong for them.

They walked slowly around the trailer as Dan described his search for Craig Killingworth and the events that had led him to contact Magnus. As they walked, Magnus appeared to be taking inventory of what he'd left behind on this plot of land as much as the measure of Dan's intentions.

Dan tried to look interested when Magnus pointed out the stubby basil and flat-leafed parsley. "They don't thrive here — not enough light except in the morning. Then the deer eat the leaves down to the stems."

Crows hung and dipped their heads in the rust-flecked fronds of Western Redcedar waving overhead. "You must enjoy the solitude out here," Dan said.

Magnus scratched his chin. "Tell you the truth, most days I hate it. It's a lonely life. Blacker than black. People always romanticize places like this. You're still stuck with your own company, whether you like it or not."

He turned away and looked into the forest as though searching for a sign, some encouragement that what he'd endured hadn't been in vain, or maybe just wanting a reason to go on. When he turned back, his face was set. "All right — I guess I trust your motives. Ask me what you want to know."

Dan nodded. "When we spoke on the phone, you said you had proof that Craig Killingworth was dead."

"I do."

"I was hoping you could show it to me."

Magnus waved him around to the front of the yard. He walked up to the steps of the trailer and pulled the door open.

Inside was a world in decline. Everywhere were signs of hopelessness: cramped quarters that bulged with household goods, piles of discarded clothing, boxes making an obstacle run of the trailer's length. The interior had been turned into a museum, a monument to lost time. There was more than a hint of mould in the air. Papers languished on shelves, letters whose corners had been nibbled by mice thieving for their nests, with droppings left on the counters and on the unwashed vinyl floor curling at the edges. It was a catalogue of despair, a last refuge of broken dreams.

Dan watched Magnus insert his hand into a pile of papers and turn something over. A bundle of letters teetered and splashed to the floor. Magnus looked down at them with contempt, scratching through the refuse flattened into piles on the shelves. For a moment, Dan was afraid he'd come all this way to interview a crazy person who just wanted a little company.

"Here — look at this." Magnus handed him a photograph. Dan was expecting a picture of Craig Killingworth, but the attractive young man standing in a rose garden was a complete stranger. Dan stared at it, hoping to glean its significance.

"Hard to believe that's me, isn't it?" Magnus said. "You wouldn't know it to look at me now, but I used to be very good looking. Turned a few heads in my day. Forty years of smoking will do it to you. I quit the day I got my death sentence." Dan looked up from the photograph to the emaciated skull regarding him. Magnus nodded. "Terminal lung cancer. Well, here I am five years later with everyone telling me how lucky I am to be alive. 'What's so lucky about it?' I ask them. 'I haven't had a cigarette in five years.'"

His fingers went on scratching through the piles. He plucked out a page and stopped to read it, the contents unknowable from his expression. It could have been a laundry list or a love letter, an unpaid bill or an obituary. His hands shook with the weight of all those years of missing cigarettes. A tremendous burden.

From out of the mire he lifted another picture, this one of two young men. Dan recognized a slightly older Magnus standing beside Craig Killingworth at roughly the age he'd appeared in the missing person report. But this was a transformed Craig Killingworth, smiling broadly and looking for once as though he knew how to enjoy life rather than just endure it. He seemed alive and vibrant. Dan thought of the hushed light falling in the Adolphustown sitting room.

Magnus's rasp intruded on his thoughts. "That's Craig."

"Where was this taken?"

He filched the photograph out of Dan's hands and squinted, though he seemed to be focusing his memory more than his eyes. "Picton Town Fair sometime in June — maybe '84 or '85."

Dan looked up. "Do you recall the last time you saw him?"

Magnus screwed up his face, summoning the recall. "Yes, I do. Twenty years ago this coming November first. That was the day I left Prince Edward County. I never saw him again."

It jived with the police reports, Dan noted. "Did you expect to?"

Magnus turned a sorrowful gaze on him. "Son, I expected to hear from him every day for ten, maybe fifteen years. On a bad day, I still do."

"Why is that, if I may ask?"

A spasm of emotion charged Magnus's face. "That's the day we were supposed to leave together." He looked at Dan. "Me and Craig ..."

For a moment, nothing registered. Then suddenly the piece fell into place. "You were ... together?"

Magnus nodded. His eyes misted over, his voice came out a croak. "We had it planned. I couldn't believe when he didn't go through with it." He sniffled. "It was Craig's idea. He wanted us to be together, but because of his family we had to go far away. It's why we planned to come out here. So that's why I wondered, when you said his name on the phone, if you had some news of him...."

Dan leaned against the counter. Somewhere far away a dog howled. Twenty years ago a man had planned his escape, chosen his companion for another chance at life, and disappeared. An hour ago Dan had had no clue what had been going on in Craig Killingworth's mind. Now here was the answer, but he was still no closer to knowing what had happened to him.

"Did you ever try to get in touch with him again?"

Magnus shook his head softly. "No."

"Why not?"

"At first I just assumed he'd either ditched me or decided not to leave his family. He was awfully keen on his boys. It was harder back then to make such life-altering decisions. It's easier today. Kids nowadays know what they want and go out and get it. *Will and Grace* and all that."

Easier for some, maybe, but not all. Dan thought of Richard Philips, newly christened Lester Higgins.

"Back then if you were gay, you constructed a family life on top of what you were inside and prayed no one ever found out. We had no choice, see? We covered our tracks so no one would know. If you weren't careful, you could get fired or beaten up. Or, if you were someone like Craig Killingworth, you could lose your family. Oh, yeah, the authorities were only too happy to take your kids away from you. It happened all the time."

Dan felt shot through with emotion. What would have become of him and Kedrick twenty years ago? Impossible to say. He considered the question before he spoke. "Did you ever suspect that Craig was murdered?"

Magnus's face exploded with anger. "Oh, he was murdered all right." Dan was startled by the vehemence in his voice. "But you'll never be able to pin it on the bitch!"

"Lucille?"

Magnus nodded. "Oh, no — she was too smart. And she had help in high places."

Dan wondered if Magnus was referring to Burgess, the OPP commissioner with the barracuda eyes. "But why do you still hope he'll turn up alive if you know he's dead?"

"I'm getting ahead of myself." Magnus nodded toward the creased piles on the shelf. "The letter. I got it two, maybe three weeks later. It took me a while to get out here, but it was waiting for me when I did." He held up the piece of paper he'd been scratching through the debris for and offered it to Dan. "You can read it for yourself."

November 1st

My dearest, darling Magnus,

Forgive me. I should be with you instead of sending you this sorry letter. I know how hard this is going to be for you. I am a weak man. I can't spend the rest of my life with you.

An hour ago I told you I was leaving with you tonight. I lied. I know now I can never do that. She's won. I cannot live without my sons. It's all in the diary. Do what you see fit with it.

Please forgive me. I'm going to give her what she's always wanted. By the time you get this, I will be a dead man.

Love always, Craig

Dan looked up. "Suicide?"

Magnus nodded. "It's what she wanted. Craig talked about it often enough. Even said how he'd do it, if it came to that. He said if he ever disappeared, he'd be under the ice in the bay. In the winter the reach freezes over. Only the ferry passing through every half hour keeps the channel open. The ice is thick. Thick enough to keep you under till it thawed. It would keep you down all right. Your bones would stay covered over till spring."

"You think he's at the bottom of the Bay of Quinte?"

"He told me he'd kill himself if she managed to keep him from his sons. And she did." Magnus nodded to the picture in his hands. "And she did."

Dan was prepared for a long wait, but Magnus started in again, the telling easier now. "Twenty-three years ago we met at Lake on the Mountain. I was the gardener up at the lodge. Have you been there?"

Dan nodded.

"He'd just separated from his wife, but he hadn't told her he was gay — just said he had things he needed to work out. We had an affair. It was going along fine until he decided to tell her about it. He thought she'd understand. So he told her — and she threatened him. She said she'd never let him see his sons again. And she had ways to make sure that happened. He was terrified. He broke things off with me and went back to her. It hurt, but I understood how he felt. I didn't hear from him for a year. She got him into some kind of therapy, one of those programs where they try to change you. But you can't change these things. I know it's hard for your sort to understand, but that's just how it is...."

"I'm gay, Magnus."

Magnus gave him an appraising stare. He nodded. "All right. Then you know."

"And I also have a son who means more to me than anything in the world. So I know what that would mean to a man like Craig Killingworth."

Magnus nodded. "Anyway, he wasn't cured. He just buried it inside. One day he snapped. He drove his car over the side of the road trying to kill himself. For four days they couldn't find him. He lay in that car, pinned against the steering wheel, hidden by the brush around it. Some kids picking blueberries spotted it and called the police to get him out."

"But he survived?"

"That time, yes. Anyway, he went back to her again. Crazy — just plain crazy. She'd been happy thinking he was dead. Now she had to worry about him all over again. That's when I came to work for them. He thought it might help him get better if he had me around, at least part-time, puttering around the grounds, though he was still pretending to be what she wanted him to be. I think it made things worse for him, though. It was harder for him to have me there and not be with me."

"And she didn't suspect you?"

"I think she knew something was up. That's why she concocted that story about him attacking her and claiming he was mentally unstable."

"It wasn't true?"

"Nah, it's a lie. They were arguing and she started to beat him with her fists. He put up his hand to stop her from hitting him. She called it assault."

"He told you that?"

"I was there. I saw it! Right after that, she fired me."

Dan flashed on the OPP report stating Magnus had been fired by Craig Killingworth. "Did you tell this to the police?"

"I tried. They didn't care. I think that was when she decided to kill him. She vowed that if she couldn't have him, no one would. 'If I can't have you, nobody will!' She actually said those words to his face. That's when Craig got suspicious and started taping her phone conversations. He got her on tape asking a friend how she could drive him to suicide. He'd tried it once — she knew it wouldn't take much to make him try again."

"Why didn't he go to his family for help?"

"Oh, she was right tricky. When he was in the hospital recovering from the car crash, Lucille told Craig his family had turned against him because he was gay. And then she phoned his family and said Craig didn't want to hear from them any more because they'd caused the trauma he was going through. Anyway, they all believed her stories." He clucked his tongue. "She was a monster!"

Dan thought of Trevor's story about how his mother had stopped talking to her brother when he first left home.

"This was back in the eighties. It was all AIDS-this and AIDS-that. They were pointing fingers, blaming us for the epidemic. 'God's wrath on queers' and all that rot. Nothing but ignorance and superstition."

"The old man — Nathaniel Macaulay. Did he know what was going on?"

"He surely did. He hated the fact that his son-in-law was a hell-bound faggot. Worried himself sick one of the grandsons might catch it. Never stopped nagging his daughter about it."

Which explained the will, Dan realized. "What happened the last time you saw Craig?"

"We spoke on the phone that morning. He sounded moody and went on for a long time about not wanting to leave his sons. It was killing him, I could tell. Craig was living in Bloomfield by then. Because of the assault charges, he wasn't allowed to see his sons at all. The court had stayed that verdict the day before we were to leave. He'd also been suspended from his job as principal at the high school. Shocked them all, too — everybody loved Craig." His voice caught again. "Anyway, I convinced him that leaving was for the best. I told him there was no telling what else she might do. Better to get away and deal with it from a distance. We'd talked about it a million times already. I was just repeating myself."

"When did you last see him?"

"Around noon. I went over and helped him get ready. I remember we had a little fight over it, because I was in a hurry and he was terribly fussy about packing his clothes, so I did it for him. He was always a very smart dresser, and it was the only thing I've known him to get cranky about."

"How were you going to leave?"

"By car. I was supposed to do all the driving, take our time to get here. He still couldn't drive after his accident."

And thus the bicycle, Dan thought. "Then what?"

"I called him again in the afternoon, maybe five o'clock. I just had a feeling he might change his mind. But he didn't answer."

Because by then he'd been spotted on the ferry to Adolphustown, Dan thought. Maybe he was already scouting out a place to throw himself under the ice. Only he couldn't do it in the light of day with everyone watching. He'd have waited till it was dark, when no one would see. "What then?"

"I went and waited for him up at Lake on the Mountain as we'd planned. He was supposed to be there by eight. I got there an hour early, I was so nervous. I sat in the parking lot and waited for nearly five hours, but he never showed. It was cold that night. I kept running the engine then turning it off again to save gas to make sure we had enough to leave."

"Did you see anything while you were waiting?"

Magnus shook his head. "The place was deserted. It was eerie and dark. It was past season and there were no lights on at the resort. A couple of cars drove past. One pulled into the parking lot and stopped for a second, then drove away again when they saw me. Probably lovers looking for a make-out place. Then nothing for almost an hour. I was ready to give up. Then a kid came by on a bike and I split. It was nearly midnight by then and I figured Craig had changed his mind. I was crying and pretty confused. I couldn't believe he'd decided not to come with me. There was a couple walking up the hill. I passed them on the way down. I didn't recognize them. I don't think they were townies. Not sure who they were. It was odd to see people out walking at that time of year."

And by then Craig Killingworth had succeeded in killing himself, Dan calculated. "And after that?"

"After that I drove by his place in Bloomfield, but all the lights were off and I just kept heading west. Didn't stop till I hit the Sault thirteen hours later. I pulled into a motel, cried for an hour and then slept. I made it out here a little over two weeks later. I didn't even know he was missing till I got here and found his letter. Then I knew what he'd done."

Twilight had come and gone. The sky was black outside the trailer, as dark as Dan remembered from his time on Mayne Island. Magnus lit a lamp — the power hadn't been reconnected. Their faces were orange moons in the dark. Moths batted themselves senseless against the screen outside.

"You see what I'm saying. No one looked for him. No one cared. No one wanted him found but me. And who was I? Just some faggot gardener who got involved with a man and tried to help him understand himself. I wouldn't do it today, let me tell you."

Craig Killingworth's suicide note lay on the table before them. Dan fingered it. "This diary he mentions. Do you know where it is now?"

Magnus pondered this. "Probably still in a locked box in the Bloomfield bank where he left it. I opened the account for him in my name, but only Craig used it. He was documenting evidence of Lucille's campaign against him. I think he put the tapes in there too. He didn't want anything to be associated with him. He thought they might come looking for it and he was still pretty scared of her. But they didn't know him in Bloomfield, so he'd go in with his key and forge my signature whenever he wanted access to the box. He sent me the key in the letter."

"You never opened the box?"

Magnus sat back and sighed heavily. "Even now, after all these years, I still haven't the heart."

"Do you think it might still be there?"

Magnus squinted at Dan in the false light. "Hard to say. I paid the account up until about five years ago, then I got sick and moved and the bank lost track of where I was. I've thought of it many's a time, but never did a thing about it."

"Would you agree to help me get it out? For Craig? Maybe to help his sons understand what happened to their father?"

Magnus regarded him for a second. "I'll do anything I can to help him, and if it hurts her, even better. I could write a letter for you telling them to release it. The key's long gone, though. I haven't seen it in years."

TWENTY-FIVE

Deplorable, Nasty, Unsettling, Sick

BLOOMFIELD WAS EVEN MORE NONDESCRIPT and reserved than Picton or Glenora. Dan found the town's only bank, still located on the main drag, and held his breath. He went in and offered the letter from Magnus granting him permission to access the box's contents. The clerk gave him a suspicious look, impatiently adjusting her glasses as Dan explained that he'd been given the letter from his uncle, who had spent the past half-decade fighting a serious illness.

"Sir — this account hasn't been paid in more than five years," she said, as though he were personally accountable for its dereliction. "We cannot be held responsible for the contents of a safety deposit box that has not been paid for any length of time exceeding two years."

"I understand that," Dan said. "I just wondered if you could check to see what happened to the box's contents."

"I can tell you what would have happened." Her face wore the look of a teacher speaking to a particularly dull three-year-old. "The bank would have sent out several letters requesting payment, and then, receiving no answer from you, we would have extended a courtesy time of two years' wait. After that, the box would have been drilled open and the contents removed." She stared him down, the better to make her point. "You understand, of course, that we do not keep spare copies of the keys. Once you have opened the account with us, no one can access the box but you."

"Or in this case, my aged and infirm uncle."

"Be that as it may," another teacher-child look passed over her face, this one more wrathful in its proportions, "we cannot access the box without the key your uncle was given when he opened the account with us. Even if we needed to, we could not see what was inside the box without it."

The reasoning went on like this for some time until the clerk seemed satisfied that Dan had been apprised of official banking procedures and was thoroughly taken to task over his shameful neglect-by-proxy on behalf of his uncle's account.

"But if the box has already been drilled, might I not have access to the contents without the key?"

She peered at him closely, her face a reminder of the ignominy of all that was implicit about irresponsibility in regard to past due accounts. "I will speak with my manager."

The manager, a thin-faced and surprisingly pleasant young man in an out-of-season linen suit, came forward and shook Dan's hand. He looked over the letter and nodded. "We don't get many requests going back that far," he said. "Though oddly, someone was in here last week looking for something in another name from this same time period."

Dan felt the chill crawl up his spine as he wondered about the coincidence of the timing. "Family looking for a long-lost will?" he asked casually.

"Not at all. Police business, actually. Though I had to turn them away empty-handed."

"That's a shame," Dan said.

"In any case," the man said, turning to his clerk. "I believe we can help Mr. Sharp, Karen." He turned back to Dan. "We don't actually dispose of the contents of safety deposit boxes ever. No matter how long the account has been derelict." He smiled at this revelation of the bank's good graces and nodded to the vault at the back. "We have a special place where we keep the contents in a sealed envelope, hoping that someone will show up one day — just as you have done — and that we will be able to return the items to their rightful owners."

He gave Karen the nod and she went off to retrieve the contents, returning in less than a minute with a manila envelope and what Dan hoped was Craig Killingworth's diary. She was all smiles as she asked him to sign a register acknowledging that he had picked up the box's contents five years late. He paid the penalty fee and left, feeling like a neglectful library user who'd returned a book so long overdue it had gone out of print.

Outside in the parking lot, he slit the seal on the envelope and let its contents fall into his hands: a single cassette tape and a thick notebook puckered with the weight of Craig Killingworth's entries. The creased pages held together for another instant then opened to reveal their long-unread secrets.

†

Dan was exhausted. He'd spent the past eight hours reading Craig Killingworth's diary — a litany of fear, confusion, regret, and loss. It was the last testament of a man who had bound up all hope for the future in being reunited with his boys and who could never stop hoping for that day as long as he lived. He'd been tortured by his inability to change the one thing that defined him.

Dan read as Craig outlined his decision to reveal his secret torment to his wife, the one person he felt he could trust, setting in motion his betrayal at her hand. For more than a year, entry after entry detailed the torture he'd endured trying to be what she wanted him to be. This was followed by a hiatus of four months during which he added not a single entry. It resumed with the title "Crash," as he described his recovery from the botched suicide attempt.

As Magnus suspected, that was when his wife's plan had taken hold. She knew that nothing but death would stop Craig from exposing her lies and her efforts to separate him from what he loved most. *If I can't have you, nobody will!* He'd inscribed these chilling words in the diary, the words Magnus claimed were Lucille's, as she blackmailed him into being what she wanted him to be — lover, father, family man. Straight in every way. But ultimately he'd been unable to keep up the facade. And Lucille Killingworth had responded by separating him from his sons, knowing it would destroy him. Magnus was right. She was a monster, plain and simple.

The diary told Dan little he didn't already know or suspect. Still, a man didn't fill in a diary entry on the day of his death, walk over to the bank to deposit it safe and sound in a security bin before giving up the ghost. Craig

Killingworth had made plans to secure the record of his ordeals long before whatever had happened to him. He'd even given Magnus the key to make sure it was followed up. Except Magnus hadn't been able to do that for the last twenty years. Sometimes better never than late.

Clearly, Craig Killingworth had planned his death to the final detail. An orderly man, his writing showed that same attention to detail as his mind trod the many possible solutions to his problem and its likely outcome. Even while detailing his plans to leave with Magnus, and the brief blossoming of hope he saw in that, his diary entries vacillated daily between leaving and killing himself. *As much as I love Magnus,* he wrote, *without my sons, I have nothing. Most days I think it would be easier to end the struggle. To give her the thing she wants most — my death.*

Craig Killingworth had preferred death to a life without his sons. Lucille Killingworth had sensed that. She'd asked herself how she could drive him to suicide, and that was the answer she received. She'd systematically lied to the courts and taken away what mattered most to him. Dan imagined him standing on that lonely shore by the bay as he looked into the void his life had become and decided it was no longer worth it. A few hesitant steps onto the ice, a crack as it gave under his weight, and he would be gone. The trail would die out. The sun would come up the next day, and a man who'd touched hundreds of lives would no longer be there. They would think he'd left home on his bicycle, taken the ferry across the river, and vanished.

Love's a terrible fever. It burns when it's new and aches when it's old. It tempts and taunts, beguiles and bewilders, before leaving you high and dry with the worst hangover you've ever experienced. It's a whore and a thief, a liar and a sinner, though it goes by many names. Are there ever any survivors?

Sometimes, Craig Killingworth wrote near the end of his account, *I think the only things that matter are the choices we make, for better or worse, for right or wrong.* But he'd struggled with his choices for too long. The last entry, made the day of the hearing right after the court stayed the order separating him from his sons, contained a simple sentence: *She's won.* Craig Killingworth had known then what the story held for him. He'd already made his choice. He simply hadn't wanted to tell Magnus that it left him without a future.

What Lucille had driven her husband to do was terrible, but in the end he had been the architect of his own demise. Whatever had finally befallen Craig Killingworth had clearly been perpetrated by his own hand. It was too late to save him now, to point twenty years down the road and say, *Here are your boys — live for them: the drug addict who needs you to love him so he won't destroy himself, the arrogant one who needs to know that he doesn't have to be insensitive to be a man.*

Dan turned to the beginning of the diary and reread Craig Killingworth's determined first entry. In a strong script he had written: *Whatever happens I will never give up my fight.* But he had. In the end, he hadn't found the determination to live.

Donny buzzed him in.

Dan brandished the diary as he came through the door. "You've got to read this. It even describes his sudden impulse just before he drove off the road rather than undergo any more torture at the hands of that woman and her barbaric therapist who promised to help him change his orientation."

"Whoa!" Donny said, taken aback. "First ask how the boy is doing."

"Sorry. How are things with Lester? How are you two getting along?"

"Fine. We're getting along fine. Thank you."

Dan glanced around. Nothing had changed in the condo. For having a teenage terror under his roof, Donny seemed to have maintained remarkable control of his premises. For a moment Dan wondered if "fine" meant more than it said. Should he ask for reassurance that Lester hadn't come onto him, as he had with Dan, and that Donny hadn't succumbed to the boy's charms, such as they were? Then he remembered who he was talking to: Donny the wise, Donny the compassionate. The look of disdain that would greet the question stopped him dead. He already knew the answer. Better yet, he knew himself. He would never have entrusted Lester to Donny if he'd had any doubts. A father's work was never done, it seemed.

"Great — I'm glad to hear. Where is he?"

"In bed. It's past eleven o'clock, and those are the rules. He goes to bed by ten thirty." Dan gave Donny a bemused look. Donny nodded. "Which also means you will have to contain yourself and keep your voice down."

"Got it."

He followed Donny into the kitchen and placed the diary on the table beside a yawning pile of unopened mail. Dan glanced at it. Neglect of self was one of the prime signs of depression. Was he seeing the outward clues of self-destruction? But no — Donny was past that. He had a cause now. Dan stood looking down at the book, as though waiting for it to speak.

"Go through it," Dan said. "She drove him to suicide. Even after he and Magnus had planned their departure, he was still tormented by it. It's sad, but he realized he couldn't live without his kids, and the courts helped her take them from him."

Donny nodded slowly. "I'll read it — but I don't like the look on your face."

"What look?"

"The one that threatens to take on the world to save someone who died twenty years ago." Donny shook his head. "Life's always going to be harder than you expect. I don't know why you want to make it worse."

"Just call me Angela Davis."

Donny shot him a glance. "You're going to have to work on the 'fro."

Dan pulled out the cassette and laid it beside the diary. "He even taped her phone conversations. He knew she was up to something. I had it transcribed and copied onto CD."

Donny took the tape to the stereo and popped it in. It crackled to life, the years and cheap celluloid having left their mark. The voices were scratchy here, muffled there, but by straining an ear you could make out the words. A twenty-year-old conversation brought to life, the layers of time peeled back to reveal dust, but no tears. Not for Craig Killingworth. They listened to Lucille coolly discussing her husband's fragile mental state with her friend, a woman named Bernice, whose smoke-tinged voice contributed to the conversation hesitantly, not convinced she wanted to be part of it, but reluctant to pull away.

Bernice suggested pressuring him to come back; Lucille declared she'd had enough of him and simply wanted him dead. The tape came to an end with the conclusion hanging in the air.

"I think if a judge hears this he'll have to conclude that Lucille Killingworth contributed to her husband's suicide. If we can't get her up on murder charges, then this will at least do something."

Donny gave Dan a sober look of appraisal. "Except that there's still no body."

"I know that."

"No proof of death. On the other hand, if he really is dead, he might just as easily have been hit by a car while leaving town on his bike. Have you considered that? Or maybe he lives somewhere on Cape Breton Island raising goats. Who knows? Besides stirring up a great deal of trouble, what good do you really think this is going to do?"

It was past two a.m. when he left Donny's place, the downtown core illuminated by bleached rectangles of light where over-zealous office workers toiled late into the night. He thought again of the missing part of the police file that hadn't made it into his hands. He was convinced it told Craig Killingworth's side of the story: his battle to regain custody of his children, his tortured efforts to change his sexuality despite the fact that he'd already attempted suicide, and Lucille Killingworth's threats to keep him from his sons and expose him to the world, adding cruelty on top of cruelty. He was sure now that

Commissioner Burgess, or possibly someone under him, had repressed the report.

He was sitting in a café in Bloomfield reading a blank menu. The front door opened. When he looked up, his mother stood next to him. She hadn't changed a bit in all those years. He invited her to take a seat. She smiled and sat down, leaning in to speak in a low voice. "How are you doing with it?" she asked with a knowing look.

"Not drinking? It's a bitch, but I can make it."

She laughed — a raucous, throat-racking laugh. The kind of laugh you'd expect of the dead. So far, Dan told her, he'd had it relatively easy: no chills, no shakes, no scary bugs crawling over his skin at night. Only a slight hand wobble and a constant urge to do something — anything — to keep his mind off what he couldn't have. Alcohol. The god-demon-lover-bitch.

"I never did get the hang of it myself." She held a hand in front of him. "How many fingers do you see, Danny?"

Dan squinted. The fingers kept changing. "Four. No, five."

"Are you sure?"

"No."

"Look again. How many fingers?"

He looked and was surprised by what he saw. "Thirteen. At least."

Look ma, no hands.

He was a zombie at work the next morning. But a dry zombie. Normally a slug of Scotch from the bottom drawer would have revved his motor for an hour. Without it he felt beat. But he was determined not to break his promise to Ked.

He played his messages after lunch. Pete Saylor had called to say he'd learned what the missing Killingworth file contained. M.H. Not someone's initials, but "Medical History." Dan was elated — that meant it contained Craig Killingworth's side of the story. So there was hope. Saylor had called a second time a few minutes later, his voice sounding more urgent, saying he needed to talk to Dan as soon as possible, but not to call him at work. He could be reached at home later that afternoon. He left his number. The message made Dan curious, but it would have to wait.

Sally had left a new batch of files on his desk. The one on top was for another missing runaway — this one a nine-year-old girl. At three o'clock, he had a meeting with a client who wanted to update Dan on the status of her son, whom Dan had successfully tracked down a month earlier, only to have him vanish again. Still, it was good news, of a sort. He'd used his health card at a walk-in clinic in another city and been referred to a depression specialist. It seemed to be catching, Dan noted.

The day spun itself out and Dan left early. He'd just taken off his jacket and hung it up in the hall closet when he remembered Saylor's message. He fished in his pocket for the number he'd scribbled on the back of an envelope.

The knock came before he could find the number. The officer was polite. He offered Dan a dopey grin as he flashed a copy of the search warrant. Without a look at Dan, his team swarmed into the house.

Dan watched, his face set to impassive as they tore apart his home. He wouldn't give them the satisfaction of letting them see him disturbed. Larry Fiske came to mind first, followed by Commissioner Burgess and the surprising news that someone had been to the same bank in Bloomfield on "police business" a week before Dan got there. He seethed in silence. Nothing was spared. They were surprisingly methodical. At least his sofa cushions were zip-ins. They hadn't had to slice them open and toss the stuffing around in the process.

In the middle of it, Dan checked his watch: he was due to pick Ked up in twenty minutes. He caught Kendra at home and told her what was going on. She agreed to take Ked for the next little while and asked if he wanted her to contact a lawyer.

"Not yet," he said.

Ralph growled every time something got toppled to the floor, eyeing Dan as though waiting for the command to attack. Dan felt proud of him. Shoes ended up beside cushions and books and household cleaning products, making a total hodge-podge of things. They even upended his plants, dumping the soil onto a plastic roll. The place was a Robert Rauschenberg universe of mismatched items.

"If you tell me what you're looking for, I might spare you the bother."

"Sorry, sir — it's just orders. I really can't say more than that."

"There are no drugs in my house," Dan said, though he doubted that was what they were really after. "Who authorized this?"

The officer shook his head. "Just orders, sir."

Dan knew he'd get nothing out of him. He let them do their dirty work. It was more than four hours before the officer nodded ruefully at him and they left empty-handed. He thought of Saylor's message again. No need to call back now.

Dan felt sickened and violated as he surveyed the state of his home. He made a half-hearted attempt to restore order then gave up. It was impossible to decide where to start. Even the wall calendar was ajar, as if the wise mother and her joyful brood had lost their taste for gravity. He gave up and took Ralph for a much-needed walk.

Upstairs at Spring Rolls, lunch hour was in full swing. Donny listened to Dan describe the previous night's events as he struggled with his chopsticks. It was the only thing Dan had ever seen him look incompetent at.

"They did everything but crawl up my ass."

"That would have been cosy."

Dan cocked a baleful eye at him.

"And what were they looking for, do you think? Pirated DVDs? Stolen iPods? Teenage runaways?"

"I think they were looking for Craig Killingworth's diary," Dan said.

"Yeah — me too. Funny, that." Donny raised a noodle to his face. It fell just before it reached his mouth.

Dan watched impatiently. "So — what did you think?"

"I read it." Donny reached for a fork and speared a cut of chicken.

"And?"

"Deplorable, nasty, unsettling, sick. I wouldn't wish his wife on my worst enemy."

"But do you agree she was directly responsible for his suicide?"

Donny chewed contemplatively, buying time before he spoke. "I think Craig Killingworth sounds like a man who was desperate. A man who had tried to commit suicide once and failed, and might very well try again. But what good is it going to do you to track this down? Why not just hand it over to the family and be done with it? *Before* you get arrested for handling stolen property. Or worse," he added darkly.

Dan stared in disbelief. "The family? Have you heard a word I said? The family is who I'm keeping it from!"

"Why can't you just accept that the man changed his mind and went east instead of west? It wouldn't be the first time a man living under duress made a snap decision. He was feeling pressured by his wife as well as his lover and he just couldn't handle it. So he got on the ferry, crossed to the other side and disappeared down the road."

Dan shook his head. "There are so many things that don't make sense. He was leaving town on a bicycle without taking any of his belongings? Give me a break! And why not stay and fight it out?"

"The diary tells you why — he'd cracked. She'd won. He just gave up the battle, rode out of town on his bicycle...."

"...and was never heard from again. Come on! You don't believe that any more than I do."

Donny held up a finger. "It's not what I believe. It's what makes sense for you to live with. That may be as close to an answer as you get. There's no proof he's dead. And if he is, there's no proof she knowingly participated in his suicide or even that she handed him the razor blades and stood by and watched."

Dan narrowed his eyes. "So what are you saying?"

"Think about why you're doing this."

Dan shook his head in exasperation.

"No, really," Donny said. "If you go down this road any further, you'll be stuck in a dead man's world." Dan grimaced at the words. "Whatever happened, it was his choice. If he died, he died by his own hand. It was terrible what she drove him to, but it's too late to save him now."

Dan looked out the window and watched the sprawl of traffic. The waiter gathered Dan's empty plate and gave a look of contempt at Donny's half-full one. Donny uncharacteristically waited till the man left before speaking again, this time in softer tones.

"Think about it. They've torn apart your house and threatened you with a lawsuit — which by your own admission you came close to deserving." Dan glanced up sharply, but Donny silenced him. "Who's the one person you've really been scratching around in the dirt trying to find all these years?" Dan shook his head. "Well, let me tell you, Daniel. That person is you. That's who you really need to find. And before it's too late." Donny handed over the diary. "For now, I'd say you're very lucky they didn't find this."

"Did you make the copies?"

Donny sighed and nodded his head. "Yes, I made the copies. I stood in Kinko's for an hour and a half turning pages. You owe me big time again. Not to mention the mounting babysitting charges."

He'd walked Ralph and was nearly ready to settle in himself. The phone rang and Ked's excited voice cut through the wires. "Hey, Dad!"

"Hey, Ked. How are things at your mom's?"

"Fine. She's not as good a cook as you, though. When can I come home?"

"Not yet, but soon."

Dan thought how much he'd missed his son in the few days they'd been apart.

"Are you going to tell me what's going on then?"

"Soon … real soon."

"Is it some kind of secret mission you're on?"

"Something like that. Listen, how's school?"

"Good. Eph got an A+ in English. His paper on *Blade Runner* blew us all away. The teacher made him read it aloud in class. She said it was the best paper she'd ever had."

Dan thought about this for a moment. "Why wasn't your paper that good?"

"Give me a break! Isn't it enough that I have a genius for a best friend? Do I have to be one too?" Ked thought about for it a moment. "He sucks at basketball, though."

TWENTY-SIX

Restoration

DAN GOT UP BEFORE SIX, in the dark. He called to leave a message for Sally saying he was taking a few days off and asking her to cancel his appointments. He set the diary on his desk in his calm, green-toned office. He'd thought long and hard about what he was about to do. He picked up the phone again and dialled the law firm that had requested him to find Craig Killingworth. He heard it ringing in someone's empty office until the answering service picked up. He spoke slowly and clearly. He had proof of what happened to Craig Killingworth, he said, and would turn it over once the person who was paying him revealed him or herself, but not before. Fuck his job — he'd quit before he went any further without knowing who wanted him to prove that a man was dead.

He spent the morning restoring his home to some semblance of order. He discovered things he'd forgot he had, including a few knick-knacks going back all the way to his time with Bob. It was unsettling how physical objects brought back the past, as if it lay waiting around the corner and could return of its own volition at any time.

A solicitor called in the afternoon. His client had agreed to meet with Dan the following afternoon. When he hung up, Dan wasn't a hundred percent sure which one it would be, but he had a pretty good idea.

He'd just sat down to supper when he was startled by the doorbell. Had the police returned? This time they *would* find Craig's diary, if they had. He pulled the curtains aside carefully and looked out. At first it didn't register. There was a gathering of small figures, including a miniature nun and several others wearing animal masks. He opened the door.

"Trick or treat!" they screamed.

He'd forgotten entirely. He went back in and scrounged around the kitchen, still very much in disarray. At first he couldn't find what he wanted. Then he saw it, overturned and dumped on the shelf under the sink. It was intact. Even Ked hadn't been able to find it. He returned to the porch and handed over his secret stash of Kit Kat chocolate bars.

The following day at three o'clock, Dan turned up at the coffee shop on College Street to find Ted Killingworth waiting. He looked much as Dan remembered — black turtleneck, rock star glasses, and a silver strand around his neck. Everything pricey. Everything annoying.

"Surprised?" Ted asked from behind the cobalt glare of his lenses.

"Should I be?"

"No. You're a very smart man. That's why I hired you."

Dan waited. He wasn't going to make things easy for Ted.

"I suppose you're wondering why I hired you to find my father after all these years."

"It's not my business to know why."

"No, but I have a strong suspicion that you find me a trifle on the despicable side." Ted waited, but Dan gave no response. "I'd like very much to reassure you as to my motives."

Dan nodded. "Shoot."

"I spent years trying to understand why my father left, but I never found a satisfactory answer. Sometimes I hated him" — he shrugged — "mostly I hated him. But other times I wondered and even worried about him. Why didn't he care enough to let us know how he was? The days of wondering are mostly behind me now, but I've been an addict for most of my adult life and I feel as though I've spent too many years paying for something that wasn't my fault." He removed his sunglasses. The dull glaze was gone. "For the record, I'm in recovery. At least that's what they call it."

Dan offered a smile, his first concession in Ted's direction. "How's it been so far?"

"The first week was like a year in hell, the second even longer. Some days it rains fire in my hands and back, other times I feel like I might implode." He looked at Dan. "You've caught me at a vulnerable moment. I think that's the reason I'm here right now."

"You think that learning what happened to your father will undo some of the damage?"

"Maybe. At the very least I'm hoping it will give me some peace of mind." Ted suddenly looked worried. "Will I be shocked by what you've found?"

"You might. What are you expecting?"

Ted considered this. "I don't think he's alive. I'd be very surprised if you told me otherwise. I never really bought the story that he left us for another woman. I think we would have heard from him eventually. I think *something* happened to him, but I don't know what."

"Your instincts were right. As far as I can tell, he isn't alive. When I said I had proof, I meant proof of a sort. I can't produce his body. As for why he left, it wasn't for another woman." Dan caught Ted's glance and held it. "Your father was planning to leave your mother for another man: a gardener named Magnus Ferguson."

Ted's mouth gaped. He recovered quickly. "Okay, well — you've delivered on your promise to shock me. Can you prove it?"

Dan walked him through the evidence, explaining his father's relationship with Magnus, the false charges concerning the assault on his mother. He brought out the letter Ted's father had sent to Magnus the day he killed himself, laying it on the table as Dan explained what he knew and what he'd merely surmised.

Ted looked at it for a moment then looked away, marshalling his composure. "I assumed he was dead, but it never occurred to me that he might have killed himself." He smiled ruefully. "I shouldn't have had a hard time coming to that conclusion. Like father, like son. I've been trying to kill myself for years."

Dan handed him the diary along with his father's letter. Ted pushed them back across the table. "You keep them," he said.

"I've got copies on file."

Ted shook his head. His voice came out a crabbed whisper. "You keep them. I can't bear to touch them."

Dan returned the diary and letter to his case. "What are you going to do now?"

Ted looked out the window. "I'm going to tell her that I know."

"You'll destroy whatever relationships exist in your family."

"I know," Ted said, looking back at Dan. "It's what I intend to do. At least I'll have the satisfaction of knowing I've destroyed her in return. And I won't stop there. I'll make sure everyone she knows and respects hears what she did."

"It won't bring your father back."

"No, it won't." Ted seemed to be considering this. "Is there any chance of reopening the case?"

"To bring criminal charges against your mother?"

Ted nodded.

"She could probably be charged with aggravated assault or causing mental anguish with intent to harm. Something like that."

"But you don't think it's very strong." It wasn't a question.

"I'm not a lawyer, Ted. You'd have to ask someone better informed about such things. The diary and tape are pretty strong evidence, but there's still no body. No proof."

"She didn't kill him with her own hands, but she might as well have. Why is there no justice for such things? All these years she let us think …"

"What? That he was alive? That he left because of another woman? Would it have made a difference if you'd known the truth?"

403

"Look at me!" The voice was quiet, but insistent. "Look at what I've become. This is what not knowing has done. She told me … she told me he left because he didn't give a fuck about us. And I believed her. Thom and I both believed her. I spent twenty years believing it, and hating him for it, and this is what it's done to me."

"I understand. But you might want to think about it, all the same."

"I'll think about it." Ted got unsteadily to his feet. "Believe it or not, I'm very glad to have met you." He pulled on his overcoat and nodded at Dan. "It's my birthday today," he said. "I'm thirty-five years old. Time to start living."

The door closed behind him. Avril Lavigne droned under the whir of a cappuccino machine grinding the coffee to strength. Dan was glad finally to be able to call the case closed. He hadn't found Craig Killingworth, but what he'd found had brought the man back to one of his sons, at least. Where there had been a blackened reputation — shame and hatred and a damaged psyche — now there could begin the restoration of a proper memory, for whatever it was worth.

If and when the day came that Craig Killingworth's bones could be scooped out of the bay, Dan thought, that part of him could be put to rest as well. Till then, at least, there was this small triumph to be thankful for.

TWENTY-SEVEN

Goodbye, Again

A WEEK WENT BY, followed by another. He heard nothing further from Pete Saylor or Ted Killingworth, though every time his phone rang he half-expected to hear Larry Fiske's oily rasp threatening him with legal action for his part in helping Ted confront his mother. Even if Ted said nothing to implicate him, they would know Dan had helped in some way to restore his father's legacy.

Ked stayed on at Kendra's for the time being, at least until Dan could be sure everything had returned to normal and there were no further risks to him or his son. One night he saw Bill out surrounded by friends at a crowded Danforth bar, but either Bill hadn't seen him or he discreetly avoided looking in his direction till he left.

Dan had returned to his work, but most evenings he spent alone at home. He'd had enough of other people's company for now. He seldom answered the phone, though the one time he did he was surprised to hear the voice of his former neighbour, Steve.

"How are you?" Dan asked, genuinely pleased.

"I'm fine. Really well, Dan!" There was enthusiasm and warmth in the voice. It sounded like the old Steve again.

Steve thanked him again for having met with him that late night in the fall. It had made all the difference, he said. Just knowing there was someone who cared whether he lived or died had made him want to get back on his feet.

"Things are going better then?"

"Yes. I started back at work last week." He paused. "And I've met someone … she's fantastic!"

It was as simple as that, Dan thought. Steve's real medicine was a new love. He suspected Steve had dependency issues among his other problems. *Maybe you're being cynical,* he told himself. *Stop searching for the cloud behind every silver lining.*

Steve insisted on a get-together. He wanted Dan to meet his new girlfriend, who, Steve assured him, would just love Dan. Yes, she was that terrific. They chatted for a while and exchanged promises to hook up. Later, Dan walked Ralph and then turned on the television to pass the time. He'd just turned it off and gone upstairs to check his email when the phone rang again.

"Oh, god, Daniel," he heard Kendra croak out.

His heart leaped into his throat. A dozen scenarios, all ending in Ked's death, careened through his mind. "What is it?" He envisioned a photograph of his son beneath a headline outlining the city's latest traffic fatality. Something to do with a faulty skateboard or a bicycle spoke left unmended that had caused a fatal spill.

"Something terrible's happened to Ked's best friend."

"Who?" he said, uncomprehending. "Who is his best friend?"

Kendra's voice shook. "A boy he goes to school with. I thought you would know who it is."

Dan felt sick. "I can't think right now. What happened?"

"It was a drive-by shooting. Ked's friend was shot and killed." She paused. "He's very broken up. I don't know what to tell him."

Dan heard her speaking to Ked. "Sweetheart? Do you want to speak to your father?"

Dan waited while the phone was passed.

"Dad?"

"I'm here."

Ked was whimpering into the phone. "Someone killed Eph!"

An image of the skinny black kid on the corner flashed before Dan's eyes.

"We heard about it after school," Ked said, breaking into sobs.

"I'm so sorry, Ked."

Dan had no idea what to say to his son to console him for his loss, for the encroaching edges of life bearing down on him. He was also terrifyingly grateful it had not been his son who had been killed, though he could scarcely bring himself to think this. He couldn't remember ever feeling so helpless.

Kendra came back on the line. "Danny, he's too upset to talk."

"Should I wait?"

"No. I'll get him to call back later when he's feeling better."

"Okay. Tell him I love him."

"All right."

Dan held onto the receiver until the line went dead. He went back to the TV and turned it on, waiting for the news.

There was a new receptionist behind the glass at Martin's office, though she wore the same blank look as her predecessor. Martin didn't mention the change and Dan didn't ask.

The topic most on Dan's mind was the death of Ked's friend, Ephraim Adituye, a bright kid seemingly with everything to live for. Martin nodded in understanding. He'd heard the news reports. The entire city was reeling from the killing — not the first of its kind in recent memory.

"How are you feeling about this?" Martin asked solemnly.

Dan sat crumpled in the chair. He shook his head, bewildered by the question. How would anyone feel? Shocked. Angered. Vulnerable. At last, he said, "In a world where kids get shot by absolute strangers ... why is it I scare my own son? Why is that?"

Martin stared without answering.

"I saved a kid the other day," Dan went on. "And I had to break the law to do it." He hadn't intended to say anything about Lester, but there it was. Dan waited for Martin to write this down, but he simply sat there.

At last, Martin said, "Why did you have to break the law to do it?"

"Because his parents would have destroyed him. Because in order to save him, I had to keep him from his family. Some people would call me a monster for doing that."

"Some might call you a hero for making a moral choice."

Dan looked up. "I'm not sure it was a choice. Something needed to be done to save him."

"Why do you need to save people?" Martin asked.

Dan shook his head. "That's what I do — I save people. From themselves. From their shitty lives. From the world."

"You save them or you locate them?"

"Same thing, isn't it?"

"Is it?"

Dan had come here to talk about the death of a fourteen-year-old boy and all that Ephraim's death said about a corrupt and seemingly pointless world. He hoped this wasn't about to become another meaningless conversation. Neither he nor Martin spoke for a full minute. Martin had never let him sit in unbroken silence for so long.

Martin cleared his throat. "Is there anything else you'd like to talk about today?" he said at last.

Dan shook his head. "Actually, no." He stood and reached for his coat, then paused at the door. After a moment, he turned back to Martin. "I don't think I'll be coming here again."

Martin looked down at his sheet. "I'll have to fill out the report," he said.

Dan nodded. "It's what you get paid for." He stood there trying to think of something to say. He thought Martin looked scared. Had he never had a patient walk out on him before?

Martin looked up again. "Did you ever think of saving yourself for once?"

"Am I supposed to have an epiphany on that one, Martin?"

Martin stared, blinking his incomprehension. "Is that a rhetorical question?"

"No."

"Then maybe you are. Supposed to have an epiphany. Maybe that's what you need — an epiphany to tell you how to save your own life. Something to tell you that it's worth saving."

"And what exactly would that be?" Dan heard the anger surge in his voice. "All you ever do is ask questions, Martin. Don't you ever have any fucking answers?"

Martin stared until Dan felt uncomfortable. He leaned forward. "What's the one thing that matters most to you?" Martin asked. "Whatever it is, hold fast to it."

Dan had a sudden glimpse of this pathetic little man returning to his empty house and his lonely life every single evening for the rest of his days. A man who had no friends and who suspected the motives of everyone he met. A man who probably had never been happy and who had once turned to his profession hoping it might save him from himself, only to discover it couldn't save anyone. All his hope dying with it.

"I'll do that." Dan turned the handle and the door opened. The lights were off in the waiting room. "Thank you, Martin," he said. "I'll see myself out."

Craig stayed with him all that long month of no drink, no news. A month of Dan thinking about who the man had really been. Father, teacher, lover. Remarkable by any account, despite his undeservedly sad ending. Dan tried to imagine what might still remain of him — a soul, maybe, or just some essential spark if you were less inclined to go in for sentiment. Whatever it was would have been hovering over his sons, if it wasn't busy haunting his wife in some spooky supernatural capacity. Somehow, that last thought appealed to Dan.

Ed called Dan to his office the day after he informed Martin he would no longer be attending the weekly therapy sessions. Dan had his resignation letter ready.

"You're my best investigator, Dan. I was going to tell you it was time to stop that nonsense anyway. Won't you give this another think?"

"Not at present, Ed. Sorry."

Whatever the future might hold, he told himself, he was going to get in a whole lot of jogging. He might even welcome a lascivious proposition or two, though none came his way. Sobriety was having a strange effect on him.

Though Ked was still at Kendra's, Dan was making the effort to see more of him. Even Ralph began to weary of all the walks he now received, turning his head when Dan opened his arms wide with a "What do you want, boy?"

The rain was coming higgledy-piggledy down the windshield, a composition in silver and grey, liquid and changing. Enigmatic codes, scribbles darting across the screen, with the wipers batting the way. *Then maybe you are. Supposed to have an epiphany. Then maybe you are. Supposed to have an epiphany.* Martin's words came back to him, insistent, keeping time with the wipers. The bright effervescence of October, that final burst of summer-not-quite-over, had led to the dreariness of November's bride-stripped-bare before slipping into December's oncoming winter-never-ending. By the time Dan reached the wind-riven shores of Prince Edward County, the rain had turned into wet, sloppy flakes that splatted against the windshield all along the Loyalist Parkway.

Ted had telephoned unexpectedly, asking for Dan's company. Not his help, but his company. His strength: "I can't do this alone. Will you go with me?" He'd put off confronting his mother till he had a bit more solid ground — meaning drug-free time — under his feet before tackling her. But now he felt ready. Sunday.

He'd chosen the weekend when both she and Thom would be at Adolphustown closing the house down for the winter. Perhaps subconsciously he'd wanted to confront her where the crimes against his father had been perpetrated. To face her on her own turf. Never a wise decision, Dan thought. But it was Ted's choice.

Dan had agreed to accompany him. It was odd how straight men turned to him as though he were innately more competent than them. Or maybe it was so they could finally stop pretending to be competent and let someone else do the job for once.

They met at a café in downtown Picton. Not the Murky Turkey. Better for both of them to avoid even the hint of temptation, surrounded instead by sandwiches and bright little pastries and coffee, sweets and caffeine still being the only socially acceptable addictions.

Ted looked clean, far better than when he and Dan had last met. He confirmed it had been six long, difficult weeks. But with the knowledge that he could pull himself through came the strength of self-confidence. He was finally starting to feel better for it. He smiled. He seemed in remarkably good spirits for a man who was about to blow apart his entire family. Though in some way or other he'd been preparing for this moment for most of his adult life.

He pocketed his cell phone as Dan walked in. He'd been talking to Thom, he said, trying to prepare his brother for what was coming. At first Thom hung up in disbelief, but he called back within minutes. He was ready to hear the truth. And Ted had delivered it. Give him till one o'clock, Thom said. They would confront her together. Ted agreed.

"It took me a while to convince him. I think it was harder for him to believe our father was gay than that he'd killed himself. I don't think I would have believed it either, but for the diary." He shrugged philosophically. "He found it particularly hard to accept the story about the assault charges. I assured him Magnus had witnessed the altercation and that he was still very much alive to tell the tale."

"What was his reaction?"

"He was in a rage. It wasn't loud, but I could tell. He fumes quietly, my brother. We're both practised at repressing our emotions. We've always been a family of liars, especially when it comes to our feelings, and damn good at it too. I think the legacy goes back to our grandfather, if not well before that."

Dan remembered standing by Nathaniel Macaulay's grave outside the Church of St. Mary Magdalene in the long shadows of morning. A man whose intolerance and prejudice had reached so far as to touch the lives of his own grandchildren, long after his death. Was that the Presbyterian idea of immortality?

"Can I ask something…?"

"Shoot."

"On the last page in the police report, you were quoted as saying your dad was a liar. What did you mean by it?"

Ted gave a bitter laugh. "My father showed up at home right before he disappeared. I hadn't known he was coming and I was thrilled to see him. It was my birthday and I thought he'd come for that. He came into my bedroom. I remember he was crying. He held me a long time and said he was coming back to us and that everything was going to be the way it had been. But he never came back again, and I couldn't understand why he didn't keep his promise."

Dan nodded. "Not much of a birthday present."

Ted looked at his watch. "Twenty minutes."

"Sure you don't want to rethink this?"

"No — I can't."

They finished their coffee and got ready. Ted wanted to stop for cigarettes. He couldn't give up every addiction, he told Dan with a smile. That would still give him time to get to the ferry and over to the house while Thom did whatever he needed to prepare himself. They stepped out into the whiteness of a flurry. Dan hesitated on the steps of the café before heading for his car. He watched Ted head out, shoulder to the wind, waiting till he drove off.

Dan started up the engine, the wipers taking right off again, picking up the old refrain: *Then maybe you are. Supposed to have an epiphany. Then maybe you are. Supposed to have an epiphany.* Craig Killingworth's face bobbed up and down like a sideshow clown at the midway, a moving target in the Shoot-'Em-Up galleries. In the background, Dan imagined Craig's father-in-law, Nathaniel Macaulay, holding a gun to his shoulder and squeezing the trigger again and again.

Dan slowed the car as he approached Glenora. No line-up. He glanced across the water where the ferry was just reaching the far shore. There was still time. He found himself turning around and heading back up County Road 7 to Lake on the Mountain. He thought of its subterranean aquifers travelling hundreds of miles unseen, only to emerge again somewhere strange, mysterious and unexpected, like a father's love for his child.

The lake suddenly came into view. Dan pulled into the empty parking lot. The sleet was bashing against the windshield, insistent, like something trying to pound its way into his brain, thousands of little pieces of a giant puzzle flinging themselves at him, getting closer and closer but not quite reaching him.

After all these years, he thought, it was strange how the past still held sway over the present, like hands reaching out from the grave. An old man's prejudices had stained and perverted his grandson's lives, and a father's diary that had lain unread for more than twenty years was about to destroy his family. From this day forward, Dan promised himself, he'd think more about the here-and-now. Donny was right — he'd been caught in a dead man's world after all.

He sat looking over the Bay of Quinte, with its breathtaking views. If he tried, he could probably pick out the Killingworth mansion on the far side hidden by its copse of pine trees. Were Craig Killingworth's remains out there, his final resting spot somewhere just offshore from his wife's cheerless estate? What had gone through his head in those final moments as he stood saying goodbye to all the things he was giving up? How did you say goodbye to your life, letting go of everything that mattered?

What is the one thing that matters most to you? Whatever it is, hold fast to it. Martin's words again. Thank god for Kedrick. In all those years, his son was the one thing that had kept Dan's head above water — at times only just above, but still. Dan had promised himself nothing would ever come between him and Ked. Even alcohol hadn't made him break that promise. So there was hope, he knew. There would always be hope, so long as love remained. Then what had happened to Craig Killingworth, a man who claimed his sons mattered more to him than anything, even life itself? Why hadn't he chosen to live for them?

Something … something … something was driving at him, ticking at the back of his brain with an insistent rhythm. Whatever it was, he couldn't ignore it. It held there, waiting for him to find it.

Dan recalled his momentous meeting with Ted a month earlier as he'd unravelled the secrets of the past, unlocking the mysteries of the long-dead. *It's my birthday,* Ted had said, just before going out the door. *Time to start living.*

Dan thought back. It had been the day after Halloween, making it … November First. The date Craig Killingworth had planned to leave town twenty years earlier. The same date on which he'd disappeared forever. If Dan were ever to leave Ked, for any reason on earth, it wouldn't be on his son's birthday.

Or any other day.

Because a man who loved his children that much could never abandon them, not even for a pact to begin a new life with another man. Earlier that day Craig Killingworth had said his real goodbyes, to his friend and lover, Magnus Ferguson. Magnus hadn't known it at the time, but he'd suspected something was wrong when he spoke with Craig on the phone in the morning. So he'd gone to the house and helped him pack. Craig had always been fussy about his clothes, he'd said. A fussy man, who got cranky about packing....

Dan looked down at the cell phone resting on the passenger seat. *Yes or no?* he asked himself. *Yes or no?* It had to be … *yes!* He picked it up, flipped it open with one hand and dialled. *Yes! Yes!* It screamed at him now. Why? Why hadn't he seen it in all this time?

Saylor answered. Dan spoke quickly, trying to convince the Picton cop that what he was saying was really true this time. Because he'd just grasped the one thing that was bothering him in all this mess. Despite the apparent suicide letter to Magnus, despite the eyewitness reports and the numerous sightings following Craig Killingworth's disappearance, leaving just a trace of hope that he might still be alive somewhere, something had been nagging at him. Because despite even what the diary said, he'd felt it in his bones … the one thing out of place in all this sordid sadness.

He'd finally found the unexpected: a suitcase. Standing empty behind a door in a police file, but packed earlier that day according to Magnus. It was the one thing awry in the report. A man had packed his suitcase to go away. Why would he bother to unpack it if he was going to kill himself? Dan's instincts had been right all along. Ted said his father had come back to see him the day of his birthday. He would never have left on his son's birthday after promising Ted he was coming back to stay: *I'm going to give her what she's always wanted. By the time you get this, I will be a dead man.*

Craig Killingworth hadn't decided to kill himself. He was a dead man because he knew he couldn't live without his sons. That meant for the rest of his life he would have to endure whatever his wife had in store for him. He'd unpacked his suitcase — because he'd finally made up his mind to return. Just as he'd promised Ted.

Grief. A powerful word beginning with a soft utterance and ending in a feather's caress. There's no way to say it without beginning and ending in a sibilant whisper. Intake of breath or out, it's still the same — like a verbal palindrome. Craig Killingworth had felt its pull, soft and seductive enough to make him sacrifice himself. He'd given in to its drowning embrace, giving up what he wanted most — his freedom — for what he couldn't live without: his boys. In doing so, he'd lost both. There wasn't a prayer or lamentation or elegy in the world that could convey, in words or music, the tragedy that this had brought about. There was nothing that could revoke or undo the senseless horror of what had happened to him: *If I can't have you, nobody will!*

Craig Killingworth had unpacked his suitcase that day and then sat down and written his letter to tell Magnus the truth, a truth that even he hadn't fully comprehended: that he wasn't leaving. Not because he'd decided to return to his family, but because he would be dead by the end of the day. He couldn't have known that he was setting his own death in motion when he got on his bicycle and took the ferry to Adolphustown to tell his boys and his wife that he was coming back to live with them.

Terry Piers said that Craig Killingworth hadn't returned on the ferry with his bicycle. But someone had. A boy. The same boy Magnus had seen riding a bicycle up the hill to Lake on the Mountain. A dutiful son removing the evidence that his father had been there that night.

She was pure evil, a woman who destroyed to suit her own ego. She'd even enlisted her son to help her. Murder: the one unforgivable sin. Because she had taken away something she could never replace: her husband's life.

At least I'll have the satisfaction of knowing I've destroyed her in return. Had Ted known all along what he was doing?

The ferry was agonizingly slow approaching the dock. Dan waited in unbearable torment as the crew in fluorescent orange coats with fluty stripes slid open the gate and waved the cars off-ship before calling in the oncoming group. He felt the vibrating charge as his wheels hit the loading ramp, second-last to board. And then there was nothing to do but wait as the boat ploughed into the reach and plied the waves, carving its way through the jagged ice locking the passage.

His car sat next to a muster station with its yellow boogie board life preservers. Dan stepped out and looked over the side at the chunks of ice floating in black water. At this time of year he could almost have run across faster, if the ice would have held. His mind screamed for speed, but the boat kept up its steady crawl. Ahead, he saw the Royal Union flag waving them on to the Kingston side. The last gasp of the United Empire Loyalists. To his left, a sign read *MV Quinte Loyalist, rebuilt by Cartier Construction Inc 1992.* What had happened to the previous incarnation,

Dan wondered, and why had it had to be rebuilt? He tried to keep his mind off what lay ahead. Whatever it might be was now out of his control.

The Killingworth estate sat undiminished by rain or time or encroaching cold, the pines still greenly watching his approach. It had eluded him before, but Dan knew now what the look of the house signified: death waiting.

Saylor had got there first. His car, door wide open, sat in the circular drive with lights flashing and the radio emitting useless sounds that went unanswered. Beneath the front window the garden was ravaged, plants torn out by their roots as though a demon wind had ripped things asunder.

Dan's footsteps pounded a futile path up the stairs and across the porch. The front hall was stacked with boxes and containers. In the drawing room, the afternoon light still held its hushed somnolence. The furniture had been draped with sheets in preparation for closing the house down for the winter. Ironically, it looked as if the owners had gone into mourning.

The body was in the hall next to a bouquet of faded Monkshood, the delicately hooded flowers wilting as they thawed in the warmth. Lucille Killingworth lay across the carpet, her compact form neatly blending into its patterns and colours. She seemed to be camouflaged, as though the carpet were shielding her while she slept. As though she'd planned her death in advance to be as comfortable and well-coordinated as possible. A designer end. Suitable as any artist's rendition of what death should look like. The effect was both comforting and eerie.

Ted was crouched on his haunches, watching. Saylor stood over him, regarding Dan with an air of regret. Thom had been detained upstairs in the bathroom, either not man enough to finish the job or so mentally destitute he didn't realize he hadn't accomplished it all yet.

TWENTY-EIGHT

Cures

THEY'D BEEN TOO LATE. Aconite has no known antidote, and chances were non-existent that anyone could have survived such a massive dose. Thom's arrest for the murder of his mother was almost secondary to the shock that a twelve-year-old boy had poisoned his father and then got away with it for twenty years. He might find sympathy with a jury on the plea that his mother had encouraged him to kill his father, turning his young mind against him, but he would have a hard time getting out of the charge of murdering Lucille Killingworth two decades later. The fate of Daniella Ballancourt remained undecided, though Thom stuck to the story that he was innocent of any wrongdoing in connection with her death, and Dr. Bill McFarland, more than a good friend, stood firmly by his man in vouching for him. Dan was quietly surprised by Bill's steadfastness.

He wondered briefly about Lucille Killingworth's request for his help back in the fall. Had it merely been a ploy to find out about Daniella's pregnancy, so she could truthfully say that he, Dan, had told them, if asked? *A woman knows these things.* She'd probably just wanted to be sure, in case the investigation turned up anything. Thom probably hadn't known till Dan came by that afternoon. In a way, Dan felt sorry for him. What chance had he had with a mother like that? Then again, he'd had a good father. A very good father, who had loved him beyond all knowing. On some level, even the boy Thom must have known that. Shaken by what he'd done, the twelve-year-old had tried to destroy all remnants of his father's memory, beginning with his horses, before retreating into a life of showy but mostly superficial physical accomplishments.

The pre-trial publicity kept the presses raging for a few weeks before other matters began to turn the tide of interest. All in all, the length of his sentence wouldn't matter much to Dan one way or another.

Dan was backing out of his driveway when he heard the tear of metal against metal. He jammed on the brakes, got out of his car and looked back to see a ten-inch gouge running across his rear door. His neighbour's car, unapologetically parked with a foot of overhang on his drive, hidden by the drifts, stood in the thin wintry sunlight.

Glenda came out of her house wearing an annoyed look. "That's gonna cost you!" She ran over and saw that her own vehicle had sustained no damage. She turned meekly to Dan who stood glaring. She seemed to wilt.

"Sorry — I guess I was careless...."

"How many times have I asked you to park your car so it doesn't block my driveway?"

"Don't worry, these things happen." Suddenly, she was all charm. "I'm having a party tonight. You wanna drop by?"

"You're trying to buy me off with a party invitation?" Dan demanded, more amused than insulted by her colossal lack of respect and consideration.

"There are going to be a couple of gay guys from my work. I'm sure they'd love to meet you."

I'm not falling for this girly-girl routine, Dan thought. *It may have worked on Steve and probably every other straight man you've ever flirted with, but it doesn't work on me. That's at least one advantage gay men still hold over straight men.*

"It's a theme party," Glenda went on, ignoring his glare. "It's a come-as-someone-you-hate party. It'll be fun."

"Sounds like a riot," Dan snapped, stepping back in his car. "Can I come as you?"

He left his damaged vehicle on the street and buzzed himself up to Donny's condo. Donny stood just inside the door, grinning from ear to ear. He looked, Dan thought, suspiciously like a proud parent.

"Guess what Lester said when I asked what he wanted to be when he grew up."

"No idea. I hope he didn't say a machine or a porn star."

"Neither of the above. Cut the kid some slack." Donny gave Dan a withering look he saved for those few times when he wanted to annihilate with a glance.

"So, are you going to tell me or what?"

"He said — and I quote — 'When I grow up I want to be *Miles Fucking Davis.*'" Donny was grinning. "Is that unbelievable or what?"

"That he wants to be Miles Davis?"

Donny nodded.

"Well, I guess a jazz superstar crackhead is better than just a crackhead."

"Oh, fuck you, Snow White."

Dan grinned. "So, is he good?"

"What — on the horn? I don't know."

"What do you mean you don't know? Did you let him play a few licks?"

"Of course. I let him lean on my horn — after I dusted it off a bit."

"And?"

Donny was evasive. "I don't know."

"What do you mean you don't know? You know what good horn playing is. Either he was good or he wasn't."

"Well … I guess he wasn't too good. *But!* Even Miles must have wondered what he was going to make of that piece of metal the first time he pressed it to his lips. I mean, can you imagine what Miles Davis was thinking as he raised a horn to his lips for the very first time?"

"An historic moment." Dan waited a beat. "So, dare we hope that Angela Davis will inspire you to become a surrogate father to a needy boy with musical talent just waiting to be developed?"

Donny toed the edge of a counter. "That's the question, isn't it? I mean, we can't just send him back to his parents. That would be … like a life sentence. Wouldn't it?"

Dan nodded, waiting.

"And I guess I've kind of gotten used to having him around."

"So…?"

Donny shrugged. "So, I guess … whatever."

"Whatever? Just like that?" Dan said.

"Do you want me to say I'll think about it?"

"Definitely not."

Ked had been home a week. He was still on edge over Ephraim's death, though the last few days had seen him returning to his old self. But he was changed, Dan knew. Older, sadder. Death had whispered in his ear then driven the knife blade in a little, under the skin. The experience would leave him marked, but not, Dan hoped, permanently damaged. Maybe it was too soon to be doing this. He went upstairs and knocked on his son's door.

"Come in, Dad!"

Dan pushed the door open with his foot, avoiding the maze of clothes and school reports sliding over the carpet. Ked removed his earphones, his head still swaying to whatever unheard pulse he'd just been connected to.

"I need to speak with you about something," Dan said, hoping his timing wasn't completely off. "I'm thinking about going away for a while."

Ked just sat there. This wasn't going to be easy. "I'm thinking of going back to B.C. For a couple of weeks — maybe a little longer."

"Uh-huh."

"I know it's been a difficult time for you, and I don't want to do anything to upset you." Memories of promising

Ked never to desert him clouded his mind; was that what he was doing? He retreated. This was all wrong. "But anyway, it can probably wait...."

Ked's voice intruded. "What's in B.C.?"

"Oh. Well. I was ... I mean, there's someone I met there I like a lot. I want to get to know him better. But of course my home is here — with you." Dan watched closely, trying to read that inscrutable teenage face that seemed to follow him with X-ray vision, as though his son knew his deepest secrets.

"That's cool."

"What's cool?"

"That you want to go to B.C. Especially if there's some-one you like." Ked cocked his head. "Is he nice?"

Dan nodded. "Yes. He is. Thanks for asking."

"Just checking up on you."

"And anyway, it's just a thought. I mean, I might not go —"

Ked fixed him with a stare. "Dad, I just want you to be happy. Have you ever been happy in your entire life?"

"What?" Dan looked intently at his son. "Of course I've been happy." He stopped and thought about it. "Maybe not for a while, but I will be again."

Ked sat watching him. "What makes you happy?"

"Did your Uncle Donny tell you to ask me this?" Dan said, suspicion clouding his mind.

"No."

"Okay. Well, you make me happy, for one."

"What else?"

Dan thought it over. Not much came to mind. Could he add Trevor to the list? What was he expecting of Trevor anyway? Salvation? Love everlasting? Supernatural sex?

What happened when the sex slowed and the boredom quickened? When the perfect life became perfectly boring? The picture clouded. What would he do about the weight gain from not dancing or working out every other day and one too many hot chocolates before the fire? Or just from not having enough to get up and get done in the morning. These were precisely the kinds of things that destroyed relationships. And would Trevor still respect him no matter what tricks Dan came up with to booby-trap their rose-strewn path ahead? He was only now becoming aware of all the ways he sabotaged his own best intentions. Did he, Dan, even have what it took to make a go of things without fucking up, throwing up his hands, and moving on?

He smiled. *Listen to me,* he thought. *I've already moved in with him in my mind and we're having our first fight, all without him even being there. Who says I'm not complex?*

"I don't know what else at this moment. It's hard to say right now. It's been a rough year for me too." He shrugged and tried to cover his seriousness.

Ked watched him. "So just me? One thing?"

Dan nodded.

"Is that enough?"

"What do you mean?"

Ked looked around. "I mean … well, I'm happy living here with you, but Ralph makes me happy and I like playing basketball, and Mom makes me happy, and Uncle Donny too. There's lots of things that make me happy —"

"And you think I need to have lots of things too?"

"Maybe you just need a few more."

Dan watched his son watching him.

"I know you hate Toronto...."

"It doesn't mean I want to leave."

"I'll be fine if you do."

Dan stared at him.

"Dad — I'm almost done high school. I just have a few years left, and then I'll be going to university somewhere."

Dan was shocked to realize it was as close in time as that. He tried not to let the surprise sound in his voice. "Where will you go?"

Ked made a face. "I don't know. Geez! I haven't even started to apply. The one I want to go to most is in B.C., though, so if you moved there —"

"Who said anything about moving?"

"No one." Ked shrugged.

"Good, because I'm just going for a trip." *And to try to talk someone into coming back with me,* Dan thought. Maybe his son was right. Didn't he deserve a happy ending? Still, he couldn't abandon Ked. Couldn't, wouldn't — it was all the same. For some things, there were no second chances. "I'm going, but I'll be back. Don't even think of trying to get out of doing the housework."

He would not leave for now, though Ked was right — one day, he would. That didn't mean Dan was stuck here till he died, however. Vancouver was only five hours away, and Air Canada had non-stop flights every day of the week. What more could you ask?

"Anyway," Ked continued, "if I go to school in B.C., I might see you hanging out there."

Dan snorted. "Hanging out? Is that what you think you'll be doing in university?"

"Dad! Relax, would you?"

"I'm relaxed!"

"Yeah?" Ked eyed his father. "Okay, then. Let's see you."

Dan knew this would be hard to do without a drink, but he was only two months into his promise to Ked and he wasn't going to break it. Six months wasn't that long — not when you really thought about it. He felt himself dialling the number before he'd consciously made the decision.

Trevor answered. "Don't tell me — you're on a ferry that's just pulling into harbour."

"No, not this time."

"Good. Because the place is a mess and I'd hate to think you were coming out here just to cheer me up. You don't have some scheme to come and save me from loneliness or something, do you? I don't need to be saved."

"Not at all," Dan said. "But I've been thinking a lot about how that gong sounded in the Japanese garden and how dark it gets there at night."

"Does that mean you're coming for another visit?"

"I'd like to." Dan faltered. Words were failing him. "I've been thinking that my mind needs a break ... before I start to hate everything here again. And it so happens there's a seat sale on right now."

"Fantastic!" Trevor jumped on it. "But I'm not pressuring you. I'd love to see you. Any time — I told you that. I've got the cure for whatever ails you."

"Just so you know, I haven't had a drink in two months, so I'm a total basket case, but a committed one."

He was wrapping a box with a miniature Pride flag rolled up inside and a note that said, "I hope that's enough colour for you." Before he left, he'd drop it off at the office with a thank you note for Sally.

"I'm not selling the house or committing myself to anything … well, apart from spending the night with a cup of hot chocolate in front of your fireplace now and again. Preferably with lots of marshmallows."

"You're travelling 4,300 kilometres to have a cup of hot chocolate?"

"With *you*. A cup of hot chocolate with you. Any problem with that?"

Trevor laughed. "None whatsoever."

"Fine. Then wish me luck —"

"Good luck."

"— and I'll see you soon. Can I bring you anything?"

"Yeah. Bring your tool belt. You can read into that whatever you like."

Downstairs Ralph sat looking at him. "What do you want?" Dan asked, opening his arms wide. The dog leapt to the door and waited while Dan put the leash on him. Outside he trotted briskly along without pulling. He seemed to know where he wanted to go, as though he'd sniffed the wind, and it had told him something.

How do you gauge what lies ahead? How do you choose?

Sometimes, Craig Killingworth had written in his diary, *I think the only things that matter are the choices we make, for better or worse, for right or wrong.* He had chosen the love of his sons and walked into the open arms of death. As sad and unfair as it was, nothing could change that. Craig

Killingworth had let duty — an all-consuming duty of fatherhood coupled with a love for his sons — kill him. He'd tried to escape his fate and walked right into it. And here, twenty years later, Dan Sharp walked his dog across a bridge in one of the world's largest metropolises, contemplating his future. His own choices. He, at least, could still make them. And they would be as wrong or as right as could be. There was no telling until he made them.

The man and dog passed over the Don Valley Bridge. Snow fell lightly. Below, a flow of red taillights winked and twitched its way up the constipated fracture that divided the city. A river of flame that would be cold as ash tomorrow. A river of escapees. Those who couldn't take the city any more — this place that was supposed to be friendly and safe, a haven for like-minded souls who wanted to live together in peace and harmony — were slowly making their way to a new land, leaving behind the tyranny of mob rule. Somehow in the course of the last century, as the city became a garbage bin for the tortured and angst-ridden, the uncaring and soulless, the promise had all gone wrong.

Dan heard voices and turned to watch three kids cutting across to his left, sharing some childhood joke. There were two boys, one black and one white, running alongside an Asian girl, laughing as they went. Citizens of the new century. The very essence of diversity.

Well, maybe not all wrong, then. Somewhere there was hope.

ACKNOWLEDGEMENTS

Thanks to Navigator Shane McConnell, Captain Russell Sergiates, and First Mate Timothy Pinnell of the *Outward Bound,* for that eye-opening trip to the Bay of Quinte, Fisheries Officer Brian Round for his explanation of marine rescue operations, Constable Lyn Nottingham and Sergeant Mark Round for their advice on policing strategies, and Group Manager Barbara York for shedding light on the intricate mysteries of banking protocol. Any errors or inaccuracies in such matters are of my own purposeful and fanciful invention.

Thanks are also due to Peter Hawkins and Arnon Melo for inviting me on their lovely, non-fatal wedding cruise, Richard Armstrong and Peter Nosalik for having me as a guest in their charming Forest Hill home, Dean Gregory and Drew Elvin, each for their own brand of west coast hospitality, Bob MacGregor of FSA Toronto for helping me sort out my own messes, Kevin Hartley and Eric Wegler for enlightening me on the perils of being a gay dad, and the delightful and ever-lovely Gail Bowen for her additional insights into parenthood.

Cheers to Michael Carroll, Allister Thompson, Margaret Bryant, and the team at Dundurn for making me feel welcome. As well, I salute my boyhood friends Johnny S, Ed T, Joan M, Sharon W, Harris G, Jamie V, Gail and Brenda R, Lynn and Gary D, Junior and Rachel T, aunts Shirley, Elsie, Evie, Kathy, and Helen, uncles Don, Edgar, and Jim, grandmother Evelyn, and cousins Susan, Judy, Steve, Barb, Diane, and David, each of whom contributed something of value to my wayward Sudbury years. And finally, to the memory of Allen Brooker, whose struggle to be with his sons tragically led him to take his life.

MYSTERY AND CRIME FICTION FROM DUNDURN PRESS

Birder Murder Mysteries
by Steve Burrows
(BIRDING, BRITISH COASTAL TOWN MYSTERIES)
A Siege of Bitterns
A Pitying of Doves
A Cast of Falcons
A Shimmer of Hummingbirds
A Tiding of Magpies
A Dance of Cranes

Amanda Doucette Mysteries
by Barbara Fradkin
(PTSD, CROSS-CANADA TOUR)
Fire in the Stars
The Trickster's Lullaby
Prisoners of Hope

B.C. Blues Crime Novels
by R.M. Greenaway
(BRITISH COLUMBIA, POLICE PROCEDURAL)
Cold Girl
Undertow
Creep
Flights and Falls
Coming soon: *River of Lies*

Stonechild & Rouleau Mysteries
by Brenda Chapman
(FIRST NATIONS, KINGSTON, POLICE PROCEDURAL)
Cold Mourning
Butterfly Kills
Tumbled Graves
Shallow End
Bleeding Darkness
Turning Secrets

Jack Palace Series
by A.G. Pasquella
(NOIR, TORONTO, MOB)
Yard Dog
Coming soon: *Carve the Heart*

Jenny Willson Mysteries
by Dave Butler
(NATIONAL PARKS, ANIMAL PROTECTION)
Full Curl
No Place for Wolverines
In Rhino We Trust

Falls Mysteries
by J.E. Barnard
(RURAL ALBERTA, FEMALE SLEUTH)
When the Flood Falls
Where the Ice Falls

Foreign Affairs Mysteries
by Nick Wilkshire
(GLOBAL CRIME FICTION, HUMOUR)
Escape to Havana
The Moscow Code
Remember Tokyo

Dan Sharp Mysteries
by Jeffrey Round
(LGBTQ, TORONTO)
Lake on the Mountain
Pumpkin Eater
The Jade Butterfly
After the Horses
The God Game
Shadow Puppet
Coming soon: *Lion's Head Revisited*

Max O'Brien Mysteries
by Mario Bolduc
(TRANSLATION, POLITICAL THRILLER, CON MAN)
The Kashmir Trap
The Roma Plot
The Tanzania Conspiracy

Cullen and Cobb Mysteries
by David A. Poulsen
(CALGARY, PRIVATE INVESTIGATORS, ORGANIZED CRIME)
Serpents Rising
Dead Air
Last Song Sung
None So Deadly